# BOOK T[WO]
## OF THE BLOODBO[RN]
# HELLHO[UND]

# DEVIN THORPE

Copyright © 2024 by Devin Thorpe

All rights reserved.

No part of this publication may be reproduced, distributed, or transmitted in any form or by any means, including photocopying, recording, or other electronic or mechanical methods, without the prior written permission of the publisher, except as permitted by U.S. copyright law. For permission requests, contact devinthorpewrites@gmail.com.

The story, all names, characters, and incidents portrayed in this production are fictitious. No identification with actual persons (living or deceased), places, buildings, and products is intended or should be inferred.

Book Cover by Black Veil Arts

Illustrations by Sienna Arts

1st edition 2024

To the literary agents and publishers that rejected me.
*insert middle finger emoji here*

## Contents

| | |
|---|---|
| Trigger Warnings | IX |
| Reading Order | XI |
| Fullpage image | XIII |
| Verbiage Glossary | 1 |
| Character Glossary | 3 |
| The Story So Far... | 7 |
| The Creator's Prophecy | 11 |
| 1. Wolf Among Sheep | 15 |
| 2. Grand Tichu | 24 |
| 3. Varne | 37 |
| 4. Wishing Well | 40 |
| 5. Piss Slave | 46 |
| 6. Rats and Cockroaches | 56 |
| 7. The Witch | 63 |
| 8. Newborn | 75 |
| 9. Peanut Butter & Jelly | 78 |
| 10. Mammoth | 84 |
| 11. Home Sweet Home | 99 |

| | | |
|---|---|---|
| 12. | The Price for Blindness | 102 |
| 13. | Regicide | 114 |
| 14. | Wolves & Ravens | 121 |
| 15. | Ghosts of the Past | 126 |
| 16. | Two Enemies, One Body | 131 |
| 17. | I Told Them You Would Come For Me | 142 |
| 18. | Ventur & Bloodlust | 150 |
| 19. | Heart of a Leader | 156 |
| 20. | Battle of Alphas | 167 |
| 21. | One Wish | 177 |
| 22. | Nightfall | 184 |
| 23. | Fervent | 192 |
| 24. | The Culling | 197 |
| 25. | Skathen | 209 |
| 26. | Eighteen Maidens | 215 |
| 27. | Humanity's Savior | 227 |
| 28. | No One is Coming to Save Us | 234 |
| 29. | Skathen Mori Vere | 238 |
| 30. | My True Enemy | 251 |
| 31. | The Temple of the Acolytes | 254 |
| 32. | The Man Beneath the Hood | 259 |
| 33. | Scared Little Boy | 265 |
| 34. | Defeater of Death | 277 |

| | |
|---|---|
| 35. Valor's Vengeance | 284 |
| 36. The Hellhounds | 291 |
| 37. Wolfsbane Warfare | 299 |
| 38. The Bigger They Are, The Harder They Fall | 306 |
| 39. A True Leader | 314 |
| 40. Revenge. Revenge. Revenge. | 320 |
| 41. Selena & Sephora | 327 |
| 42. Ghost of the Future | 332 |
| 43. Bloody-Eyed Monster | 341 |
| 44. Crixus vs. Chimel | 350 |
| 45. Remember Who You Are | 358 |
| 46. Equinox | 363 |
| 47. Till My Heart Beats No More | 372 |
| 48. Retreat | 379 |
| Epilogue 1 | 385 |
| Epilogue 2 | 393 |
| Epilogue 3 | 399 |
| About the author | 405 |

## Trigger Warnings

This is the part of the book that is eerily similar to pharmaceutical drug advertisements. You know, the ones that act like the prescription they're promoting is the best thing since sliced bread, but then tell you in the last ten seconds all the horrific symptoms the medication could potentially inflict.

Obviously, I want you to read this book.

With that being said, if you have an aversion to—blood, death, nudity, sexual assault, body horror, human trafficking, or gore—this book probably won't be your cup of tea, and that's completely fine!

Now, if you're convinced you're ready to take the path less traveled...

"Beware all hope, ye who enter here..."

-Dante, *Inferno*

# Reading Order

I'd be remiss to let you dive into this book without giving you my wisdom, as its author.

First, I published "Bloodlust," the first book in this trilogy.

However, I subsequently published "Huntress," a prequel novella which takes place in this universe. Reading "Huntress" is not required to enjoy and understand "Hellhound;" however, it introduced new characters that appear in this story. It's my recommendation as the author of this universe that you read "Huntress" before "Hellhound" in order to get the maximum amount of enjoyment from this book. Further, "Huntress" is available via ebook completely free, now and forever. It is a short, fast-paced read, and I don't think you'll regret sinking your fangs into its contents.

That's my one and only soapbox; do with it what you will.

# AREOPAGUS

**BLOODY TOWER**

**NORTHERN MILITARY SECTOR**

**THE CAPITAL**

**WESTERN MILITARY SECTOR**

**EASTERN MILITARY SECTOR**

**SOUTHERN MILITARY SECTOR**

**RED GATE**

# Verbiage Glossary

Areopagus – The central kingdom in this world; the Areopagus is home to the Sylvians' long-established reign over the many fiefdoms in its immediate control.

Blackblood Virus – A vicious pandemic that swept over the Undead civilization centuries ago; the Blackblood virus is an infectious disease that turns Undead into demon spawn. The virus turns the blood in their veins black, but it also perverts their minds and fills them with unquenchable bloodlust.

Cardone – An ancient city that exists no more; Cardone was once the central kingdom that ruled the nation until a war between Dagon and Damon broke out, reducing its buildings to rubble and its population to genocide.

Creator – The central god in the pantheon this world worships. The Creator is a mysterious being who rules over this world from detached indifference. He is responsible for creating everything the eye can see—from the world we live on to the stars in the sky. Smitten with righteous superiority, he's cursed the offspring of Dagon and Damon to pay for Solis and Luna's sins.

Dagon – The first ever Lycan this world has seen who is now worshipped by Lycans as a god; Dagon is a child of Solis and Luna's eclipse, and after the Creator learned of their treachery, he cursed Dagon to turn into a wolfish beast whenever the moon is full.

Damon – The first ever Undead this world has seen who is now worshipped by the Undead as a god; Damon is a child of Solis and Luna's eclipse, and after the Creator learned of their treachery, he cursed Damon to never walk in the sunlight again, and also to forever thirst for the taste of blood.

Luna – The name of the moon and the goddess of night; Luna is worshipped by some and feared by many.

Lycan – Man by day, wolfman by night, the Lycans are a truly fearsome creature infected with an inability to control the beast that dwells within. The full moon calls to the monster inside them, and they are powerless to keep it at bay.

Solis – The name of the sun and the god of the day; Solis turns Undead to ash and provides comfort to Lycans.

Sylvians – A royal family whose bloodline stretches back to the creation of mankind. Known best for their iconic silver eyes, Sylvians are the world's only Undead-Lycan hybrid, and because these curses cancel out in their bodies, they have the ability to call on the powers of both the Undead and the Lycan while retaining full autonomy.

Sylvian the First – After Dagon and Damon were cursed by the Creator, Luna and Solis eclipsed a third time, thus creating Sylvian the First. In him, he possessed both curses his elder brothers suffered from, but in him, these curses cancelled out. Sylvian is worshipped as the god who brought order to earth's people, and it's his offspring who have forever ruled over the kingdom he built.

Undead – Characterized by their purple eyes and silver hair, the Undead are this world's version of vampires.

# Character Glossary

Atlas – Charismatic, psychotic leader of the Acolytes—Atlas was the descendant of Sylvian the First from Dagon's daughter, a bloodline thought to be extinct. After losing his father to Bloodlust's cruelty, the Sylvian was groomed by Blackblood forces to take the kingdom over for Bloodlust. That is, until Syrus Sylvian buried him in Lake Askamyre.

Bloodlust – Once known as an Undead named Lundis, Bloodlust is the resurrection of Marduk, the first Blackblood to ever walk this earth. As the leader of the Blackblood Legion, Bloodlust is hellbent to subvert creation to his will, no matter how many must bleed in the process.

Chimel – Father of Crixus; he sold his daughter to the Blackbloods for a pretty penny, but not before pimping her out as a sex slave to deplorable men in order to turn a quick profit.

Creon – Syrus Sylvian's right hand man; Creon is a former Muzzled slave of the Blackbloods, who now spends his second chance at freedom doing all in his power to earn the approval of his pack leader, Syrus Sylvian.

Crixus – The only Muzzled slave to survive more full moons under Bloodlust's tyranny than Syrus; Crixus is best described as a rose covered with thorns. She is beautiful to look at, but few have laid hands on her who weren't left bleeding.

Enchantress – Also known as the old hag, Enchantress was once a living person, cursed by Solis to kill everything she touched. After ascending death, she's become this world's version of the devil, and she's chosen Syrus Sylvian as her chief Hellhound.

Lysander – Known as the ancient Acolyte who slayed Marduk, Lysander is a historical figure who symbolizes hope for humanity. He is also, several generations removed, Syrus Sylvian's ancestor on his mother's side.

Marduk – The first ever Blackblood to walk the earth, not much is known about Marduk's origin. However, much is known about the bloody genocide he caused once raising an army of Blackbloods.

Saunter – Half-sister to Syrus Sylvian, Saunter was the product of Silenius Sylvian and Ventur's wife. After learning of his future demise, Silenius Sylvian impregnated Ventur's wife as a final 'fuck you' to the Undead Emperor.

Scar – A native to the Skaarian Isles, Scar is a tongueless Lycan whose sheer size and strength, coupled with his unmatched loyalty, have proven a considerable asset to Syrus Sylvian's objectives.

Sephora – Daughter of Syrus Sylvian and his wife Vesper, Sephora was presumed dead after Syrus watched her neck get snapped by Blackbloods. However, thanks to her Sylvian powers, Sephora survived death and is now in the protection of the Fang Clan.

Syrus Sylvian – A man haunted by his past, Syrus Sylvian is the heir to the Areopagan Throne. After being betrayed by Ventur, the Undead Emperor, Syrus has returned to the Areopagus to take back what is his.

Ventur – Once the right-hand man to Syrus's father, Silenius, Ventur betrayed the Sylvians to take the Areopagan Throne for himself. Ever since then, his only regret has been leaving Syrus Sylvian alive to one day seek revenge for Ventur's treachery.

Vesper – Wife to Syrus Sylvian, Vesper died fighting to save Syrus's life. After discovering the rebirth of the Blackblood virus, Vesper died on the battlefield, dragging as many Blackbloods into the afterlife as she could possibly manage. As an Undead herself, she has shown Syrus that not all bloodsuckers are evil, though her death has turned her husband into a monster not even she would recognize.

Wolfsram – Syrus Sylvian's personal raven, Wolfsram is a vengeful bird who is loyal in this world to Syrus Sylvian, and Syrus Sylvian only. After being separated from his owner for more than a decade, Wolfsram is finally reunited with his master, and nothing on this earth will separate the raven from his highly-esteemed Hellhound.

# The Story So Far...

Syrus Sylvian's life has not been one most would envy.

Born as a prince into a long line of Lycan-Undead hybrids, Syrus expected his life to be one of grandeur as a child. That is, until he awoke one morning covered in the blood of his father, mother, and sister.

Ever since that day, Syrus's life has been one crippling tragedy after another. In order to save himself from the repercussions of killing the royal family, he ran from his kingdom, and he never looked back.

In the course of twenty years, Syrus lived as most outcasts do—bouncing from one unstable situation to another, all in an attempt to outrun his past.

For several years, he was raised by a pack of Lycans known as Wolf's Blood, learning how to tame the beast that lived inside him as hope of his Sylvian powers appearing slowly faded. But all good things in life must come to an end, and end they did for Syrus when he returned from a hunting trip as a teenager to find his wolfpack slaughtered.

Hellbent on revenge, Syrus and his pet raven, Wolfsram, hunted the Undead responsible for his packs' genocide into the Thoren Mountains, where he ultimately found an Undead girl named Vesper.

After enacting his revenge, Vesper's cohort of Undead took Syrus in. Despite the fact that he was a Lycan, they wanted to thank Syrus for saving Vesper's life, and as a consequence of these circumstances, Syrus and Vesper fell in love and got married.

Years later, Syrus and Vesper had their first daughter, whom they named Sephora. Having a daughter while being wanted for political treason was not an ideal lifestyle, but Syrus did everything in his power to make it work—until he couldn't.

An ancient evil known as the Blackblood virus reawakened, and it was this evil that led to Vesper's death, taking the few shambles that remained of Syrus's life and shattering them further. Syrus and Sephora became enslaved by the demonic Undead—monsters whose skin had turned as black as their souls. For two years, Syrus was forced to fight in their gladiator ring amongst other Lycans. With every passing full moon, Syrus rose victorious, yet wished more than anything he hadn't.

But everything changed the night Syrus unlocked his Sylvian powers, granting him silver eyes and an uncanny ability to quell the Curse of Dagon and Damon that lurked within him. Honing in on Syrus's silver eyes, Bloodlust, the leader of the Blackblood horde, saw an opportunity to use Syrus Sylvian as a weapon in his war against the Undead Empire.

After revealing his true identity to Syrus (that before becoming Bloodlust, he was Syrus's childhood tutor, Lundis), Bloodlust leveraged Syrus's daughter against him to gain the Sylvian's cooperation. With the help of Lycans named Crixus, Creon, Scar, and Lockjaw, Syrus traversed the known world from the Blackblood's mountainous siege to the city of Sygon, where Princess Saunter of the Undead Empire exerted control of the west coast in an attempt to vanquish Bloodlust and his Blackbloods.

Along the journey, Syrus unlocked the answers to both old and new secrets. Upon meeting an ancient being known as Enchantress, he learned the death of his parents and sister were not his own doing as a child, but instead a coordinated assassination attempt led by Ventur, the current Emperor of the Undead Empire. Further, he learned Enchantress was the being who had been systematically pulling the strings of Syrus's fate, though to what extent, Syrus was unaware.

Upon taking an Undead named Wilhelm prisoner, Syrus was informed that the Undead Empire had discovered a cure to the Blackblood virus, which was why the Undead no longer feared the possibility of contagion and actively took up arms against their legions.

Upon saving at the hands of Atlas and his Acolytes in Yueltope, Syrus made his way to Sygon, where he used a vile of black blood to infect the Undead's fighting forces. Using chaos as his ally, he launched an attack on Princess Saunter, who revealed to him everything he thought he knew was wrong.

Not only had Bloodlust lied about Syrus's role in taking Sygon, but history had lied to Syrus about being the only remaining Sylvian. Unbeknownst to him, Syrus's father had foreseen his death and impregnated Ventur's wife, producing Saunter as a means of revenge—making Saunter Syrus's half-sister. In addition to that, Atlas, leader of the Acolytes, possessed the powers of Sylvian the First and was a descendant of Sylvian from a fractured lineage long-thought extinct.

The parties stood at odds, each one claiming a right to the Areopagan Throne, and so Atlas and Syrus went to battle in order to determine which Sylvian was fit to rule.

The story concluded with Syrus victorious, and Atlas dead.

As the fog of battle settled, Enchantress appeared to Syrus, prompting him to go to the Areopagus to oppose Bloodlust and Ventur in their war, where only one fighter will earn the crown to the kingdom.

Our story continues...

# THE CREATOR'S PROPHECY

*From life, comes death.*
*From death, comes life.*
*The two cannot exist without each other.*
*Creation cannot thrive without destruction.*
*And so Death will come for Creation.*
*And the Creator will send an Omen.*
*To warn his Creation.*
*For it will come from the Sea; the Air; the Ground; from Hearts;*
*In this time, Death will claim her mortal body;*
*And the Creator will send His Death-Defeater;*
*All the world will witness Her terror,*
*All the world will testify to His splendor.*
*Gods will die.*
*Devils will perish.*
*Creation's light has tempted death to come.*
*Come She will.*
*Life has had its turn to reign.*
*The cycle of Death is all to remain.*
*From life, comes Death.*
*And from Death, comes life.*
- An excerpt from Alabastur's play, *Equinox*.

# PART ONE

# 1

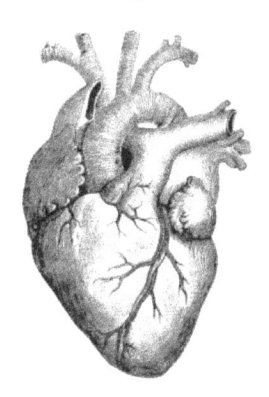

## WOLF AMONG SHEEP

My body jolts with every rocky bump the wagon strikes. The sheep are packed around me so tight that I am smothered in wool on all sides. The air in here is stale. The heat of the day is merciless. Though we are covered with a thick canvas tarp, I bake among these sheep like insulation in an oven. They smell of manure and sour grass.

Every bump in the road causes several of them to bleat with anxiety. I can't imagine how hot it is in here for them. I am barely clothed myself and am on the brink of heat stroke.

Sweat drips from my bangs into my eyes, stinging my vision.

Every time I wipe the moisture from my face it returns almost instantly. I have no way of knowing how close we are to our destination. All I have are my thoughts, and those are as manic and nervous as the wavering cries of my traveling companions.

I am a wolf among sheep.

These livestock know it as well as I do.

Animals have a way of sensing when they're in the midst of a predator. A sixth sense when danger lurks nearby. And though sheep are stupid, their survival instincts are sharper than most swords.

In the heated darkness I'm forced to reflect on Sygon's downfall.

I can still see Atlas's silver eyes sinking into the waters of Askamyre. I can still see Creon's butchered body on the cross. Sephora's broken figure at the base of the throne. Saunter's wicked grin as I saw the trap close around me.

I was not supposed to survive last night, yet here I am. All of creation came together to stack the odds against me, yet creation lost.

Though I once doubted the existence of gods, I now have sufficient proof that the devil is alive and well.

Alive and well, and she holds my leash.

Her name is Enchantress, and gods save whoever wants to stand in her way next.

I am her Hellhound.

Whether or not I want to accept it as the truth, the only reason I'm alive today is because of her. I cannot count on two hands the number of times I should have died in this life but didn't. That hasn't made the pain of living any more tolerable, though. My lungs yearn for their final breath. My heart envies eternal rest. My soul wants to join Vesper in whatever hell waits for me.

But the Summoner won't let me go so easy.

There are still those who must pay for their actions, and I will be the arbiter's chief executioner.

Historians will write for centuries to come of the Hellhound that made the moon bleed a second time. His name is Syrus Sylvian.

My name is Syrus Sylvian, and the wagon I stow upon will soon enter the gates of the Areopagus in plain daylight.

When I fled this city as a child, I was wanted for murdering my parents and sister.

Now I return as an adult with nothing but murder on my mind.

I can't imagine death feels much different than the numbness that throbs inside me. Flying from Askamyre to Areopagus wasn't without its punishment. Mortal man wasn't designed to defy physics of the natural world. I don't feel sore or in pain. Instead, the anatomical response of flying hollows my body and strips me of all sensory feelings.

After grounding myself, nothing feels right.

I am like a man who walks through fire yet shudders a chill. Like one trapped in a blizzard whose skin burns with frostbite. Man isn't meant to be among the clouds. Once gravity loses power over our bodies our egos can never again be grounded.

But I had no choice but to fly across the known world and return to the Areopagus. Tonight is the night of the full moon. Bloodlust's entire plan hinges on me being dead.

I have no choice but to trust my guardian demon has plans in place for me to prevail. I have no army to support me. Creon and Crixus and Scar are on the other side of the globe. The Fang Clan can provide me no aid when the moon rises tonight.

It is just me against the world, as it always has been. I return to my homeland a complete stranger. There are no cards up my sleeve. No one is coming to save me. My enemies are incalculable.

My two childhood mentors—Ventur and Lundis—will wage war tonight. Each would be as happy as the other to see me dead. But I have no choice in the matter.

The powers that be pre-ordained this day at the creation of the cosmos.

Yet there is one thing that weighs heavily in my favor.

My enemies underestimate me.

In truth, I do not need Enchantress guiding my leash to get me to join this war.

Bloodlust was mistaken to employ me in his dirty deeds. Knowing what he did, he should have killed me when I was muzzled.

And Ventur erred in helping me flee the city as a child. He should have slain me as I cradled my father's dead body. Instead he sowed a seed that has grown into a mighty tree, and tonight I will hang him from the tree's lowermost branch.

I have sufficient motivation to go to my death tonight, and neither of these monsters expect my coming.

I am a ghost roaming the earth. I will not pass on until I've collected the debts owed to me. They used my daughter against me, but now that she is safe with Crixus, there is nothing holding me back.

If Enchantress can be trusted, Bloodlust has been foolish enough to bring my fellow muzzled slaves to the Areopagus. Like me, they have no say in the matter. But I do know one thing. They are much more likely to bite the hand that enslaves them than the man who sets them free.

The wagon ceases all movement beneath me. The bumps in the road come to a halt. The sheep stir anxiously around me. I run my hand through the wool of one close to me to calm its nerves. Still, the bleating increases in volume. They are dumb creatures, but I am a capable shepherd. Though they know it not, these animals have no idea how integral a part they are in this war. It's for the best. If they knew how much rests on their shoulders, they would faint at the prospect of what needs to be done.

Best to let animals be animals.

They are the sheep.

I am the wolf.

We stand on opposite sides of the circle of life.

But today our purposes are aligned.

Sheep do not concern themselves with war, but wolves cannot afford this luxury.

A squawk sounds from outside the caravan. Wolfsram is ahead of schedule it seems. I didn't expect his arrival until early evening. Better to be ahead of schedule than behind, though.

The rusty latch squeals as the wagoneer opens the back gate of the wagon. Daylight pours in and punctures my eyes. I curse under my breath at the light's violence. The sheep around me spasm as they all fight for freedom simultaneously.

I cradle myself and close my eyes as they pour out the back of the wagon like sand from a broken hourglass. When the wagon ceases its shaking I stand to face the light, then hop out the back gate after my army of livestock.

My bare feet tingle as soon as they hit the ground. I breathe in deeply the fresh, unpolluted air. I exhale the staleness of the cramped wagon.

"Droppin' you off right where you asked, chief," the wagoneer grunts. "Can't go no farther anyway without being spotted by Scouts. You'll wanna remain undetected as long as you can, though. Grazin' animals strictly prohibited in these parts. Not much they can do to stop you with the sun in the sky though, I reckon."

"You have my deepest gratitude, good sir. I wish there was some way I could repay you for loaning your sheep and wagon on this endeavor," I say.

"No need for that. Bloodsuckers killed my wife n' son. If the things you say are true, I hope these damn wolves rip them apart tonight."

"There will be no favorable outcome for any party involved," I reply. "But the Undead will have the worst of it, that much is guaranteed."

I look down at the high grass around me. Purple flowers bloom in every direction my eye can see. The air is filled with their potent aroma. It enters my nostrils and causes my eyes to water. My skin itches the longer I stand stagnant.

It's called Wolfsbane, and the Undead have planted it in a crop circle around the entire perimeter of the Areopagus.

It is supposed to be lethally toxic to my kind, the same as silver.

But I am no average Lycan, and even if I was it wouldn't matter. I was trained long ago how to temporarily defeat the effects of the poisonous bud. I have microdosed on the herb for decades now. My body has been taught how to survive in its presence.

And now the powers of Sylvian the First pulse in my veins. Silver has no hold over me, and Wolfsbane is stripped of its dangerous potency.

Ventur is not a dumb man.

I heard rumors years ago about him having wolfsbane planted around the Areopagus, but now I see it is true firsthand. Is this what Dagon's wolves saw before the Walk of the Wolves? I stare at the field of blooming beauty. How can something so beautiful be so deadly?

The purple offshoots dance in the breeze. They're mesmerizing to watch. But I don't have the luxury of frolicking through the meadows. I am here on a mission. This wolfsbane stands directly opposed to my plan tonight. Ventur has planted it with the explicit intention of keeping Lycans out of the Areopagus.

But luckily for Lycans, sheep love the taste of wolfsbane, and there is little more in this world they like more than grazing. I watch as the animals go to work doing what they do best. Instinctively, the wooly creatures rip the beautiful flowers from the ground and grind it between their molars.

I don't know how Bloodlust was planning on getting the Muzzled into the city, but I will make my own path for them. I have learned from history. Tonight will not be a repeat of the Walk of Wolves.

The Undead won't win this battle on a technicality.

If they want to win this war it will require flesh and blood.

"Revenge!" Wolfsram squawks, descending from the sky to land on my shoulder.

"Good to see you ahead of schedule, Wolfsram. Did you reach our friends on the west coast?"

"Creon!"

"Yes, Creon and Scar and the Fang Clan."

"Creon! Creon! Creon!" the bird croaks rapidly.

"Well did you reach them? Did you tell them the reason I haven't returned?"

"Revenge!"

"Use your words, Wolfsram."

The bird twists its dark eyes to patronize me. He is smarter than most humans I know, yet he insists on recycling the same twenty words to me over and over. The gods have gifted him with the ability to say more with less, but he enjoys saying only the words he thinks will get a reaction out of me.

"Wolves coming," Wolfsram replies.

"Nonsense, they are on the other side of the world. They won't be here in time for the full moon tonight."

"Wolves coming," Wolfram insists, doubling down on his statement.

"And how do you suppose they'll be able to traverse over a thousand miles, huh?"

"Boats!"

I scoff briefly. I am like a man speaking with a toddler.

"And where exactly did they procure boats? I was just in Sygon last night and didn't see anything that resembled so much as a floating piece of driftwood."

"Acolyte boats," Wolfsram barks, shaking his feathers and picking with his beak at a spot under his wing.

I stop for a moment of reflection. The notion Wolfsram proposes isn't entirely impossible. Theoretically speaking, the rapids of the Kieran could very well be how the Acolytes were able to conquer so many cities in such a little amount of time. The great river cuts across the entire landscape of the west like a ghastly scar, then dumps directly into the Black Sea, the same sea that is an hour's march from where I stand. If the Acolytes did indeed anchor their boats in the Kieran, Fang Clan may be able to arrive at Areopagus before the sun sets.

It would be close, and the risk of having several hundred Lycans aboard boats is a dangerous prospect with the full moon so close. But either way, there is a chance Wolfsram isn't spewing total nonsense. Besides, he's a bird. He is merely reciting the words others told him. Birds, unlike humans, can't lie.

Perhaps I won't be as alone tonight as I thought.

Perhaps this path the sheep pave for me will need to be wide enough for two armies.

The strength of the pack is the wolf, and the strength of the wolf is the pack, Mordecai used to say.

Maybe my pessimism in creation is unwarranted. If Wolfsram's words are true, I may win tonight. Why hundreds of wolves would voyage to their deaths to aid a man like myself makes no sense to me. I have done nothing to earn such trust. I am a wretched man who has done nothing but serve my own interests in life.

Still, perhaps the gods don't hate me as much as I was led to believe.

Or perhaps the gods want all Lycans to be eradicated in one fell swoop.

Either way, there is no telling what will happen until Solis rises on the morrow.

In the meantime, there is much work to be done and little time to do it. I will not bank on having any assistance tonight, that way if such assistance does arrive my plans will be all the more successful.

I pull a piece of parchment paper from inside my sweaty tunic and present it to the raven. I say, "Wolfsram, this is a letter I wrote for a woman that lives a few miles south of here in a village called Rendir. Her hut is located in a grove of Bloodmaples. You'll know you're at the right place if you see a manmade pond on the premise stocked with glass vipers. I need you to deliver this message to her."

"Name?" the bird asks.

"She has many. You may call her Skillah. Deliver this letter to her, then scout where Bloodlust is keeping the Muzzled. I suspect they will be somewhere in a fifty mile radius. You can narrow your search to places the Blackbloods can hide during daylight. Caves, forests, crypts. When you've found them, meet me just inside the Red Gate at a pub called Worshire's. It is the one with a naked woman on the sign."

I smile for the first time in a long time as Wolfsram steals the letter from my palm and takes flight. Though I will more than likely die tonight, things have never gone so far in my favor. There is something exhilarating about living as though today will be my last. And there is something satisfying about tonight being the one where I finally have my revenge.

## 2

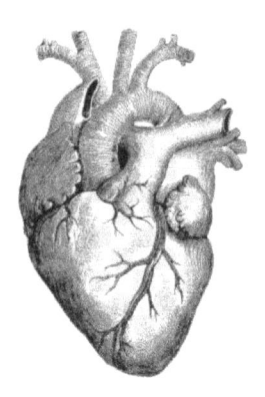

## GRAND TICHU

Lundis and Ventur both taught me an invaluable lesson as a child—a mighty kingdom cannot be destroyed from extraneous threats. A mighty kingdom can only be destroyed by tearing itself apart internally.

Tonight it is my plan to do both.

I will simultaneously sow discord and violence amongst the citizens of Areopagus while Bloodlust brings his army of bloodthirsty demons to the kingdom's doorstep. Ventur may have the homefield advantage, but Bloodlust and I are no stranger to this kingdom. I was raised in these streets. And all three of us know the many strengths and little weaknesses the Areopagus possesses as a military stronghold.

But I possess one strategic advantage my enemies don't.

Where each one of them wishes to preserve the city so they have a throne to rule upon, I will feel no remorse watching every last stone come crumbling down.

Nearly every city within a thousand miles of here has been pillaged and destroyed, why should the Areopagus have any different a fate?

Though this was my first home, I feel no attachment to this place.

The years I spent as a vagabond have taught me a place can never be a home. To think so is foolish. We people put our hopes in feeble walls that succumb to storms and fires and poor construction. We spend our whole life savings on the ability to call a tract of land our own, only for it to become devastated in an earthquake.

Home has no locations. It isn't built in brick and mortar.

Home is the tender embrace of a lover after a long day toiling under the sun. Home is the familiar scent of fresh bread being baked after several days without eating. Home is holding your daughter for the first time and looking into her innocent eyes. Home is the things that follow you no matter where you travel, no matter how destitute a land you own, no matter how poor you are. This world has stripped me of all I call home. My wife is gone. My daughter's innocence is damaged. My enemies have made me a hollow, homeless man.

For this very reason, I will teach the citizens of Areopagus that this kingdom is no home to them, and I will teach my enemies that a throne cannot be commanded if it is crushed to rubble.

"Well?" a strange man asks me through the fog of tobacco smoke. "Staring at your cards won't make it any better a hand, friend," he continues.

I look up from my eight cards and into the eyes of my opponents. "Grand Tichu," I call, grabbing the remaining six face down cards off the coarse table.

"Dagon's sake, man," my partner sighs. "We have a three-hundred-point lead, moron. Now's not the time to grow a pair of balls."

"Ah, but I respect him for it all the more. I like a man with a little gusto!" Nikolai sits up eagerly. "Why win by three hundred when you can win by five? That's what this table has been missing all these years, someone with a little confidence, eh?"

I have no idea why Nikolai cheers me on, seeing that he needs me to lose for him to win. The strange man twists incessantly at his overgrown mustache as if he is attempting to rip it straight off his lip. Since sitting down at this table with him he has single handedly drank enough dark liquor to get all four of us drunk, yet his speech doesn't skip a beat and his wit only seems to increase.

"I'll call your bluff then and call Tichu myself," Nikolai announces. "A little friendly competition never hurt anyone."

"Except Dagon and Damon," Nikolai's partner replies. "You've lost the past two times you called Tichu. I'm starting to wonder if you even know how the game is played."

"You just worry about your own hand, my friend, and pass me something good during the exchange."

I look down at my added cards. The hand isn't much better than what the gods dealt me in life. Though I have a low full house and a high straight, I have no high cards to win the lead. My partner is right. Calling Grand Tichu was unnecessary, but fate fortunes the bold. I've played games of Tichu in the past where no one is brave enough to bet on themselves. It is always those games that drag on hours as a result of cowardice.

I've placed a bet on myself that I will play all my cards before anyone else at the table. So has Nikolai, but that will only be true for one of us. My bet is worth two hundred points because I made it before I looked at my entire hand. Nikolai's is worth a single hundred because he already had all fourteen cards when he made it. Whichever of us fails to go out first receives negative points. Me, two hundred, and Nikolai, a single hundred.

I select the worst cards in my hand and slide them face down to my two opponents, making sure to give Nikolai the worst of the worst. I give my partner a card I have no use for and pray a silent prayer to the gods he is giving me something that will give me the lead, preferably the dragon or phoenix.

I look at all three cards given to me and oddly enough, the most useful one comes from my direct opponent, Nikolai. Surely he meant to give me the low two as a way to put me at a disadvantage. What he's done instead is give me a natural straight, otherwise known as a bomb.

"Good luck getting rid of that, old friend," he grimaces at me through a cloud of smoke he blows. I don't let my face reveal my excitement. He's single-handedly just lost the round for himself.

My partner hasn't given me the dragon or phoenix, but he managed to give me the lead another way. I look at the mahjong he slid me, the lowest card in the deck. Whoever possesses the mahjong gets the first play in a game. Normally, people play the mahjong first if they have it in their hand since it is the lowest card in the game, but I have other intentions.

"I have the mahjong," I announce to the men around me, indicating I will make the first play. My full house is ruined now that I have the bomb. It would be pointless to play three sixes and two fives when I need a single five and six to complete my ultimate hand. I play the high straight first. Eight through queen.

"Now that's what I call gusto, gentlemen," Nikolai exclaims, scooching to the edge of his seat in excitement.

For someone to beat it they will need a nine through king or a ten through ace. Nikolai's partner folds, then my partner, then Nikolai. Easy enough. I collect the cards and lay down my pair of sixes next. Nikolai's partner tops it with a pair of jacks, then my partner lays down a pair of kings. Nikolai eyes me curiously with his purple eyes. Two aces is a lot to dispense with this early in the game, but he plays them anyway.

We all fold and Nikolai takes the lead.

He plays the three I gave him during the exchange, and I lay down my useless five on top. Now all I have left are my bomb and the mahjong. This game is mine for the taking. After my partner goes, Nikolai plays the dragon and wins back the lead.

"Been a pleasure, boys, but it's time for this man to cash in," Nikolai says, laying down a pair of fours and a pair of fives. He has six cards left but talks as if this play has just won him the game. I shift uneasily in my seat, wondering what the reason for his false confidence is. I stare directly at him, dissecting the smoke with my calm eyes. He eyes me mischievously from his spot at the table. His purple eyeballs are covered with a film of hazy glaucoma as if the smoke from his lungs has coiled into his skull. He has the face of a man who has a tapeworm in his stomach. His cheeks are sunken in and the bags under his eyes are like grooves in a dune of sand. Liver spots litter his pale flesh like ugly, expansive freckles fighting to take over his entire face. At one time in his life he was likely a handsome man, but the booze and blood and drugs have made him a hollow man and will send him to an early grave.

"What say you, traveller? Six cards left to the both of us, make your move." His smirk is evil in a way and playful in another.

Either way, there is only one play left that I can make and there is no use putting it off any longer. I put down the natural straight on his two pairs and hold up the single card left in my hand. I look back at Nikolai to watch his reaction to my bomb, but the stupid smirk refuses to leave his face.

My partner lets out a sigh of relief to see my bomb and slams his fist down on the table. "Looks like the next round of drinks will be on you, Nikolai!" he exclaims, laying down his cards as if the game is over.

"Not so fast, gentleman," Nikolai mutters slyly through his teeth. Above all else, he is a showman. The old man brings the pipe back to his lips and takes a deep inhale, then blows the smoke directly in my unflinching face as he lays down a natural straight from nine to king.

I look down at the cards that trump my own and my blood pressure rises.

All four of us stare down at the high bomb as if Nikolai has placed the heart of Marduk before us. I am dumbfounded. People warned me this man was a cheater, but I had no idea he would go to this extent to throw a game.

Did he add a card from his sleeve when I was blinded by smoke?

Did his partner slip him what he needed under the table?

Nikolai looks at me and raises the single card left in his hand to remind me he is about to go out. Everyone at this table knows exactly which card I have left in my hand since I started the game but chose not to play the mahjong. Now, not only will I not go out first like I bet I would, but I will go out last since there are no cards lower than mine that I can play on top of.

"It was a good attempt, lad, but you put too much faith in your cards being better than mine," Nikolai scoffs.

Now my partner and I will lose two hundred points and our opponents will gain one hundred, earning them the lead. I am left to sit here silently, avoiding eye contact with my partner, who no doubt scowls at me from across the table for my naivety. You can't beat a cheater playing honestly.

Nikolai goes to collect the cards laid down on the table but a hand slams down on top of them. My partner speaks over the noisiness of the dimly lit bar, "I never folded, *old friend*," he whispers intimidatingly.

Nikolai's eyes shift as my partner lays down a natural straight from ten to ace, trumping the bomb Nikolai beat me with. My heart skips a beat to see the five cards laid on the table.

What are the odds?

Near impossible.

I have seen a game before with two natural straights, but never three.

And to make things more poetic, the queen of diamonds that connects the natural straight is the queen I gave him. Perhaps the gods favor me more than I'd care to admit.

Nikolai's smile instantly turns to a venomous glare. "Cheater!" he shouts at my partner. "I'll have your hands for cheating!"

"Don't project your shortcomings onto me, old man. Not everyone has to cheat to win. My hand is as fair and clean as Fates dealt it."

My partner collects the cards and lays down the dog, which transfers the lead across the table to me. I stare Nikolai dead in the eyes as I lay down the mahjong and then innocently hold up both my empty hands.

"That's game," I say, trying to hold back the flood of excitement that surges to my head. "And I'd suggest you don't forget what you wagered as a bet now that you've lost."

Nikolai sinks back in his chair and stares at me in disbelief. He likely searches his mind for where he went wrong. Like anyone who loses in Tichu, he likely thinks back on how he could have played his hands differently. But there is no play he could have made that would have led to a better outcome. He knows it as well as I do.

He was merely dealt worse cards than myself, and so the glory is mine to reap.

I would say I'm surprised to have pulled out this victory, but this has been my whole life. Placing side bets on myself to arise victorious before looking at the hand the gods dealt me. Truthfully, Nikolai never stood a chance in the first place.

With Enchantress on my side deciding what cards are dealt to those around me, how can I expect any different outcome other than me ending up on top?

"I'll go get us a round of drinks on Nikolai's tab," my partner says, throwing his remaining cards on the table. Nikolai's partner spits on the table and leaves without another word, then disappears into the fog of smoke to another sector of the bar.

Now it is just me and Nikolai, and I've never looked in the eyes of a man who's wanted to kill me more.

"Who are you, stranger?" Nikolai growls at me. "I see through your coyness. Your eyes may be human, but you are no human. I smell something on your person. Smelled it the second you walked in this bar, daywalker."

"It doesn't matter who I am," I dismiss. "All that matters is that you hold up your end of the bargain."

"And if I don't?" The smile returns to his face as the Undead man leans back and twists his mustache once more.

"Do you still live in that little shack off Griffeth Ave?" I threaten, staring at him more violently than before.

Though the Undead are cold-blooded creatures, I watch as a sheet of redness blushes to the man's cheeks. "How do you know that, stranger?"

"Never mind how I know that," I reply coldly. "I may be a stranger to you, but you are no stranger to me, Nikolai Von Haus of Tribe Celestial."

"Whatever game you're playing—"

"I'm done playing games, Undead. All my cards are on the table. Now I am talking strictly business, and you have something I need. Now that you've lost, you will deliver it to me, and we will go our separate ways."

"I'll report you to the high council..." Nikolai stammers, "I'll... I'll report you to—"

"You'll do no such thing, soldier. You are wanted for crimes of treachery. If you turned me in, you'd be turning yourself in."

The Undead man leans across the table and whispers into my ear, "You're playing with fire right now, human."

"No, Nikolai. I *am* the fire."

We sit in silence and stare at each other from a fist's punch length away. He sizes me up. Unlike my winning hand in Tichu, the Undead doesn't know if he should bet on himself in this situation. I hold all the cards now and he has no idea what I've been dealt. Only now it's his life on the line, and though his life is worthless to the rest of the world, it is the only important thing he still possesses.

"May I ask what a man like you would want with a suit of armor?" Nikolai asks, the smile slowly returning to his face.

"Not just any armor, Nikolai. You were once a Black Knight, one of the most feared warriors in the entire realm."

"And you are a strange man who looks like he's never held a sword in his entire life. So I will ask again, what do you want with my old armor?"

"I don't need to explain what uses I have planned for it. You wagered your armor and I wagered my estate in Queensmyre," I reply, knowing the news of Queensmyre's demise hasn't reached Areopagus yet. "You lost, I won. Now tell me where to find the armor and I'll leave you alone with your booze and cards."

"Ah, but it is my business, because even though I have been dishonorably discharged from the Black Knights, if that armor fell into the wrong hands it could be used for dastardly intentions. And you, my friend, have *wrong hands* written all over you."

"You want to know who I am?" I ask, repeating the question for the stubborn drunk. "I'll tell you exactly who I am, Nikolai. I'm the lesser of two evils. There's a war coming for Areopagus, tonight. If you haven't gathered that by now you either live under a rock or you're stupid. But I know you, Nikolai, and you're neither. When I last saw you, you were one of the only Black Knights who was worth his weight in silver. But that was long ago, and like myself, the years have not been kind to you. To see you like this is disappointing. Word around town is you spend all day every day in the pubs pissing away the small fortune you accrued from your time as a royal guard. You're a drunk. A drug addict. A gambler. A crook. A petty thief. Everything you once stood for is so trampled by your own feet that the mud has sucked it up."

"You don't know what the hell you're talking about!" he screams, no longer willing to play in a friendly game of banter with me. He points an accusatory finger in my direction. The veins bulge from his neck and temple with anger. His lips raise to expose yellowed fangs inside his mouth. "I demand to know the truth of who you are, now! Or else I'll—I—erm..."

The man's voice trails off as the darkness between us illuminates in silver light. My body throbs with euphoria as the powers of Sylvian the First come over me. There is no one in this part of the pub to witness me revealing myself other than Nikolai. I can see the reflection of my gleaming eyes in his irises. I watch the anger in his demeanor evaporate in the blink of an eye.

"You know who I am, Nikolai," I growl in a low tone. "And you know why I'm here."

"But... No... You... I don't—"

"My father held the Black Knights in a low regard," I continue, "But he saw value in a select few of them, Nikolai. You were one of the good ones. One of the ones who defected after his death. You, along with a select few, refused to serve Ventur when he ascended the throne. And for that you were sentenced to death for charges of treachery. Since then you've hidden in plain sight, wasting the daylight away in pubs and spending the night nursing your hangovers."

"I have nowhere else to go... But I learned shortly after what Ventur did to your father. That he used the Black Knights to execute the royal family and frame it on you... A mere child at the time... You have to believe me that I wanted nothing to do with it, Syrus, you must!"

"Lower your voice," I warn. "I know you had no part in my family's demise. You wouldn't be alive right now if you did. But still, you know why I'm here. I need your armor for tonight. I need them to think I'm one of them."

Nikolai looks at me like I'm a ghost. In all honesty, I'm not sure how I expected him to react. I heavily weighed the pros and cons of seeking him out, then only followed through because I figured I have little to lose. But I watch a hardened, jaded man be restored of life in less time than it takes for Nikolai to take a shot of whiskey.

When Nikolai last saw me I was only a child, innocent as the sun is bright. Now I am as monstrous and sinful as he is, corrupted by the darkness I harbor in my heart. Though I spent the morning having my hair and beard cut to a much more manageable length, I'm sure I'm not a sight for sore eyes.

I am fresh off twenty-four moons of slavery and a brutal beating from Atlas. I've walked through a burning city, swam in bacteria infected waters, basked in the decay of burning Undead, and bloodied my hands with the death of dozens. No amount of hot baths can wash my skin of the sin I wear.

I let the silver light between us dissipate for fear of being spotted by bar patrons. The darkness settles between us again, bringing with it silence. Nikolai's glazed, purple eyes stare at me with a mixture of admiration and horror.

"The armor is buried under the tobacco pasture outside my homestead," Nikolai whispers, still in disbelief. "I've marked its burial with a hawkmoth hive. They pollinate the tobacco. You'll need to smoke them out if you're going to dig up the armor."

"Right, thank you." I stand from the table and disengage from the conversation.

"What will you do, Syr... stranger?"

"When the sun sets tonight, I suggest you flee this city immediately if you want to live. Evil is coming."

"But I can help," Nikolai stammers, half standing from the table and nearly tripping over as a wave of drunkenness washes over him. He quickly falls back into his seat and continues on without missing a beat. "I have allies! There are others who would join you in your fight for the crown. Other Undead who defected when your father died. I could gather them! I could—"

"I need the Nikolai Von Haus from twenty years ago," I reply cruelly. "Not the sad mess of a man you've become. Look at yourself. You can barely stand. You expect me to trust you leading other men into battle? No, it's nonsense. Your fighting days are over. The only use I have for you is the hollow armor you've buried to forget about your past."

"But I—"

"I said no. Now drink and be merry. Celebrate the last day of peace while the sun is still in the sky."

My Tichu partner returns to the table with three pints of poldir. "Off so soon, partner? We can find someone else and get another game started."

"I have business to attend to. Give my pint to my old friend Nikolai as gratitude for the good sportsmanship."

Without another word said, I walk out of the bar into the intense daylight. Nikolai stares at me entering the sun's deadly rays, knowing he cannot follow where I go. He is a ghost of my past; one of the few I will need to resurrect if I'm to be successful tonight. I will let my words sit in his mind and marinate the rest of the day. Reverse psychology, Lundis called it in my lessons. The easiest way to get someone to join your cause without lifting a single finger. I have bruised Nikolai's ego enough to awaken the warrior that sleeps within. Slowly but surely my plan comes another step closer to completion.

# 3

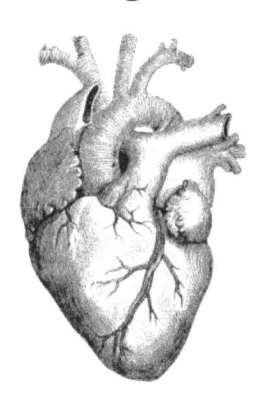

## Varne

A shadow descends from the sky and lands on my shoulder. I look back at the naked woman on Worshire's sign as the door closes. The Undead inside breathe a sigh of relief.

"Worshire's!" Wolfsram calls, "Naked woman!"

I stroke the feathers along the raven's back and pull out a piece of buttered bread I took from someone's plate inside the pub. I lift it to Wolfsram's beak and let him have at it. Another bloke inside the pub already paid for my meal after I beat him in a game of Gondall.

Wolfsram eats graciously while I allow the sun to warm my hollow bones.

"Did you find the recipient of my letter with ease, Wolfsram?"

"Skillah!" the bird squawks between beakfuls of bread.

"Did she seem to take its contents well?"

"Dam be damned," Wolfsram croaks, likely mimicking the words of Skillah.

"Good," I say through a smirk. I am not used to things going in my favor this well. If this dumb luck can continue into the night I may still be alive by the time the sun rises.

"And the Muzzled?"

"Muzzled!"

"Yes, did you find them?"

"Varne! Muzzled in Varne!"

I sigh inwardly. I should have known my luck could only go so far. This entire time I secretly knew in the back of my mind that's where they would be. There are only so many cesspool cities in this world that would allow Blackbloods to cohabitate with them. I was retaining hope it wouldn't be Varne, but evil attracts evil.

Crixus's image briefly flashes in my mind. Varne is her hometown. The place she was trafficked by her own father. The city where men paid money in exchange for her sexual favors. The city where men held her down and treated her like an object. Beat her. Bruised her. Spit on her. Laughed at her. Forced themselves on her. My mind races with thoughts of what occurred to Crixus in her time living there.

I push the thoughts away.

Picturing her hurts.

I miss her already.

I wish she was here by my side.

Part of me wonders if I should even be here in the first place. I could go back to Sygon and find Crixus and Sephora and continue running away. We could retreat to a small coastal town in the west. I could fish for a living and make enough money at the local farmer's market to support us three.

The war in the Areopagus could be nothing but distant news that takes months to reach my ears. The blood spilled tonight could be spilled by people other than me. No more listening to the gnashing of fangs or the flapping of leathery wings. No more agendas for power or crusades for authority. The petty wars fought so one man may sit atop a throne instead of another would no longer be my business.

But I've lived that life before.

I've run before and look where that led me.

Wolves don't run.

Nature punishes wolves that try.

I've learned my lesson.

No more running.

And so I will face the thyrops head on instead of waiting for it to catch up to me some day. Better yet, I'll travel to its den while it sleeps and kill it while it hibernates the day away.

"To Varne we go, then, Wolfsram. Hopefully you like debauchery. Plenty of that where we're going."

"Debauchery!"

# 4

## WISHING WELL

There is evil, and then there is Varne.

A city all gods simultaneously chose to avert their eyes from. There is no recourse for justice in Varne. It is a place where morality goes to die. Men fuck men here. Women fuck women. And men and women fuck women and men.

It is said Varne has something for everyone.

Sex for the touch depraved.

Gambling for the financially struggling.

Drinking for those who need an escape.

Every drug imaginable for those who don't want to return from their escape.

Only false idols are worthy of worship in these city gates.

It is said someone doesn't know who they really are until they've been to Varne. It is the place where people can freely let out their monsters. It is the place where they can take off the mask society told them to wear. It is hell on earth to some, but for others it is the only refuge of heaven they will ever see. Most people who enter Varne die in Varne. They let the vices take control of them. They give their inner demons too much slack on the leash. They make foolish decisions, and their foolishness leads to their lethal demise.

Truthfully, it is the perfect place for Bloodlust to keep his forces in preparation for his march on Areopagus. Varne was originated as a mining colony hundreds of years ago. Its founder discovered gold in the ground and set up camps to excavate the treasure. Before long, an intricate network of tunnels and paths were carved under the earth and those who invested in the mining operation quickly became wealthy. They re-invested the riches into the erection of a city of casinos and bars and brothels. Word spread that Varne was a place to retreat for those who had voids to fill in their lives.

Soon after the launch of the city's grand opening, the gold underground dried up and the tunnels were sealed shut. Most forgot that Varne was built on hollow earth held up by rotting beams and termite-infested boards. But not Lundis, who taught me from an early age that he had advocated father to collapse the town by caving in the ground.

Father refused to see Varne be demolished. From a military aspect, it was too valuable a town to destroy for surveillance purposes. Father sent spies into the city to walk amongst the people and collect intel. Only there could he be informed of rumors on rebellion and whispers of treachery. The painful tradeoff for this information, though, was the continued exploitation of sex slaves and minor children, like my beloved Crixus.

Now that Lundis is dead and Bloodlust is alive, I have no doubt that's where his demons wait in dark silence, patiently waiting for the sun to set.

They are sitting ducks to a wolf like me. If they were nice enough to bury themselves for their funeral, I will be nice enough to fill in the dirt over their grave.

I faced no trouble entering the city. There is no military presence patrolling the cesspool's borders. This is a place dedicated to anarchy. Only those with enough money to bribe or enough strength to kill will survive.

Its streets are filled with trash and human excrement. Rats the size of small dogs sprint from rubble pile to rubble pile. Parasitic insects buzz in the humid, polluted air looking for hosts to feed from. Even walking through the city's streets is enough to make me feel as though I need a hot bath to scrub the smog off my skin.

The buildings were once elaborate towers built to reach the heavens. Now they are dilapidated, run down pillars of filth. Some have collapsed and fallen to the ground. Others still cling desperately to their foundation like trees ready to be uprooted by the next hurricane. The air reeks of feces and urination. Homeless addicts lay in the streets strung out on whatever drugs they could get their hands on in exchange for sexual favors.

Some of them smile up at me with toothless grins. They think I am their next ticket to a cheap high. It would be a mercy for me to bury them alongside the Blackbloods that creep below.

There are fewer innocent souls in this city than I can count on one hand. Mice do not willingly live among rats.

The hollow earth beneath is symbolic of the weak foundation these people base their lives upon. They all build towers and aim for their place among the stars while ignoring the sinking ground beneath their feet.

I slow my stride as I pass a wishing well. A man is bent over its basin. I can hear his hands splashing in the water below as he fishes out the coins lining the bottom. He is a junkie, surely, stealing people's wishes so he can fulfill his own. The scene is almost entertaining to me, watching the man's clothes become soaked as he stashes the coins in his pockets.

After he has stolen all he can, the man straightens himself up. Water drips from his heavy pockets as he looks around for anyone watching him, then leaves a puddle behind as he quickly sprints away from the crime scene.

Several minutes later, I watch a woman approach the coinless well. She kneels beside it, cupping her hands in front of her face like she's praying. After a few moments of silent meditation, the woman in rags stands and tosses a coin into the well. My ears twitch as its echoes ring out. I watch her scurry off, wondering what it is she wished for.

There isn't much sadder that comes to mind than an adult who believes the tossing of a coin can grant their wishes.

"Say," I call out to a man stumbling by. He looks up from his bare feet and stares at me like an Undead at the sight of fresh blood. He is strung out on some drug that makes his eyes hazy. The bloodshot and irritation make his eyes look as if they're bleeding. I continue, "I'll pay you a copper to help me find a man."

His eyes light up at the sound of money. "A copper?" he repeats. "Who you lookin' for? I'll find 'em alright."

"He's a man who loans sex slaves. A few years back he let me borrow a feisty she-wolf named Crixus. I think it was his daughter. Woman had a fine ass on her too."

"Ah," the man moans, his eyes lighting up with recognition. "I know Crixus. I know Crixus real good," he says, implying to me he knows her better than I hoped. "O' course, I preferred using her more when she was a youngin'. Wasn't much interested once she grew up on us."

I clench my fists and flex my jaw. It is taking everything in my power to not strangle this man dead where he stands.

"You're lookin' for Chimel. That's her pops. Don't think she's around no more. Heard she passed on. Chimel's here though. Just saw him at the cock fight. Man put ten shillings on the gators. Placed a bet they'd catch the cock in only ten minutes. Told him not to do it. Gamecocks are bred faster these days than they use to be."

"And where might I find this cock fight?" I ask through gritted teeth.

The man is swaying as if he can feel the earth moving beneath his feet.

The thought of this man laying hands on Crixus as a child makes me feel like a volcano ready to erupt. I haven't desired murdering a bystander in cold blood to this degree ever before. Love drives men to madness. Makes us do things only the devil can appreciate. Some of the worst things I've done in life have been justified by my love for others. Maybe the devil sees it as my weakness. Turns me into his greatest foot soldier through emotion alone.

Gods and devils are all one in the same.

They have the power to stop me from committing evil but both stay their hands.

I once thought it was because it was a part of some divine plan.

I now realize it's because they enjoy the entertainment after eons of boredom.

"Fighting pit is in Eastern Varne. Street's name is Hillsborough. Just outside a brothel named Paradise and a saloon named Thirsty Monk," the man states, itching a patch of leprous sores on his forearm.

I turn from him and start heading east. I hear him mumble and call after me.

"Aye!" he screams, his feet tripping over one another as he shuffles after me. "What about my copper?"

I continue walking, not looking back. If I look back it won't end well for either of us.

"Liar!" he screams, his exaggerated breath loud enough to be heard from afar. "You promised a copper!"

"It's in the wishing well," I shout, not turning to face the man. "If you want it, fish it out yourself!"

I listen as I hear the man sprint manically to the well's basin, followed by frenzied splashing as he throws his whole body into the water. He thrashes like a fish on a hook as he searches for the copper along the basin's floor. He is just as determined to find the coin as I am to defeat my enemies. I have no doubt he will find it.

I have no idea what the woman wished for when she cast the coin, but it won't come true anymore. Her sacrifice is my gain. Another human's future I've manipulated to further my cause.

# 5

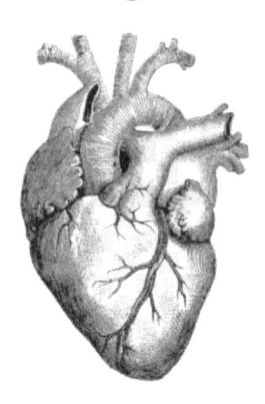

## Piss Slave

"I'm looking for a man," I whisper into the ear of another over the roaring crowd.

He looks up at me with whimsical eyes, like I've just told him some sort of joke. I smile, flashing my enlarged, sharpened canines to reassure I'm not joking in the slightest. He composes himself and replies with a laugh, "Then you're in the right town, but I don't swing that way, good man. I'm afraid I don't engage with faggots. Don't frown upon it of course! Whoever you stick your dick in doesn't matter to me, but I'm not your guy."

This warrants a laugh from me. I wrap my arm around the stranger's shoulders and bring him close, tightening my grip so as to inflict pain in him. He grimaces through gritted teeth and looks around at the crowd. They are all too preoccupied watching the fighting ring as a chicken evades ten hungry alligators. Unfortunately for my victim, they likely all have money at stake on the chicken's survival or demise. Their eyes wouldn't leave the ring if the sky were to fall right now. By the time I'm done with my acquaintance I doubt he will care whether the rooster lives or dies. By the time I'm done with my acquaintance, he will wish he were in the alligator pit himself.

Claws grow from my fingertips as I cling tightly to the man's shoulder. The tips inevitably penetrate his flesh and draw blood. I take great pleasure in watching his face light up with pain.

I look down at the chicken as it leaps from the back of one alligator onto the back of another. The fearsome beasts are too bulky to intercept the agile cock. It runs like someone who is running for their life. By the time the fearsome predators clamp their mighty jaws shut, their fangs close around nothing more than air and floating feathers.

Is this how the Blackbloods felt watching us Muzzled fight to the death against our own kind? Did they cheer and place wagers on who would win like these demented townsfolk do?

Do they do this out of boredom?

The sight of such an event makes me sick to my stomach.

It is one thing to kill a man.

It is another to defy nature in forcing prey to fend for its life in stakes weighed unfairly against it. But then again, I guess this shouldn't surprise me. I've been the chicken more times than I can count in life. Placed against predators whose survival counted on my demise. The cruel gods gathered around, all of them placing bets to see if the underdog could thwart its enemy and defy the odds stacked against it.

If I had so much as a copper on me now, I'd place it on the chicken. But I don't, so I'll leave the betting to the wicked men and women who have rents to pay.

"How about we go somewhere quieter, eh?" I ask. "Somewhere us gentlemen can talk."

My victim grunts loudly to acknowledge the question.

I drag him from the crowd like a lion drags a gazelle's panic-filled body away from a pack of hyenas. He follows like the subservient, worthless piece of prey he is. I push open the door of a nearby saloon. Luckily for me, most of the pub's usuals are outside watching a chicken run for its life. Unfortunately for my guest, there are little to no witnesses to observe what's about to happen.

Immediately, I throw the man into the closest table. His body collides awkwardly and sends the chairs toppling over. The table flips atop his grunting body. I watch him struggle to push it off with his frail frame and weak limbs.

The remaining patrons of the saloon go running out the front door as I rip the table off him and press the sole of my boot into his sternum. I look down at him and am almost disappointed at the lack of a fight he puts up.

The man's skin is bronze and stained by the sun. His hair is thinning but black in the places its thickness remains. His eyes are two separate colors—one brown and one blue, each covered with thick, bushy eyebrows that are close enough to nearly form a unibrow. He has an innocent look about him—not the sort of face you'd expect to find on a hardened criminal.

The look of fear in his eyes suggests he's either innocent or cowardly, or both. His clothes are made from fine cloth. His nails are freshly manicured. His face is clean shaven. He looks more like a wealthy merchant to me than a glorified pimp. And yet, I can see the striking resemblance between him and the woman I love. The symmetry of his face. The lining of his lips. The petite nose. The defined jawline.

"Please, whatever you want, I have money! I—erm—I know men who are into that sort of stuff... I meant no offense when I..."

"Shut up," I scoff, cutting off his wind as I press harder into his sternum. He is a man used to being able to bribe his way out of these situations. Unfortunately for him, not all the possessions in the world could prevent me from doing what I came to do. "Sit up," I command, releasing my foot from his chest and taking a step back.

The man quickly scoots his arse several feet away from me and props his back against the nearest wall. Blood seeps through his fine clothes from where I cut open his shoulder. It's comforting to know that blood stains even the wealthiest of cloths in this world.

"It is my understanding you have an assortment of children you loan to men with dark, twisted needs," I start. I stare at the man as he quivers unabashedly in the corner of the room.

"Is that what this is about?" he asks. "All you had to do was ask, good sir. There was no need for brutality in the matter. There is nothing to be ashamed about if you—"

"You misunderstand me. I am no pedophile, nor am I a faggot. Now, is it true?"

"You must understand..."

"Yes or no, is it true? And I can hear your heartbeat. Even though it races a mile a minute, I will know if you are lying."

"It is true, but such a thing is a common trade of practice this side of the Black Sea... There are a dozen—no—two dozen others who..."

"I didn't ask what others do, nor did I ask for a lesson in local industry practices."

"Then why did you—"

"Do you ever wonder why people are so evil?" I ask, pausing for a moment of reflection. I watch as confusion infects his face. To him, he likely thinks I'm some deranged lunatic. After all, he is not accustomed to being held hostage against his will like the children he sells for sex.

"Erm, I... I don't know..."

"I don't know either, yet they are evil nonetheless. It's funny, though. A good friend of mine once told me she thinks people are so evil because they are all searching for something that isn't out there."

"Uh..."

"They all think there is some universal answer waiting for their discovery. They do anything and everything they can to claw themselves closer. They turn themselves from men into monsters... Tell me, do you ever feel like a monster?"

"I suppose we are all monsters at times," he whimpers, hoping to answer my question in the way I want it answered. Men of his particular station are accustomed to changing the way they talk to the people around them.

"Some more than others, I'd say." I stare directly at him with more hatred welling inside me than he can fathom. "Nevertheless, when they realize this is all meaningless, they give in to their fleshly desires. They rape and murder and steal to fill the void inside. Convince themselves that they must fuck the world before the world fucks them. I, for one, resonate with my friend's sentiment. Do you?"

"Are you going to kill me, sir?"

"I asked you a question. It is impolite to talk out of turn," I growl. "What would you do to one of your child slaves if they didn't answer your questions, eh? Would you beat them? Let their disobedience be a message to the other kids?"

"Fucking the world is the only option men like me have," the man jumps back to answering the first question instead of the latter. "Every choice I've made, even the horrible ones, were done for self-preservation. There isn't a single thing I've done to those children that my master didn't do to me as a child."

"Ah, so the world fucking you is your justification for fucking it right back, eh?"

"You're damn right it is. The fact that you even have the audacity to accuse me of being a monster shows me you've never had to serve one yourself!"

"Twenty-four bloody months, you bastard!" I scream at him for no reason other than an inability to control my rage. "Twenty-four months I had a fucking muzzle around my mouth and chains around my wrists!" My eyes glow silver now, though through no conscious summoning of my own. "There are monsters in this world worse than mortal men, I assure you."

My body shifts before the man's eyes. Clothes tear. Black fur grows. Whiskers sprout from my snout. I don't let a single yelp escape my quivering lips as my bones shatter and rearrange. The pain only further fuels the anger I feel in the pit of my stomach. But it is nothing like the pain I will make this man feel.

After several seconds of agonizing transformation, I stand before the man I've identified to be Crixus's father. The man cowers in the corner like a child who fears a beating. This is the man who sold my Crixus for sex. This is the man who gave her up to the Blackbloods for a quick penny. This is the man who runs one of the largest child prostitution rings this side of the Black Sea.

I wish more than anything that I could ascend outside my body and watch what's about to happen from an unbiased perspective. I wish to see my demented, wolf-like body standing before him—the man who's just peed himself. I want to see what he sees. I want to feel the fear he feels. I want to dread the justice that's coming for him.

I am no god, but if I was, I'd be an unforgiving one.

"Who are you!" he screams at me.

I am a wolf, and wolves can't communicate with humans, so I leave him alone with his questions and thoughts.

I walk right up to him, fists clenched, fangs exposed. A low growl vibrates from my throat, unceasing for even a second. I get really close to him, close enough for my legs to straddle around his hunched, quivering body. There is a sting in my bladder. I release the tension in my lower abdomen and let my bodily fluids loose upon the man. The warm piss flows over him like a bucket of water dumped after a hot summer day.

He shrieks in disgust as my piss douses his expensive garb. Unfortunately for him, opening his lips to scream allows the piss to fill his mouth accordingly. He spits and gasps and holds his hands up to block the heavy stream that flows upon him. He learns his lesson and keeps his mouth shut from that moment on.

It takes longer for me to empty my bladder than I thought. The remainder of the time I just stand there, not averting my eyes for the briefest second as I watch this man take a shower in the liquid that wasn't good enough to be absorbed by my body. By the time I'm done, there isn't an inch of him that isn't soaked in the steaming, yellow fluid. I can smell the pungent odor of urine permeating in the air around us. It is a scent well-known to me. The same scent I've smelled upon trees I've marked my entire life.

By the time the man is able to collect himself and wipe his eyes clean of the piss, I'm once again standing several feet away from him, once more a human. My silver eyes are gone, along with the fur and fangs. I am as naked as the day I was born. I almost like the feeling of wearing no clothes. No cloth to restrict my skin's ability to breathe. I can feel the air moving around me in all directions. Nothing can restrain me from moving freely.

But I can sense how uncomfortable and frightened my guest is as he looks up at me. Though he is expecting to see a Lycan, he is left to deal with my nudity instead. He looks up at me with a million emotions. Words racing through his mind that he can't bring himself to speak.

The stench of urine burns my nostrils. It makes me smile.

"You might have heard us wolves mark our territory using the pheromones in our piss," I announce, then continue, "To answer your earlier question, no, I'm not going to kill you. You are not mine to kill. What I have planned for you is much worse than death."

"Then… Why… The pee… Your eyes… Silver? There's no moon… I don't understand…"

"I am here because of your daughter, Crixus."

"Crixus?" I watch the man's eyes light up at the mention of her name, then dim immediately when he realizes the repercussions of my statement. Horror quickly takes over his face. He winces in fear though I make no advance toward him. "Please, you have to believe me, I didn't want to sell her! I had no choice! They—"

"She is alive and well, cretin. I am not here to avenge her, and like I said, you are not mine to kill. If she wants you dead, I will preserve your life so she may issue your final judgment. But in the meantime, I have marked you as my territory, cretin. There is not a place in a thousand leagues you can go now where my species won't smell my markings. No amount of bathing will scrub clean the claim I've laid over you today. You are mine to control. And like the children you slave for profit, you now belong to me. You see, I did not come here to kill you. I came here to teach you a lesson. Before you die, I will see to it that you understand the feeling of answering to a master who doesn't care whether you live or die. That way when Crixus arrives you will understand the hell you put her through. And then, and only then, do you have my permission to die."

"Crixus? She's coming here?" The man's teeth chatter like the thought of his daughter is more horrifying than anything he's ever contemplated.

"Oh yes, good sir," I reply through a perverted grin. "I have fallen for your daughter sir, and she loves me in return. Our souls are mated. No force in this world will prevent her from finding me. But in the meantime, there is work to be done. The full moon is only a few hours away. We must be ready for Luna's ascent."

The man pushes himself onto his feet, his clothes dripping as he does so. He stands in a puddle of my piss and his feet splash as they collect themselves.

"But I've already asked you," he stutters, "What is it you want from me if not money?"

"You are going to help me collapse the mines that cut under Varne," I state simply, no emotion on my face.

Crixus's father stares at me as if I've just grown two heads. He is many things, but stupid is not one of them. He knows as well as I what monsters lurk beneath our feet. Every citizen of Varne knows what resides in the darkness underground. In a single sentence I've communicated my intentions of waging war against the Blackbloods without so much as mentioning their name. I watch as a new look of fear takes hold of the man's eyes.

This is not the same fear he felt when I stood before him as a Lycan, nor is it the fear he experienced when I uttered his daughter's name. This fear is something more. It is a fear of something far more sinister than the thought of dying. This is a man who understands what the Blackbloods are capable of, and in a single sentence I watch his life flash before his eyes.

The order I've just given him is like hearing his own death sentence. After all, I've just commanded him to close the gates of hell on the devil himself.

"Follow me," I say, not waiting for my slave to pause for reflection. I walk out the pub's door in time to see the crowd dispersing from the fighting ring. There is no more cheering, no more frenzy-filled madness. Nearby, a woman counts a large wad of crumpled bills and assorted coins.

"Who won?" I ask.

"Rooster lasted the full half hour and took home all the winnings!" she shouts at me through rotted teeth. I stare down at the pit of defeated reptiles. They sulk after the loss of a fresh meal. The results cause me to smile as I watch dozens of gamblers shuffle away. I can tell by their demeanors who bet on the alligator and who bet on the chicken.

"Always bet on the underdog," I whisper to myself.

"You're damn right!" the woman shouts through a toothless grin, shaking the crumpled dollars in her hand.

# 6

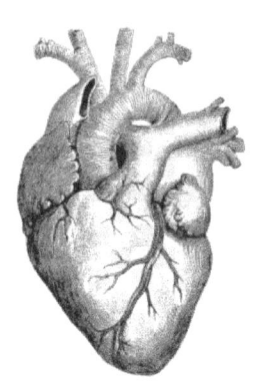

## RATS AND COCKROACHES

"You unlucky lot of men and women have been gathered here today because of your common acquaintance, Chimel," I announce, looking each person in their eyes as I walk back and forth between the line of them. Chimel squirms uncomfortably at the mention of his name. Each of my prisoners direct their looks of hatred in the slaver's direction.

"He has ratted each and every one of you out as frequent clientele of child trafficking," I continue, pausing so the gravity of the situation can settle in. The group of prisoners before me are each bloodied and battered. Not a single one of them allowed me to detain them without a fight. Some fought more gallantly than others, but all ultimately lost.

"I do not care what you were in a past life. Each and every single one of you has the opportunity to be reborn today. If you choose to defy me, you will die. If you try to betray me, you will die. If you don't do exactly what I say, when I say it, you will die."

The ragtag group of pedophiles sulk like a cooler of fish after being pulled from the lake. They stare at me with big eyes as the futility of the situation sinks in. But it is their own fault for biting down on my hook. I ripped them from their comfortable, lush lives into an environment where it's impossible for them to breathe. "Don't look so gloomy," I scoff. "You each have an opportunity before you to rectify your sins. If you do what I command of you, we will all part ways before the sun can set tonight."

"Get on with it then!" an impatient man with a double chin yells at me. I remember him distinctly. He was the only person present who wet his pants when I came to detain him for his crimes. He puts on a front for his fellow noble companions, but I see him for the coward he is. I wish he hadn't interrupted me. Now I must make an example of him for everyone present to see what I'm capable of.

The prisoners stand shoulder to shoulder before me inside the same saloon where I conquered Chimel. My silver eyes persuaded the bartender to close up shop for the day. There are no witnesses except for all those I've collected for my mission.

I approach the overweight man. I can still smell the urine in his britches. I can hear his heart struggling to pump blood through his obese veins. There could not be a better man to make an example of, since this man is likely not fit enough to carry out what I'd ask of him. More likely to drop dead of a heart attack than be of any use to me.

I hear the saliva gulp in his gullet as I stand before him. His heart is racing. Does he know those words he yelled would be his last?

"Oh, I'll get on with it," I whisper. My claws lash out faster than the man can blink. His rubbery neck opens like gelatin with a strawberry purée filling. Blood splashes onto my tunic before he has time to wrap his fat, sausage fingers over the lacerations. Those standing directly next to him jump away in surprise at what's just happened. We all listen to the gurgle of blood as he chokes and suffocates on the uncontainable fluid. He drops to his knees before me as he becomes too light-headed to support the great weight upon his knees. His dying body leans into me. When I step away from him, we all listen to the sound of his obese body thudding to the ground face down in a pile of his own blood.

I lock eyes with Chimel as I move away from the heavy corpse. The man has a look of horror written plainly on his face, as do all those he ratted out. The sight of death is still something new to them. Watching someone die still has an effect on them. Yet it frightens them even more to see how little an effect it has on me.

They can tell from my body language this is not the first life I've taken. I straighten myself up and lean into my indifference. I want each and every one of them to know I am willing to send them into the afterlife to join this man. Fear forces loyalty, and each of these people are more fearful than they've ever been before.

"I have no tolerance for impatience," I continue. "I am offering all of you a second chance, but if you'd prefer to join this man in whatever hell awaits you, say so now, and I will send you on your way."

Silence penetrates the room. The prisoners all avert their eyes from me, each of them too afraid to meet my gaze of condemnation. They are the perfect group of people to carry out the mission I have planned. They are each more afraid of the devil they know than the devil they don't.

"Very well," I continue as if I didn't just kill a man in cold blood. "As I was saying, you are each equally deserving of hellish deaths. You have each committed sins unspeakable to mankind. You are each rapists of childhood innocence. But luckily for you, I am not a god, and therefore I do not have the authority to pass judgment. Instead, I am sending you each with an opportunity to defeat a devil that walks on this very earth. I'm sure most of you know what force hibernates under the same ground we walk upon."

I watch this statement cause the prisoners to look at one another. I don't have to speak in exact terms for them to know what I'm referring to. The arrival of Blackbloods in Varne was likely an event all locals witnessed. No one is likely to forget a swarm of demons descending from the sky to seek refuge in one's own town.

"You are going to help me collapse the mines they currently slumber in," I announce, cutting straight to the purpose of my mission. I watch each of their faces become contorted with dread at the prospect. Several of them want to interrupt me and impulsively speak what's on their minds. The dead body at their feet deters them.

"There are eleven known entrances to the gold mines that tunnel beneath our feet. Now that your comrade is dead, there are sixteen of you remaining. I made sure to employ more of you than what was necessary as a reminder that you are all expendable to me. I need eleven of you, but if your number dwindles for disobeying me, Chimel has a long list of clients I can recruit in your stead. Is that understood?"

The group collectively nods their heads like a batch of disciplined school children.

"Great," I cheer sarcastically. "Now, Chimel, please uncover the means of our mission." Chimel scurries across the room and pulls a tarp off a pallet of burlap bags. It is bizarre to see the man who birthed Crixus be so subservient. Having known his daughter, I imagined he would have more of a backbone. She is everything he isn't. Brave and cunning. Fierce and loyal. She could kill her father as easily as a winemaker squishes grapes.

"With the help of Chimel's connections, I have acquired twenty burlap bags of black powder. As some of you may or may not know, black powder is one of the most flammable and volatile substances sold on the black market. Luckily for us, Varne is home to one of the largest black market arms dealers in the world, so obtaining it was no difficult matter."

The group of prisoners stare at the burlap sacks like open nooses on a gallows. Now that I've revealed to them the means of collapsing the mines, they are smart enough to know what I have in store for them.

"I have laid out a map along the bar that has each of your names on it assigned with a specific entrance of the mine. The plan is simple in execution. Each of you will carry a sack of black powder to your designated entry. I have taken the liberty to travel to each one and stash a book of matches. All you have to do is light the knotted end of the burlap and throw it into the mine. Now, we will need to do this at the same time so the Blackbloods aren't free to flee from different entrances, so you all have approximately a half hour to get to your spots. Then, when the town bell rings at the stroke of a new hour, you will have until the fifth chime to light your sacks.

"The explosion will likely cause a surface landslide. Everything you know and love about Varne will become consumed by the earth. All the towers your ancestors built to be seated amongst the gods will be sucked into the pits of hell. Anyone you know or love too slow to race against the impact will be consumed. Consider it a mercy I've brought you in on my plan, for you are the ones who will have enough notice to escape."

"Right," Chimel chimes in, "The longer the lot of you wait here the less time you have to reach your positions! Get in line to grab your burlap bag, then go to the bar to see where your assignment is. No talking to one another! You only have a half hour, I don't want anyone thinking they have time for funny business! The man has an army of ravens in the sky reporting your every move. If you even think about defying him, it will mean the death of us all!"

"Death!" Wolfsram repeats from outside the saloon's dusty glass window. He pecks at the glass to catch the attention of all those present.

All things considered, planning Varne's destruction was almost easier than herding sheep this morning. People like this only want one thing—to survive. They are cockroaches that don't mind betraying their own species for a chance to live. I could have told them they were to assist me in overthrowing the Undead Empire itself and they would have fallen in line so long as I had a plan laid out for them that guaranteed preservation.

None of them say a word as they fall in behind one another to grab their burlap bag, some of them having to step over the bloody bastard's corpse to do so. Chimel gently tosses one bag to each person in line. Their hands cradle the bags delicately as if it could catch fire with only the slightest misstep. I watch from a distance as they huddle around the map I've laid out for them. Chimel assists them in deciphering who needs to go where. He is the leader of the misfits, even though they all hate him for implicating them.

"All right, out the door the lot of ya!" Chimel shouts. They each look directly at me for approval. I nod at them and gesture toward the door without another word. Wolfsram takes to the sky as they enter the city streets. I have no army of ravens with me, but Wolfsram's presence will be enough to make them think I do.

I stand in silence until all of them have disappeared from sight, then ask Chimel, "Do you think they'll all go through with it?"

"I haven't a doubt in my mind. The lot of them are all of noble birth. They've given orders their whole lives. Now that their lives and reputations hang in the balance, they'd damn near kill a king if it allowed them to keep their skeletons in the closet."

"Good," I respond. "Did you speak to the arms dealer about supplying archers?"

"You mean the ones that cost fifty golden eagles to hire? Yes. Eleven archers, each positioned outside the mines and ready to kill the second they see someone light a burlap bag on fire. Not a single one of them will know their deaths will be the first of thousands," Chimel informs, then looks at me seriously. He asks, "And how am I supposed to know you don't have plans to betray me so soon?"

"I told you. You aren't mine to kill. Until I've reunited you with your daughter, there is no need to watch your back. None of this would have been possible without you. You are the rat that single-handedly destroyed an entire city."

"Splendid," Chimel whispers to himself.

"We'd better get going," I say, "There are a few more things that need to be done before the sun sets."

"And what of the wolves being held captive by the Blackbloods underground?" Chimel chimes in. "Will you so easily leave them behind to die?"

"I was once one of those wolves," I reply coldly. "And believe me when I tell you, a quick death by suffocation is more of a mercy than anything they've experienced since their bondage. Besides, you're a fool if you think this will kill the Blackblood army. This plan was merely meant to slow them down. They are already dead inside. Burying them will do little to deter the war tonight. I have no doubt the Muzzled prisoners with them will emerge from the earthquake. Bloodlust won't let them die so easily."

"You mean... You think they'll survive the landslide?" Chimel gulps.

"Oh," I reply through a smirk, "I'm counting on it."

# 7

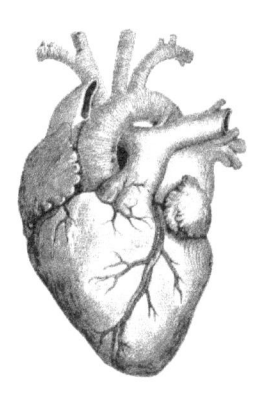

## The Witch

"I didn't think you'd come," I say, greeting someone I never thought I'd ever see again. I stand beside the Wirewood River, its rapid waters instilling a sense of serenity in my soul. In less than an hour, I've traveled from the turmoil and filth of Varne to the peace and quiet of nature's solitude.

I've reached the calm before the storm, I think to myself.

"I didn't think you were alive," Skillah grumbles with less enthusiasm than I'd hoped. I see now the years have been kind to her. Though she nears her seventieth birthday, she still appears to look a few days younger than thirty. Gossipers can say what they want about alchemy, but this woman seems to have discovered the fountain of youth.

"You seem disappointed that I am," I reply.

"Disappointed? No," she laughs. "Surprised? Very much so."

"Well it's nice to see life still has a way of surprising you after all these years."

"The problem is that life never seems to stop surprising me. And yet here you are, standing on the outskirts of Areopagus looking like the ghost of your murdered father. The resemblance is striking, I'll give you that. I had my doubts when I read the letter, but I no longer need you to prove your bloodline... Now that I gaze upon you, I see you are Sylvian."

"Still, I'd submit to whatever test you request," I admit, knowing it must be hard to believe Syrus Sylvian would return to this kingdom after all these years.

"I'd sooner request you to explain the reason for your presence. Every second I speak to you is an act of treachery."

"I didn't know you held yourself to such a high moral standard," I reply. "Seems you've done everything in your power to distance yourself from the kingdom short of moving across the nation."

"Ventur wouldn't allow it. I'd be dead if I tried. He knows what secrets I hold. His Scouts keep tabs on me and report back to him regularly. We both pretend one another don't exist and carry on with our miserable lives. He doesn't ask for my services anymore though. I've made it clear I am not his to control."

"Well, then I'll just come out and say it. I'm here in need of your services."

"I figured as much," Skillah sighs. "I am not dumb. Full moon tonight. Bloodlust lurks in the south. Ventur readies his forces. A war is coming tonight. But what I didn't anticipate was for you to return."

"Death didn't suit me as well as I'd hoped," I reply.

"And yet you have brought it to our kingdom with you."

"It was coming for this city regardless."

"And you want me to help you retake your father's throne, I'm guessing?"

I look around us. The banks of the river at our feet are gorgeous. The landscape sprawls with wildlife in every direction I turn. The water flows with little current. The early evening breeze causes the high grass to dance. The air smells of honeysuckle and pinecones. I can hear the footsteps of wild game rummaging through the forest. The Areopagus looms in the southwest several miles away, and we stand elevated above it by several hundred feet.

All of this will soon be plagued by war.

The vibrant greens and crystal blue water will lose their color. Soon blood will fill the water and bodies will litter the grass.

Us mortals are so fickle. Whatever destruction we cause tonight will be erased by nature's healing. The vines will overcome the rubble. Rain will put out the fires. The dead will fertilize autumn's flowers. Winter's snow will purify all that was defiled.

"Tell me, do you still see colors around people?" I ask.

"I told you as a child, Syrus. They are more than just colors. They are auras, and yes, I still see them."

"Repeat what you told me as a child."

"You had the most unique aura I've ever seen. Most people only have one, maybe two colors making up their aura. Yours was multicolored. Radiated so bright it was almost blinding."

"And now?"

"Now?" she repeats. "Now I only see black surrounding you."

"And what does that color mean?"

"Black is not a color, Syrus," she clarifies, "It is an absence of color. Whatever you've done, whoever you've been dealing with... They have ruined you, Syrus. Whatever devil you've made a deal with, they've taken your soul."

The statement is so absurd it almost makes me laugh. Even as a kid I doubted this woman's ability to see colors surrounding people. Lundis taught me to believe in logic and order. To put my faith in the natural world, not the things we cannot see. Yet every time he turned me over to Skillah for my lessons in alchemy, this woman tried to fill my head with nonsense on witchcraft. It was laughable then, and it is laughable now.

"They've taken more than just my soul, Skillah. The thing is, there is only so much you can lose before you no longer fear death. That's what makes me different from Bloodlust and Ventur in the coming war. They both value survival. Winning the throne wouldn't be a victory if they died in the process. But me? I don't care whether I live to see the sun rise on the morrow, so long as I've dragged my enemies to hell with me."

"And how do you intend on doing that?" She eyes me skeptically. Now is the time for me to cut to the chase.

I squat beside the river and dip my hand in it. Its coolness is calming to me. Unlike fire, water is the ultimate equalizer. Where fire scorches, water cleanses. And Areopagus needs a cleansing more than any city I know.

I point downriver to Skillah, then say, "I need your help tonight. I need you to destroy the dam that holds the Wirewood River at bay." I say the words matter-of-factly, as if there is little implication to be drawn from the statement.

I see the strain that overcomes Skillah's face. She can read between the lines. Wirewood is the second largest river in all the realms. Only the Pagean is bigger. Consequentially, the dam that holds back the floodgates were built generations ago by the brightest engineers available to the Areopagus.

The pitfall of any metropolis is its need for nearby freshwater sources. The larger the city, the more water necessary to sustain rapid population expansion. Areopagus's success is due in part to its close proximity to Wirewood, but it is this same advantage that began endangering citizens a few hundred years ago.

After a season of flooding brought a plague carried by mosquitos, the kingdom decided it was in its own best interest to distance themselves from the water source, keeping it close enough for easy access but far enough to keep the flooding and wetland erosion away. Though it has been generations since the river flowed freely, the impressions of erosion still cut through the rock opposite the dam.

"I heard rumors of an earthquake in Varne," Skillah announces, deflecting my request.

"Rumors spread much faster in the east," I reply.

She looks at me with an accusatory scowl. "They say the mines caved in and nearly the entire city sank into a natural landfill. An entire city erased off the map in the blink of an eye. I'm guessing you had some hand in that as well?"

"The entire realm is better off without Varne," I justify.

"Maybe so," she admits, "But the destruction the Wirewood would cause the Areopagus if this dam was destroyed... It would flood the entire city, Syrus."

"That's why I asked you to destroy it."

"The Undead and Blackbloods can fly, Syrus. The only people your flood would harm are the innocent citizens of Areopagus."

"Can it be done?" I ask, not commenting on her train of logic.

"The real question is *should* it be done," Skillah corrects me.

"Your trade is alchemy, not philosophy, Skillah."

"I'll be damned if I let you use me like some puppet and be the reason why thousands of innocent men and women perish. If you don't want to explain the purpose behind your mission, you came to the wrong woman." She's more stubborn than a heifer in mating season.

"Have you heard what happened in Queensmyre?" I ask candidly.

Skillah curtly nods her head.

"That was me, Skillah. I burned an entire city down in one night just so I could decrease the odds of being attacked by Undead in the west." I take several steps toward her, my eyes burning into hers with intensity. "I didn't think before I did it. I just did it. I burned an entire city full of innocent people down to the ground to increase my odds of survival." I point to the river without breaking eye contact. "I don't care if it's by water or fire, Skillah. The Areopagus will fall tonight. Let me make it clear that I do not need you to accomplish my mission. But just know that if you refuse me, the innocent lives of the Areopagus will face a far worse tragedy than flooding. It is called natural selection, Skillah. Those smart enough will have already fled the city. When the war breaks loose tonight, even more will flee. And those remaining by the time this dam breaks... Well, they better hope they know how to swim."

Skillah looks at me with pain in her eyes. It is as if she doesn't recognize me. She lifts a hand to her heart as if it is broken. In the blink of an eye, it looks as if she has aged eighty years. Her youthful look fades momentarily and exposes the stress and anguish the last twenty years have caused her. Tears form in her eyes at the sight of what I've become. I'm no longer the innocent child she taught. There is no elixir of chemicals she can mix to fix the void inside me. I may look like my father to her, but I do not have my father's soul. She was right. Whatever devil I've made a deal with, they've darkened me. In its place they've left nothing but cold bitterness.

"I will do what you ask of me," she replies, a single tear rolling down her cheek. "But I ask for a favor in return."

"And what is that?"

She stares at me longingly, biting her tongue to hold back the words a moment longer. "I still love him, Syrus," she admits. Now the dam that breaks is the one behind her eyes. She loses composure and lets the tears roll down her cheeks without restraint.

I shake my head. "No," I reply. "It isn't possible."

"It is!" she shouts, reaching into a small purse that hangs from her necklace. "Look! Have a look for yourself!"

She tosses me a small vial containing a red, gelatinous liquid inside. I catch it with one hand and examine it closer. It looks like stale blood at first sight. "What is this?"

"The cure," Skillah replies.

My mind goes back to what an Undead named Wilhelm once told me. *We have discovered the cure to the Blackblood virus, Sylvian. Your questions reveal how little you know, exiled prince.* I dismissed the accusation as a bluff at the time. If there was a cure, I'd know about it. Better yet, if there was a cure, the Acolytes would have discovered it in the Crusades. Yet here is Skillah, the most talented alchemist in all the realms, once more challenging my ignorance on the matter.

"Nonsense," I reply. "There is no cure."

"There is," Skillah asserts. "I've tested it myself on an injured Blackblood. It works, Syrus."

"How?" I look up from the vial to examine her face for lies.

"Sylvian blood," she answers, sadness written on her face.

"Ah," I sigh, finally understanding how all these pieces come together. All at once, a dozen unsolved mysteries become solved in a single utterance. Saunter, my sister. Atlas, Bloodlust's soldier. Me, still alive.

Sylvian blood is the cure to the Blackblood virus, and everyone has known it this whole time. Well, everyone but me.

It finally makes sense. Ventur must have learned that Sylvian blood can reverse the curse from Saunter in battle. Likewise, Bloodlust must have tested Atlas's blood on his own soldiers. Together, Ventur and Bloodlust likely saw the utility and danger posed by the Sylvians, all before I stumbled across their paths at an opportune time, clueless of their schemes.

And better yet, Ventur and Bloodlust think they got rid of us three for tonight's war. Unfortunately for them, the devil I serve is a clever bitch.

I stare back down at the vial of Sylvian blood Skillah provided and consider her request once more. "I cannot do what you ask, Skillah. He must die," I confirm, tossing the vial back to her.

"Think about the man he was before the virus, Syrus! He was your greatest mentor! A teacher to us all," she begs, doing everything she can to tug at my heart strings. She is right. Before becoming Bloodlust, Lundis was many things. A wise teacher, a caring friend, a fearsome warrior, but above all else, he was Skillah's lover.

Skillah catches the vial frantically like her life depends on it. I don't care to ask how she obtained the Sylvian blood. Ironic, how I thought a vial of black blood would be my savior in Sygon. Now Skillah thinks a vial of red blood will be hers. But Bloodlust must answer for the crimes of this life, not find redemption from his actions in a past one.

"Lundis is dead, Skillah. There is no bringing him back, cure or no cure. You knew Lundis better than me, but even I know Lundis wouldn't be able to live with himself after seeing the atrocities he's committed. You'd be bringing him back to live in eternal guilt, Skillah. For what? So you have someone to warm your side in bed at night? I fear his cold heart won't be capable of doing even that."

"There is still good in him, Syrus!"

"Then hell will gain an angel tonight," I reply.

"You need me," Skillah counters.

hers do what I've asked of you."

...ing her head. "For the Dybbuk Box

...hten subconsciously. I haven't
...ttle boy. Even then, the idea of
...ories. Skillah sees she's caught
...his information to wrap me around

..., "You were too young as a child to know the truth of ...matter, but the rumors you heard of me were true. Before your father brought me in to tutor you and Selena in alchemy, I was sentenced to death by gallows for witchcraft."

We lock eyes with one another to share the sincerity of the moment. She's right, my father's staff caused an uproar over her pardoning and subsequent employment within the castle. I don't know what crimes she was sentenced to be hanged for, but criminals rarely draw such a penalty for trivial matters.

"I left that life behind me at the request of your father. He gave me a second chance. But since his passing, Ventur has pushed me to use my abilities for the betterment of the Undead Empire. The point is, I have information you need, Syrus. You were wise to send a raven to me before tonight. I am caught between this war as much as you are. But luckily for you, I haven't chosen who I want to help win as of yet. I am giving you the opportunity to be the victor. All you have to do is promise to spare Bloodlust. You don't even have to be the one to administer the cure—just get me in a room with him. I know he will remember me. Deep, deep inside the monster he's become is the man I once loved."

"You don't know Blackbloods like I do, Skillah. I was a slave to them for twenty-four moons. The virus... it does terrible things to them. It is like

being possessed by a demon. They are like Lycans, o[...]
come once a month when the moon is full—it is never-[...]

"You haven't seen what Sylvian blood can do to reverse t[...]
I have seen it firsthand!"

"Whose blood is that, Skillah?" I ask, my curiosity getting th[...]
me as I stare at the vial in her hand. It is a fifty-fifty chance it is Sau[...]
Atlas's. But how Ventur discovered such a cure is a mystery. Like ponder[...]
who the first man was that discovered that cow milk was edible. No one[...]
stops to question why a man dared to drink the liquid from another
species' body. Nor do we ask how he came to know, we only care that we
can obtain nutrition from an animal's udder.

Skillah replies nonchalantly, "Ventur's Scouts captured a dying Blackblood out west. She was nearly dead when they found her. Her smoking
corpse had spent all day in the sun. They found her in a valley surrounded
by mountains. The desert floor was littered with nearly a thousand slaughtered Blackbloods, most of which were vaporized by the direct sunlight.
The clever beast had managed to pile enough bodies on top of her to
protect her from the daylight. The Scouts found her delirious body at the
bottom of the pile of corpses and realized she was still alive. Brought her
back to Areopagus for questioning."

My ears prick up at the story being told. I realize I'm holding my breath
involuntarily. My heart is racing at the words being told to me. I know
this story, though I was not there to experience its conclusion. Valley
surrounded by mountains. Desert floor. Nearly a thousand slaughtered
Blackbloods. No. It can't be. It's utterly impossible. But Skillah has no
reason to lie to me. The witch has no knowledge of my connection with
these events. Her words make me feel like I am a kid again exchanging
glances with Vesper for the first time on the outskirts of the Neverglades. I
want to strangle the words out of Skillah faster than she is speaking them.

"They locked her in the Bloody Tower until she awoke. Took nearly a week for her to come conscious, and when she did, the bitch was rabid with the virus. It was consuming her body faster than Ventur could get information out of her. She wouldn't talk. She killed three interrogators before Ventur gave up hope and ordered her to be executed."

At this point it is taking everything inside of me to not beg Skillah to get to the end of the story. My mouth fills with blood from where my molars bite down on my tongue. I do everything in my power to hide the look of crazed desperation I feel inside. But each sentence makes me feel more alive as Skillah comes closer to a conclusion. All I can do is hope that the conclusion is one favorable to me.

"But then something changed after several weeks," Skillah continues. "The virus stopped spreading in the woman's body. In fact, after a few months, her body started reversing the curse. It was miraculous. And then we noticed the lump in her stomach. She was pregnant, Syrus, all while her body was healing itself of the Blackblood virus!"

The weight of the news is enough to bring me to my knees. I collapse to the ground involuntarily. If the things Skillah says nonchalantly are true, Vesper is not only alive, but she has bore me another child. Tonight marks twenty-five moons since I saw her last. Twenty-five moons I've assumed she was dead. Twenty-five moons I've cursed myself for not being strong enough to save her.

"Oh gods," Skillah sighs with realization. My buckling knees have given me away. She connects the dots faster than the time it takes for my tears to hit the ground. I can't breathe. My life is some sort of cruel joke. I spent twenty years thinking I was the cause for my family's death only to learn I was framed by Ventur. I spent twenty-five moons thinking I was the reason Vesper and Sephora died only to learn Enchantress has spared them.

"I had no idea, Syrus," Skillah exclaims. "Even Ventur... I mean... We naturally assumed the child belonged to Atlas! Your name hasn't been uttered in these parts for years! And seeing it was a Blackblood that was pregnant—well—naturally we assumed Bloodlust's adopted son to be the babe's father. He is descendant from Sylvian the First, after all. The child was born with silver eyes. The mother wouldn't tell us who the father was... Atlas was the most obvious answer... But... you mean to tell me that the woman is... The child is..." Skillah is equally as lost for words as me.

Vesper is alive.

My wife is alive.

And I am the father to a second child.

I have cursed the gods countless times throughout my life, and now they pay me back for all they've taken.

It must have been our intimacy—before I faced the Blackbloods—that conceived the child. I should have known Vesper's unwillingness to die would have preserved her. Throughout my entire life, the woman has been a survivor. Even when I first found her in that dark cave all those years ago, she was a survivor. As the Blackbloods pulled me into their caves while I watched the sun kill my wife, I concluded all hope was lost.

It wasn't.

She pulled other corpses on top of her to block out the light.

She weathered away the day under the shade of the dead.

She survived as she always has.

And she is alive.

She is alive.

This changes everything.

# 8

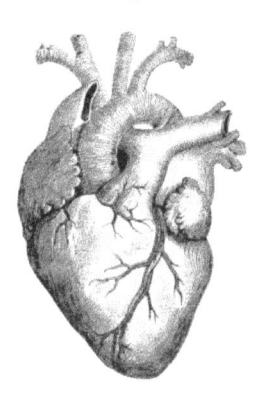

## Newborn

"What of the child?" I ask, pushing myself back onto my feet. The emotions come in waves, but I must weather through the storm. Enchantress has just given me an opportunity to win back my wife and my throne in the same night. Much more is riding on this mission than I could have imagined.

"Alive and healthy," Skillah mutters sympathetically. It is like she is my teacher and I am a child once again. I can sense the empathy in her tone. She realizes she's just delivered news to me that will cause irreparable damage to my enemies, her lover included. "But Syrus-"

"Boy or girl?" I interrupt, wiping the tears from my eyes. I curse inwardly at the sign of weakness. Now is not the time to be weak. Wolves don't cry.

"A little boy," she whispers fearfully, watching as the calculated anger takes over my expression. I am the father to a son. And it is the blood of my son that saved Vesper. Sylvian blood has been the answer this entire time to eradicating the Blackbloods. This war can either end by the spilling of my own blood or the spilling of an entire kingdom's. I choose the latter of the two.

"Syrus, whatever you're thinking-"

My eyes burn into her with a lifetime's worth of pent-up rage. The look instantly shuts her up. It is like a punch straight to her gut—for the first time since our reunion began, I let her see who I truly am behind the mask I wear. And though I only let her into my soul for the briefest moment, that is enough to strike the fear of hell into her.

"You said earlier the devil I serve has ruined me," I growl from my diaphragm. "But now I know you are wrong. For twenty years now the gods have done nothing but take everything I love away from me. For twenty years now the gods have given my natural birthright to my enemies. Everything my father stood for has been disgraced. The Creator has kicked me to the ground and pinned me there while Ventur and Bloodlust continue to betray my father's memory. And now, as soon as I return, you have the gall to look me in my eyes and tell me the devil who holds my leash has ruined me? No, Skillah. I realize now that I owe my entire life to the devil who holds my leash. I am her Hellhound, and I will drag to hell whoever she commands me to.

"When I was a child, you told me you see colors around people—you called them auras. You said the colors around my body were unlike any you'd ever seen, and now you tell me they've been consumed by darkness... Let me assure you, my aura may be gone, but my resolve has never been greater. So go home, Skillah. If you will not blow the dam I will do it myself. Better yet, tell Ventur I have returned and I am coming for him. Because the next time you see me I will be wearing your lover's skull as a crown of my victory."

"Gods be good," Skillah moans as she sees the conviction on my face. Though this woman hasn't seen me for twenty years, she knew my father and mother personally, so she knows better than most what I'm capable of. Skillah looked youthful and beautiful when this conversation began. Now she looks like a woman who should have died ten years ago. Her appearance before was all an illusion. A mask, like the one I wear for bystanders. But now we let each other in to show our true identities. She sees the beast that lurks inside me, and I see that she is so old and feeble, the wind could blow her over if it wanted to.

She continues, "I'm so sorry, Syrus… You didn't deserve what happened to you."

"If you are truly sorry, you'll tell me the nature of the Dybbuk Box before you take leave," I assert. I know as well as her that such a mystery could be detrimental to my plans.

"If the things you say are true, we are now enemies, Syrus," Skillah informs. "I cannot reveal what you ask of me."

"Then be gone," I order.

"For what it's worth, I am sorry it has to come to this," she whispers as tears reemerge on her face.

"Save your apologies for my father," I reply coldly. "For he is the one that saved you from the gallows, and I will be the one that corrects his mistake."

I don't wait for a response before taking flight. I let anger fuel me as passion and pain boil beneath my skin. There is much to be done and little daylight left to achieve it.

But under all the anger that burns inside me lies a feeling I haven't felt in many moons.

Hope.

## 9

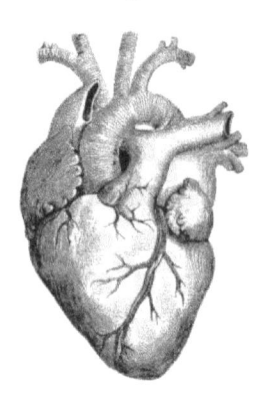

### Peanut Butter & Jelly

"It's like a real life telling of the damsel in distress," Chimel exclaims.

"Another word and I'll cut your tongue from your mouth," I threaten, tightening the vambrace around my forearm. Nikolai's Black Knight armor fits my body like a glove, and Chimel has done a stupendous job washing the dirt from it. It sparkles under the sunset with accent hues of dark purple. I stare down at the obsidian plates that cover my body. As a child, the Black Knights terrified me. Now I am one of them. A false member of the most elite group of warriors this world has seen.

Once I put on the knight helm, my identity will be hidden from all. No one will know that I am not Undead. My eye color will be indistinguishable beneath the cold metal. I can slip into the city without suspicion and enter the most safeguarded areas without being questioned. This armor is a VIP ticket to go wherever I want, when I want.

The ironic thing about war is, they are easier to win when you don't have an army. The more people you have following your cause, the more attention you bring to yourself. Ventur and his generals will be able to see Bloodlust's forces coming from miles away.

And me?

I'll take the throne back in plain sight.

I lift the helmet and stare at my reflection in its dark surface. Will Vesper even recognize the man I've become? I am not the man I was twenty-five moons ago. It feels as though I've lived several lifetimes in the span of two years, and my face reflects such. And even worse, will I even recognize her?

There is no telling what happens to a body after shifting into a Blackblood and then back into an Undead. Not to mention she smoldered in the heat of the sun for an entire day before being found. What if she is so scarred I don't even recognize her?

These are all things I don't have the luxury to worry about. I made vows to my wife on our wedding day. When wolves mate, they mate for life. Though she is Undead, she is my she-wolf. It is my duty to protect her with life and limb so long as her heart has a pulse.

There is now a knot in my stomach that wasn't there an hour ago. News of Vesper's resurrection has filled me with nerves. I am no longer a man who has nothing to lose. Instead, I realize now that I have everything to lose all over again. If I do not win tonight, I will merely repeat my failure from twenty-five moons ago and be forced to grapple with the loss of my loved ones all over again.

I cannot let that happen.

I slowly lower the helm over my head and let it encapsulate me in darkness. I watch Chimel through the slitted visor as he gets a first glance at the completed armor. Instead of fear, the man smiles.

"Speak," I command.

He lets out a laugh, "I was just thinking that I would hate to be the one who crosses you in battle tonight."

"Are there any gaps in the armor I need to cover?" My voice echoes inside the helm.

"Every inch of you is horrifying from head to toe, good sir."

"Good," I reply, bringing my hand to the sword hilt at my hip. I draw it for the first time. It is deadly light in my grip. Though it's been many years since I've held a sword, my muscle memory has hardly faded. I give the blade a few test swings with both arms, then swing it with my dominant hand only. I parry the air, then practice blocking oncoming attacks.

When I'm satisfied I return the blade to the sheath on my hip and look back at Chimel. We are a team of two, and now that Skillah has rejected me, I'm forced to rely on this miscreant more than I wanted to.

"Do you have everything you need for tonight?" I ask. He cannot see my eyes beneath this mask, but hopefully he can feel their intensity on him.

"I will not let you down," he bows his head before me. "I will use the remaining black powder from Varne to blow the base of the dam as soon as the sun hits the horizon."

"And then?" I don't know why I drill the plan into him like he is a child. He is much smarter than I give him credit for. Regardless of the man's sins, the man is better at this line of criminal work than me.

"And then I go spy on the alchemist to make sure she doesn't interfere in your plans."

"And if she does?" I ask, my gut swelling with nerves as I await his answer.

"I kill her," he answers candidly.

"Good," I reaffirm.

"Can I ask something?" Chimel interjects before the silence ruins our conversation.

I nod.

"Why do you do this?" he asks. "I mean, why put your life on the line when you can flee now and die happy somewhere else?"

I stare at him through the slitted visor and look him over. Him and I are not so different. Standing before me is a man who has prioritized survival his whole life, as have I. But the means in which we have survived could not be more different. I find my strength in my loved ones and launched this crusade to avenge them. Chimel, on the other hand, will sacrifice anyone and everything to save himself. Doesn't matter if it is sex slaves or children or his own daughter.

"When I was a child, my favorite thing to eat was peanut butter and jam sandwiches," I say, my voice echoing all around us. Chimel looks at me with amused confusion. I continue, "And though we had royal chefs, I would often make the sandwiches myself. I'd sneak in the kitchen after hours when it got dark and make them as a midnight snack. And when I made them, I would always lick the knife to clean it of peanut butter and again to taste the jam. One evening, my mother saw me licking the knife at the dinner table and reprimanded me. She warned me to not lick the knife, Chimel, because it could cut my tongue severely. But the problem was, I had already licked the knife a hundred times without getting cut, so her warning meant nothing to me. It was like warning a monkey not to climb a tree because it could fall.

"Men like me and you, Chimel, we continue to lick the knife because something deep inside us wants to see if it will cut us. We are not ordinary men who listen and obey and do as we're told. The gods have hardened our hearts—we cannot help the evil we commit. You traffic slaves for money. I kill anyone who obstructs my path. Our tongues run along the length of the blade secretly wishing it would draw blood. But it never has, and men like us won't stop our wanton ways until it does."

For a brief moment I watch the mask Chimel has been wearing in my presence slip ever so slightly. Though he is not a Lycan or Undead, there is a monster inside of him he hides from the world. And like us Lycans, he does everything he can to hold it back so it cannot roam freely. But I see through his façade. I know the sort of depraved demon he hides from me. The kind of demon that profits off selling his own daughter for sex. I don't buy the fake smiles and charismatic charm he flashes my way. I am not like the rest of the population. No, it takes a monster to know a monster. There is no mask this man can hide behind that I won't see through.

Chimel quickly composes himself and chuckles, "I do love a good allegory, good sir, but you make one mistake. You are right that I lick the knife because it has yet to cut me, but it appears you lick the knife and then purposefully gouge it into your own heart. Where I seek survival by running away from the storm, you do everything in your power to chase tornadoes. Excuse my candidness, but you compose yourself like a man with a death wish."

I chuckle at the man's honesty. For a commoner, he is smarter than most. Maybe that's why he's gotten away with his criminality for so long. But his words certainly have a way of making the truth sound whimsical.

I match his candidness in my response, "Like I peed on you, so too has the devil left her mark on me, Chimel. I don't have her permission to die until I've carried out her work. Until then, my death wish will never be granted."

I turn from him and feel my feet lift from the ground. The sky wraps around me as the sun burns closer toward the edge of the atmosphere. In less than an hour, the moon will rise. By the time the bell rings next, the earth will be dark.

I can feel the wolf within baying for blood.

The gates of hell will soon be opened, and I am the hound unleashed upon earth to collect its souls.

# 10

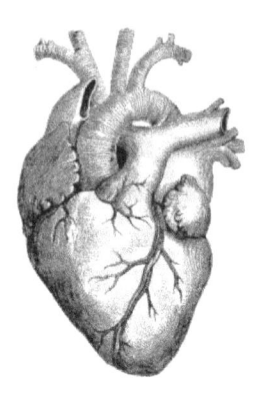

## Mammoth

The Bloody Tower is one of the oldest buildings still standing from Areopagus's founding. As a child, it was the only part of the kingdom explicitly off limits to me, for good reason. If the Black Knights are the kingdom's greatest warriors, the Bloody Tower is home to the kingdom's most dangerous criminals.

To this day I know little about it. By the time I fled the Areopagus, I wasn't old enough to have its mysticism explained to me. Those locked away in its keep never see the light of day again. For whatever reason, these are the criminals who committed atrocities where death was too lenient a punishment. Lundis rarely hinted at the sorts of torture that occurred inside its walls but never gave details. Every once in a while I could hear echoing screams from inside its bowels, but always kept my head to the ground and walked on.

All I know for sure is one thing. If the things Skillah spoke are true—if Vesper truly is inside the Bloody Tower—there isn't a single force in heaven or hell that can keep me from finding her. I have been to many dark places in life. I have known many evil people. I have committed enough crimes myself that likely warrant me to be a prisoner. There is nothing inside this tower that can surprise me.

At the end of the day, crime is crime.

Once you've seen it all firsthand, there are no new crimes to discover. And if my wife is in there, I'd be willing to bet she isn't the only person falsely accused. But still, the shroud of mysticism lingers in the back of my mind as I approach the building's massive entrance. It is taller and wider than a lighthouse on an island but similar in overall shape. Its outside is archaic, nothing more than stone and concrete. Though it is nothing special to behold, the fact that it has been standing for hundreds of years is a testament to the builder responsible for construction.

The tower's pointed top reaches toward the heavens like a spear planted firmly in the ground. It scrapes the sky and kisses the clouds—plenty tall enough to house an entire civilization of miscreants. Fitting for its name, blood ivy climbs its sides, sinking its roots along aging cracks as the ivy seeks to suffocate the building until its inhabitants can no longer breathe. The early evening breeze jostles the leaves, giving the appearance of blood flowing down its veiny facade.

My arrival makes me nervous. There could be hundreds of prisoners trapped inside this fortress. With each door I break open, my heart will flutter with the doubt of Vesper's presence. Now that my hopes have been raised, what will I do if I knock down the final door and I haven't locked eyes with her?

Will I still have the strength to then go to war?

I soar among the clouds so scouts on the ground don't spot someone flying during the day. Only Undead fly, and their flight is limited to the darkness of night. Being spotted among the clouds at this hour would tell my enemy directly a Sylvian is in their midst. And though they'd likely think it is Saunter or Atlas, my Black Knight disguise would be nonetheless useless.

I make no spectacle of my landing to avoid drawing attention. The only two men who see me are the human knights standing at guard outside the tower's entrance. They both look at me, then look at each other with confusion. Seeing a Black Knight while the sun is still in the sky is like seeing a fish walking out of water. It doesn't compute.

I use their confusion against them and knock the consciousness from their skulls. I watch their bodies tumble down the steps in front of the tower. By the time they awake, war will engulf them.

I push open the wooden doors and enter the prison. It's funny, the kingdom's most dangerous criminals are guarded by less than a dozen jailers and two knights posted at the front door. Luckily for me, people normally only try to break *out* of prison, not *into* it. Because of that, I face little opposition at all. I quickly look around to gain my bearings. The inside is exactly what I anticipated it would be. The middle column of the tower is a hollow spire that models the outside of the tower. The cells are rooms littering the cavernous womb of the tower with a set of spiraling stairs scaling the wall to reach them.

None of this was a part of my original plan. I don't have long to find her, if she's here. The sun will set soon and I need her to be far from here with our child. But before I go busting doors down, there are witnesses that must be taken care of.

"Oi!" a jailer yells down at me from his post a few floors above. "What's your business here, Soulless? It is still daytime!"

Maybe I don't have to break doors down after all. I look up at the filthy jailer and sense he fears me. Not because he knows I'm Syrus Sylvian, but because I'm a Black Knight in his eyes. My eyes flicker to the other jailers. They each come to the edge of the stairs to see what the cause of commotion is. They aren't accustomed to visitors inside the Bloody Tower. For good reason.

There are ten total from my counting. From what I can tell, their posts are staggered every other floor for the twenty total floors. If it comes to it, it won't be difficult disposing of them. They will each be equipped with no more than a sword and dagger. Jailers aren't soldiers. They are torturers. They are not drilled to fight a fair fight. They are trained to attack restrained, helpless individuals. They know their place. I am their superior.

"The Emperor has called for the transfer of an inmate!" I call out to them with all the authority I can muster. They look at me with equal confusion in their eyes. I'm guessing this never happens, but I double down on my lie. I'll play on their ignorance. "The Undead woman who bore the Sylvian child! The Emperor seeks her audience immediately!"

This causes each jailer to furrow their brows with even more confusion. The one who spoke first replies, "Emperor came and got her and the whelp himself last night, Black Knight. Surely there's been some kind of miscommunication on your end."

So she was here, I curse inwardly. And now she is gone.

Ventur must have taken her last night in preparation for the war. Our child is too great a resource for him to lose with Saunter gone. Who would have thought *my* child would be the only thing left to save Ventur from the Blackblood virus? The same bloodline he tried to extinguish is the only one that can save him.

"My mistake," I call out, "I have my orders mixed up. I've been so busy it is all becoming a blur." I watch relief wash over the men's faces as my comment melts away their suspicion. "The Emperor did request the release of another prisoner, however," I shout.

"Name them and we will release them for your supervision!" the guard replies.

Maybe my trip to the Bloody Tower won't be wasted after all. Though I was never educated on the contents of the Bloody Tower as a child, there was one prisoner in particular whose reputation superseded himself.

It was only a legend, but the story goes something like this… Father's forces were sent to claim a small village called Greylock as a military stronghold on the eastern coast. It was hardly a mission, since scouting reports estimated there were only a few dozen men of military fighting age. It's likely father only sent expendable troops to take over the land and seize it for strategic purposes.

But days passed, then weeks, all with no word on the status of the mission. Father sent another scouting party out to Greylock to confirm the operation was complete, but those scouts never returned. Frustrated by the hold up, father sent another battalion, this time with heavy calvary and Undead archers to determine the reason for delay.

Not a single soldier returned alive. Instead, a courier was sent from Greylock with a bloodied package for father. Inside the box was the decapitated head of a knight. Etched in the knight's forehead was five words forming a single question: "Is that all you got?"

Infuriated, father led the final battalion himself. They stormed Greylock during the night to catch its inhabitants off guard. To his surprise, they were awaiting his arrival. Father ordered his troops to advance and watched the battle unfold from a vantage point. It didn't take long to determine Greylock's greatest warrior—a giant so large he used a mammoth's ivory tusk as a spear. The armor of mortal men could not fit the giant's physique.

Instead, the troll of a human donned quilted fabric with iron plates sewn together.

The admirable foe slaughtered father's army before his eyes. Though other villagers of Greylock assisted in the defensive operation, it was plain to see Greylock would have fallen if it wasn't for the giant known as Mammoth.

Because of one man's actions, Greylock was wiped off the map. In truth, I don't even know if this man is still alive. If he is, he's somehow survived nearly thirty years of torture. If he is, he's just the kind of man I need for a night like tonight.

"He requests Mammoth!" I call out bravely. My voice echoes off the inner walls of the Bloody Tower. It becomes so silent I can hear the beating of jailers' hearts escalate. I can tell almost instantly these men not only know who I'm talking about, but that this man is still alive after all these years. I smile widely beneath my helm at their reactions. There are few men in this world whose name alone can strike fear into the hearts of those who hear it.

"What would His Excellency want with a murderer like Mammoth?" a guard asks timidly as if he can talk me out of my request.

"He will go to war for us tonight against the Blackbloods," I answer. It's only half a lie. With Mammoth on my side, he will surely kill Blackbloods. That is, after he's gotten his revenge on the Undead, I'm sure.

"The man is a bloodthirsty lunatic!" a jailer shouts.

"He cannot be controlled!" another adds.

Imagine being paid by the kingdom to torture prisoners and failing to submit one into subordination. Lundis was right—whoever Mammoth is, there is a reason why he is locked away for life.

"You leave controlling him to me. All I need is for you to unlock his cell," I reply. "Or I can return to the Emperor with word that you have refused his request."

Time to see who they fear more. A human prisoner, or the seemingly immortal leader of the Undead Empire. I discover the answer almost immediately as the sound of keys jingling rings out.

I may not have reunited with Vesper, but I've gained the next best thing: A soldier to help me find her.

A jailer descends the spiral staircase to meet me on the bottom floor. I see the look of fearful hesitation written on his face. It's like I've just asked him to stab himself in the gut with his own dagger. I step aside as he eyes a keyhole on the ground.

"We keep him under earth," the jailer says sternly. "The man broke through the rock wall and nearly jumped to freedom when we kept him in the upper cells."

This elicits another smile from me. I love a soldier who cannot be held down. The jailer kneels down and inserts the largest key on his set into the hole. As the key twists, a metal handle emerges from the ground. The jailer grips it and yanks it to the side. The jailer squats down and pulls the trapdoor open, lifting the heavy rock floor to expose a cavernous cell beneath.

I squint my eyes as I peer in. It is dark inside, so dark I can barely see past the first step down. The jailer leans over the hole in the earth with furrowed brows.

"Hmmmm," he exhales. "Normally he is—"

A hand shoots out of the darkness fast as lightning and grabs hold of the jailer's ankle. A worried squeal leaves the jailer's mouth as his body disappears. I watch the jailer's hands clutch the edge of the top step as he is dragged beneath by some demon below. The fingers disappear into the darkness. I hear a muffled scream, then nothing. I look up at the other jailers. Each of them sits uncomfortably on their respective perches. Their faces are each pinched with worry. It is like they've just woke from a nightmare, only to realize they were never sleeping in the first place.

Their amethyst eyes look down at the trap door like purple stars peering down at the gates of hell. I can feel their fear radiating throughout the tower. I stand in silence and bask in it. War is not far. There soon won't be an ounce of silence throughout the kingdom. Better enjoy it now.

I watch the monster lift himself up from the rocky enclosure etched in the ground. Two ginormous, meaty hands anchor into the ground to pull the giant's body from the earth's womb. My brain processes the ghastly figure piece by piece as it rises from the dungeon. Though the giant's skin hugs his bones from decades of starvation, the man's height is otherworldly. I have never seen a human so large as this. Not even my Lycan form is this tall.

Mammoth plants his blistered, callous feet on the stone and stands upright. I am glad the Black Knight helm blocks my face from onlookers. It is better off for my look of dumbfounded naivety to be concealed as I take in the sight. The jailers above look at Mammoth like a fight that has already been lost.

Looking at him is like looking at something that shouldn't exist. Although I never thought much about giants, I realize now they belong on the same pages of fiction as unicorns. Mammoth towers over me by several feet as he straightens himself. His hair is so long it hangs down to his waist. His gangly arms extend to his kneecaps. It is as if he stands on artificial stilts. It is like looking at someone condemned to death on the rack, but instead of being torn in two they merely stretched like taffy.

Part of me didn't even think he would exist. The other part of me now wonders how I will get a man like this to join my side. Mammoth is an anarchist; he does not follow orders. That is the reason why he was locked up thirty years ago. Here stands the man who retaliated against everything my father threw at him and lived to tell the tale.

My identity will find no sympathy with him. Mammoth hates the Sylvians as much as the Undead. Likewise, I doubt he even knows what's happened the last thirty years. My father's demise and Ventur's rise to power are meaningless to him. The war tonight holds no value. Everyone from Greylock Mammoth knew or loved is long gone.

I was locked away in the darkness for twenty-four moons and nearly went insane.

Before me is a man who was locked in darkness for thirty years.

There is no telling the delirium that's rotted Mammoth's brain. I may have stabbed myself in the foot by releasing him, but there's only one way to find out.

"Mammoth of Greylock," I call out as if I'm greeting an old friend. The giant twists his head to face me. I am the size of a dwarf next to him. "I come with an offer… Your freedom for a night of fighting."

An amused grin curls across the giant's face. He is only a few feet taller than me, but I imagine I must look like a toy soldier from his perspective. In truth, I feel silly acting like I have the high ground in this conversation when my opponent could squish my skull like a grape.

"Mammoth fight for Mammoth!" he shouts at me. His breath is so rank it burns my nostrils through my helm.

"I told you!" a jailer shouts. Mammoth looks up at the amethyst eyes above us and notices the men who've caused him considerable agony the last three decades. The grin melts from his face and he forgets about me entirely. I take a few steps back as I watch the giant become animated with fury at the sight of his torturers. Thirty years of pain and misery makes for grotesque revenge.

The jailers draw swords as Mammoth climbs the stairs. His legs are so long he skips four steps with every stride. They raise the toothpicks and ready themselves for death's coming.

I remain silent as the screams of men fill the chambers around me. Prisoners come forward from their cells to experience the massacre. Together they chant for their comrade. Fists beat against the rocky walls. Mammoth is the champion of these people, and now he attains vengeance for those who cannot. The jailers scream in agony as they go to their deaths one by one, but the screams are swallowed by the audience's chanting. These walls have heard the screams of agony for centuries. These walls take no sides. Like me, they watch with amusement as the rock is fed more meaningless blood.

Mammoth's shit-stained loincloth becomes spattered with the blood of his enemies. Watching him crush these men is like watching a poorly written play, as if the playwright gave Mammoth entirely too much power. Only this is reality, and this man's overwhelming strength is not a plot hole in the overarching story of history.

I look at the faces of all those who chant Mammoth's name. Their eyes are each filled with the same lunacy that possessed me during my own captivity. I wonder how many of these men and women truly deserve to be here. Knowing Mammoth's past, is it really a crime to stand against oppression? It's what I do every damn day of my life, yet he was imprisoned thirty years for it. Treason is a crime made up by weak, insecure forms of government. Condemning one for treason is no better than children playing capture the flag. Men fear those who oppose them, so they lock them away where the daylight doesn't shine as a deterrence method to others.

The show is over before I can appreciate the fact that it started. Blood drips from the steps above me and fall to the rocky ground like fat raindrops. I can hear Mammoth's labored breathing though he is at the top of the keep. The prisoners cease their chanting and now beg for the giant to free them. He pays no attention to them as he descends the rocky staircase to join my side once more.

The giant's face is beaming with perverted pride. I have experienced the joy of killing for revenge like he has. I know the surge of adrenaline that pulses through his veins right now. It is that very feeling I chase after tonight. Mammoth has slain his captors, and now it is my turn to go after those who've caused my afflictions.

"Mammoth wins," the giant sighs triumphantly as he stands before me. He eyes me curiously. The warrior in him senses the warrior in me. We share an unspoken connection that separates us from ordinary men. The man looks like someone possessed with a demon. Blood drips from his palms. Gashes cover his body from where the jailers were able to find their mark before dying. His breath wheezes through his weak lungs. His muscles strain with their first real labor in over thirty years.

"I am going to war tonight against the men who held you captive," I say stoically. "That is why I've freed you, Mammoth."

"Mammoth fight for Mammoth," he repeats, shaking his head angrily. "Mammoth no fight for you."

"Do you remember the man who defeated you?" I ask.

I see a look of confusion on the giant's face, then reflection. Anger quickly takes over his demeanor, coupled with thirty years of stewing on the memory.

"Silver eye man kill everyone," Mammoth growls, gritting his rotted teeth. "Silver eye demon from sky destroy Mammoth's home!"

Though I don't know the full story of Greylock, I figured as much. My father was not the sort of man to kill a warrior like this. If the legend is true, my father defeated Mammoth after Greylock's genocide, then imprisoned him for life. He was of the opinion that it's better for a monster to live with his sins and regrets than to grant them death.

But the man before me isn't a monster. When I look at Mammoth it's like looking into a reflection. Though he is bigger and stronger and mightier than I'll ever be, at the end of the day he is a man who lost everything, and a man who will make others pay for all he's lost.

I remove my helmet and let it crash to the ground between us. I open my eyes and let their silver glow illuminate Mammoth's face. This is the moment of truth. He will either kill me for who I am or bow before me.

"I killed the silver demon you speak of," I announce, stretching the truth. The likelihood of Mammoth finding out is small, since the entire kingdom thinks I am responsible for my father's death. I continue, "Then his power passed to me, Mammoth. I am here to take this kingdom as my own, and with you by my side, all will fear the ground upon which we walk."

A look of muffled horror slowly wipes away Mammoth's grin as we lock eyes. His bloodlust from killing the jailers melts away instantly. He transforms before me into an innocent child. His knees shake beneath him, as if the weight of his bondage has suddenly become too heavy to bear. He mutters beneath his breath, "Silver eyes…" All that talk he was doing before was nothing more than baseless threats. Now that he sees my eyes, I see who Mammoth truly is.

This is a man who fears me.

What did my father do to this man to deserve such a reaction?

Fascinating, I think to myself. Lundis once taught me of elephants in the circus. Their masters tether them to poles with nothing more than twine to hold them back. When I asked Lundis why the enslaved elephants didn't break the restraint and run away, he replied it was in their subconscious nature. As babies, the masters tie the elephants to trees with chains. The toddlers try running away, but they are not strong enough to break the chains. Over and over they strain their neck as they try to build enough momentum to break away. But the elephant is a smart creature, so after a few dozen times it learns escape is futile, and it accepts the bondage. Then, as they grow older, the master doesn't even need to use chains anymore. A simple piece of string tied to a pole will do, because the elephant has been conditioned to think it cannot break free.

Like the elephant with string, Mammoth has been conditioned to cower before my silver eyes. I watch the strain in his body go limp. Whatever hatred boiled within him toward the jailers, my silver eyes pour ice onto his emotions.

"I will not hurt you," I tell him. "I am not like the silver-eyed demon. I do not come to destroy your home. If you help me, we can rebuild Greylock, together."

"Greylock?" Mammoth repeats the word like it is a warm blanket placed around his shoulders. This man is not a monster. This is a man who watched his entire community become slaughtered—all so the Areopagus could have a military stronghold it never needed in the first place. Twenty years I've wandered this earth, and twenty years has taught me how the other side lives.

People like my father rule their kingdom without tolerance for disobedience. To men like Mammoth, they must bow or die. Men like us choose the silent third option—rebellion. Better to die fighting than to live oppressed.

I no longer wonder why people hate kings and queens. I have been a commoner twice as long as I was royalty. I despise the lineage I came from. I'm embarrassed of the blood that flows in my veins. What benefit can be gained from ruling the world if it means trampling all those who follow? There is no such thing as a monarchy. There is only tyranny. A political system designed to make one man happy at the expense of everyone else's misery.

"A new Greylock, free from oppression," I reiterate. The man seems to have the emotional IQ of a toddler. I can see the thoughts racing behind his eyes but he lacks the ability to process them quickly. It is like I've just asked him to solve a calculus question without an abacus. The lights are on but no one's home it seems.

In the span of a few seconds Mammoth faces an existential crisis. The last time he fought someone with silver eyes he lost miserably. These silver eyes that shine on him are the only light he's seen in the last thirty years of darkness. They have kept him going all this time, fueling his lust and preservation for revenge. But the man responsible for his bondage is dead, and so he must see reason and evolve or die by my blade. I will kill him if he refuses me, I realize. Releasing a monster like him back into society isn't an option. It is sad how much I take after my own father.

A loud bang echoes in the distance. The ground beneath our feet shakes. The walls around us tremble. My feet stagger to keep myself from falling. The prisoners scream out as the tower feels as if it will collapse. But Mammoth doesn't seem to notice the sensory overload as he becomes lost in his thoughts. I run to the tower's doors and throw them open. The sun is on the horizon. Chimel has blown the dam. This city will soon be flooded with water.

I see a plume of smoke in the distance.

Citizens far away join the prisoners in their screaming.

I turn to face Mammoth. I do not have all day for him to make a decision. My hand instinctively hovers near my sword's hilt, readying myself for his inevitable rejection of my offer.

"New Greylock," Mammoth says to himself, then focuses on me once more. "Mammoth fight for New Greylock." The giant extends his bloody hand toward me as a gesture of agreement. I go to shake it and feel his massive palm wrap around my hand, wrist, and forearm.

The giant retreats to the dungeon he was previously locked in. I watch him disappear under the earth momentarily. The sounds of chains echo as the giant busies himself in the darkness. When he returns from the dungeon, I see he holds a set of massive chains in his hands. Each link is thicker than the steel that makes up my armor. Mammoth takes one set of chains and wraps it around his knuckles and fist. He holds the other set loosely in his dominant hand like a whip.

The same chains that bound him all these years will now be his only weapon in the coming war. The dying sunlight enters the tower and shines on Mammoth's body. The giant stares at the outside world with an uncontainable smile on his face. I still remember how I felt after seeing the night sky after twenty-four moons of slavery. I can only imagine how Mammoth now feels.

I grab my helm from the ground and slowly place it back on my head. My silver vision disappears. Ready or not, war is here. "Kill anyone with purple eyes or black wings, Mammoth. If you see any wolves, leave them be. The wolves are on our side."

Though the giant is intellectually slow, he is a warrior that knows war. There is no need to explain the complexities involved with tonight's battle. Tell him who needs to be killed and he will fight faithfully. I see the look of understanding on his face as he nods gently.

He whispers under his breath, "Purple eyes. Black wings. Mammoth kill."

"Very good," I reply. "Now let's go to war."

# 11

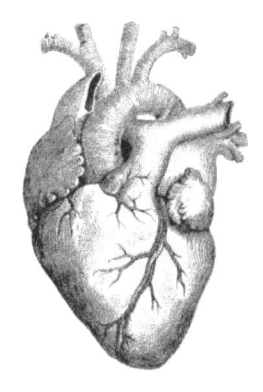

## HOME SWEET HOME

The moon rises in the distance. My face is illuminated by its company. Darkness settles. Howls echo from the gates of hell. I feel a force pulling deep within me. The beast. It claws and gnaws for freedom. My Sylvian blood holds it at bay. Fever burns beneath my cheeks from the inner conflict. Two identities trapped in the same body. Yin and yang forever fighting for control.

Exactly a month ago I was a slave to the Blackbloods. A gladiator in their fighting pits for their amusement. We Lycans were like dogs forced to fight. Starved so our bloodlust was indifferent to killing our own kind. Beaten so we were never strong enough to bite the hand that muzzled us. So much can change in a single cycle of the moon. Instead of killing my own kind tonight, I will be calling them to my aid to face the real enemy. I stand in my home kingdom for the first time in twenty years. I wear the armor of those who killed my family. My only allies are outcasts and criminals. There is no one better to have in your corner on a night of utter anarchy.

My plan is self-executing at this point. The Blackbloods are significantly delayed from the mine collapse. They will come soon, but until then, I will infiltrate Ventur's imperial guards. Mammoth has been left to lead a fighting force of criminals from the Bloody Tower. I gave him full autonomy to go after the Undead in any manner he saw fit. I am not his babysitter.

The streets already flood with water. Those who haven't locked their doors for the night wander in confusion and panic. A tsunami winds its way through Areopagus street by street like a river seeking to claim what once belonged to it.

I stand at the base of the Areopagus castle and look up at it with nostalgia. Other than the Undead banners that stream from its windows, the place hasn't changed one bit in twenty years. It was a marvel to behold as a child, but after wandering the poverty stricken lands across the globe for decades, I finally see the great disparity of a building like this existing while so many sleep in clay huts across the land. It is as if the keep's builders intended to defy the gods with their architectural prowess. The castle is as wide as it is tall and tall as it is long. The sort of building so massive someone could become lost within its innards and never see the light of day again. All the homeless of the world could seek refuge inside and the castle would still be far from filled.

It makes me feel sick to know I once took living here for granted. I was a child. I didn't know any better. But I don't miss this lifestyle. This place always felt more like a prison than a home. We mortals are never comfortable in life. The poor will always want riches. The rich will never have enough. I have now lived both lives and learned the truth to happiness. It is not found in castles and treasuries, nor derived from fame and status. True joy is having the ones you love by your side. It is laying beside them in front of a fire on a cruel winter night. It is knowing no material item will ever make me feel as warm as the kiss of one I love.

But the gods are cruel. They take away the things we love to get a reaction. They introduce suffering so we never feel complete. Fine by me. Tonight they will have their reaction. This castle I once called home will not stand by the time the sun looks upon it on the morrow.

I listen to the desperate cries of others in the distance. Undead soldiers take to the sky now that the sun has departed. Chaos reigns. A swollen river crashes from the imploded dam. Even the strongest swimmers drown. Buildings collapse beneath its weight. Screams turn into gargles in its maelstrom. I am safe at the castle's entrance. The flood's effects will take time to reach the royal keep. But the parts of the city closest to the Wirewood will not survive the rapid's vengeance. Like a hurricane on land, the immediate destruction will be the most devastating.

Was I wrong for unleashing such chaos?

Was Skillah right?

No. This flood may not kill the Undead who fill the sky now, but it will confuse them greatly. Confusion is a powerful weapon on the brink of war. Chaos spreads like bacteria in darkness. Chaos is the reason I walk up the front steps to my childhood home. Chaos is the reason no one opposes me as I open the front gates.

No one would be crazy enough to attempt assassinating the Emperor in his own castle.

Well, no one except me, I suppose.

I walk through the doors of the castle and take a deep breath.

Home sweet home.

## 12

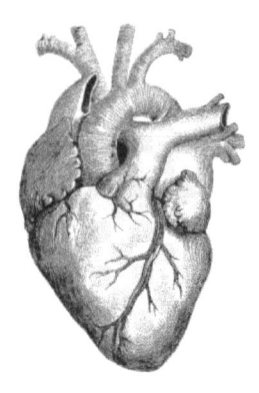

## THE PRICE FOR BLINDNESS

*Traitor*, a distant, familiar voice growls from the depths of my soul.

I cannot take my eyes off the Emperor's face. He sits upon the throne where my father once rocked me on his knee. He wears the same crown smelted to fit my father's head. The same scepter of authority my father wielded now lies across Ventur's lap. Looking at the man who betrayed me makes me feel as though I've slipped into some alternate universe. The hood that shades his scarred figure hides nothing from me. Now that I see the Emperor for the first time since his rise to power, I know Enchantress's vision of my past was accurate. Without her I likely would have spent my life in Sygon to end my misery. But revenge mandated that I be more, and so here I am to rise to its occasion. My gaze doesn't waver from the Emperor's hazy, amethyst eyes. Every second I stare at him my rage grows exponentially.

*Traitor*, the beast within howls, closer this time.

All these years I thought he was dead—a loyal servant who sacrificed his life so that I may live.

It was all a lie fabricated to get rid of Ventur's unfinished dirty work.

The feelings that well up inside me are nearly unbearable. My skin itches in Ventur's presence. My muscles spasm with restraint. My face is hot with fever. The Hellhound within howls uncontrollably. Standing motionless in file with the Black Knights is like standing on a great hill of fire ants. Though I want to lash out and scream and lose all composure, now is when I must contain myself.

"My lord," the leader of the Undead Scouts kneels before the hooded Emperor. "My Scouts report an earthquake brought Varne to the ground. There is no sight of the Blackbloods in the sky."

The leader of the Scouts is a ghastly man, as is the case with all Scouts. Wrapped in the mummified remains of a dozen unidentifiable hides, he's one of the few Undead able to walk in the light of day without being burned alive. Fastened around his neck is the pelt of some brown bear—perhaps a grizzly. It drapes to the ground, its matted fur covered with mange and fleas.

The Scouts are pathetic excuses for living beings, but for the Undead Empire, their service is priceless. They are the Emperor's only trustworthy avenue for gathering intel during the heat of daytime. The Emperor relies on humans for information, sure, but humans can rarely be trusted to stick their necks out for those inclined to sink fangs into them.

"This is no coincidence," Ventur replies coldly. His voice is not what it once was. His vocal cords sound as if they've been seared by hot coals. "We would have felt seismic activity in Areopagus if this was true. What else have your Scouts reported that is of use to me?"

"My lord, by the time the ground caved it swallowed whole the vast population of Varne entirely. There were no survivors left to interview. We were unable to investigate the natural causes that led to the catastrophe."

"Several thousand criminals I've pardoned for you to command," Ventur growls violently. "Several thousand eyes I've given you to survey the kingdoms, and you bring me information no more relevant than what a common courier could tell me."

"My lord—"

"Meanwhile," Ventur interjects, "The Wirewood dam has magically exploded and flooded our kingdom with the Blackbloods camped on our very doorstep. Would your Scouts happen to have investigated this, or do they chalk this up to natural disaster as well?"

The Scouting leader replies nervously, "We, er, the investigation is ongoing, my lord. We—"

"Save your breath," Ventur chuckles, "I prefer confident answers to rank bullshit. I won't inquire to your knowledge on the events of Mammoth's release and the slaughtered jailers discovered, though it is your duty to know such things. Tell me, how am I supposed to lead a kingdom when my informants are blind as bats?"

"I beg your forgiveness, my lord, but—"

"I did not ask for your excuses!" Ventur screams, leaning forward on his throne. "Earthquakes! Floods! Prison breaks! All on the night of the full moon!" Ventur's voice echoes off every inch of the throne room. I have never seen him so furious. Though I only knew him as a child, Ventur was always stoic enough to keep his demeanor calm on the cusp of battle. The Emperor before me is infected by power and paranoia. I secretly burst at the seams with joy to see how my actions have caused the mighty Ventur to raise his voice. Even better, the Emperor thinks all this is some ploy put on by the Blackbloods on the eve of war.

I stand like a gear in an automaton amongst the Black Knights. After entering the castle, slipping amongst their ranks was easier than hiding a shadow amongst darkness. As expected, Ventur called us to the throne room in preparation for tonight's war. We stand in single file lines like a true military unit, each of us spaced an arm's length apart in columns and rows. The only individuals present that aren't Soulless are the Scout leader, the Queen, and a line of shackled humans tied to the throne. The humans are no doubt Ventur's feeding slaves. Their chain anchors them to the throne so the Emperor can feast at leisure.

There is no sign of Vesper anywhere. I can't even smell the faintest scent of her aroma in the throne room. If she had been here, I would know it. That means she must be in the Emperor's own quarters. A high profile prisoner like that can't be risked. By the way Ventur speaks to the Scout, I know he doesn't trust anyone, but especially not to guard the only cure he has to the Blackblood virus while Saunter is away.

I look to the Queen. Unlike Ventur, she hasn't aged a day since I last saw her. Her silver hair is braided tight and elegantly into pigtails that spill over her shoulders. I don't remember her being so beautiful, but then again I was only a child when I saw her last—I had no interest in women. Her face is sharp and regal. Its perfect symmetry suggests the gods took extra diligence when sculpting her features. Her light, lavender eyes contrast the inlaid gold of her dress. Everything about her is prim and proper, from her petite nose to her slightly pointed ears. Not a single hair lays astray atop her head and the blush upon her cheeks almost convinces me she isn't cold-blooded.

Is it true?

Is it really true?

My father bedded this woman to produce Saunter?

Everything Enchantress has told me thus far has proven to be true. I am far from the only Sylvian. Saunter is my sister. She has the silver eyes, and this woman beside the throne is the reason for it all.

Now that I lay eyes on her, can I even blame my father? She is beautiful in a way my mother never could have been. Mother was a warrior, not a princess. Her hands were calloused from swinging a sword her whole life. She never wore dresses or pretended to be something she wasn't. Mother was strong and courageous and determined. The woman beside Ventur is her opposite. The Queen is poised and proper and ladylike.

I despise the pulse in her veins. The fact that she still stands alive after all these years while my mother's corpse rots in some foreign grave makes me nauseous. This is the woman responsible for birthing Bane and Saunter, the children who replaced me in succession to the throne.

The Queen is not on my list, but if the time permits, she will be dead before the sun rises on the morrow.

"I ask for forgiveness, my lord!" The Scout squeals as he realizes he's provoked the wrath of a god on earth. I can hardly blame Ventur for his anger. What is the point of having Scouts if they cannot discern their enemy has already infiltrated the castle? Yet here I am, and not a single body in this room is aware the Emperor's assassin is in his midst. My scent is undetectable. I have consumed enough wolfsbane to kill an army of Lycans. The potent toxin chills my blood and slows my heart rate. To the untrained nostrils, I am just as dead as the army I stand among.

"Forgiveness?" Ventur asks calmly, an eery tone emanating across the chamber. "Ah, I suppose I am too hard on you, Vermouth. The long-awaited war has finally come. It is hard to have eyes in the back of your head when threats surround us on all sides, isn't it?" The Emperor laughs at his own joke. Goosebumps creep to my skin. It is chilling to see his anger dissipate and be replaced by candor in a single second. Ventur continues, "Come, approach me so that I may forgive you."

The Scout known as Vermouth stands hesitantly, looking around at the audience of Black Knights for reassurance. Our expressionless armor provides no such comfort as we watch the interaction from a neutral perspective. Vermouth laughs nervously along with the Emperor as he slowly approaches him. My heart rate elevates with every step the Scout takes. Silently, we await the inevitable.

"Stop there," Ventur orders as Vermouth remains a single stride away from the throne. Ventur leans forward and extends his scarred hand. "Give me your eyes, Vermouth." The order echoes long for the words to be cemented in our minds. The Scout shifts uncomfortably. The flesh wrapped around his body is stained by both sun and blood. Though only Vermouth's back is exposed to our sight, we can assume the look of confusion that must possess his face.

"My lord?"

"You asked for my forgiveness, did you not?" Ventur asks rhetorically.

"I did, but..." Vermouth is speechless by the request.

"As leader of the Scouts, you have assumed responsibility for all their actions, have you not?"

"I did," Vermouth confirms sullenly.

"So for their sin of blindness, I shall make their leader as blind as they are," Ventur says, elaborating on his request for the soldier's eyeballs. The Emperor's scabbed fingers gesture for Vermouth to hand over what he's been asked for. "Well, do you want forgiveness or not?"

"Surely there is some other—" Vermouth starts, then closes his mouth as Ventur stands from his throne. The Emperor's ghastly figure straightens before the Scout, towering over him like a dark silhouette.

"Turn around for my Black Knights to see your face," Ventur orders. Vermouth complies, rotating his body so we can all observe the look of fear still evident beneath the mummified flesh on his face. The only areas of Vermouth's actual face revealed are his bloodshot eyes and cracked lips, but the pungent odor of his fear fills the chambers around us. Ventur places his chapped hands on Vermouth's shoulders from behind.

"Good, now I want you to pluck your eyes out for all my knights to see, so we may all know the consequence for blindness in my service."

I look to the Queen. Her face is stone cold, as if she has seen this display of cruelty a hundred times over. She doesn't so much as blink as her husband makes a display of the Scout's failure. As a child, Ventur once taught me failure is something to be learned from. When he said it then, it seemed like an admirable lesson. As he puts it on display for all of us to watch now, I'm not so sure.

The longer Vermouth hesitates the faster my heart pounds. It isn't even my eyeballs at stake, but for the first time in twenty years I am seeing what my enemy is capable of. Like Lundis, Ventur has changed, only there is no blackening of his blood to excuse this tyranny. Maybe, just maybe, this is who Ventur always was. If so, his betrayal of my father was likely in his mind from the moment they first shook hands. Men like this cannot play servant. Their egos cannot handle it. The same hand Ventur used to shake my father's is the one he used to stab him in the back.

Vermouth raises his hands before his eyes and stares longingly at the bloody flesh wrapped around him. These seconds will be the last he will have vision. Like a man walking to the gallows appreciating life for the first time, it is too late for Vermouth to express gratitude toward his sight.

"We don't have all night, Vermouth. You must choose! Live sightless or die at the stake."

Vermouth slowly digs his clawed fingertips into the gaps of his eye sockets. A shrill scream escapes his mouth as blood starts to gush between his fingers. I clench my jaw as the Scout struggles to get a grip on the organs as they become slippery with blood. His voice shrieks involuntarily as he inflicts a pain unimaginable upon himself. The dim light illuminates the bottom half of Ventur's hooded face. The Emperor is smiling as his servant squirms in his grasp.

A gushy pop sounds loud enough for all us to hear as the eyeballs suction free from the man's sockets. Vermouth's scream turns into a violent sob as tears of blood stream relentlessly down his face. The fleshy bandages are not enough to contain the monsoon of blood. The eyeballs dangle from optic nerves in Vermouth's hands as he struggles to conjure the strength to rip them clean off. Ventur licks his lips at the scent of blood. The Queen's nostrils flare. The Undead knights around me tense as the aroma of fresh blood wafts around us. I become nauseous by the smell.

Ventur reaches over Vermouth's shoulder and grabs hold of both eyeballs while they're still attached to the nerve. The Emperor turns the eye around so Vermouth can see what his face looks like for the first time. Ventur places his face right next to Vermouth's and runs his tongue across the Scout's bloody cheek, slowly savoring the taste of fresh blood. "Shhhhh," Ventur whispers as Vermouth cries aloud. "There there, I forgive you now." The whisper is low and creepy but carries across the chamber's acoustic walls for all of us to hear.

Vermouth's lips quiver as the pain continues to register. Though he is my enemy by association, I actually feel bad for the Scout. No living being deserves treatment like this in their final moments. Only a tyrant would derive pleasure from making a show out of torture like this.

"Hell is an ugly place, Vermouth. You don't understand why I'm doing this now, but I am showing you mercy. This is a kindness, trust me. Because

Hell is not ugly for those who cannot see," Ventur whispers as he rips the eyes away clean and quickly slashes the Scout's throat open. Vermouth tries to scream out in renewed pain but blood rushes through his slashed throat instead. A thick, gurgling moan is all Vermouth can muster. Ventur lowers his cracked lips to his victim's throat and drinks deeply as the heavy current of blood flows freely. The Emperor holds the limp body up until he's had his fill, then wipes his bloody lips as the corpse drops dead at his feet. Then, without missing a beat, Ventur reclaims his throne like nothing has happened.

The human slaves on the chain beside Ventur stir uncomfortably at the sight of Vermouth's corpse near them. They each silently wonder if that's the sort of death that awaits them. After all, if the Undead Emperor is willing to do that to one of his own, how much worse an end does he send humans to?

*Traitor!* I squeeze my eyes shut. The full moon is here. The beast bays like a bloodhound. He fights for control of my body. *Submit to me, human!* No, I reply inwardly. I thought we had this worked out. I am the captain of this vessel. I am in control. *The moon is full. Luna calls me. We must kill the traitor.* I have you to thank for saving me as a child. If it wasn't for you, I'd be dead, wolf. But if we give ourselves away now, everything will be ruined.

*I will not wait much longer. Our wolfpack draws nearer by the minute. Hear them howl, human. They hunger for vengeance.*

As do I, beast. But not before we find Vesper.

"Failure is not an option tonight," Ventur addresses us for the first time since we entered the chambers. He now knows the severity the kingdom is in and must course correct his plans for warfare. Ventur continues, "The moon is full. The Blackbloods march and they bring their filthy wolves with them. Our streets are flooded. Criminals from the Bloody Tower are loose. No one is coming to save us, Black Knights. But do not fear. I know the enemy, and there is nothing they can do that we cannot overcome. We know why Bloodlust and his barbaric horde come to the Areopagus. That is why I have called you all here, Black Knights. You are to be the last line of defense should we lose the battle. Tonight is the night. Bloodlust has come for the Dybbuk Box."

The Dybbuk Box... So Skillah wasn't lying to me after all. Such a revelation makes me realize how little I know. I foolishly assumed this war between Undead and Blackbloods was like all other wars—a useless tug-o-war for the power over all dominion. But what if Bloodlust had no interest in authority in the first place? Could it be as simple as Ventur possessing something Bloodlust wants? Something Bloodlust needs?

It is said Dybbuk Boxes are containers which trap malevolent spirits. Only the strongest witches and sorceresses have the power to separate soul from body, and even more strength is required to seal a soul inside a Dybbuk. I should have heeded Skillah's warnings. I let my passion for Vesper blind me. The alchemist possessed the very knowledge I need to understand the cause of this war, and like Vermouth, I was too blind to see it.

Ventur continues, "Every Undead archer and calvary man has returned to the Areopagus for this long-anticipated battle. We will leave nothing to chance. They stand ready and await the coming of our enemy. No flood or criminal horde can deter our resolve. No enemy known to man can taint our conviction. No demon sent from the Devil himself can tarnish our Empire!"

The Black Knights around me pound their breastplates vigorously. Wanting to deter suspicion, I do the same. How foolish will they seem when historians write of their downfall? I'll see to it the entire world is told the truth: While the Undead Empire preached their immortality, their greatest enemy was in their midst cheering for their foolishness. I let the thought of Ventur's death by my doing escalate my pounding. I cherish the thought of Bloodlust's skull as my crown echo in my armor as I beat against my chest. Not a single soul present knows what's coming tonight. This is a war of proportion the kingdom has not seen since the fall of Cardone.

Tonight, Enchantress seeks revenge against the Creator.

Tonight, I seek revenge against my oppressors.

And tonight, Hell itself will not be spacious enough for the bodies I send through its gates.

My thoughts are interrupted by a distant screech. A commotion stirs as the doors to the throne room crash open. A feral scream echoes over our ceremonious pounding. I follow suit as the Black Knights around me swivel and draw their swords instinctively. The Emperor gazes curiously over our masses to identify the intruder.

She screams like a harpy, like a spoiled brat whose parents just told her no. Veins protrude from her neck. Fangs hang from her mouth like icicles. I can smell her fury and fear from here. There are only so many people in this world with the balls to storm into the Emperor's throne room as he prepares for war. I recognize her scent from Queensmyre and Yueltope. But more than that, every knight in her midst recognizes her furious silver eyes as she scans the room.

*Traitor!* The beast howls again, but this time directed at the newly arrived guest. My nose twitches at her scent. I know this woman. She is my enemy.

"Daughter," Ventur calls aloud. "Your arrival is most unexpected. What brings you back from Sygon in such dismay?"

"Sygon is lost!" She screams, "The Sylvian is alive and his wolves are only miles away! I just barely escaped their control in time to come and warn you, Father!"

So the Fang Clan made it after all, I reflect inwardly. Music to my ears. This keep's walls are sound proof, but I can imagine the sound of howling inside my head. The moon is full. My army is here. The city is flooding. The Undead are caught unprepared.

This war is by no means won, but this is a hell of a good start.

## 13

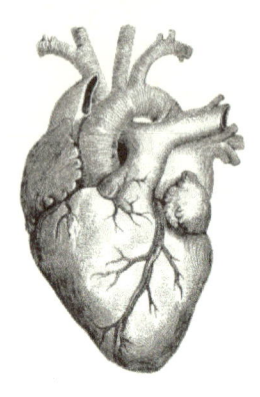

## Regicide

My head is swimming. So many ways this night could end... There are so many moving parts to this machine that it is easy to get caught staring at the gears. Full moon. Wolves coming. Blackbloods versus Undead. Saunter Sylvian. Vesper imprisoned. So many small, intricate factors that will determine who will live to see the sun rise.

But Ventur taught me as a child the greatest military commanders are successful because of their ability to step back and view the war zone from the bigger picture. Focus on one thing at a time. Ventur and Saunter can wait. I need to find Vesper and secure her safety before I think about anything else.

I never returned to Sygon after putting Atlas to eternal rest. With Saunter surrounded by the Fang Clan, I didn't anticipate she'd be able to break free from my Hellhounds.

But the sun has set, and my wolves no longer have the mental faculties to keep prisoners.

So be it. She has escaped my wolfpack, but she is too late to thwart my plans. There's nothing she can say or do to stop what I've put in motion.

And after seeing what Ventur did to Vermouth, I have a feeling she was safer in captivity than she is from her pending judgment.

The Emperor embraces Saunter before the entire Black Knight battalion. She shivers in his arms—not because she is cold, not because she is overwhelmed.

No.

Saunter trembles with fear.

She fears this man. I can smell the pheromones radiating from her. I can hear her heart rate elevating. Now I will get to learn about the relationship my half-sister shares with her fake father.

"I sent you to complete an easy mission for me, Princess Saunter, and you were not even capable of securing Sygon for my Empire," Ventur says in an accusatory manner. He does not shout but his voice carries to fill the room nonetheless. Saunter moves to break free from Ventur's hug, but the Emperor tightens his grip around her shoulders and pulls her closer. Ventur leans in and smells the girl's neck. The inhale of her aroma is entirely too long and drawn out. I cringe inwardly.

"You know," Ventur continues, finally releasing Saunter so he can stare at her in full from the darkness of his hood. "When your mother had you, I knew what you were the moment I laid eyes on you. From the moment you entered this world, I knew you were not mine. You have always been, and always will be, a child of the enemy. But I let you live, Princess Saunter, and be raised under the spoils of my many successes. Not because your mother begged me. Not because I pitied your innocence. Not because you deserved to live. No," Ventur asserts, grabbing hold of Saunter's hips intimately. The

Princess I knew from last night is gone. All confidence has washed away. Saunter flinches in the face of her ultimate master.

"I have killed Sylvians before," Ventur continues, "Though they are stronger than I, though they are smarter than I, though they are superior in every way to the Undead, I have killed them and stolen the power they hold over this world. And yet, there you were, an innocent babe used to defile my wife from beyond my enemy's grave. No, death was not a severe enough punishment for you, Saunter Sylvian. I wanted Silenius Sylvian to watch me defile his attempt to ruin my life from whatever Hell he resides."

The Queen averts her eyes uncomfortably as Ventur slowly gropes Saunter. The man's scarred hand slowly glides from her hip to the space between her legs. Saunter makes no effort to prevent the Emperor from touching her in her most intimate parts. And though the Princess stands before us fully clothed, I can't help but notice how Ventur's glowing eyes undress her as he fondles her privates. Her shoulders tremble fearfully. This is not the first time this has happened. She submits herself fully to his dominion, knowing fully well the consequences that come with retaliating.

"You were most unwise to come back to Areopagus after failing me yet again, Princess. I did everything to set you up for success short of killing the Sylvian Prince myself. Not only have you shamed me, but you have brought shame to the great Empire I've built. Your weakness has been imputed to our great nation. If you were anything less than my wife's daughter, I would burn you at the stake for your miserable attempt at winning my favor."

Ventur slowly unbuttons the Princess's pants and hastily rips them from her body. A shrill cry escapes her mouth as the cold air of the room makes contact with her flesh. Her pale skin gleams in the dim light of the surrounding torches. Goosebumps cover her lower body. Not a single knight present makes the slightest attempt to save the damsel in distress. No one is coming to save this woman. The Emperor gets what the Emperor wants.

Though she was my enemy this time last night, I suddenly feel bad for the Princess. Though she wished me dead and threatened my daughter, I now see the reason for her crazed ambition. Here is a woman raised by the Undead Emperor's evil intent. But I see now the dynamic these two have shared, and it is not one of father and daughter. No, standing vulnerable with her bare ass exposed to Ventur's militia is a woman raised in bondage and suffering. Where I was raised by wolves, my half-sister was raised by demons. And though I've never fit in, Saunter has been made aware of her treacherous blood every waking moment she's drawn breath on this earth.

"It is that time of the month again," Ventur chuckles, sliding his fingers between her legs and pulling them away covered in blood. The Emperor licks the blood from his fingers while Saunter watches his tongue savor the treat. Blood glides down the inside of her leg. I can smell it from here, and no doubt the Undead knights around me feel like sharks in the presence of injured prey. Women bleed once a month, and now Ventur uses Saunter's most vulnerable moment to humiliate her in front of hundreds. No person present will ever respect Saunter or come to her aid now that she's been made a mockery of. And this is only my first time witnessing it. Who's to say Ventur hasn't treated her like this Saunter's whole life?

Everywhere I go in this world I'm reminded only the strong prevail. Unfortunately for Saunter, Ventur has let his strength pervert his soul.

I realize now how urgent it is to find Vesper. If Ventur is willing to do this to his wife's child, there's no telling what he will do to my wife.

Ventur kneels before Princess Saunter and brings his mouth in contact with her bleeding vagina. A chill runs down the enslaved woman's body. She makes no noise. The only noise made is the soft suckling of the Emperor's fangs as they savor the blood. I clench my fists. Warm blood rushes to my cheeks. My skin is on fire.

*Let me out*, the beast within howls.

Not yet.

*Do something!*

It will give us away!

*She is your sister!*

She tried to kill us!

My mind is a maelstrom of violence and agony. If pain is suffering, I am torn in two. Sephora's lifeless body flashes before my eyes. Saving Saunter will put my entire mission at stake. She is my enemy, but she is also my sister. Ventur's tongue echoes as it flicks. He slurps the blood obnoxiously loud for all to hear. Every passing second draws forward a monster I cannot control. Unlike the Queen who averts her eyes, my vision is glued to the cruelty on display. This man cannot be allowed to live. He stands for everything my father opposed.

*You are no better than him if you don't stop this.*

It isn't that black and white.

*Your father did not die for this.*

We will be the ones who die if we so much as move a muscle.

*I did not save you as a boy so you could grow to be a coward.*

Coward? Take a look at where we are. I have marched into the belly of the beast. I have traveled across the globe to put an end to this man's tyranny and you would have me throw it all away for some spoiled brat that tried to feed me to her maniac boyfriend? Shut up so I can focus.

My heart races. My skin is clammy. I am feverish from the effort it takes to hold back the beast from his moondance. This is the first full moon I've had access to my Sylvian powers. Even so, wielding control over the beast is harder than I thought. He stirs like a bull before a rodeo.

Ventur loses himself in Saunter's crotch. Animalistic snorts sound from his bloodlust-fueled frenzy. Saunter has little recourse but to bite down on her tongue and bear the painful embarrassment. The sex slaves chained to the throne whisper silent prayers of gratitude to not be subject to such torture. I watch the blood drip from Saunter's lady parts down Ventur's chin. I can't bear this much longer.

*Stand up to him, Sylvian!*

My brain is screaming. My skin burns. My insides do backflips. My eyeballs itch. Can't contain. Hold it! Don't!

*Stand aside*, the beast growls.

My hand instinctively grabs the dagger sheathed at my hip. I curse inwardly as I draw it from the scabbard. It is like my hand has a mind of its own. I bite down on my tongue hard enough to draw blood. I scream at the beast inwardly to stop this nonsense. The scream echoes throughout the corridors of my soul. My eyes leave the Princess and lock onto the Queen standing several feet away from the throne. No!

*He took your wife*, the beast growls. *Now we take his!*

My arm draws back fast as a whip and throttles forward. It is like watching my body move, yet I'm not the operator behind the movements. I dissociate from reality as I feel the dagger leave my palm. Time slows as I watch the torchlight reflect off the silver blade as it somersaults through the air. I have compromised myself. Knights around me slowly turn to identify the cause of the commotion. But no one will be able to stop the inevitable chain of events I've set in motion.

It's gut-wrenching how fast a plan can go horribly wrong. I did not account for the beast within to meddle in my affairs. I thought I had control. I thought those days were behind me. I couldn't have been more wrong.

The dagger sails through the air to find its target. All I can hear is the wind leave the Queen's surprised mouth as the hilt buries itself in her left breast, right where her heart beats.

Unfortunately for her, the Queen's lavish dress does little to thwart the dagger's impact. Blood stains immediately as she tries to muster the air to scream. Ventur is ripped from his trance of bloodlust when Saunter screams at the sight. The Queen drops to her knees, then straight onto her face. I savor the look within Ventur's perplexed eyes as his hood slips from his head. The Emperor licks his lips and wipes the blood that drips from his chin. His wife's dead body lays next to him. Saunter takes this as an opportunity to step away from her assailant. She covers her privates shamefully as if we have not already seen every inch of her naked body.

I watch the anger fill Ventur's eyes. Confusion turns to rage. Rage turns to calculated plotting.

*If he wants blood,* the beast howls, *We will give him blood.*

# 14

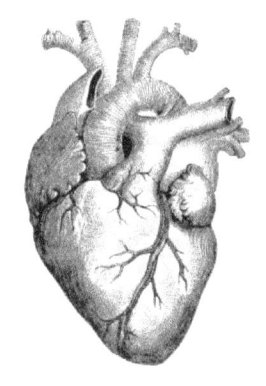

## WOLVES & RAVENS

It only took a half dozen Black Knights to kill my father and mother. I am now surrounded by several hundred, and I've just assassinated the Queen they've sworn to protect.

"Assassin!" a knight to my left screams.

Bastard! I curse inwardly at the beast within.

*We need unity if we are going to survive this,* the beast replies. The comment catches me off guard. It almost comes off as wisdom. The sort of profound, introspective thought I've never thought him to be capable of. Though it has only been a month since I've heard him speak to me, and though it's been a sporadic, rocky relationship, I'm taken back by the comment. He continues, *Only those around us know we are the aggressor. Everyone else is confused, Emperor included. We can use this confusion to our advantage. Follow my lead.*

"Assassins!" I shout involuntarily. I draw my sword and plunge it into the man to my left before he can grip his hilt. The blade enters his throat and cuts off his ability to single me out. With his body pressed close to mine, I remove the dagger from the sheath at his hip and slide it into my own. I pull the blade from his body. Blood spatters from his gushing neck. I pivot quickly and pierce the helm of the man behind me just as he pulls his sword to defend himself. The blade drops from his hand as mine splits his head from his shoulders. I catch his falling blade with my non dominant hand and use it to block a strike from the man to my right. I whip the duel blades off the parry and insert them both into the opponent's armor.

Mass hysteria breaks out among the forces. A mosh pit forms around us. Knights scramble to guard the Emperor. Saunter retreats behind the throne to conceal her vulnerability. The sound of several hundred swords drawing becomes deafening. All who personally witnessed me throw a dagger are dead. My blades are the only two covered with blood, but no one can be certain who is responsible for the Queen's death. We turn against each other. All faces are covered by helms. There is no way for these men to measure my guilt by facial recognition.

"Check the bodies for a missing dagger!" I shout at a knight approaching me. Though I cannot read his face, his body language looks as if he means to single me out. The foe hesitantly bends over and checks the three crumpled bodies, eventually coming to the man I stabbed through the throat.

"His sheath is empty!" The Black Knight barks at us, "This is the assassin!"

"There could be more!" I yell, then order, "Protect the Emperor! We must escort him to safety!" Without a moment to spare, I jump into the air and take flight toward the throne. Several other knights now surround Ventur in a protective circle. I quickly praise the gods beneath my breath as I land before the throne, a few short strides from my greatest enemy.

Without the mass confusion and sense of urgency, these soldiers may have been able to see through my lie. Hell, when the panic subsides, some may see reason and come to the conclusion that I am the real traitor. If not for the beast's quick thinking and sleight of hand, it would be me that lies in a puddle of his own blood right now.

Before joining the Emperor's party, I stare longingly at the Queen. Saunter now kneels by her side, blood pooling around them both. Though the woman was pale before the dagger hit her heart, her body is now devoid of all liveliness. Saunter's face looks so much like her mother's, yet so much like my father's at the same time. Though I have not seen him in twenty years, her sharp cheekbones and set jawline remind me of him. Saunter's silver hair and petite nose are from her mother.

The Queen made no attempt to shield her one and only daughter from the Emperor's molestation. And yet, Saunter mourns the woman's death anyway.

I feel no pain for the woman Saunter cradles in her arms. I did not know the Queen as a child. When my father sat on the throne, the woman always seemed recluse. Maybe it was because of her love affair with my father, or maybe it was because she knew Ventur planned to betray us. Either way, the woman never showed kindness to me. She was a snake in the grass, so I gave her a cold-blooded death accordingly.

A Scout emerges through the double doors Saunter left open. The Scout is accompanied by several infantrymen, each of them heavily clad with enough armor to cover an elephant tusk to tail. Still dismayed and befuddled, approximately half the Black Knights turn to determine the meaning of this intrusion. The other half still think through the death of their assassin comrades. The Scout speaks frantically with a battalion leader of the Black Knights, then rushes out of the room with his heavyset juggernauts leading the way.

I am one of seven who move in to secure the Emperor. I watch the Black Knight who spoke with the Scout quickly make his way to the elevated platform the throne sits upon.

Ventur's scent fills my nostrils.

My head is spinning. The last time I smelled this scent was when he carried me from the city in the light of the rising sun. I can feel my soul dissociating from my body. The beast wants control. I mustn't let him take over. But the smell of revenge burns my eyes with how close I am. Ventur is a single arm's distance from me. A single arm's distance, and he doesn't even know I'm here. My teeth itch for his blood.

Not here. Not now. There are things he knows that I must uncover. The location of my wife. My child. The Dybbuk Box. His knowledge is the only thing keeping him alive.

"My Lord," a Black Knight whispers. It is the one who spoke with the Scout. Ventur peers at him curiously through the shadow of his hood, not speaking. "My Lord," he repeats, "Wolves have arrived in the city." The knight's voice seems panicked. "It appears a path was cut through the Wolfsbane border during daylight. It led straight through the Red Gates. Ravens swarm in the sky. Still no sign of the Blackbloods, but our forces are struggling to ward off the unanticipated attack."

My eyes don't leave Ventur as he receives the fatal news. It was Ventur himself who taught me the measure of a man rests with how he reacts to adversity. I watch a sly smile spread across the bottom half of his face. His glazed, half-blind, purple eyes cut through the darkness with radiant joy.

"So the Sylvian Prince sent his Hellhounds on foot because he knew our eyes would be on the skies," Ventur remarks, almost proud. It is weird to hear him speak of me as if I am not by his side. Weirder still to see him react like a father whose prodigal son has returned. The Emperor continues, "Take five battalions to welcome the wolves, Commander. Find their leader. He will be the only one with silver eyes. I want him brought to me alive. Syrus Sylvian is mine to deal with. Kill the rest."

"Yes, My Lord," the Black Knight salutes, then bows away to gather his forces.

"So the boy has come to finish what I started," Ventur whispers to himself. "Seems the gods have elected me to teach him his final lesson."

I clench the hilts of each sword tight. The man's arrogance will be his downfall. I want to cleave his head off where his lips smile. How many lives will die tonight from my patience in killing him?

Howls echo in the distance. They pierce through the thick walls of this empty keep. My spine tingles at the sound. Pheromones fill the air. I breathe it in deeply. The kingdom's greatest warriors have been assembled together in the same room, and all I smell is fear. The knight's words replay in my mind. Wolves have arrived in the city. Ravens swarm in the sky.

"The war has begun, gentlemen," Ventur announces aloud. "You have your orders. Protect the city at all costs. No survivors. By the time the sun rises, the whole world will know why the Undead Empire reigns supreme."

Ventur lowers his voice and addresses us around him quietly, "You seven, escort me to our guests. I have a few final questions for the Sylvian toddler's mother."

I watch as Ventur strides off, intentionally stepping over the corpse of the Queen like she is nothing more than a lowly servant. Saunter looks up at her step father with animosity burning in her eyes. Tears stream down her face. Hatred exposes itself in her shivering. "Bring my illegitimate daughter with you," Ventur orders without turning. "I intend for her to watch me fix yet another one of her failures."

## 15

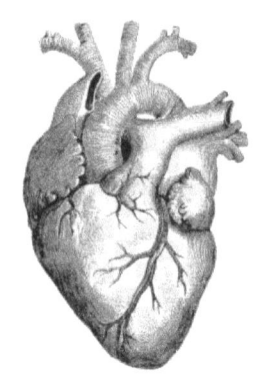

## GHOSTS OF THE PAST

I know where we are going before we get there. As kids, Selena and I would play hide and seek throughout sectors of the castle, scouring every nook and cranny until the ultimate hiding spot was uncovered. Like muscle memory, I still know these hallways like the back of my hand. Walking through them is like seeing a ghost of the past.

A moon's cycle ago I was in the pits of hell killing demon dogs to survive. Now I am a single stroke of my blade away from killing the traitor responsible for my afflictions. Ventur walks—no—floats before me like some mystical being beyond the bounds of reality. I cannot hold back the beast much longer. It is like knowing you must sneeze but attempting to hold it back to the last possible moment. My eyes water. Steam billows inside my armor from my fever-evaporated sweat. My bones ache at the prospect of shifting. With every window we pass, I'm filled with agony as the moon's light beckons me.

The howls in the distance grow closer and closer. Animalistic sounds permeate the atmosphere as the Fang Clan goes to work. Yelps and growls and snarls followed by the clapping of drooling jaws.

Is Crixus here? Is Scar? Is Creon?

I hope not. Though I tried to remain emotionally distant from them, the three members of my pack have earned a place in my heart. I do not want to lose anymore loved ones, especially not Crixus. My face blushes at the thought of her. Now that I know Vesper is alive, I can no longer be with Crixus how I imagined. Still, though, the love I feel for her is not one capable of fading. She came into my life at a time where my heart was nothing more than a void. Her words and actions mended me as close to whole as I thought possible. She made me feel again. When I looked up at the stars with her by my side, I imagined a future with her that I must now divorce. The prospect of it pains me. She is the first loved one I will be forced to lose from my own doing.

It has been twenty-five moons since I last saw Vesper.

Will she even recognize me? And I, her?

I'm no longer the man she married, nor the father she created. I have become a slave to dark forces beyond this world. I have been beaten and tortured and enslaved. I have done terrible things in the name of revenge. I am no longer worthy of her love, and it fills me with deep anxiety at the prospect of her seeing me once again.

But fear of the future won't stop it from happening, so all I can do is follow through with what the Fates have preordained.

The further we walk, the more sure I become of where we are headed. Leave it to Ventur to keep Vesper imprisoned in the one room that still brings me nightmares to this day. If familiarity breeds contempt, my stomach churns with how much I despise this place. Our metal boots thud awkwardly as the floor turns from stone to hardwood. We have transitioned from the main compartment of the castle to the living quarters. The brick walls no longer bear portraits of the Sylvian family. They have been painted black like the night and become filled with cobwebs and dust. Spiders stare at us innocently as we pass, each of them surprised to see visitors in this long-abandoned section of the castle.

The wood creaks with every stride I take. The air becomes colder as we reach a place where torches no longer burn. My eyes adjust to the pitch black of the night. It is more like walking through a catacomb than a castle from fairytales. Old tapestries hang in torn tatters. Mold and fungus cling to the rocky walls around us. It is like we have passed through a portal into some haunted mansion. Why Ventur has let this wing of the castle deteriorate beyond repair is beyond me. Does he feel any remorse passing through these halls? Or is he letting the past rot along with the Sylvian legacy?

The air smells of mildew and mothballs. Rats scurry along at our feet. Termites return to their burrows at our arrival. Bats stare at us with malevolent, beady eyes as they hang upside down from the ceiling. The only thing these halls are missing is a moaning ghost—then we would be living out a childish horror story.

There are ghosts here, but they are not the ones average mortals can see. Ghosts of my past flicker transiently before my eyes. Selena running past me with two dolls gripped tightly in her hands. Our family dog—Baxter—runs after her. A maid hustles from room to room changing bedsheets. Konnie was her name. My first childhood crush. She was only a few years older than me. An Undead refugee that father took pity on. Pale face with shadowy dimples beside her lips. Dark mascara smothered over her emotional eyes. I wonder what happened to her. Probably dead—one of many souls lost the day Ventur took over the kingdom. Does her actual ghost watch these halls, or is seeing her just a figment of my imagination?

The closer we get the more specters of the past bring life to these dead walls. Mother and father walking hand in hand. The sun streaming through the now boarded windows to illuminate their faces. Father intentionally built the Sylvian living quarters to let light in so the Undead could not venture there at all hours of the day. The sun hasn't kissed these stone walls in nearly two decades. Its cold caress reflects such.

Two of the guards in our sect rush forward to surround a door. The saliva dries in my mouth as I see my suspicions are confirmed. Is this excitement that pulses through my veins, or anxiety? My senses are hyper focused as the full moon fuels my tension. I've come so far in such short time, but now it's me that has the home field advantage.

A grin spreads from cheek to cheek along my face. The Black Knights open the door for Ventur. Together, with Ventur at the head of our party, we enter the room I spent many nights sleeping in as a child. Everything that once connected this castle to the Sylvian legacy, Ventur has let die. But more than that, the innocence that once filled these halls is now demented with the torment of countless haunted souls. I now stand in the same room I nearly died in as a child. I stare at its altered interior and still remember the sight of my sister's bed soaked in blood. My mother's headless body. My father's lifeless corpse.

We stand in my childhood bedroom, the place where Ventur made his move for the throne. But instead of the twin-sized beds and children toys, I see Ventur has put this room to use as a torture dungeon with a population of one. I smell her before I see her through the darkness. Her scent is barely the same yet unmistakable nonetheless. Cloves and cinnamon. The scent wafts through my helm on the frigid night air. Vesper. My chest is so tight I can barely breathe. My eyes adjust to the darkness and spot her chained to a stone pillar on the opposite side of the room.

"Well," Ventur breaks the silence, "Although your vow of silence has been impeccable, my daughter has all but confirmed my suspicions. You are not one of Atlas's playthings, my dear. You and your little whelp belong to the one and only Syrus Sylvian!"

I watch as a look of horror takes over Vesper's eyes.

Ventur exclaims, "It looks like I may have a use for you after all, my dear."

Fifteen years later and here we are, just like our origin. Me finding her chained up and saving her from her oppressors. Hatred burning in her eyes. She is even more beautiful than the day I first laid eyes on her. Where age damns most, it has given Vesper a look of dignified wisdom. Where age makes most flowers wither and die, she is like a mighty oak that has used it to her advantage. These last fifteen years have only added to her strength and beauty. The very sight of her makes me want to rip off this armor and slaughter those around me. But if I don't time this perfectly, Sephora could end up an orphan by the end of the night. If patience is a virtue, tonight I must be a saint.

Ventur thinks I'm out there trying to get in. He will try to use Vesper against me to win this battle. I will let him go along with this ploy, never knowing I am by his side the entire time. Then, when he least expects it, I will stab him in the back like he did to my father.

# 16

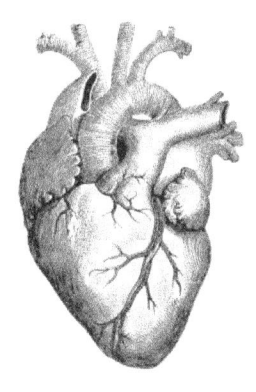

## Two Enemies, One Body

"Syrus is here?" Vesper asks. Her face lights up with the faintest glimmer of hope at the mention of my name.

"As Fates would have it, he is," Ventur replies, "But don't flatter yourself. He doesn't even know you're still alive. He did not come all this way to save you. He is here for one reason only—revenge."

I clench my fists and tighten my jaw as I listen to Ventur slander my name in front of my wife.

"You and your husband were unfortunate enough to get caught in the middle of this war, and if you think you've had it bad being imprisoned in the Bloody Tower all this time, you have no idea what your counterpart has endured."

"What have you done to him!" Vesper shouts.

"Shhhh," Ventur whispers calmly as he approaches Vesper's side. The Emperor runs his hand down Vesper's chained arm. I see Saunter shudder out of the corner of my eye as she stares at the man's creepy, consoling touch. Vesper, on the other hand, doesn't even flinch. Her eyes are locked violently on the man beneath the hood. Her eyes are like stars on the verge of exploding into volatile suns.

"I haven't done anything to him. In fact, I didn't even know he was still alive until Bloodlust sent word of a curious Muzzled he'd watched fight. Said the wolf demonstrated superior close combat skills. The kind that can only be taught by me. Turns out, the wolf was your husband, my former pupil in a past life. Bloodlust sent him and a pack of wolves to capture Sygon to distract me while he advances his forces on Areopagus. Classic diversion tactic. I knew Bloodlust before he was infected by the Blackblood virus. Back then, he was a scholar named Lundis... His head was always buried in books. Life was just a strand of theories to him. His practical knowledge was always lacking. He must have thought I'd succumb to my personal emotions around Syrus and travel to Sygon myself to vanquish him. Instead, I sent my daughter here," Ventur says, pointing to Saunter's quivering frame. The poor girl stands detached from us knights. Her false father has stripped her of all the strength she displayed in Sygon. In Ventur's presence, she is just a molested child too scared to fight back.

"I am surprised she is alive then," Vesper laughs coarsely. "My husband is not one accustomed to forgiveness."

"He killed Atlas," Saunter murmurs weakly. "Atlas was the strongest person I've ever met, and Syrus killed him." Saunter's eyes stare frightfully in the distance like the fight is unfolding before her as she speaks.

"Who the devil is Atlas?" Vesper croaks.

"Just some Sylvian bastard," Ventur chuckles.

"I loved him!" Saunter shrieks with tears in her eyes.

"Ah, yes, you always did have a thing for stray mutts you found on the road as a child," Ventur quips back. "But Syrus did me a favor putting the mutt down. One less Sylvian for me to worry about."

"I thought Syrus was the only remaining Sylvian?" Vesper asks.

"As did I, two decades ago. But it turns out the lineage is like an insufferable weed. Burn it, dig at its roots, poison the ground, and yet it somehow finds a way to prosper. Take Saunter for example. She is not even my natural daughter. Your husband's father defiled my wife before his demise. Saunter is a product of rape and adultery. Technically speaking, she is your sister-in-law."

Vesper's eyes widen at the sight of Saunter's haunted presence in the corner of the room. The information is just as shocking to her as it was to me. This moment is all too ironic. Here we stand in the same room where my childhood sister was murdered. Now my wife is chained where Selena's bed once lay as she learns the existence of my half-sister.

"And Atlas?" Vesper asks. "Is he Syrus's brother?"

"No, he is wholly different. His ancestry stretched back to Sylvian the First but takes a different path through history. The brute's wolfpack was no more than a band of primitives living off the land. Bloodlust discovered them and slaughtered them in front of the child's eyes, then took Atlas in as his own. Saunter is right though—I was quite surprised to hear Syrus prevailed in a fight to the death. Atlas was not the sort of monster one wants as their enemy."

"And my husband is not the sort of enemy a monster wants," Vesper replies coldly. I smirk beneath my helm.

"Touche," Ventur laughs the comment away, then continues, "But alas, there is no way he will survive the night. I have planned for every contingency."

"And how do you know you've planned for *his* contingencies?" Vesper asks.

"Is that what you do to sound smart?" Ventur laughs, "Does flipping my prose make you feel intelligent?"

Vesper smiles, then replies, "Do you feel intelligent criticizing my flipped prose?"

"I see now why Syrus married you. You remind me of him as a child. You have a fire inside of you. Such a shame I'll snuff it out just to cause him pain. Now that you've bore him a child, I no longer have the need for any Sylvians. The Sylvian bloodline provides us Undead a cure from the Blackblood virus, a discovery which will be the saving grace for our race. I no longer have a need for Syrus, or Atlas, or even my bastard daughter. The babe is a blank canvas—a youth ready to have my ideologies impressed upon him."

Vesper snorts mucus and spits it directly inside the Emperor's hood as he continues to grope her restrained figure. She fights against the chains briefly at the mention of our child. Ventur doesn't bother wiping the spit from his face. He's amused by Vesper's resolve. It isn't every day he finds someone willing to spit in his face. Such an offense would be punishable by worse than death if any other civilian did it. The Emperor likely gets off on the fact that it's my imprisoned wife that conjured the saliva.

"Granted, I failed with Saunter," Ventur gestures at his demented daughter standing in the dark corner of the room. I glance at her briefly. Tears fall from her cheeks but her face is devoid of emotion. There is something wrong with her. I can't shake the feeling. Every time I see her, it's like her soul is broken. She was manic and crazed in Sygon—now she stares at Vesper like there is a fracture in her psyche. The girl isn't right in the head. Whatever Ventur did to her, it's left her broken on the inside. The worst kind of wounds are the ones invisible to the human eye. Cracks in the mind and soul wide enough for darkness to seep through. Fissures deep enough for dark spirits to build dwellings.

Ventur continues, "But I will learn from my failure and raise your child differently. He will be stronger. I will raise him the way I raised Syrus. He has the genes to be the greatest soldier this kingdom has ever seen. I will send him to kill every enemy that dares to threaten my empire."

"And what makes you think he will listen to you?" Vesper spits. "You aren't exactly a spring chicken, Emperor. You look about a dozen full moons from death's door."

"Ah, it pleases me so much to hear you ask that! You see, I nearly died trying to save my reputation twenty years ago. I tried to kill your husband along with his family. Stabbed him right in the back with a silver dagger. So it was quite surprising to see him alive and well when I returned at sunrise. I had to think quick, so I aided him in his escape from the castle, then framed the murder of his family on him. It was the best I could come up with with the time I had. I needed my reputation intact if the leadership of the kingdom was to pass to me, so I couldn't have anyone knowing I was the one responsible for usurping Silenius Sylvian. But as I carried your fragile husband from the castle, the rising sun nearly scorched my flesh irreparably. If it wasn't for the shade of a bloodmaple, I would have turned into a charred corpse that day twenty years ago. But alas, ever since that tragic day my body has been horribly disfigured. And you know what? I almost gave up on getting a chance to get revenge on the little brat, but here we are! You see, I know something you don't."

The knights around me take a step back and surround me.

Ventur continues, "Your husband is in this room."

The Emperor ceases his fondling of Vesper and turns around to face me. The old, scarred man slowly pulls his hood away from his face. I watch as his lavender eyes reveal themselves from the darkness. Glaucoma makes them hazy, making it hard to tell if he can even see me. His bald, horribly maimed face looks as if someone lit him on fire in a past life. My heart freezes in my chest as I realize too late what's happening.

"Welcome home, Syrus Sylvian," Ventur says through his chapped-lip smile. "I do apologize for letting your room deteriorate in your absence. I hope your wife's breathing is a consolation, if anything."

*He knows!* The beast within howls inwardly.

No shit, I reply.

I look around at the knights spread around me as they draw their swords simultaneously. I curse under my breath. How long have they known? Within the blink of an eye, I go from perceiving myself as the smartest man in the room to the most foolish on the planet.

"Go ahead, Syrus. It has been quite some time since your wife and I have seen that handsome face. Remove your helm like a gentleman so we may have the honor of seeing those beautiful silver eyes."

For the first time in decades I am frozen with fear. In the light of Ventur's eyes, it feels as if I am a powerless child again. He's been playing me for the fool this entire time! How did he know? What gave it away? I feel like a deer the second it hears the twang of a bowstring. There is no retreating. There is no fleeing. I am no stronger or smarter than I was the last time I stood face to face with Ventur in this very room. I have the power of Sylvian the First and yet he was still cunning enough to trap me. How stupid could I be? This is the man treacherous enough to betray my father and steal the throne for himself. If he beat my father at his peak, why did I think I could defeat him at his?

*Snap out of it!* The beast growls violently, *If you don't recall, we defeated this man once already, and we will do it again.*

We didn't defeat him. He stabbed us in the back with a silver dagger.

*And yet we lived to face him today. We are the one with the advantage. We are a Hellhound, Syrus.*

I am failing to see how that is an advantage here.

*He is alpha of his race. We are alpha of ours. His followers follow him because they have to. Ours follow us because they want to.*

I listen to the howls raging in the distance. The sounds of a city under siege by Lycans is like listening to a pack of bleating sheep being torn limb from limb by ravenous wolves. Screaming. Yelping. Growling. Howls of pain. Howls of vengeance.

The beast is right. All this death and destruction is for me. The Fang Clan isn't obligated to follow me. Crixus and Creon and Scar could have left my side at any moment, yet they remained loyal the entire time. Mammoth could have bashed my head in the second I freed him, yet here I am, alive. Countless lives are counting on me. Countless lives will die tonight for me. These thoughts alone give me strength as I grip my helm and slowly lift it to reveal my face to my audience.

The room illuminates as my silver eyes gleam into the night. I look directly past Ventur straight into Vesper's beautiful eyes. She has never seen my silver vision. I watch as her face becomes mesmerized. There is more than love at first sight when I look at her, there is love at every sight. When we lock eyes, we live an eternity in only a fraction of a second. She is the sun and I am earth. Without a single word spoken, I feel my bones drawing strength from her gaze. In her presence I am reborn, baptized by fire. The months of separation melt away like time is merely a construct. She lights a fire in me that's been missing all this time. I feel it ignite and eclipse my body like a tidal wave washing over a fisherman's boat. I am not the man I was a single second ago, before I locked eyes with her. In this exact moment in time, Vesper has both sent me to my death and resurrected me from my ashes.

"It's good to be back," I sigh emphatically as my eyes hover toward Ventur. My flesh goes numb as the powers of Sylvian the First make me forget I am a mortal. The moonlight may be blotted by board covered windows, but not even concrete walls can stop me from siphoning its powers.

*Kill him. Kill him now!* the beast within demands.

Not yet. I need to find out the purpose of the Dybbuk Box. His time will come, beast.

*Look at him! He is weak and fragile. We can finish what he started. End his life now, Syrus!*

My powers make me forget Vesper is present in the room. In the light of my silver eyes, she is just another mortal. The love I feel dissipates. The anger amplifies. I am a god once more. No one can stop me. I am stronger than Ventur. I can fly. I have the demon of Dagon within me. There isn't a place he can go that I won't smell him. There isn't a soldier he can advance that I can't cut down. My eyes flicker to meet Vesper's again. It's like I can read her thoughts just from the look on her face. Despite my powers, I cannot shake the telepathy we seem to share from mating. Her scowl says it all. Since the day I met her, Vesper has always been a huntress first and a lover second. "Kill them. Kill them all, my dear," she groans from her corner of the room.

The beast within wants carnage. Vesper wants revenge. My conscience is outvoted. The Dybbuk Box will have to wait.

"Just curious," I say, looking back at Ventur. "What gave me away?" I search his eyes for any indication of fear. There is none. He has killed Sylvians before. Why would he fear one now? His naivety will be his downfall. I am not like the Sylvians he's met. My wolf within is hungry. It has been raised like a starving jackal and prodded like a circus creature. I am not like my father. And now Ventur will be forced to learn this lesson the hard way.

"I told him," a voice emerges from behind me.

I turn to face it, though I know who it is as a scent of piss floods my nostrils.

"Chimel," I chuckle, "I should have known."

"I sold my own daughter into slavery, pissmonger," he replies from the door. The coward speaks with an open tongue while hiding behind the surrounding Black Knights. "Did you seriously think I wouldn't stab you in the back the second you loosened up on my leash? I reported your plan to the Scouts the second you sent me to dig up that ridiculous armor you're wearing."

"Then it's a good thing I didn't tell you the whole plan," I reply.

"Oh well," Chimel sighs, "Your plan won't do you much good once you're dead in the ground."

"Says the man who will still smell like my urine when I'm dead in the grave," I reply with a smile. Without giving time for a witticism back, I plunge each of my swords into the two knights closest to me. I take my heel and plant it swiftly into one of them, kicking off and sending him flying back. Chimel leaps out of the door frame as the corpse soars toward the hallway window. The knight's momentum breaks through the boarded window and plummets to its death below. Wooden boards fall after him. The moon streams in, illuminating my childhood bedroom along with my silver eyes. Twenty years ago the full moon's light shined on my childish body as I tossed and turned in bed. Now it shines on me in all my glory. Everything has come full circle. Luna was there to watch my origin, and now she has returned to watch Ventur's end.

Poetic as fuck.

Four knights lunge toward me in sync, swords intent on skewing my limbs from my body. Their movements are slow as sloths. I thought these were supposed to be the kingdom's best warriors? I catch the wrist of one and redirect his blade to deflect the remaining strikes. I rip his helmet off and bash it into another knight's head, then throw his body into two others. The sound of metal knights thudding onto the concrete floor is a tremendous noise to my ears. I grab a loose blade from the ground and plunge it into the fallen knights so fast they don't even have time to pray for forgiveness.

"You misjudged me, Ventur," I growl emphatically, standing from the corpses. I turn to face his feeble body, wiping the blood of enemies from my eyes. "Where my father failed, I will prevail."

"Is that what you think?" Ventur laughs, then reaches into his pocket. When his hand returns to plain view it holds a wooden box the size of a wallet. The box is stained with blood and sealed with black gel around its edges. "Allow me to show you how wrong you are, Syrus."

Ventur throws the box at the ground violently. The wood shatters as it strikes the rock. I lose sight of the splintered wood as a black mist explodes from its contents. The mist expands exponentially. Its thickness envelopes Ventur. He vanishes from my sight as the fog fills the room. I panic. Dread enters my chest as the mist enters my nose. I know that smell. It's unmistakable. The room grows cold instantly. A shiver runs down my back. Memories of a muzzle around my mouth cause me to suffocate briefly. Thoughts of slavery flash before my traumatized eyes. I cough uncontrollably. I can't see anything. My false confidence fades. I feel like a wolf in the presence of a master hunter. I take several steps back until I run into a wall. I suddenly feel like a frightened child. I have nowhere to run. I am backed into a corner.

"I am what made you," a familiar voice growls through the mist.

A clawed hand tackles my throat and pummels my body into the wall behind me. The rock cracks as I make impact. My feet leave the ground as my assailant overwhelms me with strength. I catch a glimpse of the arm that grips me through the black mist. Its flesh is blacker than midnight. Bile rushes up my throat. I want to vomit. My silver eyes disappear. The feeling of invincibility flees. I am not a god, but my enemy is certainly the devil.

"You were supposed to die in Sygon," Bloodlust roars mightily, "But I will make use of your body now that you've so graciously returned alive."

The mist parts just enough for me to lock eyes with him. It is no longer the feeble frame of Ventur I stare at. Though this Blackblood no longer wears the mask of a Lycan's skull to cover his face, I know who this is. Bloodlust, the Blackblood responsible for my most recent afflictions. The monster I thought was Lundis. The demon who sent me to die at the hands of Atlas in Sygon.

All this time, Bloodlust was Ventur, the same man who killed my family.

Ventur, the man who wears two crowns.

Ventur, the man who has outsmarted me more times than I can count.

Ventur, the man who will send me to my death.

# 17

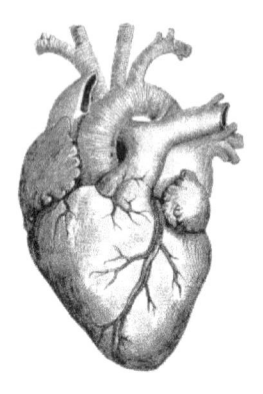

## I Told Them You Would Come For Me

How?

How has Bloodlust been behind this all?

How are Ventur and Bloodlust one and the same?

So many unanswered questions swim through my oxygen-deprived brain. What about Lundis? Have I been lied to this entire time? Why send me to Sygon if Bloodlust is just going to kill me now? Why not kill me instead of allowing me to master the Sylvian powers? Why bring my wife into all of this? There is no time to answer any of these. My vision gets narrower by the second. I am scared, I realize. The last thing I see before I die will be the devil incarnate. The ghoulish face is like a hallucination gone wrong. The suffocation makes it worse. The edges of Bloodlust's face blur. His charred flesh vibrates like unrestrained particles. His soulless eyes suck my spirit from my body. My neck creaks as his grip tightens. Will it snap before I can suffocate?

Why?

Why me?

Why couldn't I have just died in the valley of death twenty-five moons ago?

Why did Vesper have to come back?

Why was Sephora leveraged against me?

Why did I allow myself to be a pawn to the gods?

Fuck the Fates.

I won't die here.

I won't die without answers.

I'm owed answers.

*Let me out*, the beast demands. *We will get answers together.*

Poetic as fuck, I think to myself as a smile creeps onto my face. This is the perfect setting for the beast to be reunited with Ventur. The creepy smile causes Bloodlust to tilt his head in confusion. I blink, then reveal my silver eyes. I'm tapping out, I echo within my head. Protect us, I command the beast within. Protect us, like you did all those years ago.

Claws shoot out without my permission. My palm strikes Bloodlust's forearm with such ferocity that the sound of it snapping in half echoes. Before I have time to strike again, a metal chain whips around Bloodlust's neck and pulls his weight off me. I watch in euphoria as Vesper's eyes appear behind the demon as she digs her feet into his back and pulls the chain with her entire bodyweight. I look to the column she was previously tied to. It's empty, Saunter standing beside it dangling a key for me to see. The enemy of my enemy is my friend after all. The chains that were tightly secured around Vesper are now loose on the ground. I follow their links with my eyes and see it is the same chain Vesper now fastens around Bloodlust's throat.

The demon tries to get enough room to breathe but his limp arm makes it impossible. His body writhes manically while my bones break. The armor surrounding my body bends and rips at the seams. Muscles tear and expand. My facial structure shatters. My nose and mouth stretch into a snout. My human cranium distorts to that of a wolf. My ears stretch into pointed pyramids atop my head. My arms lengthen while black fur sprouts to cover my nakedness.

Vesper's purple eyes beam at me with pride. They are like orbs of violent fire. They are the same eyes that saved me twenty-five moons ago when a hurricane of Blackbloods descended on me. The same eyes that looked at me lovingly from across the altar as we uttered our wedding vows. The eyes that grimaced as she gave birth to our firstborn. These eyes will never leave me. She is like a dark guardian. A forsaken protector. Not even the Blackblood virus could prevent her from returning for vengeance.

I lift my muzzle to the air and feel a current of power surge in my lungs. A blood-curdling howl rips through my throat like a torrent of water amidst an avalanche. Saunter covers her ears and squeezes her eyes shut. Bloodlust falls to a single knee as the feral call punctures his eardrums. Vesper smiles as the cacophony allows her to tighten her grip even more on the demon.

The howl vibrates through the castle walls and reverberates throughout the kingdom. It is more than the scream of a feral predator. It is a calling to all Lycans throughout the world. It is the roar of an alpha calling to his pack members. In it is a single message concealed. *Kill.*

The atmosphere itself tears in two at the sonic boom. The walls around us shake. I am stronger than Dagon and Damon combined. I am Sylvian the First reincarnated, bred for the purpose of putting an end to the Undead Empire's tyranny. I have let them reign twenty years, and tonight

I'm here to tell them that has been twenty years too long. I will correct the sins of my father. The blood of Sylvian flows through me, communicating to my mind and soul that I am a god amongst mortals. Enchantress chose me as a vessel, and tonight, like her, everything I touch will die. Where this was a curse in my previous life, tonight, it will be a blessing to my new empire.

A thousand howls answer my call in the distance. My ears twitch with glee at the sound of the symphony.

Vesper grunts as she doubles down and pulls harder. Bloodlust's eyes are wavering as the consciousness fades. I can end him now. Separate his head from his shoulders. I grit my fangs together and snarl. Finally, this traitor will pay for all the pain he's caused me.

Just as I take my first step toward Bloodlust, I watch in horror as his wings fan to both sides and break the tension in the chain. A single link snaps and Vesper flies back as the chain whips free like a loose coil.

Bloodlust stands immediately and gasps for air. I stand in front of him in all my glory, both of us staring at each other eye to eye. Unlike the last time he saw my beast, I now have complete control, and I no longer wear a muzzle for his safety. I am not this demon's equal. I'm superior. The silver light from my eyes assaults the darkness in his own. Bloodlust doesn't utter a single word. His chest heaves for oxygen while his brain searches for a way out of confrontation. Ventur, the great military commander, has finally met his match in battle. What's even better—he's the one who first taught me to fight, and now I will be the one who overpowers him. The student becomes the teacher.

"It was supposed to be Atlas," Bloodlust grunts between spasming breaths. "Damn you, it was supposed to be Atlas!"

The comment throws me off. What was supposed to be Atlas?

"No matter," Bloodlust pants. "I will proceed with my plan and make use of you."

Time to shut him up. I raise my fist to throw the first punch. Something stabs into my side, knocking my balance. Then another. And another. I look down and see three arrows protruding from my flesh. When I look back up, I see several archers standing close to the doorway.

"Fools, move!" Bloodlust commands as his wings tuck behind his shoulder blades. The demon sprints for the open frame and dives through the open window across the hall. Fuck, I scream inwardly. I had the chance to kill him and faltered! All I can do is hope I don't pay for this mistake with my life. For now, I don't have time to beat myself up. Vesper and Saunter need me, and I can smell the Undead forces converging on us. The scent of several dozen soldiers enters the room from the hallway. We need to get out of here, fast. I look over to Vesper as she stands and dusts her body off from her fall. Saunter is only just collecting herself from my howl. For one who hasn't heard an alpha's call before, it likely scrambled her mind temporarily. Luckily for us, we have the strategic advantage. Battles were meant to be fought in battlefields, not narrow corridors and castle bedrooms. There could be a thousand enemies waiting for us in the hallway outside and it wouldn't matter—only two at a time can fit through the door.

I pull the arrows from my side and get to work while the archers re-notch arrows that will never take flight. My claws are a frenzy outside my control. All I can see is the blood splattering on my face as my hands lash out faster than I can comprehend. There is no time to think. There is no time to calculate my strikes. Primal instinct fuels me. The bloodlust of battle. My vision narrows to only those who fit inside the doorframe. Warriors come at me with spears and swords and daggers but no weapon formed against me shall prosper. The bodies slowly stack up in the hallway like a clogged artery.

The more I kill the more I lose myself. There is only the present. Wolves do not concern themselves with consequences of the future. It is kill or be killed. There is only the now. As I cut my way to freedom, the faces before me become more and more horrified. The way they see things is, if the previous hundred soldiers couldn't stop me, how can they? Some turn to run. Others throw themselves from boarded windows and take flight to fight another day. Only the fools lay down their weapons thinking I'll show them mercy. Wolves show no mercy. I take my inconsolable rage out on them. The thought of Bloodlust's escape only angers me further. The thought of him fooling me yet again makes this spiral into fury.

Before long, I lash out to cut bodies down but there are no survivors left for me to strike. I turn, my chest heaving victoriously for air, and see there is nothing left but corpses in my wake. I have subconsciously left the torture chamber and worked my way down the corridor until all opponents are annihilated.

*Damn you, it was supposed to be Atlas!*

What did Ventur mean?

So many unanswered questions.

A hand grips my shoulder and I pivot to attack. My claws lash out but a hand catches my wrist. As I turn, I lock eyes with my assailant. Even in all my rage, I cannot forget those eyes. Vesper, I sigh inwardly, reassured by her presence. The anger melts as she runs her hands through my fur. My heart rate drops drastically. The storm inside me parts before an inward sun. I cannot talk as a Lycan, but no words need to be said. She rubs my muzzle, her hands wiping the blood away from my eyes. I take in her calming scent, like a vagabond breathing in the smell of home after years on the road.

"I told them you would come for me," Vesper whispers over the sounds of war outside. "They didn't listen to me." She wraps her arms around my beastly midsection and hugs me tight. Wolves do not cry, but I am not a wolf in this moment. A single tear forms in each eye as I look down at her. All these months I thought she was dead—thought I would never see her again. My life was over. Breathing itself felt pointless. I marched toward my death, excited by the prospect of seeing her in the afterlife.

*Would you sooner go to your grave than forgive yourself?* That is the question she asked me in the darkness of my cell while I rotted away. Though I've learned it was Enchantress pretending to be her, the message is one of the only reasons I'm still alive. *If you truly love me, you'll keep fighting.*

The gods are cruel, but for the first time in my life they've shown kindness to me.

"We need to go, now," Saunter interrupts. I look up at her with mistrust in my eyes. She holds her hands out innocently. "I know you have no reason to believe me, Syrus, but there are things you don't know. I can fill you in, but it can't be here. We need to get far away from this castle. Bloodlust won't kill you. He needs your body alive."

Vesper pulls away from me and turns to face Saunter. I watch with amusement as she delivers a backhanded slap hard enough to make Saunter stagger backwards. "My child," Vesper shouts, "What have they done with my baby?"

Saunter holds her cheek as she regains her footing. When she removes her hand I can see the blood rushing to her pale flesh from the impact. "The Emperor is keeping him stored with the remaining Dybbuk Boxes in his personal quarters. The room will have more protection than even the castle's gates."

"I am not leaving without my child," Vesper says, looking from Saunter to me. I nod my head in agreement.

"You can't," Saunter counters. "Ventur will be counting on that, it's the only way he can trap Syrus. Don't you get it, Syrus? All of this, this entire war, is a decoy for a single greater goal! Ventur controls both sides of the board. He is the leader of the Undead and the leader of the Blackbloods, all without his soldiers having any clue what he's doing! They are all pawns rushing toward battle while he uses this diversion to accomplish something greater."

I tilt my head. Vesper senses my confusion and replies on my behalf: "What is the diversion for?"

"To insert his soul into Syrus's body!" Saunter shouts manically.

# 18

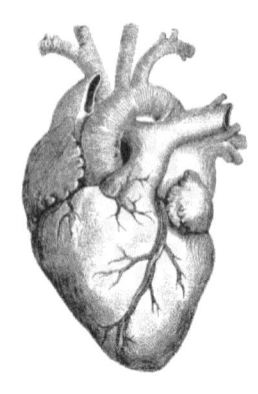

## Ventur & Bloodlust

It's all starting to make sense. The bigger picture I was too blind to see. Ventur himself taught me this lesson as a child: "If you can keep an enemy focused on small, decisive targets, they will be completely unaware of you flanking them. That is how a true commander conquers."

Ventur and Bloodlust are the same monster. The master manipulator behind this all.

Saunter continues, "He sent you to Sygon to fight with Atlas, his protege. I was just as in the dark as you, but now I know the truth. Atlas knew all of this and was planning on usurping him. It's part of the reason why I loved him so much. I knew Ventur. Atlas knew Bloodlust. But neither of us knew they were the same person. But after Atlas betrayed me, it has all been so heavy on my mind. I've been putting the pieces together, and now that Ventur has revealed his true identity, my suspicions are confirmed. It is all just a theory, but hear me out...

"Ventur's mortal body is failing, Syrus. When he saved you as a child to protect his reputation, the sun nearly killed him. He will not make it to the next age without a new vessel. So when Lundis returned from the mission your father sent him on—the mission to find Marduk's heart—Lundis discovered exactly what Ventur needed—the key to immortality. He found it in the North, in one of the last remaining Acolyte Temples from ancient times. In it was something far worse than Marduk's heart; the box contained Marduk's soul, sealed with the blood of Lysander himself. With it, Ventur was able to usher in a new age of Blackbloods and temporarily save his body from dying.

"The Emperor thought the Blackblood virus could heal his body from the wounds it incurred. He employed Skillah's black magic to divide Marduk's soul into several Dybbuk Boxes, that way he could inevitably call on the Blackblood virus whenever he wanted. Somehow, through some ancient knowledge Marduk's soul provided him, Ventur has known Sylvian blood was the cure to the virus this whole time... Again, this is just a theory, but when I was a child, I still remember him siphoning my blood into vials each month. He told me it was to ensure I was healthy, but I know better now... He was using my blood so he could cure himself of Marduk's soul whenever it was time for him to be Ventur once more.

"He didn't tell Skillah whose soul was contained within the original box, then spread propaganda throughout the realm that Lundis was Bloodlust. Your old tutor was the perfect scapegoat, but this double life was only a temporary fix... The Blackblood virus was enough to sustain the Emperor's life, but it couldn't heal him retroactively. That's when he devised a new plan... Ventur knew the only way to save himself was to insert his soul into the body of a Sylvian.

"That is why he searched for Dagon's surviving branch of kin, ultimately leading him to Atlas's tribe. He slaughtered them and took Atlas as his pupil, raising him to become stronger and mightier than you. All of it was staged, Syrus. Bloodlust forced Atlas to recommission the Acolytes and be their leader so no one would suspect him. Ventur single handedly controlled the Undead, the Blackbloods, and the Acolytes, all without a single side knowing he was moving their pieces across the board. But there was a single player he didn't account for… You.

"Everything changed when you entered the picture again Syrus. After all, you were the child that caused Ventur's body to begin failing in the first place. When the Fates saw fit to deliver you into Bloodlust's hands again, Ventur's pride caused him to become distracted. Instead of focusing on raising Atlas up to become his new vessel, he started obsessing over ways to get revenge against you. Sending you to Sygon was his way to do that—to prove his new student was better than you in every way. You were supposed to die in Sygon, Syrus.

"He played all of us. Ventur told me I would find my half-brother in Sygon and that I was to kill him. If I had to guess, Bloodlust told Atlas something similar. On the side, I conspired with Atlas to kill Ventur without knowing he was an agent of Bloodlust. Atlas and I were just brainwashed soldiers too stupid to see what was really happening. He fooled all of us, but he didn't plan for you killing Atlas. Now the only male Sylvian left is you, Syrus. Well, you and your child…"

Saunter pauses, a look of horror in her eyes. Vesper grips my arm and squeezes.

"No," Saunter continues. "He would never insert his soul into a toddler… It would make him too vulnerable. But then again, it would make him invincible against you, his eternal enemy. Ventur is the only person I know diabolical enough to claim the body of an innocent child in order to spite an enemy," Saunter says, speaking her thoughts aloud.

"We need to save our baby boy," Vesper demands, looking up at me. A low growl hums in my chest as I nod. Being a father is a strange feeling at times. Knowing there is a human out there that's half myself, being willing to sacrifice myself for it, even though I've never laid eyes on the babe before. But this child is the one thing that saved Vesper's life. Without her pregnancy, she would have never come back from the Blackblood virus. And because of that, I owe this child my undivided loyalty.

But first, I need my army. I may possess the powers of Sylvian the First, but the past month has taught me I cannot shoulder the burdens of war alone. I still possess one decisive advantage over Bloodlust, though. Winning this war is not a matter of how, but when. I don't have to kill Ventur yet, I just have to fight until the sun rises. Accomplish that and both his armies are rendered useless to open field combat. The Undead and Blackbloods will be forced to retreat to their burrows for the duration of the day, freeing me to go after Bloodlust himself. Endure until sunrise and this war is mine. Thank the gods their many tests and tribulations have produced endurance, if anything.

He won't transfer his soul into my child, not with me knocking on his doorstep. He needs to ensure I'm dead before taking such a leap of faith into a vulnerable vessel. No, Ventur will make sure I'm dead before he claims my child as his new body. Even if he doesn't have the strength to kill me himself, he will send every soldier he has to their death to accomplish it.

"You need to be safe, Syrus," Saunter interrupts. "Ventur may plan on using your child's body, but that doesn't mean today. He may still attempt transferring his soul into your body until the child is older and stronger. If you go in there hellbent on saving the child, you may open yourself up to whatever attack he has planned. If he is able to claim your body as a host, I fear there isn't a single warrior present who will be strong enough to stop him once he's claimed the powers of Sylvian the First."

I nod. Though Saunter was incoherently rabid last night in Sygon, her logic is straightforward and decisive now. Her emotion from Atlas's betrayal has had enough time to vent. Her hatred for her step father has supplanted her thinking. Whether I want to admit it or not, my half-sister is a genius. I wouldn't have been able to put these pieces together if I tried. But unlike me, she has lived under Ventur's shadow these past twenty years. She has seen all the small, decisive steps he's taken toward securing his reign. I know only the man Ventur once pretended to be, but Saunter knows how wicked this man truly is.

We may not be friends, but Saunter wants the Emperor dead just as much as me. Ventur was a fool for turning her into an enemy. Kick a dog long enough and it will snap someday and bite you. Ventur underestimated her. I hope this mistake will contribute to his downfall.

I can't speak, but I use my hands to communicate my plan. I point out the nearest window at the moon, still high in the sky. It is approximately midnight. We have half the night until the sun will rise. I indicate with my clawed fingers my intent to wait for it to shift to the horizon, then pound my fist to communicate attacking. Saunter and Vesper seem to understand the idea well enough.

Then I look to Vesper to communicate something else entirely. I rest my paw on her shoulder and point at her heart. We lock gazes. I cradle a pretend baby in my furry arms, then motion to show a toddler grown into a teenager. Vesper gasps, "Sephora..."

I nod.

Saunter jumps in to finish what I'm trying to say, "She's alive. Syrus saved her last night in Sygon. Last I saw she was in the custody of the Fang Clan."

"Gods be good," Vesper whispers, tears forming in her eyes. "Our baby is alive!" Vesper buries her head in my chest. I absorb her sobs as the trauma and shock overwhelms her. There is no time to rejoice yet. I grab her by the shoulders and break her from the trance. I point outside again at the destruction unfolding.

"I think he's trying to say the Fang Clan is the one fronting the attack, Vesper. Sephora might still be among them," Saunter explains, realizing what that means.

"We need to go now, then," Vesper demands, urgency in her tone. I nod in agreement. There will be time to process the emotions later when our family has been reunited. For now, there are many lives that must be lost still. The wolves need me. They cannot control their abilities until I've united them.

Bloodlust said it himself, *Sylvian the First turned Dagon's entire army of wolves against him. United all Lycans under his cause against their master.* Somewhere inside me is the ability to unite Lycans in a common purpose. A primordial power to control wolves and direct them in battle.

I bring a single claw under Vesper's chin, lifting her beautiful face upward. I bend down and lick her cheek with a wet, slobbery kiss. It is far from romantic, but I don't have time to shift back to my human form. Vesper grips my muzzle with both hands and kisses my nose. For now, that will have to suffice.

"I love you," Vesper says.

I touch my heart with my paw, then touch hers with the same paw. *I love you too*, I think inwardly, then jump from the window and plummet toward the earth, knowing what I must do.

# 19

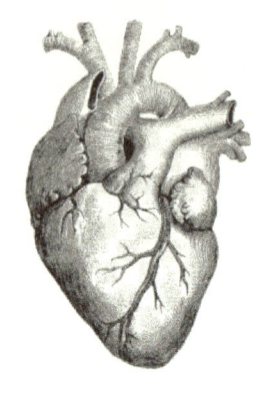

## HEART OF A LEADER

I've lost track of time being inside the castle's walls. By the time I make it to the city's capital square, I can hardly recognize the surrounding landscape. The streets are filled with water to my knees. Public sewage floats down the canals along with the dead bodies of war. The Wirewood River is looking to consume all that stands in its path. Buildings collapse. Statues fall. All firelight is doused for the night. Not a single light glows from the residential district. Not even the stars emerge to watch the horrors of the night.

Blackbloods and Undead go to war above our heads. Evidently, they are still unaware their masters are the same. The monsters collide like exploding cannons overhead. Purple eyes float in the sky. Leathery wings beat against the overcast clouds. It is like watching angels and demons go to war. Neither side will be the same by the time the sun rises. The two races will reduce their populations until Ventur puts an end to this madness.

I look around me, taking in the capital square for the first time in twenty years. Great pillars of the Sylvian Kings once stood erected here. Marble caricatures of my father and all who reigned before him. Now there is only Ventur, his likeness similar to the statue I destroyed in Sygon. Ravens flock the lower atmosphere, guiding the wolves toward me. Ventur's marble shoulder is covered in raven shit. Such a sight brings my heart warmth.

The capital square is elevated from the city streets. The ground is dry once I reach the top of the stairs, but the surrounding flood makes it look like a desolate island carved from stone. Water cascades from my drenched fur as I ascend to dry land.

This place is empty to behold. It looks like a place that is supposed to be some fantastic testament to celebrate the Undead Empire but has nothing to support such a claim. There is only the stone statue of Ventur, and nothing else. No plants or trees. No fountain laden with rich waters. No decorations or monuments. Just Ventur, emptiness, and a city slowly dissolving around him. Poetic as fuck.

I let out a series of howls, each one a calling to my Lycan soldiers to follow my voice. The calls are laced with authoritative messages. *Come, Hellhounds*, I command. *The strength of the wolf is the pack*, I explain. *Apart we will lose. Together, we are strong.* I receive howls in return that communicate their acknowledgement. It's working, I realize. They are coming.

*Coming, alpha*, one says.
*Follow the ravens*, says another.
*Wolves together, strong.*
*For Dagon!*
*We conquer our demons!*
*Vere mori skathen!*
*Death to the Blackbloods!*

*Death to the Undead!*

I'm overwhelmed with feelings of awe. Just a month ago, we Lycans were an unorganized race of savage beasts willing to kill each other for Bloodlust's amusement. With my Sylvian powers though, we are an elite pack of feral predators. I can't believe it's working. My whole life I convinced myself there was no way to control the beast within, let alone control hundreds of foreign wolves.

Bloodlust was right. Sylvian the First wielded these powers as he turned Dagon's forces against Damon's, and now I use them to liberate Lycans to a new era of freedom.

This must be how gods feel. I do not know any of these wolves, nor do they know me, yet they storm toward me ready to die for my objectives. Such a power is not one that should be taken for granted. There is a fine line between leadership and tyranny, one I must walk without stumbling.

Vesper and Saunter stand by my side as wolves lurk forward from the shadows. The moonlight reflects off their beady eyes. They approach cautiously, like clever foxes suspicious of traps. Selective breeding has taught our race to not rush into battle like foolhardy Neanderthals. The fur stands on the back of my neck as the Lycans come forth from the night. At first it is a slow trickle, then they pour into the capital square faster than I can account for them. Tens of dozens turn into hundreds. Their furs range between neutral colors and create a patchwork of diversity. Browns and whites and blacks. Tans and greys and autumns. Some walk solely on their hindlegs, others hunch over and walk on all fours. No two wolves look the same.

A select few are taller than even me and so thick with muscle that I can see striations through their fur. Others are thin and wiry with wingspans longer than their heights. The capital square is only big enough to fit a few hundred. Water drips from our soaked coats. Some of the wolves are injured already. Their blood mixes in with the pooled water beneath us, turning it bright red. The wolves who cannot fit on the elevated platform wade in the roaring waters around us, staring up like grizzly bears searching for salmon. The only common characteristic the wolves share is the same look of hunger that permeates their stares. For too long, Lycans have been forced to live lives of exile.

Tonight is the Undead's reckoning. Our bondage has been burned into our DNA. The atrocities our ancestors incurred are among us in spirit. We are surrounded by their vengeful ghosts in such a quantity one could not count in a single lifetime.

My whole life I wanted to be as righteous as my father, but I now realize I've surpassed him. Father had the ability to bring Lycans out of bondage in his lifetime, as did his father before him. Instead, our family made an unholy pact with the Undead, and it led to our downfall.

Since the fall of Dagon, Lycans have been cursed with the inability to control their inner demons. But with the help of a Sylvian, I now see wolves live their lives ready to submit themselves to a greater purpose. Without leadership, our race is like a caged animal, lashing out in fear of what we don't understand. We kill everything in our path, not because we hate it, but because we know no other way to overcome it. But my powers are the great equalizer. Solis and Luna overcame the Creator's curses by birthing Sylvian the First. And so the Sons of Dagon have never been the monsters this world has painted them to be. The real monster this entire time has been my family, for we are the ones who turned a blind eye to a race we could free from their curse.

I listen to Vesper's heartbeat as it quickens by the minute. She is not afraid of what's happening. She is in awe. Like me, her worldview is evolving second by second. She too realizes the things she's been told about Lycans since birth were a lie. These are not monsters. They humbly submit themselves before me, tails tucked between their legs as they paw at the ground I stand on.

Saunter herself is struck with equal disbelief. Though she has the ability to shift into a Lycan this very second, she retains her human form and takes in what's happening. She looks up at me and whispers, "I was wrong about you. For that, I'm sorry. It had to be you. Atlas could not have done this. It... It had to be you." Her lavender eyes are sincere and brimmed with guilt.

There is a shifting in the crowd as a select few wolves shuffle forward through their bowing comrades. My heart sinks as I analyze their faces. Although I've never seen these wolves before, I know exactly who they are. They may be animalistic now, but they share enough similarities with their human counterparts to be unmistakable. The four wolves make their way to me like divine prophets approaching a god. Slowly, cautiously, but with a familiarity unparalleled by any others present.

At their head is a jet black she-wolf leading the way through the crowd. She is tone and nimble on her hindlegs. She has the look of a warrior in her eyes. A crazed look that has seen more death and tragedy than a human heart is made to handle. Yet at the same time, I feel a deep connection with her, an admiration I have only experienced with a single female before.

*Crixus?*

*Syrus*, she replies, not speaking with her mouth, but instead with her heart. It is her voice, one that cannot be mistaken with any other. My eyes shift quickly to Vesper at my side, then dart back to the she-wolf. Crixus does the same. An awkward tension rises in my gut. Just yesterday, I was in love with Crixus—thought she was the woman I would mate with for the remainder of my life. But now that Vesper has returned, so has my love and affection for my wife.

*Is this...* Crixus stammers.

*Yes.*

*I'm happy for you*, she replies with sorrow in her tone. Instantly, I feel the she-wolf's walls grow around her heart. She must shut me out and shun me from witnessing her vulnerability. My heart is torn in two at the prospect of losing her, but a single glance at Vesper washes the pain away. Some men search their whole life for a woman who would lay down her life for them, yet the Fates have given me two.

*What is she doing here?* Crixus growls, now looking skeptically at Saunter. She pauses in her stride. Her hackles raise like the needles on a porcupine's back. I can't blame her; her only impression of Saunter is the batshit crazy woman we met last night. Crixus hasn't had the chance to see the complexities of my sister's character yet. The abuse she's endured as Ventur's daughter. The trauma she's endured throughout her lifetime.

*She's on our side now that Atlas is dead. She wants the Emperor dead just as much as us.*

Another voice interrupts the conversation. *The crazy bitch crucified me,* Creon cackles as if the attempt on his life was a mere joke. *Her deranged plaything of a boyfriend pinned me to a cross and now you expect me to trust her?*

*I may not be in Lycan form, but I can still hear you*, Saunter interjects.

*Then I'll say it to your face*, Creon continues, *I think you're a crazy bitch!*

*I've been called worse*, Saunter replies, shrugging off the comment.

*Mom?* a voice calls, shuffling from the back of the crowd. The voice comes from a she-wolf completely covered in sparkling silver hair, an appearance I've never seen in a Lycan before. But I recognize her voice. It is the same voice I've fallen in love with since she was a baby crying as I cradled her in my arms. Vesper cannot hear her. She doesn't share the ability to communicate with Lycans like I do. But still, Sephora has been sequestered in bondage as long as I have, so news of her mother's resurrection hasn't reached her yet.

*Sephora?* I respond, leaving Vesper's side to march into the crowd toward her. A rush of giddiness rises in my chest at the sight of the young female. Her Lycan form is thin and wiry yet strong and poised. Her silver fur gleams in the moonlight. Her silver eyes cast a powerful glow as I enter her view.

I don't give her time to respond. I wrap her up in my monstrous arms, embracing her like a shepherd who's lost his most prized sheep. Her hocks leave the ground as I pick her weight up like she's as light as a feather. A purr of delight rumbles through my chest. Sephora lets out a wolfish whine as we reunite, a canine who cannot contain her excitement. Where her fragile figure shook with fear and cold exposure in Bloodlust's lair the last time I held her, her body now trembles in my arms with love and elation.

Arms wrap around both of us from my side. Sephora and I both look down and see Vesper. Though Vesper has no way of knowing this is her daughter, mother's intuition needs no direct line of communication. Sephora fights free of my arms and embraces her mother, leaving me to be the one who wraps both of them in my arms. No one says a word. Sephora doesn't ask me to explain the impossible. There will be time for explanations later. For now, we rekindle our familial love while war wages around us. We stand in the eye of the storm, knowing only more death awaits us once we break this embrace.

There is so much Sephora doesn't know. She is a big sister now. The existence of her younger brother isn't an inkling of an idea in her mind. Vesper's survival remains a mystery to her. The things I've done to win her back—Gall, Queensmyre, Yueltope—are all unknown to my daughter. The same goes for me; I have no idea what my daughter has fully endured.

Although I want to barrage her with questions to fill the gap in my mind, there simply isn't enough time.

Intimate embraces never last long enough. I squeeze Vesper and Sephora tight, then release them altogether. War will not wait for us. I must address my army. Vesper and Sephora join my side. Another wolf approaches me as Creon and Crixus kneel in submission before me.

*Syrus*, the third wolf calls out. This one is covered in a dark chocolate coat of luxurious fur. He is taller and leaner than me. Longer arms and legs. Thicker muscles. Sharper claws and fangs. The Lycan looks like the ultimate warrior, the sort of soldier you thank the gods is on your side.

The wolfman's mouth is open, revealing his missing tongue for me to see. *Scar?* I ask, knowing the answer to my question.

*At your service, master*, the wolf replies. His voice is foreign to me, thick with the accent native to the Isles of Skaar. This is the first time I've ever heard him speak. As humans, we could not communicate telepathically as we do now. But wolves do not need tongues to speak to one another, I realize. My jowls lift into a smile at the sight of him.

If it wasn't for Scar, none of this would be possible. I sent him on a seemingly impossible mission to find the ancient Fang Clan. He delivered on the mission unscathed. If not for Scar, we would not have this army. If not for Scar, this war would be lost.

I have no idea how he did it, but one thing remains true. This man may not be able to speak, but his loyalty speaks volumes. His actions alone prove his allegiance. If not for him, I would have died in Sygon.

I approach the wolf and grip the back of his neck. He has to lean down to accept the embrace. Our muzzles angle down as our foreheads rest against one another. *I cannot thank you enough for what you've done. I am not your master. We are equals.*

Scar puts his claws around the back of my neck and presses his skull into mine harder. He replies, *You saved me from hell. For that, I would gladly dive back into its depths in your place.* We squeeze each other's necks, then release the embrace. Scar steps back and kneels beside Crixus and Creon. For the first time in a long time, I am happy.

Although the world around us is ending, I wouldn't want it to end while in the presence of anyone else. I have everyone I love gathered around me. Everyone except my son, that is. I'll make sure that's fixed by sunrise.

*Wolves,* I announce, casting my thoughts to encapsulate the hundreds of Lycans around me. They look up at me with sophistication. We are no longer the savage beasts we've been painted as by society. *Tonight, there is much more at stake than our freedom. Tonight, the fate of all living souls hangs in the balance.*

*For generations, our kind has been banished to live in the shadows while the Undead cinches its grip on the throne. Since the dawn of mankind, the Sons of Dagon and Damon have watered the earth with blood to grow their dominion. The Sylvians, my father included, did nothing to stop this genocide. But I have been raised by the wolves and I have lived amongst the Undead. I am here to tell you that our differences are not so great that we cannot live in peace, together. There is good in both species, and there is evil in both species.*

*Tonight, we must endure bloodshed a final time. But unlike our ancestors, this blood will not be in vain. Together we will usher in a new age of peace, one where Lycans and Undead live amongst each other in fellowship. We will see that the monsters inside us do not dictate our abilities to love one another. Solis and Luna created us to be guardians of this world, and we alone have let these curses turn us into demons. Our curse only has the power we give it. But when the sun rises on the morrow, we—*

My voice catches in my chest as a force pierces my lungs from behind. An involuntary grunt exhales as claws puncture my flesh beneath my ribcage and tunnel toward my heart. My world spins out of control. My vision narrows. Weakness injects itself into my veins. My knees wobble with the weight of my body. A hand wraps itself around my heart from behind. I cannot breathe. I cannot move. I am completely paralyzed.

"Oh brother," Saunter whispers in my ear from behind.

Vesper shrieks somewhere in the distance. "If you so much as move a muscle, I will crush your husband's heart," Saunter tells her. I don't have the energy to even look at my wife. My chest cavity tries to heal but is prevented from doing so. The foreign invader is too strong to be expelled from my body. "You speak like a king," Saunter says, "A true leader."

I curse inwardly. I have just enough brainpower to realize I'm being betrayed. The same woman who tried to kill me last night is following through with her plan. Why did I trust her? I can't seem to recall. I barely have the willpower to stand, much less meditate on my decisions.

How foolish could I be?

I thought the enemy of my enemy is my friend. I realize now, too late, I couldn't have been more wrong.

"I want to thank you for assembling this army of Hellhounds for me, brother," Saunter whispers. "Like I said, I was wrong about you. It had to be you. Atlas could not have done this. I, like you, have spent my whole life wanting to kill the Emperor. Your only mistake was thinking I'd allow *you* to take his place. Do you have any idea what it was like being raised in your shadow, brother? Ventur didn't let a single day pass without reminding me how inferior I was to you as a student. In fact, I almost hate you more than I hate him.

"I will finish what Atlas was too weak to do. But there are too many Sylvians on the board, so now I will kill you and your daughter and take what's mine."

# 20

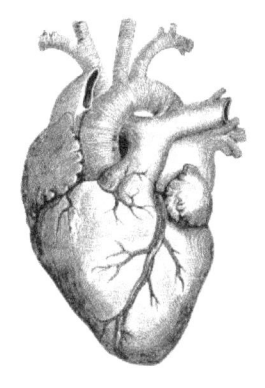

## BATTLE OF ALPHAS

I want to scream but all I can manage is an exacerbated gasp. Wolves all around me raise from their knees and snarl. Creon and Crixus and Scar rush forward like avenging angels.

*BOW TO ME!* Saunter screams telepathically. I can see the light from her silver eyes radiating over my shoulder. Creon and Crixus and Scar stop in their tracks. Like brainwashed soldiers, the hatred melts away from their faces as they bow obediently. I watch in horror as the hundreds of wolves around us obey Saunter's orders.

*I am your new alpha*, Saunter screams violently to my army. *You will obey my every command, filthy Hellhounds!* Meanwhile, I am mounted on her fist like a puppet controlled by a ventriloquist. I cannot move without my master's permission.

"I will show you why we Undead have exiled these fleabags all this time, brother."

*You there, she-wolf,* Saunter calls to Crixus. Crixus looks up with recognition, looking past me as if I'm merely a stranger. *I order you to kill this man's bitch of a wife.*

No!

Crixus stands again, this time doing so to serve her new master. I can hardly think. My body's remaining energy is channeled to combat the invading attack. Trying to heal what can't be healed. It is pitch black. The only light is the hanging moon and its army of stars. My lungs cannot inflate or deflate. It feels like balloons are being squeezed in my chest and the air pressure has nowhere to go. Bloody vomit surges up my throat and washes my tongue. My eyes feel like they will soon explode from the lack of oxygen.

The surrounding army fades to black. All I can see are my immediate surroundings. Crixus approaches Vesper like a she-wolf who's lost her man to an Undead—because that's exactly what she is. Whatever safeguards Crixus employed to repress her feelings for me, Saunter's command blew them away with black powder.

"They are not the innocent slaves to society you've painted them as," Saunter explains, "They are only as good as their alpha." Vesper panics as her eyes snap from my dying body to her incoming attacker. Crixus lands the first strike as she catches Vesper vulnerable and unaware. Her claws dig into Vesper's cheek and rip open her face from ear to nose in a devastating slap. Vesper's unbalanced body absorbs the blow and is catapulted to the ground.

It was commonly known among the Muzzled that Crixus was the longest surviving Lycan amongst us. Although I've never seen her beast before, that fact alone tells me what I need to know. Crixus is the most lethal threat among us. No one can survive the hell we went through for as long as she did without becoming a devil.

"Now watch this," Saunter laughs. *Hellhounds! I command you to kill each other! Do not stop until every last one of you is dead!*

I turn from Vesper's struggling body and expand my vision as far as it will go. I watch as the docile wolves from before stand from submission and turn into vicious jackals. It is like a switch has been flipped in their brains. They forget everything I've said about peace and devote themselves to destruction. My ears twitch as a cacophony of snarls and growls dominates the air. The horde around us becomes a warzone in the blink of an eye.

Wolves leap on one another and tear into each other's flesh. Yelps of pain reverberate into the ozone. Their shadows dance in the dark like shadow puppets cast from dying firelight. In the dark, there is no certainty what's happening. Our minds play tricks on us in the dark. Make us see things that aren't there.

All I can see is the knotted clump of demons piling higher and higher. I cannot tell where some bodies end and others begin. White fangs gleam in the moonlight. Rabid eyes twinkle in the night. Black holes that only know how to consume. Wolves make a distinct sound when they fight to the death. Jaws snap like skeleton fingers. Yelps and growls and snarls hum like a disjointed orchestra.

Saunter has unleashed civil war. This is what the Blackbloods watched in the fighting pits taken to a greater scale. Spectators can ascertain who is winning when two wolves fight to the death. But when wolves go to war with each other, no one wins.

I was a fool for thinking I could play the role of Sylvian the First. Undead and Lycans have not evolved. We are just the same sorry species we were thousands of years ago. Undead and Blackbloods slaughter each other in the air above. Lycans rip each other to shreds below. It is like watching the ingredients of dough be folded in layers. The feral predators lose their identities as they fall on one another, slowly becoming an unidentifiable mass of carnage.

Creon and Scar are consumed by Saunter's command. Because the two knelt side by side, they go for each other's throats now. I see why Bloodlust chose them as companions for me. They do not fight like the other wolves who throw caution to the wind to deal death. Creon and Scar circle each other like calculated warriors. They exchange blows like true gladiators. Scar uses his long arms to keep space. He lands several blows despite Creon's shifty dodging. Bloody saliva hangs from their jowls like they've swallowed a child with red shoelaces. Creon ducks under Scar's swatting claws and goes for the takedown. The two fall to the ground and grapple, jaws searching for vulnerable tissue, claws clamping for the jugular.

Vesper and Crixus fight their own war beside me. My ear twitches with every labored grunt from Vesper. My soul strains every time I hear Crixus's jaws clamp down on flesh. Everything I know and love collides like comets crashing. Crixus and Vesper exchange blows like master swordsmen measuring their opponent. Vesper dive bombs Crixus from the air. Crixus invites the attack and drags my wife to the ground. Vesper sinks her fangs into Crixus's neck. Crixus opens Vesper's stomach with her claws. They become so bloody that I can no longer determine who is winning or who has more wounds.

"When I was a little girl," Saunter whispers in my ear, "Ventur learned quickly that I was not his daughter. To teach me why Lycans cannot be trusted, he got me a wolf pup for my birthday. He let me raise it as my own pet. Her name was Valor, and in my miserable childhood, she quickly became the only thing I loved. But then, one day, when Valor had grown so big that I could ride her like a horse, Ventur locked me in my room with her and starved us both. I didn't know what I had done wrong to deserve this. After a few days with no food, Valor started turning feral as my body grew weak. We went from cuddling in my bed to standing on opposite sides of the room. The longer we went, the more manic we became. It didn't take long for Valor to betray me. She would stare at me from the dark corners of the room licking her muzzle, stomach growling. And when I least expected it, she turned on me. I had to snap her neck and feed on her blood to survive. I assure you, we are not the same Syrus Sylvian. We are creatures of our environment, and my environment has taught me how fatal a mistake it can be to trust a filthy beast."

My heart is broken in more ways than one. It hurts worse to know this is all my fault. I am the one who decided to trust Saunter. I erroneously believed her hatred for Ventur would bond us together. She even freed Vesper from bondage to save me from Bloodlust's attack. Why did I think we were on the same side now? This is the same woman who tried to kill me a single night ago. The same woman deranged enough to date Atlas.

Saunter's grip tightens around my feeble heart. I am hardly conscious. I walk a tightrope thread between the land of the living and the realm of the dead. Among the carnage, I see an old hag standing atop the pile of dead wolves. Am I hallucinating? Enchantress watches me intently, and I watch her. No one else seems to notice her. The moonlight shines through her like she is an ethereal specter. Is she here because my time has come? Death incarnate arrived to claim the soul of the soldier that failed her.

Her face is constantly shifting. It is like a kaleidoscope of endless morphing. A head emerges from her mouth and mounts on her neck, then another head emerges from that mouth. On and on and on she sheds the identities of others so fast I cannot see anything but her blurry face. But her eyes remain constant, glaring into my soul. The particles that make up her face vibrate through time and space, but those eyes, those eyes are like staring into eternal damnation.

Everything around me fades subtly.

The fighting, the bloodshed, the pain in my chest.

*Stop!* A voice shouts from amidst the chaos. A spotlight illuminates Sephora in her Lycan form. The fighting ceases. All wolves stand down. Motion becomes idle everywhere. Crixus regains composure.

I cannot see anyone else. Death is overtaking me.

*Sephora,* I call out desperately. It takes everything in me to channel my last thoughts. These will be the last words I speak before Enchantress claims my soul. My daughter looks to me for aid. Her eyes gleam a violent shade of silver. Her Sylvian powers… I nearly forgot… She has the power to command these wolves…

*Dad! What do I do?* Her voice is panicked. These powers are new to her, just as they are to me. We are learning on the fly. But the only certainty I know is, Sephora is our last chance of winning this war. Soon I will be dead, and it will be her word against Saunter's. Only the stronger of the two will control this army.

I lock eyes with Enchantress. The old hag mouths something to me that only I can hear. "I am not here for you," she calls out. "I've come to claim another."

Huh?

Enchantress raises a feeble, wrinkled finger and points at the woman standing behind me. Saunter. The reaper is here for Saunter.

I see Vesper move in my peripheral. Crixus's beast is dazed and confused by the ceasefire. The she-wolf staggers with a limp, moving away from her target as Vesper realizes the battle has paused.

"That bitch!" Saunter screams, then orders to the wolves, *Lycans, kill the Sylvian bitch!*

The wolves stagger in confusion. Their bodies are cut open from the civil war amongst themselves. Half of them lie on the ground bleeding out. The survivors turn to face Sephora, savagery returning to their eyes.

*Dad?* Sephora cries. I lock eyes with Enchantress. The wicked woman has a smile on her face as she watches Vesper take flight. I look up at the night sky. Vesper's eyes are like flaming heliotrope. I can feel her anger from here. I look back to Sephora, a smile growing on my jowls.

*Don't worry Sephora*, I whisper calmly, my chest ready to explode as Saunter's fist tenses around my heart. *After your mother makes her move, this army will be without an alpha.*

"Huh?" Saunter grunts, distracted by my statement. Vesper swoops down from above with the vengeance only a mother can possess. Harnessed in her strike is twenty-five months of repressed rage and grieving. Pain and torment and anguish. She has been to hell and back, and she's brought her demons with her.

The earth explodes behind me.

The pressure in my chest rips free.

*Wolves*, Sephora screams at the top of her childish lungs. *Rip that traitor apart limb from limb!*

I fall to my face. My head twists sideways so my muzzle can breathe. When I do, I realize there is a blurry red glob of flesh lying beside me. It pulses rapidly, pushing out blood from its pores. It almost looks like a heart.

Oh wait.

It is a heart, I realize.

My heart.

Saunter must have ripped it clean out of my chest when Vesper made contact.

My vision blurs as the heart slowly beats its final rhythm. It contracts, expands, then ceases all movement. Darkness converges. What a worthy thing to die for. I have regained all that I lost. My daughter is reunited with her mother. I hugged them both a final time. My soul will rest in peace knowing all that I've done has not been in vain.

# PART TWO

# 21

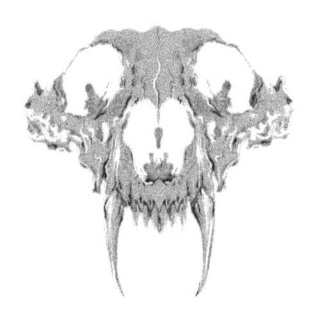

## ONE WISH

"Where... Where am I?" I ask, "And why is it so goddamn bright?" I squint my eyes like they are the last remaining floodgates saving my corneas from burning. It feels like I am staring straight at the sun despite my attempt to block the blinding glare. I shade my face with my hands and feel the flesh on flesh contact. I am no longer in Lycan form. There is no fur covering my hands. No claws protruding from fingertips. With my eyes closed, I run my hands down the length of my body and realize I'm naked. But I don't feel any particular sensation. There is no wind to chill my bones. No heat that accompanies the ghastly light outside my eyelids.

"You are dead," a familiar voice replies. It is the voice of the old hag. Enchantress. The woman who personally commandeered my rise from the ashes. Though she is the embodiment of death, her voice is somewhat soothing to me. She has never proven to be malignant toward me. If anything, I wouldn't have lived this long without her.

"Who would've thought death would be so bright," I complain.

"Us creatures of hell aren't accustomed to witnessing heaven. But everything is going according to its plan, my fallen prince."

With time, my eyes adjust to the world of white. My eyelashes flutter violently to combat the exposure. Images become apparent. At first, just shapes and lines. My brain deciphers the form of objects around me. I spot Enchantress's humanoid shape not far from me. This must be amusing to her. Only a moment ago, all I had to guide me through the pitch black was the moon. Now, it looks like I'm staring straight at an exploding star.

I'm not sure what I thought the afterlife would look like, but this wasn't it. Crazed prophets blurt about streets of gold and rivers of milk and honey. All I see are trees—ugly ones at that.

The world around me is monochrome. I stand on a line of equinox where two forests converge. The one on my right is where the intolerable light radiates from. The trees are white as ash with bark like valiant armor. The trunks are thick as redwoods and reach so high their end cannot be seen. White leaves cover the sturdy branches. White leaves with white veins. It is unnatural looking. Like a painter came through and painted the world black and white. Even the light itself, the light my eyes struggle to filter, is white. It has no color, unlike the amber sun.

The forest of white is so sterile and perfect that my mind can hardly process it. It is like staring at a paradox that shouldn't exist. An optical illusion my brain could stare at for eternity and not discern the bigger picture.

My toes sink into the fertile soil. It feels like sand, yet there is no coarseness. It is like standing on whipped, creamy butter. Soft and moist and comforting. Of course, when I look down I'm not surprised to see the soil itself is white. Tutor Lundis taught me once some people see the world this way, devoid of color. Color blindness—that's what he called it. Severe forms of color blindness left someone only able to see trees without their greens and oceans without their blues.

Rising from the white soil, surprise surprise, are white roots. Gorgeous white roots, at that. Strong healthy serpents coiling up and down across the ground. Like the curled back of a leviathan as it comes up for air only to dive back into the depths of the ocean.

Interlocked with the roots of perfection are their antithesis. Gnarled, plagued roots with a complexion black as midnight intertwine with the roots of pale ash. Every gap and loop of one root is filled by the other like ten thousand snakes fucking.

Where the fuck am I?

I follow the demonic roots to their side of the equinox line and see I'm surrounded by a forest of death. The light of the heavenly forest was initially potent enough to blot it from sight, but now its sinister details make themselves known. The roots from the converging forests strangle each other in a chokehold for control of the ground. The strong, thick ashen tubers, though mightier in appearance, make little progress in their tug-of-war against the termite-infested, leprous rhizomes. Nor does the obnoxious light from my right side breach the transient darkness of the forest to my left.

The darkness and light come to a stalemate exactly where I stand, both forces biding for my eternal soul.

"Alabastur was quite the playwright," Enchantress mutters from the palpable shadows to my left. "Somehow, despite him being born hundreds of years after my death, he was able to depict the tragedy of my being in *Equinox*... And here we stand, at the exact equinox between life and death."

"You mean to tell me *Equinox* was real?" I ask, astonished at the embodiment of what a writer's words cannot justify.

"The playwright took certain liberties, but yes. The story of Luna's affair with Cratos was real, as was her illegitimate daughter, me."

What spans before me is nothing like the earthly interpretation I saw in Queensmyre as a child. Although I was in awe of Alabastur's play then, I am incomprehensibly smitten now. Human dialect cannot fathom what I feel. All the forces of life and death converge in one point. Dread and regret invade my body, countered by love and courage. The entire spectrum of human emotions flood within me. I am cold and warm and fragile and infinite. Not a single experience can scratch what I feel now. Contradictions pulse through my veins. Meaning and despair fight a hopeless war for control of my vessel.

Trees to my left are like empty gallows. My brain anthropomorphizes them. Sees their many sticks like looming claws. Spots gnashing fangs amidst their gnarled bark. Projects my worst nightmares into their shadows. Layers upon layers of swirling darkness. No moon to illuminate. No candle to seek reassurance. The forest is filled with the same darkness that hid under my bed as a child.

The trees are like skeletons swaying in the wicked wind. The more I concentrate on them, the more I can hear their pain. They creak and cry for an audience to feel their suffering. Tears bubble in my eyes as I realize I cannot run from their infectious gaze. Their roots wrap around my ankles like venomous shackles.

I turn to face the holy forest to my right. The light burns the tears from my eyes and fills my mind with peace and assurance. White coils wrap around my legs like liberating safeguards. A white stag beckons to me from the trees. Its antlers are too large to differentiate from the branches around it. The creature is too mighty to be anything other than a figment of my imagination. Light seeps from its eyes. Safety radiates from its presence. I go to approach it but realize I am trapped by the roots that ensnare me. They are up to my waist now, growing to consume me more by the second.

Alabaster and onyx snakes entangle me. Porcelain and charcoal roots envelope my body like a cocoon. I am being devoured alive.

I turn to Enchantress. I can barely see her as she conceals herself among the shadows. "Is this it? I thought you hadn't come to claim my soul?"

"I didn't lie to you, my soldier. I have brought you here to thank you. A few moments of reprieve from all the pain. A retreat to purgatory before I send you back to hell. These roots have healing properties. You will soon be reborn from death and life. Death-Defeater, they will call you. But I am not a cruel master, so I wish to repay you for your service before we depart. Tell me one thing you wish to know, and I will make it known to you. This is my gift to you, for ignorance brings death, but knowledge brings life."

Confusion is an understatement. But then again, mortal minds aren't meant to master metaphysics.

"What are you, a fucking genie now? Saunter ripped my heart from my chest. There is no coming back to life after that."

"You've only seen a fraction of what's possible when I hold the reins of your life. The Creator no longer dictates what I can do. Outside the control of Solis and Luna, the world is mine to meddle. Besides, you are a Sylvian. Your body cannot perish without my say so."

"And then what? You're just going to toss me to the side like a broken marionette? Just like you did to my father?"

"Your father did everything I asked of him," Enchantress replies coldly, "And that alone is what's allowed you to be where you are."

"Why make him lose a kingdom just to force me to retake it? Huh? If you're so goddamn powerful, explain that to me!"

"It's so humorous, watching you humans speak as if you know the meaning of life, as if you have all the answers." The Summoner's voice is suddenly ethereal. It pierces the air around me. It causes my eardrums to vibrate. It makes the earth quake. It's beautiful. It's horrifying. It's equal parts dreadful and exhilarating. "You have no idea how many beings want you dead, Syrus Sylvian. Not just mortals. When you transcend the land of living like I have and pull back the veil that separates life from death, you emerge into a world your mind cannot comprehend. Solis cursed me with this ability from birth. Because of Luna's affair, Solis channeled all his hatred and envy into hurting me—an innocent byproduct of my mother's sins. My earliest memories in life were seeing dead people. Demons. Ghosts. Ghouls. They called to me. Some hunted me. Others protected me. But this is the way things had to be, Syrus.

"Time is not linear. I met certain spirits who, even though they were dead already, they had never even been born on earth yet. When you die, you exist at all points of time—from the dawn of creation until its end. I knew your father before he was even born into his flesh. I knew you, too, Syrus, though you can't remember it. Because of Solis's curse, I walked with the dead, even those who had never lived, and from their ranks I carefully selected my soldiers. The champions who would help me get revenge against Solis, against the Creator. Your father was one of these soldiers. You were another. It doesn't make sense now. But it will when my plan is complete. Your fickle mind is still finite. But soon it will see the meaning behind life. Because only in death can we truly appreciate life. So again, I ask you. What is it you desire to know, and I will make it known to you."

The air around me vibrates in euphoric ecstasy. I can no longer feel my body. It feels like I'm floating. I'm being resurrected. Soon, my soul will awaken in its mortal body. The darkness of the forest to my left blurs with the blinding light from my right. They converge on me like a violent tornado. The black and white are no longer polarized. I cannot make out Enchantress's figure anymore. The trees are gone. Everything is blurred as my vision is consumed by the swirling chaos of eternal suffering and joy. Everything that is pure and innocent mixes with everything that is evil and maleficent. Everything that was and ever will be surrounds me. Time is not linear. I exist in a moment that spans centuries of human history. From its inception to its extinction.

"Speak it, and I will make it known," Enchantress's voice breaches the whirlwind.

"My enemy," I gasp, the wind around me pulling the request from my lungs. "Show me my enemy, so I may know my enemy. Only then can I defeat them."

"Your wish is my command, but I warn you... You will not like what you see."

I don't have time to reply, though her warning begs a single question. When have I ever liked what she has to show me?

## 22

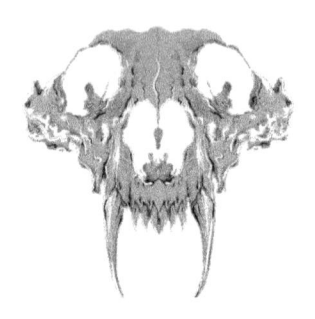

### NIGHTFALL

A bright light flashes, then darkness settles.

"Where are we?" I stutter as air returns to my lungs. Everything around me is washed in white as my eyes digest the scene. I have an uneasy pit in my stomach. I am no longer a floating conscience. I have returned to my body, but something feels off. I still feel weightless, though I can feel the ground with my feet. I wiggle my toes. They crunch a thick layer of snow beneath them. Odd, I think to myself.

It isn't that my vision is washed in white, it's that my surroundings are being bombarded by a blizzard. I freeze up for a second, expecting my naked flesh to be hit by a wave of bone-chattering frost, but no such feeling comes. Though the raining ice is enough to make my mind remember what cold feels like, my body feels no such sensation. My nipples are not hard. My dick does not shrink. Goosebumps do not cover my body. All the anatomical indications of being cold are absent.

"You are in a memory," Enchantress replies, then adds, "But more specifically, you are on the island of Nightfall, the land of frost and tundra."

Nightfall? She brought me to Nightfall? Why the hell are we in Nightfall? The island is damn near inhabitable. Even I've never traveled to Nightfall, and I've traveled to almost every city inside the Areopagus's domain.

The best way to experience Nightfall is on a map. Well, it's at least the warmest way. The geography is like any normal continent, except it's completely frozen. Snow dunes and frost forests and icy lakes. Permafrost soil and hailstone blizzards and iceberg-filled oceans. On maps, it's easy to gloss over as no more than a speck of white. But it is a remarkably large island smudged between the Areopagus and Sygon. A considerable chunk of land used for nothing more than ignoring altogether for fear of freezing to death. Or at least, that's what I thought.

"The sun will be setting soon," Enchantress announces from my left, "Then, the culling will begin."

"What are you talking about? What culling? There is no one here…"

"No one you can see. They ready themselves like soldiers before war. By the time the sun rises on the morrow, only one will be left standing."

"What does this have to do with my enemy? Bloodlust would never travel to Nightfall. He craves power. There is no one to control in Nightfall."

"Bloodlust, maybe not," the old hag rebuts, "But to know your enemy, you must know their origin. This, Syrus, is where the Blackblood virus began. Here, in Nightfall."

Gods be good. Enchantress is going to show me the birthplace of Marduk, the first Blackblood to ever become infected. Though their existence has been shrouded in mysticism for centuries, the old hag now plans on revealing knowledge that's been lost throughout history. Marduk. The Blackblood virus. Bloodlust. Dybbuk Boxes. Ventur. Lundis. There is so much I don't know, but by the time I'm resurrected I will gain understanding.

"Then what is this culling?" I ask solemnly, looking up to the sky to determine how many hours are left before nightfall.

"To understand the culling, you must open your mind to the possibility that your father hid certain details of history from you," Enchantress begins. "Not to keep you ignorant, but to protect you from their savagery. To ensure history does not repeat itself."

"By now I've determined there is a fair amount my father left out of my lessons as a child. The man I've come to know him as is basically a stranger. His withholding of knowledge may have protected me as a child, but all he did was delay the trauma to my years as an adult."

"Well," Enchantress sighs, "That trauma will only expand now, but it is time you learned this. Without the culling, there would be no Marduk. No Blackblood virus. No Bloodlust."

I hear the sound of snow crunching nearby. I turn to find its origin, then spot a human bundled in a white wolf pelt walking our way. I stand amongst snow dunes, right in the middle of nowhere. The hills of ice and snow rise and fall as far as my eyes can see. It is like being in the middle of the Scorpos desert, only someone replaced the sand with snow.

The man who approaches is young. Still a teenager, if I had to guess, but the terrain makes it difficult to determine exactly how old he is. Snow is caked in his premature beard and eyebrows. Icicles hang from his long, black hair. His face is beat red from wind burn. His hands are well on their way to being frostbitten. The wolf pelt that clings to his shoulders is thick, but it can only do so much to protect this man from the environment. The wolf's head is drawn over his own like a hood. He holds each side of the cowl to keep it in place as the howling wind seeks to expose his face.

Tied to the bottom of his fur boots are evergreen branches to provide traction in the snow. The rest of his tunic is crusted with ice, causing him to blend in with the environment like a mirage. The enveloping blizzard conceals him well. He is like a ghost, but ghosts do not chatter their teeth as loud as this man. I know what it is like to experience the cold, but not nearly to the degree this man does. Nights in winter I spent on the run were the worst. The chill of darkness is so fierce it penetrates a person's bones. It sets in slowly, then all at once. Attacks the extremities first, then inches toward the core.

I instantly feel sympathy for the man. When you are in a desert of heat, all you want is water. But when you are in a desert of snow, all you want is warmth. Each step the man takes is a protest to death. He walks like his joints are frozen and his bones are aching. Ice does not bend. It breaks. This man's body is being turned to an ice sculpture before my eyes and is one blow away from shattering like glass.

Still though, some inexorable will continues to propel one foot after the other as the man trudges through the snow dunes.

"Who is this man?" I watch his every step with sympathy. For some reason, I inwardly cheer for him to keep moving forward. Something within feels connected to him. Maybe it's because I, too, have fought the elements of life. I, too, have felt the pain it requires to simply keep moving forward.

"His name is Savrian Sylvian," Enchantress replies.

"A Sylvian? What is a Sylvian doing in Nightfall?"

"What is your understanding of the Sylvian succession line?"

I avert my eyes from Savrian to Enchantress. "The firstborn male in the family inherits the throne. If he dies without heir, it passes to a younger brother, and if there is no brother, it goes to the oldest living sister."

"It was not always this way, Syrus."

"What do you mean?"

"Not all Sylvians were as stoic as your father. Several generations before him, the Sylvians adopted more savage means of determining the successor. For several hundred years, children bickered over who deserved the throne. Animosity grew between siblings who were passed over just because they were born later than others. Sisters cursed the sex their flesh embraced. They became power hungry. Assassination attempts on the Sylvian Kings became a thing of normal life. Siblings smiled at their ruler in the day and sharpened their daggers at night."

"This is nonsense. Lundis would have taught me about this in history lessons if it were true."

"History is a fickle thing, Syrus. It is malleable, constantly manipulated by the scribes who are paid handsomely to write a certain way. To address the growing discord amongst Sylvian heirs, King Skain created the Culling. For several generations, the heir to the Sylvian Throne was decided by bloodshed. All children of the king and queen were sent to Nightfall to determine who was fittest for leadership. Those who wanted to rule had to earn the throne by killing their siblings."

"You expect me to believe these heirs wanted the throne so bad they were willing to massacre their own flesh and blood for a meaningless crown?"

"In the beginning, yes. But after several generations of the Culling, the heirs slowly realized the brutality of the situation. Some, like you, realized early on ruling wasn't worth selling their soul for."

I look back at Savrian and realize Enchantress is speaking about him. "I don't know anyone by the name King Savrian. Does that mean this man loses this Culling?"

"Your question will soon be answered. You must accept that the Culling became a social norm within the Kingdom. Although it was frowned upon at its inception, citizens of the kingdom soon grew excited at its prospect. They made bets on its outcome. Sylvian Kings began breeding out of competition, not love. The way they saw it, the more heirs they produced, the greater likelihood they had of producing stronger stock. Survival of the fittest requires participants. King Solos produced nearly thirty heirs from six different wives and handmaids just to create a greater spectacle of the Culling. For many generations of kings, having children was not about rearing a family. It was about experimenting with the genetic pool to create stronger kings. Selective breeding. Maidens throughout the kingdom would compete in games just to win the opportunity to bed the King. That was the way of life."

"It's barbaric," I say. "The strongest is rarely the most fit to lead. It's a fallacious logic that creates tyrants. Leading is more than someone's ability to kill. Raising heirs to believe savagery is the only way to secure power is a formula for disaster."

"You are wiser than your ancestors, Syrus Sylvian. But unfortunately for your ancestors, it took them much longer to come to this realization. Although they finally outlawed the Culling and returned to the natural line of succession you grew up in, the Culling was a destitute reality for many generations. And so here we are, experiencing the Culling of Savrian Sylvian. His father, Skoryx, had twelve children. All have tapped into their Sylvian powers. All except Savrian."

I look at the frostbitten man again. He's made little progress in his march in the passing minutes. The howling wind pushes against him. The swarming blizzard does all it can to push him back. He is like a salmon swimming upstream. The environment seeks to freeze him alive. I feel nothing less than pity for him. He is one against eleven, and without Sylvian powers, he is the weakest of his siblings.

He will not survive the night.

Whether his siblings find him or not, his body will be buried in snow by the morrow, never to be seen again.

I know what it is like to be cursed by the gods as this man has. To have the cards of life stacked against you. To face death head first and still move forward. A rational man would accept their fate. Lay down in the snow and let the cold consume the soul. But men like me and him are not rational. There is something else that propels us onward, something otherworldly.

The sun sets in the distance and the moon rises to replace it. Luna is full. Her light shimmers off the snow as the Northern Lights of Nightfall streak through the air above like streamers at a parade. It is a beautiful place to die, I admit. But men like me and him do not die so easily.

"Savrian!" a voice shouts across the expanse of ice. The man wrapped in wolf pelt finishes his rusty stride and freezes. He doesn't look up. It is his sibling that calls to him, and he recognizes her voice without looking. My eyes search the darkness for his challenger. I spot silver eyes sparkling a quarter mile away.

"Sister," Savrian mutters through chattering teeth.

"I was hoping for a more formidable opponent to stumble on first. But I will settle for you."

"So sorry to disappoint," Savrian replies.

I watch as the woman in the distance doubles over and shifts into a monster I'm familiar seeing. Her black hair grows to cover her whole body. The many layers of clothes that cover her rip open and fall to the icy ground. Fur sprouts to warm the areas of exposed nakedness. In only a few seconds, she shifts into a hellish wolf that blends into the darkness of night. She stands at the edge of an evergreen forest, the snow-covered trees exposing her shadowy silhouette. Her silver eyes tear through the night with malevolent pride.

Savrian has fought all day just to die at the paws of his own sister.

"Here goes nothing," Savrian whispers to himself, drawing a blade at his hip from its sheath.

## 23

### Fervent

I stare in confusion as the sword's blade ignites with colors more vibrant than the Northern Lights of Nightfall above. First, the blade is blue, then purple, then crimson. But I watch as the red hue glows brighter and brighter, shifting slowly to vibrant orange like the burning glow of a blacksmith's forge.

"That's my mother's blade, Fervent," I stammer.

"Did you think your mother was the first to handle such a weapon?" Enchantress questions.

Thoughts of Atlas wielding the blade come to mind. The old hag is right. Surely my mother wasn't the first to wield the iconic blade, but I never learned where it came from or how it descended to her hands.

"It belonged to the Sylvians?"

"Fervent is one of five weapons created that possesses the power to kill a Sylvian," Enchantress informs.

How did I not know this? It makes sense. No one in this world is invincible. Lycans have affinities to silver, and Undead can die by wooden stake. I guess the thought of Sylvians having fatal flaws never occurred to me. As a child, I always viewed my father as impenetrable. And mother possessed Fervent at that time, so it's not like the blade was in the hands of someone set on killing Sylvians.

Damn, I reflect. How much did my father shield my learning as a child to hide the truth from me?

"You said it is one of five weapons... There are others out there that can kill a Sylvian?"

"Yes, one which has already been used on you."

"What do you mean?" I search my mind. I have encountered death so many times that it's hard to pinpoint the weapons used against me. Then a memory strikes me like a bolt of lighting. "Ventur's dagger," I say.

"Ventur's dagger," Enchantress confirms. "Its name is Fang, and it is one of the five."

"But it looked like any other silver dagger."

"If it was silver, you would not be here today. That is where he went wrong when you were a boy of ten. He stabbed you through the back thinking the dagger would surely kill a Lycan if it could kill a Sylvian. But this is not the case. The Deicides—Fervent, Fang, Exile, Reclaimer, and Sun Piercer—were forged by humans long ago as a check against the Sylvians' godly powers."

"What gives them the ability to kill Sylvians?"

"Long ago, the humans raised up a maiden for the sole purpose of seducing Sylvian the First. When she went to bed him, she pricked his finger while he slept, and collected a sample of his blood. Witches later used the blood to imbue the weapons with cursed abilities to counteract Sylvian powers. It was the same dagger, Fang, that was plunged into your heart as a boy of ten, that slit Sylvian the First's throat from ear to ear while he slept. The Sylvians later learned of these weapons' existence and took them by force, locking them away in an armory deep in the Areopagus Castle. Ventur stole Fang from the armory in order to kill your father that night, but it was his mistake to think it would work on a boy who'd failed to come into his Sylvian powers."

"You mean to tell me the only reason I'm alive is because I was powerless as a child?"

"Being powerless has its advantages, Syrus Sylvian, as Savrian will now show you."

I turn to watch as Savrian swings Fervent through the snow at his feet in an effort to get his blood pumping. The blade melts the snow where it makes contact. Heat radiates from the sword. It turns the surrounding blizzard into evaporated steam. It makes a palpable sound as it cracks through the cold air around it, warming a microcosm of space amidst a frozen environment. It was said Fervent was forged with the heart of a dying star, hence its ability to reflect the mood of its user. I don't know if there is any truth to this rumor, but I surely can't explain its properties any other way.

The icicles hanging from Savrian's eyebrows and mustache melt. His joints loosen as the stiffness is boiled by anger. The blade looks at home in his capable hands. In seconds, Savrian Sylvian has turned from a frozen mummy to a calculated warrior. I had little to no knowledge of Fervent's properties as a child. And although I saw Atlas wield it, I have not seen what it's capable of in battle. The sword's ability to heat the atmosphere like a double-bladed torch is remarkable. I've never seen such anger channeled into the weapon.

Savrian's warmup motions are blindingly fast. He whips the blade around like it is a part of his own body. My eyes can't follow the whistling steel as it parts the blizzard with its rage.

The Lycan drops to all fours and charges Savrian like a bull after a matador. The air around Savrian glows orange off the reflection of snowflakes. He widens his stance and stands his ground. I closely examine his face. There is no fear written on it. His exterior is as cold and inhospitable as the environment he traverses.

The Lycan covers the distance fast as a cheetah. Her silver eyes don't spare a blink. Her paws are silent as they leave wolf prints in the snow. The snow collects in her fur. Drool freezes on her jowls. The wolf's jaws snap excitedly at the prospect of killing. Or perhaps they chatter from the cold. Either way, they lock in on their target.

Time slows.

The innocent snowflakes avert their eyes.

Man and monster collide.

Blade pierces flesh.

Jaws snap shut on empty air.

A shrill yelp permeates the atmosphere. The forest shivers as it echoes.

Time resumes and the two bodies become a tangled mess of bloody flesh and fur. The blood freezes instantly as it hits the icy ground. Not even the heavy snowflakes can cover the murder scene.

I watch as Savrian stands, then pulls Fervent from his sister's corpse. The wolfish features dissipate as the Sylvian Princess passes on from this life. Her body returns to its human appearance, naked and pale on the bloodied snow. A gaping hole is left between her breasts from Fervent's penetration. The Sylvian's silver eyes fade, leaving a sad shade of lifeless blue behind. The Princess's black hair lies peacefully around her body as the snowflakes begin to bury her.

"In blood, you are my sister," Savrian speaks to the corpse. "When we were children, you used to stand up for me when Syrex bullied me. Do you remember that? There was that time he tied me to the reins of a mule and had it drag me across a field of poison ivy. But you found me, and you freed me, Savannah. And then you found Syrex and beat him to a pulp, because I wasn't strong enough to stand up for myself. I miss those days, Savannah. Before the power of ruling didn't matter to any of us. Before us siblings grew distant and cold. But then you got your powers, and suddenly I was no longer worth standing up for. You were once a beautiful person, Savannah, but these powers destroyed your soul. But now it is my turn to stand up for you. For the person I know you are, deep down. I didn't want to kill you, but now you are free. Free from these powers. Because they are not a gift. They are a curse. Maybe you'll see that now that you're free from them. Maybe you won't. Either way, save me a spot in hell. Hopefully it's warmer there than it is here."

Savrian sheathes his sword and moves on from the corpse. "Syrex!" Savrian screams to the wilderness. Snow falls from tree branches in the distance as the sound waves make impact. "I'm coming for you," he whispers to himself, leaving Savannah to forever be forgotten as the Northern Lights of Nightfall dance across her cold body.

# 24

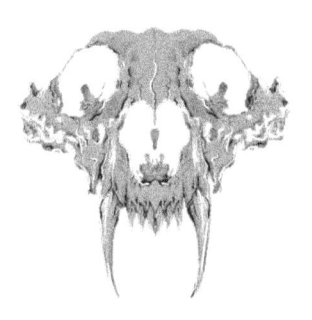

## THE CULLING

The sun has set. The sun has risen. And now, the sun sets again. Enchantress and I have followed Savrian Sylvian in his journey across the frozen wasteland, watching Fervent collect four more kills in the process. Twelve children Skoryx sired. Five are now dead at Savrian's hands. The only child of twelve who's yet to tap into Sylvian powers. Powerless, his siblings call him as they taunt him before attacking. Two sisters and three brothers, all elder. All dead.

I've grown to love Savrian like he is a brother of my own. Like me, he is prey to the circumstances life has cursed him with. I can relate. But he doesn't cower from what he's been predestined to do. Though the Fates have stacked the odds against him, he's prevailed again and again.

But he can't take much more of this brutality. Savrian hasn't emerged from these lethal battles unscathed. Lacerations litter his body. The Lycans he's sent to hell did not go willingly, and their jaws and claws tried their best to drag Savrian with them. But it isn't the bleeding that threatens him. Being slashed by claws and fangs has left his thick pelts open to the elements. The bitter cold now makes a frontal assault on his skin. Frost bites at his flesh worse than his siblings' fangs have.

Fervent is no longer sheathed. Savrian carries it just to keep warm, channeling his anger at the situation to keep the blade aflame. But he wavers. His steps are not as sure. Every few strides he stumbles, leaning on trees within the evergreen forest to stay standing. His wolf pelt whips in the wind like a tattered flag.

His hand leaves its bloody fingerprints on every tree he leans against to regain balance. If one of his siblings is near, the scent of blood will draw them in like sharks to chum. The faster they kill, the faster the Culling will be complete. Scalding baths and warm blankets wait for them in Areopagus. But not even warm food and fine wine will let these Sylvians forget what they had to do to survive. The castle will be eleven bodies emptier upon their return.

I no longer bother looking at Enchantress. She hasn't spoke since we first arrived. Like me, she floats upon the ethereal plains of the spiritual realm watching Savrian's bravery endure attack after attack. Sometimes I forget she is even here, too engrossed by the combat to pay her attention.

What Savrian's bravery has to do with Bloodlust, I'm unsure. But Enchantress's visions have a way of making sense as time passes, so I don't bother wasting my breath asking questions.

The moon pierces through the stout spruce trees. The falling snow has died down, and the fat snowflakes that fall are caught by the foliage above. Watching Savrian walk is like watching a slug slide across hot cobblestone. Painful. And although Fervent keeps his body from freezing in the night, I can't fathom this man has much willpower left in his reserves. I can still remember what it felt like marching from Queensmyre to Yueltope. My body burnt to a crisp. My legs chafed raw. Sweat stinging my cracked lips. Blisters breaking on the soles of my feet. I can only imagine the pain and numbness Savrian feels now.

"And then there was one," a voice calls from overhead, breaking me from my sympathy. My heart drops. Savrian pauses in his limping stride. A set of silver eyes peer down at him from the shadows of a pine tree above. Not even I was able to sense a threat, and I can see from Savrian's reaction he wasn't either.

"Syrex," Savrian mumbles through chattering teeth. I look up at the shadows of the pine tree. The only discernible feature of the lurking predator is his silver eyes. But I have never seen eyes so dangerous in the midst of darkness before. Though I can't make out Syrex's face, his eyes convey a thousand emotions. Comedy, because this situation is funny to him. Confusion, at how Savrian is still alive. Calmness, because this situation is under control. Confidence, because he is superior to Savrian in every way. Condemnation, because he is going to slaughter the last remaining Sylvian standing between him and the throne.

Syrex leaps from the branch and falls thirty feet to the ground. It is a graceful leap, and the only sound his feet make upon landing is the soft crunch of snow. The adversary's body is naked from previously shifting into his Lycan form. Steam rises from his feverish flesh. Though the temperature is well below freezing, a Lycan's internal temperature rises when they prepare to shift.

"Who would've thought," Syrex chuckles, "That I would kill five of our siblings just to run into you, runt, the weakest of us all. Tell me, how many have you killed?"

Savrian lowers his sword to the ground and leans on it like a cane. The snow along the ground melts away as Fervent's tip makes contact. The melting sends a palpable sizzle into the air, sending a wall of steam rising around Savrian's shivering body. Through chattering teeth, Savrian replies, "Fuh-five."

The response catches Syrex off guard. The look of surprise turns to amusement. He crunches the numbers inwardly, calculating the odds of Savrian being able to survive all that he has. Syrex looks at his prey from head to toe and sees the fatal wounds that line his brother's body. He shrugs, realizing he's indifferent to the method of Savrian's survival. If anything, it just means there's less work for him to do.

Syrex Sylvian stands a whole head taller than Savrian. His flesh doesn't bare the markings of a single injury. He carries himself like a man who has never felt pain. He is cocky from his shaggy, sandy hair to his perfectly pedicured toenails. His body is regal, carrying the sort of appearance everyone would want in a king. His eyes are fearless. He has the genetics of a Cardonian god. I instantly grow to hate him, because he reminds me of Atlas, and Savrian reminds me of myself. I need Savrian to win this fight. For once in my life, I want to see I am not the only one cursed by the gods who defied their predestined plans.

"The light of the moon makes it easy to see how pathetic you look," Syrex laughs. "Little Savrian, the youngest and weakest of us all. Your whore of a mother isn't here to protect you anymore. Can't go running to dad to snitch on me. Can't hide in your closet to avoid my wrath. Now it's just me and you, and no one will mourn your failure to return to Areopagus."

Savrian straightens up, lifting Fervent into a defensive position. The sword burns so hot with its fiery orange blade that I fear it might explode into a million pieces. The air itself is consumed by the vacuum of rage. Darkness retreats from Savrian's presence. It is like sunlight beams down on him, and him only.

"You think I'm afraid of a light-up sword?" Syrex chuckles.

"All my life you've bullied me," Savrian shouts, his face spasming with a million shades of hatred. "No one will know that I saved the kingdom from a tyrant by cutting him down before he could rule!"

"I'll make sure your tomb stone says nothing more than 'Son of a Whore' mongrel. And then, when father is dead, I will make your whore mother be my bed maid. Every night I will fuck her, and I will whisper in her ears how good it felt as I ripped you apart limb from limb. I'll tell her how you begged for mercy as my beast feasted on your carcass. I won't be gentle with her. I'll hold her down against her will and ravage her loins until she begs me for mercy. First, I'll take her son from her. Then, I'll take her will to live."

Savrian screams with agony, then charges. His limp disappears. Adrenaline and rage consumes him. His rusted movement is replaced by well-oiled mechanics. His footfall is graceful like a swan and nimble like a panther. Fervent splits the air in two. Snow melts in the presence of its hellstorm. I can't stop watching. Can't even blink. I need Savrian to win. Not just for the kingdom, but for myself. Too often the strongest are chosen to lead. Too often this leads to tyrants. For once, just once, I need to know I'm not alone in my endeavors.

Syrex smiles as his younger brother charges him. The elder Sylvian doesn't shift into his Lycan form. He doesn't even move. He just stands there, an arrogant look on his face. He has already won this battle in his mind. He's been groomed by the gods to know the outcome of this night. Steam rises from his pale shoulders. Steam rises from Fervent.

Savrian arches the sword over his head and puts all his energy and effort into delivering a devastating blow. My breath freezes in my lungs as I watch. The Culling will soon be over. The fate of the kingdom rests in Savrian's hands. Firelight reflects off Syrex's face. The light of his silver eyes repels it. The sword begins its downward trajectory. Syrex doesn't so much as flinch at the attack.

My eyes are glued so heavily to Savrian's hands that I completely miss what happens as his foot stubs into a frozen rock on the ground. The younger Sylvian's body contorts as his foot slips on the rock, throwing him off balance. He trips, then stumbles, then falls after several strides trying to catch himself. What happens next is too fast and too cruel to comprehend. Savrian moves his hands to catch himself, forgetting to release Fervent as he does so. The sword's hilt becomes wedged between the ground and Savrian's body, then pierces its wielder through the stomach as he falls to the ground.

A cry of pain exits Savrian's mouth as Fervent finishes Syrex's opponent for him. The blade rips through Savrian's bowels and protrudes from his back as he falls to the ground, defeated in a split second by nothing more than a slippery rock.

The cry of pain is overwhelmed by Syrex's laughter. The man's diaphragm shakes wildly as he releases his reaction. Savrian's body slides across the icy ground and stops short right at Syrex's feet, utterly slain. All light fades from Fervent as Savrian's emotions are consumed by death. It is just a cold blade once more, covered in the blood of its own wielder.

The Culling is over. Syrex will be the kingdom's next leader. Any hope the kingdom had of avoiding tyranny died with Savrian's defeated body.

Syrex holds his stomach as the laughter becomes painful. The irony is too great for him to bear. But the laughter is cut short as Savrian's body gains movement again.

I watch in horror and awe as the younger Sylvian rises from the ground, defeating the death that possessed him. With Fervent still in his stomach, he stands to face his opponent once more, not an ounce of suffering written on his face. Savrian's eyes are no longer the eyes of a mortal. His irises are black, blacker than the night of a new moon. He has defeated death, but death has returned to the land of the living in his body.

The horror I feel also possesses Syrex. I watch as a look of bewilderment consumes him. He staggers back a step, mumbling, "Wuh-what is this sorcery?" This is the first time in his life he's been threatened by a superior opponent.

Savrian replies coldly, "The gods have always been cruel to me, so I learned early on to pray to demons instead."

Now it is Syrex who trips as he backpedals, slipping on the icy ground to fall on his butt. The Sylvian elder does everything he can to put distance between him and his brother, scooting his body through the snow away from the walking corpse in front of him. Savrian looks at him with a queer, perverted gaze. "What's wrong, brother? You look scared."

The shadows behind Syrex materialize, turning from darkness to palpable evil. A dark mist thickens, blending into the night of the forest but standing starker than the night itself. Luna's light doesn't pierce this portal of abyss. It is a void between space and time. A gate opening to hell itself. And Syrex does not even notice its dreadful presence. The shadows make no noise as they assemble. The elder Sylvian is so preoccupied with putting space between himself and his brother that he doesn't realize he is moving closer to an otherworldly evil.

It isn't until now that I eye Enchantress, confused by the abyss. She doesn't spare me a glance in return. Whatever is going to happen, she knows already of its happening. This is not Enchantress's first time watching these events unfold. She exists in a plane where time is merely a construct. She knows all that has ever happened, and all that will ever happen. To her, this is normal.

I look back to the portal of shadows. It is the height of two men and the width of three. Although I was not susceptible to the freezing temperatures of this wasteland before, a shiver runs down my soul now. This portal exists in the realm of spirits too, and the dread it emits fills my being as I stare into its endless pit of madness.

Savrian doesn't move, doesn't bother pulling the blade from his bowels. He just stands there like a stone statue, watching a sacrificial lamb drag itself to the altar.

The shadows stir, then transform. They swirl like clouds before a hurricane, then compress into the shape of a human body. At first the body is without form or substance. But in a few short seconds, they contract until they turn into the robes of a reaper. Deafening silence fills the air as nature bows to the reaper. Silence, and the panicked breaths of a defeated Syrex.

The void of blackness still fills the reaper's drawn hood. It is the sort of darkness so apparent, so visible, it almost makes me think there is no one inside this shroud. But there is someone contained within that darkness, of that I'm sure. The cowl is not made of ordinary fabric. It still ebbs and flows with the life of darkness. Mist coils from its bottom hem, bleeding shadows into the night.

The reaper outstretches his arm and a scythe appears out of thin air, its handle made of well polished obsidian wood, its blade sharp enough to cut the night in two.

Savrian smiles at the reaper's appearance. This is not the first time he has seen this demon. The younger Sylvian is no longer the person I knew him to be. Death has demented him. Removed the admirable traits that won me over. His stare is hollow and vacant. Consumed by obscurity.

Syrex is now double-teamed by death and its reaper. All other Sylvians are dead, culled by Syrex's own hands. The murder of his siblings will now lead to his own downfall. There is strength in family, only this fool turned it into his weakness.

Savrian creeps forward slowly, black veins slowly creeping up his exposed neck. "I cried out to the gods before the Culling," Savrian growls, his voice distorted. "I begged them for mercy, but my prayers fell on deaf ears. Instead, it was a devil who heard me, and he answered me with a deal I couldn't turn down."

"Gods be good, what have you done brother!" Syrex screams, now only a few short feet away from the silent reaper.

"The gods didn't see me fit to wield the Sylvian powers before the Culling, so I took matters into my own hands." Savrian's voice is like an omniscient god. The earth itself quakes at his speech. Black veins continue to consume his face. His flesh turns black as frostbite. His body distorts. Claws sprout from his fingernails. He rips everything but the white wolf pelt off his body, revealing the transformation beneath. Muscles ripple under his skin like tumorous growths. This skin, too, is as black as the reaper's robes.

Dark, leathery wings rip from Savrian's back, sprouting like the wings of a butterfly from a caterpillar's cocoon.

"The devil who found me was Skathen, master of hell's demons, Defeater of Death," Savrian bellows as his face distorts into that of a monster. Fangs replace his canines. His lips shrivel. His nose shrinks into two distinct slits. His ears grow pointed. His eyes remain black and lifeless. This man, I realize, is the first Blackblood to ever exist. He continues, "Although Skathen could not grant me the powers of Sylvian, he offered me something better." The Blackblood rips Fervent from his stomach and throws it aside. I watch as his gut heals instantly, closing the wound like it never existed.

Syrex is speechless. Horror steals the breath from his lungs.

"Vere mori skathen, the Sylvian Creed. We conquer our demons. I sold my soul to Skathen in order to prevail in the Culling. I knew I wouldn't defeat you without powers of my own, so Skathen inverted my Sylvian blood and created something far more sinister out of me. Skathen mori vere. Our demons conquer us. Sylvians control their beasts, but now I will create a race where beasts control us. The powers of Sylvian the First have been successfully inverted in my body. Both Damon and Dagon flow through my veins. I am everything a Lycan is and more. With the help of Damon's curse, I am more intelligent than a Lycan, and I can fly while in this monstrous form. This, my brother, is the final evolution of the Sylvian namesake. Our blood is now bound to this curse. Our fates are sealed. I have won this Culling and inherited the throne. And now, Skathen will send you to hell so you can watch me rule my new kingdom."

A look of confusion and terror possesses Syrex. The sinister reaper behind him raises the scythe with effortless speed, then brings it down on Syrex's unsuspecting neck, cleaving the bully's head from his shoulders before he has time to understand he's lost.

The head tumbles to the ground, still staring in bewilderment at Savrian's beastly form. I, too, am trying to put the pieces together. The words play over and over again in my mind. *Our blood is now bound to this curse.* That is why Sylvian blood is the antidote to the Blackblood virus. *The powers of Sylvian the First have been successfully inverted in my body.* This monster is anti-Sylvian. Where Sylvian the First could control the curse of Dagon and Damon, the curse of Dagon and Damon now control his body simultaneously. He is equal parts Undead and Lycan in his beastly form. His blood has soured black at the perversion of nature. He has the body of a hairless Lycan; claws, muscle mass, hind legs. His features also resemble the Undead; fangs, pointed ears, and although Undead do not have wings, this beast has grown them so he too can fly.

This is the origin of Bloodlust. This is the origin of the Blackblood virus. Savrian Sylvian is responsible for their creation. The Sylvians are responsible for the deaths of millions. It is my ancestor that brought this curse into being.

"Kneel," the reaper commands, bringing his bloody scythe back to his side. The reaper's voice is like the wind itself, surrounding us from all directions. "You pledged your soul in exchange for my aid in the Culling, Savrian Sylvian. Now begins our dominion over earth. You will be my chief executioner in the flesh. Together, we will defeat death. We will defy the wicked Enchantress."

I watch as the reaper slowly twists his head to stare directly at Enchantress, who meanders off to my right. She stares back at him with anger on her face. They can see each other, I realize. Through time and space itself, these two know each other, like eternal enemies. Her words echo in my mind, *Now you are seeing the bigger picture, Syrus Sylvian. Hear my words, this war is much bigger than you and Bloodlust and the Areopagus Throne. This war goes back to my inception...*

The reaper turns again, this time staring directly at me. The abyss that rests within his hood looks into me, staring into my soul itself. It consumes me. The feeling of an eternity of loss and agony possesses me. Revenge. Rebellion. Resurrection. Together, we can defeat death. The thought pops in my head as if it was planted by someone else, a low whisper in the back of my mind. The reaper sees me, and I see him. For the briefest of moments,

I peer into an eternity of existence. The vision is incomprehensible chaos to my finite mind.

"Rise," the reaper commands, still staring at me. He continues, "You will now be known as Marduk, the ancient Cardonian word for rebirth. Savrian Sylvian is dead. Only you remain." The void within his hood converges on my sight. Everything is growing dark. My world is closing in around me. "Now go, spread our kingdom. Spread immortality to the masses. Create a nation that cannot die. Only then can we defeat death's mistress, Enchantress. Only then can we wipe her from existence."

The darkness consumes me.

Reality fades.

I asked Enchantress to show me my enemy.

*Your wish is my command*, she said, *but I warn you... You will not like what you see.*

I now know who my true enemy is.

It is not Bloodlust.

It is not the Blackbloods.

Skathen, the defeater of death.

That is my enemy.

That is the devil responsible for ruining my life.

As an enemy of Enchantress, he stands directly opposed to my mission.

I vow to ruin his creation in return for what he's done to me.

I am bound by blood for Savrian's weaknesses. But my blood is stronger than that coward's. So help me gods, I will set right Savrian's wrongs before I die. Even if it means the death of me.

# 25

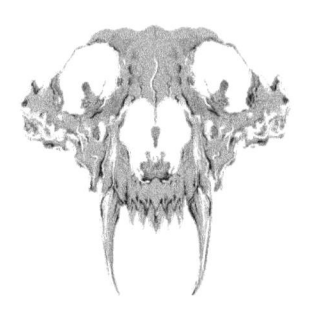

## SKATHEN

A melancholic cemetery stretches far with gravestones as far as my sight extends. This is the next scene Enchantress has chosen for me. She provides no context for our arrival. Observation is the only tool I have to put the pieces together. Fog rolls on the ground, hiding the dead grass and moldy headstones. Leafless trees stand like sharp pikes planted in the ground. Jagged branches cut across the skyline. The overcast sky blocks the moon's light with malevolent nimbostrati. A storm is coming. It brews in the distance. Lightning flashes. Thunder follows.

A little girl cries in the distance. My soul naturally gravitates to her. She curls her innocent body up in a ball against a nameless grave. Skeletal hands reach up from the unbroken ground in an attempt to grab her. They, too, are spirits. The souls of the dead and forgotten. They crawl forth from their graves, leaving the ground undisturbed as they rise from their slumber. Their collected moans fill the air. A thousand voices of eternal regret calling out to be heard.

This girl is the only living being present. She covers her ears and rocks her body as the dead call to her. She's crying, I realize. Silent sobs shake her body as tears water the dead earth under her. The ground is black and charred in the place she lays. Her dark dreadlocks blend in with the ground, accentuating her pale face.

"Please stop," she cries out, overstimulated by the army of dead calling to her. Skeletons and demons rise from the ground and converge on her. Their numbers are innumerable. Incubus, goblins, fiends, imps, beasts and brutes. They flock toward the terrified girl like angels toward heaven's gates.

"It's you," I say aloud, speaking to Enchantress. The old hag stares longingly at the child. A single tear brims in her eyes. She too is sympathetic for the innocent child.

"It is," she replies.

"How long ago was this?"

"Long ago. Not long after Damon and Dagon were killed by Sylvian the First. In the first generations of mankind."

"When Solis first cursed you; when he called the dead to haunt you..."

"I was just a child... I didn't deserve this." The tear finally forms and falls down her wrinkled cheek.

"Please! Just stop!" the girl cries out. The dead don't heed her command. They reach out to touch her. Their gnarled hands grip her extremities, causing her to shriek in terror. She screams. A pit rises in my stomach. I need to do something. I need to help her. I, too, am a spirit. I can fend these demons off. I look around, searching for a means to ward off the malignant spirits.

Lightning strikes the ground near the little girl, causing the demons to flinch back in fear. In the place the lightning strikes, a new being appears, almost as if it teleported from the atmosphere itself.

"Bow!" the savior orders, not raising his voice yet echoing loud enough for all to hear. The army of dead shrivels before the dark guardian angel, retreating from the girl's body he protects. I recognize him instantly. His dark robes are the same he wore in Nightfall. The scythe in his hand still gleams with death in its blade's reflection. The space within his drawn hood is still an eternal void of tangible darkness.

The army of dead falls silent in a split second, bowing before Skathen, Defeater of Death, master of hell's demons. They bow without hesitation, ceasing all moaning, no longer reaching out for the feeble child's body.

The little girl rolls over to her back, staring up at her savior. He stares back down at her. She is trembling with fear. Her innocent eyes peer into the abyss within Skathen's hood. The abyss stares back into her.

"Please," she begs, "Don't kill me... I... I don't want to die..."

"You are safe, child," Skathen replies, his voice calm and soothing. "I am here to protect you. Death fears what has defeated it. And like me, you too, will one day defeat death."

"Who... are you?"

"I am known as many things, child. Some confuse me with death itself. Others think I am a reaper sent to do its bidding. You may call me Skathen. So long as you are in my care, I will raise you as my own. I will take care of you, child, and no harm will befall you."

The little girl sits up and wipes the tears from her eyes. "If you aren't a bad guy, why do you dress like one?"

Skathen squats down nonchalantly, leaning his body weight against the scythe to steady himself. His hood is eye to eye with the girl who sees death. He replies, "The same reason a scarecrow looks like a bad guy... If he didn't, he wouldn't be able to protect his crops. Sometimes you can't defeat fear... The next best thing is to make others fear you... The afterlife is a scary place. If people knew my identity, they might try to find me when I was living and cut me down so I don't become the Defeater of Death."

"How can they cut you down if you are here?"

"I will teach you the ways of the afterlife, child. But for now, I will teach you about time. Do you like playing with dolls?"

The little girl nods her head, the mere mentioning of dolls lighting a sparkle in her eye.

Skathen holds out his glove-wrapped hand and darkness materializes in a confined space along his palm. The blackness compresses in an orb, then vanishes, revealing a small doll. It is by no means a beautiful toy, but its body and clothes are stitched with fabric. It resembles a girl that looks just like the child. The little girl shouts with glee at the sight of the toy, grabbing it from Skathen's hand as he offers it as a gift.

"How did you do that?" she asks excitedly.

"Because this doll exists, it has always existed," he replies. "All I did was will it into existence at this time, to exist in this place."

"How could it always exist if it didn't exist until now?"

"How can you always exist if you didn't exist until your birth?" Skathen counters whimsically, "This is the way the universe works. There is creation. There is life. There is death. But there is also existence, and all who live have also existed in a place where there is no time. This will make sense to you with time. Be patient, and I will teach everything I know to you, Enchantress."

The girl looks up at the hooded reaper with confusion. "That isn't my name."

"Then what is your name, child?"

"I... I don't know," she replies, realizing she'd never had parents to name her. She was cursed at birth and chased away from society. Never had anyone to love or care for her. It is apparent from her interactions with Skathen this is the first time she's been showed kindness. She is reluctant to accept it, not used to extended empathy.

"Everyone needs a name, child," he whispers sympathetically. "The gods cursed you, but life is about learning to turn curses to blessings. They sent the dead to haunt you, but I will teach you how to enchant the dead. So you will be known as Enchantress, a name equally as beautiful as you," he says, speaking in a fatherly tone. A tear falls from the girl's eye, but this time it is not from sadness or fear.

She pulls the doll close to her chest, nodding to Skathen's words. She sniffles as more tears release. Here is a girl who has never felt safe in this world, and Skathen has just provided a shelter of comfort for the first time in her life.

I look to the old hag and see that she, too, is crying. Confronting the memory is too much for her to bear. Seeing her younger self be shown love for the first time is overwhelming. I don't know how to react to this situation. I don't know what to think of Skathen. The same being responsible for creating the Blackblood virus is the one who saved Enchantress from her curse. Evil is not black-and-white. It is infinite shades of gray, indiscernible to my finite mind.

I want to ask the hag so many questions, but the memory fades to black before I can form an opinion on what's happening.

I'm left with the image of Enchantress's younger self throwing herself into Skathen's arms as she hugs her adoptive father with inexpressible appreciation.

Then, all I can see is darkness.

# 26

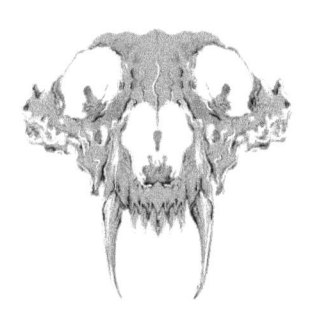

## Eighteen Maidens

I'm not given the time to reflect on what I just saw, and Enchantress provides no commentary to dilute my confusion. What does she expect me to think after showing me all this? Am I to feel hatred toward Skathen for the monsters he's created? Am I to feel admiration toward him for taking Enchantress under his protection? There is so much I don't know and too little time to find understanding.

"The preparations have been made, my Lord," a voice says. My spirit now floats in an entirely different place. The scenery is the exact opposite of the dark and depressing cemetery. I am now in the courtyard of an unfamiliar castle in the presence of regal nobility. A vanguard of soldiers march alongside a carriage, a single knight opening the carriage's door to escort its sole occupant. The man that emerges from its body is one I've seen before.

He is a man who needs no introducing.

A mural of his likeness was plastered in my study room as a child.

His armor is extravagant, polished so clean it reflects the clouds above on its surface. A regal cape floats behind him as he leaps from the carriage, clasped around his lean neck. The crest of a cross is etched plainly for all to see along his breastplate. His wavy blonde hair falls just short of his shoulders and flows in the afternoon breeze of the sunny spring day.

Before me is my childhood idol. The man I owned action figures of. The man I dreamed of one day being. The original leader of the Acolytes. A military legend. The hero that saved humanity. Slayer of Marduk. Warrior. Poet. Philosopher.

Lysander.

"It brings me no pleasure in what must be done today, Gabriel," Lysander replies to his fellow knight. "It is too beautiful a day for such dark deeds. It is a tragedy we must resort to such evil to overcome our foe."

"The maidens know what is at stake, my Lord. They know the future of humanity rests on their shoulders."

Lysander locks eyes with his comrade, then nods. His eyes are sad. Human eyes often are, living in a world filled with demons. His lips indicate there is much more he would like to say, but knows saying it would only be a waste of oxygen and time. Lysander claps his fellow Acolyte on the shoulder and orders, "Bring me to them."

"At once, my Lord."

My spirit follows the small party of Acolytes as they proceed through the courtyard. The majority of their troops remain behind to care for their horses and tend to their weapons. Lysander was right. I haven't seen this beautiful a day in a long time. Although my flesh isn't present to feel the breeze's caress, I can hear the birds chirping and the leaves dancing. Pollen floats through the air. Flowers smile toward the sky.

It has been over two years since I've seen spring bloom across creation. My mind has forgotten how beautiful it can be. I was captured by Blackbloods in summer's harsh heat, trapped in darkness, only to be released into summer's hostility once more. Us mortals must endure the extremes of summer and winter to reap the luxuries of nature's beauty.

The courtyard is filled with flowers of every color imaginable, arrayed in glamorous patterns of captivating allure. Butterflies and bees hop from petal to petal, overwhelmed by the prospects available to them. A stone fountain trickles water in the center of it all, its age apparent in the moss that consumes it. Even the grass looks soft enough to sleep on without tossing and turning. There isn't a spot of decay as far as my eye can see. Coming straight from the dreadfulness of the cemetery, this is like being in paradise.

Enchantress herself looks taken back by the nature. This is not something she was accustomed to experiencing. During her life, everything she touched died. The grass she slept on as a child turned black. Dark clouds hovered over her. Trees withered in her midst. There was no opportunity to bask in Solis's daylight or the Creator's creation because of her curse. Because of this, she is not accustomed to scenes of such beauty.

The light of day shines through her translucent spirit, revealing the smile on her face. It is much better to see her smiling than crying, as she was in the graveyard.

We follow Lysander and his escort through the moss-covered steps of the courtyard. It is hard to believe I'm here, 800 years After Sylvian. My mother was the last known descendant of Lysander. Now that she is gone,

I have taken that mantle. The same blood that flows through this warrior's veins are responsible for my genetic makeup.

It is odd to see the Acolytes in such high regard after seeing Atlas and his band of renegades. Though Atlas's warriors were no doubt fantastic fighters, they were not embraced by society as these Acolytes are. The knights before me have the best armor a blacksmith can forge. There was an element of outlawry surrounding Atlas's group, but these Acolytes have been accepted and bolstered up humanity's caste system. They are the top of their food chain, judged not by the status of their birth but by the ability of their stoic actions.

We exit the courtyard, then enter the castle's front lawn. Before us is an assembly of the kingdom's nobility, and in addition, what looks to be eighteen women standing in a line shoulder to shoulder, each more beautiful than the last. A man in a crown sees Lysander and kneels, his counterparts doing the same. I have never seen a king kneel to a knight in all my days, which speaks to the regard they hold Lysander.

"King Dexus, there is no need for that," Lysander chuckles, speaking to the man as if he's an old friend. Lysander approaches the old man and offers a hand to lift him off his knees. Dexus accepts graciously. Lysander's Acolytes follow suit and offer hands to the remaining nobility. The women, clothed from neck to toe, stand in awestruck silence in the background, the breeze revealing their curvatures as it cinches their robes tight to their bodies. They are like fangirls who've spotted their favorite celebrity. Lysander's presence causes them to blush.

Dexus, restored to his feet, replies, "It is my honor, Commander Lysander. Baptiste and its citizens are blessed by your presence. We have awaited this day for many years."

"I only wish the reasons for our meeting weren't so grave, my king. The Holy Knights are appreciative of your great hospitality. In three days, we sail for Nightfall to bring death to Marduk."

"The Creator will be with you, Holy One. He has not forsaken us humans yet. Our priests report nightly visions of your victory over the Blackbloods! Premonitions of humanity rising from its oppression once more!"

"The outcome of these visions will come at a great cost. The Creator steers our fate, but we must row nonetheless. But enough talk of what's to come. For now, let's enjoy the present. Please, introduce me to these holy women you've assembled." The statement makes the girls blush once more, their rosy cheeks the only flesh exposed for the world to see.

"Yes, of course," King Dexus responds, snapping back to composure. "We have raised these women in the Creator's Temple here in Baptiste. Each remains a maiden, committed to their Lord's calling in life. From left to right, there is Adora, daughter of Sinai, Cassandra, daughter of Lemini, Raquel, daughter of Bolene, Jezebel..."

King Dexus continues to name woman after woman, each one laser focused on Lysander. They are equally nervous and excited. Their ages vary. Some look as though they've only just reached the age of maturity, others look older than Lysander himself. Their hair is covered with hijabs, their collars with shawls, their bodies with robes. Their innocent faces and gleaming eyes are all Lysander can see.

Lysander smiles in turn at each one as their name is called, and the maidens swoon accordingly. I am unsure why we are here or what this has to do with Marduk. I asked Enchantress to show me my enemy, but I've only seen Marduk for less than a few minutes since these visions began. Nonetheless, I am grateful to be in the presence of Lysander. Historians did a poor job keeping records on his life. Jealous Sylvian leaders did all they could to smite his name from ledgers in an attempt to erase him from existence.

This is the man who defeated the Blackbloods while the Undead and Sylvians locked themselves away, unbothered by Marduk's reign. Expecting the Acolytes to fail, Lysander used this doubt to prove humanity is not the inferior race. Fearful of rebellion, the Sylvians took necessary measures to put mortal men back in their place after the Holy Crusades.

To this day, humanity has forgotten the power they once wielded.

After Dexus finishes introducing the women, Lysander addresses them as a group. "Holy maidens, we know why we are here." The smiles somewhat disappear from their faces as he cuts straight to the point. "I have engaged Marduk in battle myself, and I have learned that his evil spirit cannot be defeated without spiritual exorcism. My armies have researched extensively alongside the priests of Baptiste for ways to accomplish this, and that is what brings us here. I would not commit myself to this if I did not think it necessary. All problems point to one solution—a Dybbuk Box."

As his words settle over uneasy ears, I am left to ponder the mystery of what he's said. Is that how Lysander defeated Marduk? The histories are unclear. Some say he cut out the Blackblood leader's heart. Others say he burned his body with holy fire. There are a dozen tales of how Marduk met his demise, but none of them mention a Dybbuk Box. But it makes sense, after seeing Ventur break open his own Dybbuk to call upon the spirit of Bloodlust.

"To make a Dybbuk Box, I must fall in love with one of you," Lysander continues, unclasping the cape from his neck. I'm caught off guard as he slowly begins undressing himself while he talks. King Dexus himself blushes at the knight's nonchalantness as plates of armor come thudding to the ground. The surrounding Acolytes aren't taken back by the action at all, as if they expected to see Lysander's nakedness this entire time. After his armor is reduced to a pile of metal at his feet, Lysander removes the tunic from his skin and stands before the women in nothing but his flesh.

Their eyes collectively glare at his flaccid manhood. There is hunger in their stares. Some unknowingly drop their jaws. Others fiddle with their hands, unsure what to do. They are maidens. None of them have ever seen a man's nakedness before, and it isn't until this moment that they realize what they've been missing out on. Lysander's manhood is not the only thing impressive about him, though. His body, like Atlas's, is etched in stone. His body is everything his polished armor wasn't. Scars cover him from shoulder to calf. The only unblemished inches of skin I see are those of his manhood itself.

"You women have been told this is your duty, as followers of the Creator. As a knight, I am sympathetic to duty. But what the priests and I are asking of you is not fair, so I extend the offer to all of you now—if you want no part in what's to come, you may leave now." King Dexus gasps audibly, flabbergasted at Lysander's willingness to disobey direct orders of the priesthood. Lysander continues, ignoring Dexus, "Whatever punishment the priests hold against you, I assure will not happen under my watch. I am not a rapist. I will not bed one of you if it is not your wish."

Offering the women freedom has the opposite effect on them. Not a single one of them so much as moves an inch away from Lysander, their shining knight. The mere fact that he extends freedom makes them double down in their commitment to his cause.

"Very well, it was just something I felt needed to be said. Now, three days is not a long time to fall in love. Creator knows there is much that goes into an eternal mating. It is more than just physical. Love is emotional. It is spiritual. It is mental. By the time I leave for Nightfall, I will love one of you women more than I have ever loved another human. And it is that love that will allow us to make a Dybbuk Box as a consequence. I have strained long hours thinking of how I will select which of you are to intertwine souls with me. Please, women, remove your veils and clothes."

The maidens flush red at the command. The eighteen of them exchange glances, understandably nervous. These nuns have spent their entire lives shunning their sexual impulses, punished for lustful thoughts. No one has ever seen them naked aside from their mothers in infancy. No one has ever seen the women they've grown to be. Their bodies are hidden treasures, and Lysander has just asked for them to unlock their contents for him to explore.

"You have no need to be nervous," Lysander reassures, "Love is many things, but I decided we must deal with the physical aspect first. For there is no point in me growing to love you emotionally if I later find I am not attracted to you physically."

The maidens remove their hijabs slowly, revealing a spectrum of well-groomed, slicked back hair. They embody every color of hair possible. Blonde and brunette and ginger. Black and gray and auburn. All of their faces were beautiful, but now that their hair is drawn into the equation, they are all heavenly. Next, they remove their neck-high shawls, exposing their tender, kissable necks. Some remove their robes with more excitement and angst than others. Solis's light radiates down on their naked bodies as their tunics fall to the ground at their ankles.

My breath catches in my soul's lungs at the sight of them. I have never seen such modest personalities in women so seductive. Their bodies are inviting, each of them provocative in their own unique way. I wonder what Creon would say if he was here to witness this slice of heaven on earth. I laugh inwardly at the prospect. He would likely die a second time if he witnessed what I am.

Each of them has prepared for this day. Their bodies are hairless and bathed so clean that the sun sparkles on their oiled flesh. I have never seen women so pampered and groomed. Even when Crixus and Lockjaw stood naked before me, their bodies were malnourished and wore the scars of slavery. Vesper herself always took care to make her body comely, but after having Sephora there wasn't enough time or desire in the day to groom ourselves to this extent. Enchantress eyes me from several feet away and I do my best to hide my shock.

Lysander is not jarred to the extent I am. The sight of the voluptuous bodies do nothing to distract the stoic man. Not even his manhood stiffens. It doesn't so much as flinch in their direction. His eyes are cold and mathematic as he takes in their appearances. Several seconds pass like an eternity before Lysander approaches the bare-chested maidens.

The armorless knight walks right up to the woman on the farthest right and places his chest against hers. I can hear her gasp as their bodies make contact. He doesn't speak. He lowers his head to her neck and kisses below her ear, causing her body to break out with goosebumps. She closes her eyes and lifts her head to the sky at an angle. He runs his calloused hands down her body, not reaching for the space between her legs. Then, just as she shivers with excitement, Lysander leaves her for the next woman in line, his manhood unaffected by the first contestant's offering.

Lysander approaches the next woman from behind, making her jump as he presses into her ass. His big hands wrap around her front, fondling her petite breasts with his big hands. The contestant lets out a moan of pleasure as Lysander kisses her shoulder. His hands dance down her body from her aroused nipples to her wide hips. She places her hands around her breasts, embracing the memory of his fingerprints on her skin. She bites her lip as he presses into her harder from behind. And then, just when she's convinced she is the one, he vanishes like a distant memory from her presence, approaching the next woman in line. The second contestant lets out a feeble sigh of pleasure.

Without explanation, Lysander continues his illustrious examination of the maidens, laying hands on all of them, but only kissing a select few. For some, simply holding their hair and breathing in its fragrance is enough. For others, his fingers linger longer than they should. His face is stern, not taking this decision lightly. Though he doesn't mean to, each maiden is left more disappointed than the last. They stare at his manhood, wondering why they're unable to make it stand with their allure. Is it something wrong with them? Their collective frustration is plain to see.

But everything changes when Lysander gets to the woman known as Jezebel. With only three maidens left, I'm wondering if Lysander will even be able to find one to his suiting. Or maybe he plans to interact with each of them before rendering judgment. Jezebel doesn't give him that chance though. Lysander slowly approaches the slender brunette. She is petite. What her breasts lack in size they make up for in perkiness. What her hips lack in width her ass makes up for in roundness. The overhead sunlight gleams through her thigh gap, revealing the treasure within. She has the collarbones of an angel and the seductive gaze of a devil. There is hunger in her dark eyes. Fullness in her lips. Confidence in her stance.

Jezebel drops to her knees before Lysander has the chance to lay hands on her. With the dexterity of a practiced whore and the experience of a seductress, Jezebel grabs hold of Lysander's manhood and places it in her mouth, claiming him as her own. Gasps fill the air from the surrounding women. Lysander himself nearly trips in disbelief. But Jezebel's hands wrap around, cupping at his buttocks so he cannot escape her. She fills her mouth with his manhood, an audible slurp echoing for onlookers to hear. She doesn't stop there, though.

No, Jezebel strokes Lysander with her tongue while she runs her mouth back and forth the length of the stiffening member. Lysander betrays himself as a moan escapes his mouth. His hand shoots out to hold her hair back, his primordial instincts kicking in. The manhood grows significantly, disallowing Jezebel from fitting its entirety in her mouth. She gags in a desperate attempt to bring her lips to his pelvis once more, but its size won't allow her.

When she's sure he won't back away from her, she removes one hand from his ass and wraps it around his engorged member, stroking in tandem as her mouth bobs back and forth.

King Dexus is in disbelief, but doesn't interrupt the imprinting. Several Acolytes exchange envious glances. The other maidens don't know what to do with themselves. Some are flustered. Others are enraged. Jezebel has stolen their knight in shining armor. Lysander's moans are evident of that. But each of these women were equally capable of Jezebel's actions, only they weren't cunning enough to think to do such a thing. Because of this, they are more mad at themselves than they are at Jezebel.

Lysander's leg twitches. Jezebel has him wrapped around her finger. Her mouth dutifully serves like a pious woman before the gods. The sound of her sucking is maddening. Jezebel is a lustful glutton in the way she devours her prey. She speeds up her head's bobbing, causing Lysander to tremble. Saliva drips from Lysander's engorged member.

I watch the muscles in Lysander's back tense. He is close. Soon, his seed will spill. He clenches Jezebel's hair tighter. She runs her free hand up his abs, then toys with his nipples. Lysander lets out a muffled gasp, and then, just before he is about to sacrifice his seed to the seductress, Jezebel stops. Lysander freezes up, uncomfortable with the feeling of being so close yet so far. Jezebel stands, licking her succulent lips. She moves close to Lysander, one hand still on his excited member, and whispers, "That is but a taste of what you will get these three days if you choose me, my Lord. There is much more we can explore together."

Jezebel backs away from the Acolyte leader and returns to the lineup, her chest heaving from the labor of her services. She doesn't break eye contact with Lysander. To them, they are the only two who currently exist in this world. Though Lysander is credited in the histories for speaking like a poet, he is speechless now. The line between lust and love is often thin. Fools often confuse the two for one another. Lysander set out to find someone he loves, not knowing he would also find someone who was his weakness.

I can relate. Love is weakness, but love is also strength. Before I met Vesper, I fought like I had nothing to lose. But after her, I realized I had the whole world to lose. Love is the greatest motivator humanity has. Without it, Bloodlust couldn't manipulate me to go to Sygon. It is the only emotion that corrupts us in the most beautiful way. To love is to stare at the sun until one goes blind.

Lysander has unfinished business with Jezebel, so his interactions with the final maidens in line are nothing more than polite attempts at indifference. One maiden, bless her heart, gets on her knees in an attempt to finish what Jezebel started, but Lysander stops her, shaking his head. He will not allow her to reap the fruits of another's labor. She is ashamed of her attempt, but how else could she follow such a performance?

The decision is made long before it leaves Lysander's lips. The Acolyte leader came to Baptiste to claim a maiden—someone to fall in love with, but instead a maiden claimed him. Time passes, and as Enchantress's vision fades, it fades on the image of Jezebel finishing what she started in Lysander's tent a few short hours later.

# 27

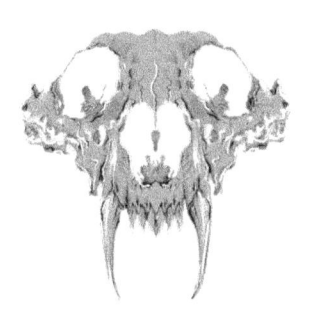

## HUMANITY'S SAVIOR

"Why did you do it," Lysander pants uncontrollably, shifting his sweat soaked body off Jezebel. They are both covered in a sheen of sweat enough to convince an onlooker they'd run through the rain for hours. Jezebel's chest heaves up and down, up and down. The two have intertwined their souls once, twice, thrice times today since Lysander picked Jezebel as his soulmate. King Dexus donated a suite in his personal wing of Baptiste's castle.

Baptiste is known as the Holy City, but the things Lysander and Jezebel have done in this room are anything but holy. There is such little time to explore each other's bodies, so they devour every inch of each other like today will be their last. Their minds transport to another place when they dance like devils. Jezebel might be a maiden, but this is not Lysander's first time feeling the touch of a woman. But he has never experienced anything like this, knowing what's to come in three day's time. What Jezebel and Lysander have done isn't sex. Lysander has had sex before. There is little special about it. Two bodies going through the motions to satisfy their selfish cravings.

This is not sex. This is sacrament. Their lust and love opposed like two candles being held together to burn against the other. The wax that drips is no longer its own. It pools below together, mixing, intertwining, creating something new. Their souls will not emerge from this interaction belonging to themselves. They leave their fingerprints on more than their partner's body. They have poured into each other's chalices until their content is diluted with something different altogether.

"To make a Dybbuk Box, it requires the maker to sacrifice something they love, or something they hate," Jezebel answers, a smile still on her face from the offering Lysander made between her legs. "But Dybbuk Boxes trap the souls of evil spirits, so the blood of hatred does little to trap them for long, because evil spirits feed off hatred. So the blood of love is the strongest seal to keep a spirit trapped. That is how you plan on stopping Marduk, after realizing he cannot be killed as ordinary mortals are."

"Yes," Lysander answers, saddened at the thought of Jezebel's blood being the requirement to reach that conclusion. "So why did you do it? I could have chosen any of the maidens."

"No, you couldn't," Jezebel replies, "It had to be me. The gods have shown me premonitions of my destiny since I was a child. Visions of you, before I even knew who you were. Visions of my death at your hands. Visions of you using my sacrifice to save humanity. It had to be me."

"And you are okay with that?" Lysander lays beside her, brushing sweaty strands of hair behind her ears.

"I have been miserable my entire life," Jezebel admits. "I was born into the Holy Order. My parents gave me up to them because they could not care for me. So the Monastery raised me as a nun, punishing me for my humanity. At first, I tried my best to do as I was told. I prayed for forgiveness. I denied gratification of my earthly desires. I fasted, I abstained, I sacrificed. But none of it was enough. I detest the gods. I have always hated them, and nothing I've done can change that. This world is too unfair to love its makers. The Sylvians, the Undead, the Lycans, the holy scriptures make them seem like they are the chosen ones, and humans are only here to satisfy their bloodlust. I cannot bring myself to bend my knees to their curses. I cannot accept the way this world would have us humans live. We are more than bloodbags and Lycan fodder. It is called the Curse of Damon and Dagon for a reason; our enemies are cursed. Yet the Holy Order would have us believe humans are the inferior ones, meant to submit to their wanton ways because we are powerless to do otherwise.

"I cannot live like this any longer, watching our species be treated like we are second class citizens. That is when my visions started making sense. Premonitions of a man that would change the natural order of this world. Prophecies of a man who would defy the natural order and reclaim humanity's potential. Omens of you, Lysander, are what I saw. When the Blackbloods arose, I finally understood why the gods chose me to suffer." Jezebel looks deeply into Lysander's sad eyes as she says the next part, "You are humanity's savior, Lysander. And I am the required sacrifice to restore humanity to its potential. Few in this world get to choose the way they die. I can think of no better way to face death than in the embrace of a man I love."

Lysander doesn't speak. His hand rests beneath her left breast, feeling her heart flutter. His face has concern written on it. He has never been snared by feelings like this before. Love is a scary realization, for those who've never felt it before.

"You believe this is preordained?" Lysander finally asks after the silence eats at him. "What if we are just two humans choosing our own fate, decision by decision?"

"You know the answer to that," Jezebel laughs the sadness away. "Freewill, predestination, they are two sides to the same coin. If a butcher throws a piece of meat in a cage and a rabid dog becomes trapped, was it the dog's freewill that snared him, or was it the butcher throwing the meat?"

Lysander is taken back by the comparison. It is not a question he's comfortable answering because of its hidden implications. If the natural world is predestined, it means there is someone—some force—responsible for all the atrocities that happen every damn day the sun rises, every dark night the moon reigns. Who that force is and what their objective is causes dread.

But the thought of there being no author for the atrocities of this world is equally terrifying. Humans, Undead, Lycans—the slaughter, the injustice, the subversion of nature—if it all points back to the freewill of creatures to commit themselves to such evil... Well, it means no one is coming to save us, and the balance of all admirable virtues are only as secure as those who stand and fight for their survival.

"Is that all I am?" Lysander asks. "A starving dog chasing after a piece of meat? A naive human chained by his unwillingness to settle for inferiority?"

"You are neither the dog nor the meat-tosser, Lysander," Jezebel replies. Her eyes peer through the darkness with tears bubbling on their surface.

"You are the one who slays the butcher and frees the dog from the cage. You are—"

Lysander's hand shoots to Jezebel's throat, a knife in his clenched fist cutting off his lover's words as it opens her neck from ear to ear. "Shhhh," Lysander whispers, crying as fear radiates in Jezebel's eyes. Fear of dying possesses her as she fights for her next breath, suffocating on blood instead. Her frail hands cling tight to Lysander's muscular arm as he throws the blade across the room, disgusted by himself.

"I'm so sorry," he whispers, his tears falling onto her face. "I'm so so sorry," he sobs. Her eyes search for an answer for his betrayal. "I had to… I… I couldn't wait any longer… I fear if I waited any longer, my love for you would grow too great for me to follow my destiny."

My breath catches in my soul's spirit. It happened so fast. I didn't even see him reach for the dagger. Don't even know where it came from. Like me, Jezebel is caught off guard, not realizing she's dying until she's taken her first step into the afterlife.

A Dybbuk Box can only be sealed shut with the sacrificial blood of a lover. For this to happen, Lysander came to Baptiste for one reason, and one reason only. To find someone he truly loved, so he could acquire the blood necessary to trap Marduk's soul for all eternity. Three days. That's all he had to form a union with a woman of his choosing. Coming here, he thought the prospect impossible. Love is something most people search their entire life for and never succeed in finding. Lysander was bleak at the possibility of finding even a fraction of such a beautiful emotion.

But alas, he has fallen in love with Jezebel in less than a single day. She has done what no other ever could—taken a piece of his heart and cursed him to forever be incomplete without her. A part of him will die with her, be buried in the ground with her, decompose with her. With love, comes fear.

Fear of loss. Fear of incompleteness—a fear of knowing what you need yet knowing you will never have it.

It is this fear that has driven Lysander to do what he must, not because he wants to, but because another second in Jezebel's presence will cause him to retreat from his fate. Another day, another minute, another second with Jezebel would force him to cave to his fears and destroy Jezebel's visions of humanity being saved.

The gods are the butcher. Humanity is the dog. And Lysander is the man who stabs the butcher in the heart.

But unfortunately, for Jezebel, she is the tremble in Lysander's wrist that tempts him to throw away the blade and run from his destiny, and because of that, she must be eliminated. Blood pours from her neck and washes over his loving hands. She understands his decision to cut their affair short, but that understanding does little to eliminate the sadness from her eyes. She wraps her dying hands around his head, then pulls him in for one last kiss. He complies, tears from his face mixing with her blood. He closes his eyes as their lips connect. He can feel her body losing life with every waking second. Lysander will never be complete again without her soul walking this earth.

Jezebel's body dies in his arms, and Lysander's cries shake her corpse.

"I am not the one who will save humanity," Lysander sobs, holding her limp head in his arms. "You, Jezebel. You are humanity's true savior."

I don't feel envy for Lysander, knowing the pain that possesses his heart. The gods took everything from me, but the gods made Lysander take everything from himself. A chance at love. A chance at a happy life. A chance at seeing the fruits of what love may produce. These seeds are now crushed to dust beneath his own feet, all so humanity can have a fighting chance against the Blackbloods.

Enchantress and I leave Lysander to mourn his loss. Whether it was the gods who predestined this moment or Lysander's own choices matters little, for a piece of Lysander will always be missing. Jezebel died so her dreams may live. All Lysander can do now is ensure his blade doesn't fail him as he rips her dreams into reality, bit by bloody bit.

# 28

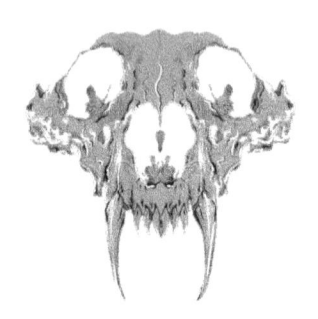

## No One is Coming to Save Us

"No one is coming to save us," Lysander shouts to his army of Acolytes. The sun sets in the distance, its light casts a warm glow off the armor of several thousand knights. The fighting force assembled is like nothing history has ever seen before or since. I can tell by our surroundings we are back in Nightfall, the birthplace of Marduk and fabled breeding ground of his horde of Blackbloods. The landscape has been washed over by several feet of snow, though the sky has paused its flurries in anticipation of the war to come. The Acolytes stand to their knees in it. The sun bounces off the ice to create a glare that is blinding.

"The Undead have locked themselves away, afraid of becoming monsters like the Blackbloods. The Lycans are of little use, unable to control their own monsters. And the Sylvians... Well, the Sylvians have never cared about anything other than their precious throne and who sits on it. But I don't give a fuck who sits on the throne. We must be our own kings tonight. Tonight, no one is coming to save us. It is only us. We are the only thing standing in the way of humanity's extinction. Let that sink in, Acolytes. Tonight, we fight not for ourselves, but for the preservation of our own species. If we fail tonight, the Blackbloods won't stop until they've fed on every drop of fresh blood our species has to offer."

The Acolytes are motionless. The cold does little to shake their bones. They are seasoned killers, no greenness behind their ears. Any inexperience they once had has been burned away by the terrors of war. They know what waits for them when the darkness settles. They embrace the possibility of dying for a chance at freedom.

"Red blood and black blood, that is what this white canvas of snow will be covered with when the sun rises tomorrow," Lysander reflects, standing stoically on a snow dune before his army, his knight helm in one hand so his comrades can see the conviction on his face. "I do not care who the Fates have preordained to win this war. Victory is up to us, and if we are to lose, we will make our enemy take their victory while looking down the length of our drawn swords. No surrender. No retreat. There is nothing our enemy has that we cannot overcome. They fly, but we will make them face us on the ground. They have claws, but we will cut their hands off at their wrists. They have size, but we are faster and more agile. They are frightening, but we are molded by Fear itself.

"The night is only so long, Acolytes. This is our greatest strength, for our enemy only has half the day to eliminate us. But we humans? We are not limited by an aversion to sunlight. We are the true apex predator, able to hunt whether or not Solis is here to watch. If we cannot finish Marduk off by the time Solis rises, no matter. We will follow these demons back to whatever hell they spawn from and bring the battle to them. Because the truth of the matter is—no one is coming to save the Blackbloods either. It is they who should be worried, for they do not know the true resolve humanity is willing to resort to in order to survive.

"Heaven waits for us, and hell for them. We have no fear in dying. They are the ones with everything to lose. So, Acolytes, paint this landscape with black blood. Be artists tonight. Find fun in killing, for there is no greater joy than sending demons back to hell. If you die, rejoice! You will be met by your loved ones in the afterlife. It has been an honor serving with you men and women. It is our sacrifice that will secure peace for our children. We will not fail tonight. This ice will forever memorialize our artistry, so the whole world can see more black blood was spilled tonight than red blood. Gather your blades, for they will become death once more."

Lysander lifts his helm into the air, the setting sun behind him painting his silhouette. The Acolytes raise their swords in unison, the sun shining on the crosses forged into their breastplates. They do not shout, nor do they cheer. Silence is their creed, for they know the loudest soldiers are often the most insecure. They need little motivation to hype themselves up for battle. They know what they are here to accomplish, and they await the sun's setting to get to work.

Lysander lowers his helm over his face, its emotionless faceplate molded like the face of a snarling lion. His long, blond hair streams out the back of it like a lion's mane. I have never seen a figure as daunting as him. Raised as a Sylvian, I fell prey to the belief humans are inferior. Lysander proves my worldview wrong, putting humanity's powers to display in a way my mind will never forget. The wind whistles as it passes through the field of sharpened blades. The whistle is a calling, like a war horn—a low-pitched beckoning to enemies. Come all who dare. Abandon all hope, ye who hears our call.

## SKATHEN MORI VERE

This is a war unlike any other I've studied. Watching the slaughter is like having a front row seat to a well-orchestrated play. The Acolytes have planned for every contingency, and now that darkness has settled, the Blackbloods throw themselves into the fray of battle without remorse.

I am in disbelief to see how savage humans are when they've committed to a cause. I was a prisoner to the Blackbloods for twenty-four moons, and though I had stood toe to toe with them in battle, I had convinced myself in twenty-four moons they were unconquerable. The Acolytes put that ideology to shame now.

They spread out across the frozen ground and ready their barbed whips. Any Blackblood that does not want to come to the ground to face them is forced to. The whips lash out into the sky, their spiked coils digging into Blackblood flesh. The more the Blackbloods try to escape the whips' grasp, the deeper the barbs dig into their flesh. Their demonic bodies are pulled down to the earth with a force their leathery wings can't overcome. Acolytes discard their whips once their enemy is felled and draw their swords, carving into the decayed flesh of their enemy like knives through rotting pumpkins.

Blackbloods are formidable opponents, as fearsome as I remember them being when I was their slave, but their attacks are too slow and awkward to best these trained fighters. The Acolytes do exactly as Lysander ordered. Their swords cut off their attacker's claws at the wrist. Loose wings fall to the ground, severed from their owners like bats being dissected strike after strike. These Acolytes are like surgeons with scalpels the way they make precise incisions along a Blackblood's body. It's like they've studied the anatomy and deduced all that makes a Blackblood superior, then get to work evening the playing field.

The Blackbloods don't roll over and die though. I can see the traces of red blood splattering across the battlefield as several Acolytes are overwhelmed by the Blackblood army. What makes matters worse is the flurry of new snow that rolls in now that the temperature has dropped with the setting of the sun. I know this from my time being Muzzled; Blackbloods thrive in the cold, making Nightfall the perfect climate for them to fight.

My eyes focus in on an Acolyte who goes toe to toe with a massive Blackblood. He swings his sword, but the demon catches his arm and counters with a violent headbutt, splitting open the beast's forehead. Black blood paints the knight's helm, but the blow is devastating to the Acolyte. He staggers back, dazed from the blow, and the Blackblood moves in on his prey. The knight makes a desperate attempt to ward off the monster with a frantic swing of his sword. The Blackblood bats the strike away and pummels his prey into the snow, driving his rotting fangs into his newly proclaimed bloodbag.

I avert my eyes and look to the nucleus of the battlefield. All forces converge around one man—Lysander, the Lion Knight. Watching him fight, it is hard to believe I am his descendant. Lysander is like an angel the way he kills. Any Blackblood he passes over falls dead swiftly, their cause of death unknown to even them until they've expired. With some, he deals death with two hands on his hilt. With others, all it takes is a flippant, one-handed strike to get the job done. Feint, spin, backslash. Dodge, advance, lunging jab. Guard into slash; block, pivot, kill. Where the Lion Knight goes, limbs sever and bodies drop, black blood painting his armor like war paint.

Everywhere Lysander goes, his Acolytes draw inspiration from his persistence. They draw strength from their leader, turning the chaos of war into a well-orchestrated symphony of killing. Snow falls faster and heavier now, but it is not enough to cover the blood on the ground. Steam rises from the Acolytes' armor.

Lysander's words still echo in my mind:

*Heaven waits for us, and hell for them.*

The Blackbloods are discharged to hell accordingly, landing from the sky to meet their makers.

*We have no fear in dying.*

The Acolytes do not retreat; their swords have no hesitation.

*They are the ones with everything to lose.*

Headless Blackbloods litter the snowy plains in such numbers that the Acolytes have to fight atop their felled bodies, trampling them into the ice to serve as platforms for further slaying.

*So, Acolytes, paint this landscape with black blood. Be artists tonight.*

I have never seen artistry like this. It is not just precision and skill. It is holy devotion coupled with calculated passion. This war is an epic fantasy—their swords are their pens, black blood their ink, and the icy ground their papyrus for recordation.

*Find fun in killing...*

I can hear their laughter echo. The knights chirp their opponents, insulting them before killing them. If my hearing doesn't deceive me, I believe I overhear some of them placing monetary bets on the quantity of enemies they slay. The Acolytes are like children left to their devices, playing a game with lethal consequences yet undeterred by the prospect of death.

But that ends when Marduk arrives.

I recognize the Blackblood leader as he lands amidst the carnage. Though Blackbloods are similar in many ways, I remember Savrian Sylvian's transformation into a bloodthirsty bat. He is not the same as his soldiers. He stands head and shoulders taller than them, towering over his enemies and going to work to even the playing field. I watch in horror as the tides of war shift. Marduk catches a blade in his bare hand and rips the head clean off an Acolyte's shoulders.

A guttural roar lifts from Marduk's diaphragm. The roar is answered by the gut-wrenching, collective hiss of his army. The Acolytes are like stuffed scarecrows to the Blackblood leader. Their armor does little to protect them from his obsidian claws. He opens their bodies with a single strike; his bloodlust strengthens him with every fallen opponent.

Marduk fights exactly how I would expect a demon to. His movements are savage and barbaric. He clubs a knight with his outstretched wing, then crushes the knight's helm inward until the skull within is like an orange squeezed of all its pulp. Marduk picks up an Acolyte by his feet and uses the knight's body like a club, swinging madly at other knights around him, bashing their bodies defenseless so other Blackbloods can feast on what Marduk has sowed. Any sword raised against the Blackblood leader does not prosper; simply being in Marduk's vicinity is a death sentence. His bony, obsidian armor deflects swords like they are wooden tools for sparring. Like the Acolytes, the Blackbloods draw motivation from their leader. So much death in such little time.

The Acolytes are losing this war, I realize. Within several blinks of an eye, Marduk's presence alone rallies his brigade into an unstoppable force. The Blackbloods still descend from the night sky, their numbers forever unending.

"Where we go!" A voice screams, answered by the unrelenting scream of Acolytes, "Humanity's strength is proven!"

I locate the chant's origins. The note hangs in the air around the Lion Knight as he cuts his way toward Marduk like a miner toward gold. Marduk sees this and sets his path toward Lysander like a cyclone destroying all in its path. One is an unstoppable force, the other is an immovable object. The laws of physics will soon be proven wrong when they meet. The lion helm snarls as it approaches its enemy. Marduk hisses as he clears a path connecting him to his target.

Fighters on both sides seem to pause as the leaders of the two armies charge one another. For the briefest moment, not a single blow is exchanged throughout the war zone. The killers watch in silence as the inevitable occurs. By the end of this altercation, one of these armies will be leaderless, and the outcome of this battle will be written in blood.

The thunder of gods could not imitate the noise that permeates when Marduk and Lysander collide.

It is like watching all heaven's angels clash headfirst with all hell's demons. A reaper stands in the distance, far on the horizon of these snowy dunes, a scythe in hand as he watches the battle from detached neutrality. Skathen, Defeater of Death, is here to watch his creation go to battle on his behalf. The reaper's robed figure is a mere silhouette on the dark horizon. Enchantress stands on the opposite side of the horizon, watching her chosen soldier Lysander do everything in his power to destroy Skathen's hellish creation.

I can sense their animosity toward each other spewing contempt from miles away. *The war you fight in the physical world is far more than flesh and blood*, Enchantress told me. Enchantress chooses soldiers to do her bidding in the mortal realm, and so does Skathen. This battle is no different than what I will face when I am resurrected. Me versus Bloodlust; Lysander versus Marduk. It is the same fight that has stretched on for generations. It is more than human nature persisting for survival in the face of monsters. It is devils meddling in the affairs of mortals for a chance to reign supreme.

Unlike the Acolytes Marduk faced before Lysander, Marduk cannot easily catch his foe's blade as it goes to work on his perverted body. The steel is too fast to block. Its echo rings out as it continually makes contact. Marduk attempts to pummel Lysander into the ground, but his fists are too slow. It is like watching a human try to swat a wasp. Marduk's fist aims for where Lysander is, but lands where Lysander was. The snarling lion helm is never in the same place long, and the blade in his hands is a mirage of strikes so fast I can barely make out their movement. Before long, Lysander finds the chinks in Marduk's impenetrable hide and draws black blood from them like water from a desert.

Marduk's bleeding sends him further into rage. Savrian did not sell his soul to the devil just to lose to a human. The dark nature of his infected heart compels his murderous intentions. Demands humanity pay for the black blood that's been spilled. But no one told Lysander this was an unwinnable fight, so in Marduk's barrage of rage, Lysander's calculated strikes draw blood a second, third, and fourth time. Marduk lets out a scream so violent even Luna above is fearful of the berserking behemoth.

Marduk is like a childish brat told he can't get his way. His host, Savrian Sylvian, was once used to losing fights; but his new identity, Marduk, is not accustomed to being put in his place. Steel echoes as Marduk catches Lysander's next strike on the hide-armor of his forearm, then grips the knight's throat with his free hand. Marduk's wings extend from his back, then catapult them both from the ground, Lysander's feet kicking at empty air beneath him.

Lysander had the advantage when the ground was beneath him, but the sky is Marduk's home-field advantage. The Lion Knight makes a desperate attempt to cut one of Marduk's wings off, but the demon catches the blade and rips it from Lysander's grip, throwing it to the ground below to never be seen again. Claws dig into Lysander's neck. The knight fights Marduk's grip by battering the hulking forearm with his gauntlets. Blood seeps over Marduk's claws, drawn from their prey's arteries.

A dagger appears from thin air in Lysander's hand, then saws through Marduk's wrist. The rotting flesh provides little resistance at the joint where there is no hide-armor. Marduk hisses as his hand is separated from his body, plummeting to the ground with its claws dug in Lysander's neck. Black blood rains from the wound and falls to the ground.

Luckily for Lysander, fighting in Nightfall has a few distinct advantages. One of which is the snow dunes, which in any other circumstance would be a hindrance, but when falling from the sky from thirty feet in the air, serve as a nice cushion. The Lion Knight's body is absorbed by the snow, making a snow angel several feet deep.

Marduk folds his wings and dives after his dropped meal in a fury. They are now on the outskirts of the warzone, on the threshold of an evergreen forest that looks oddly familiar. By the time Lysander has dug himself from his ditch, Marduk is there to greet him. The Blackblood plants his heel in Lysander's chest and kicks off, sending the Lion Knight catapulting into the forest until a sturdy pine trunk catches him. The knight leaves a trail of blood on the pine bark as he slides to the ground.

"You're making this too easy," Marduk mocks as he enters the forest. My spirit leaves the ongoing war behind and follows them into the pitch black forest. The moonlight is gone inside this new battlefield. I lose sight of Marduk's camouflaged body in the darkness. All I can hear is Lysander's strained wheezing as his lungs search for air.

Lysander stands to his feet and rips his lion helm off, throwing it to the ground so he can see. His white face and blonde hair are all I can see through the veil of darkness. The winter breeze from an incoming blizzard shakes the branches overhead, sending a cascade of collected snowflakes falling to the ground.

A shadow passes in front of Lysander. "Over here," Marduk's voice echoes. Lysander spins to face it. A shadow passes behind him. "Over here," the Blackblood repeats. Lysander swivels again, no weapons left for him to fight with besides his fisted gauntlets. The shadow passes overhead. "Over here," Marduk calls again, his voice surrounding Lysander.

Marduk laughs, "If only the moon's light could show me how pathetic you look right now." It is the same thing Syrex Sylvian told Savrian. Can Marduk remember his past life as a Sylvian, or has the curse blotted all memories that made him into this monster?

A clawed hand reaches out and grabs hold of Lysander's throat once more, but instead of choking him this time, Marduk slings the knight to the ground. A grunt leaves Lysander's lungs as his breath is stolen from him a second time. A noise rings out as metal strikes metal. I can barely make out what's happening. I hear Lysander sifting through snow, then cracking ice open with his gauntlet. He is like a kid searching for buried treasure. His hand closes around something and he pulls it from the ice.

"Dagon's mercy," I whisper to myself as the air around Lysander illuminates. The item he landed on, by the fate of the gods alone, was Fervent, one of the five weapons imbued with the power to kill a Sylvian. Its blade glows orange as the sun in Lysander's palm, exposing the delirium in his eyes. There is a look of deranged lunacy on Lysander's half-dead face. The blood from his throat has frozen twice over, stopping the wounds from bleeding altogether. His flesh is pale, like he clings to this life by failing willpower.

The light berates Marduk's night vision and exposes his ghastly appearance. The demon shrivels away from the light, hissing at the sight of the weapon that once belonged to him. Of all the places for this war to lead, what are the odds it was destined to end where Savrian once stood opposed to Syrex?

Here Fervent has rested since the final Sylvian culling, dormant in the enshrined ice for decades while Marduk raised armies. My nonexistent heart throbs out of my chest at the turn of events. The hunted becomes the hunter, and now Marduk will meet his maker.

Fervent vibrates in Lysander's hand, the color in its blade shifting altogether. The impurities burn away, and suddenly it glows so hot that it loses all color whatsoever. The light that now burns is a color I didn't know possible. In Lysander's hands, Fervent now blazes pure white, the color of innocent vengeance in a world of rampant sin.

Of all Fervent's wielders, I have never seen this before. For my mother and Atlas, the sword glowed red. For Savrian Sylvian, the blade radiated orange. But for Lysander the Acolyte, Fervent is whiter than the snow his feet stand upon.

"Impossible," Marduk hisses, staring at the stark vibrance of the blade. The air around Fervent screams in protest as it's heated. The snow falling over Lysander turns to steam before it hits the ground. The icy ground turns to suctioning mud. The wave of heat carries on the wind and hits Marduk, its impersonation of the sun causing him to leap backward in fear.

"I am Lysander, leader of the Acolytes, descendant of no noble family," Lysander announces, giving Fervent a test spin to get a feel for its weight. The air hums as the blade cuts reality in two. "Where I go, humanity's strength is proven. The gods bore me on earth for one purpose—to put an end to your tyranny, Marduk, leader of the demented horde of swine known as Blackbloods. Let this sink in, demon. No one is coming to save you."

My eyes catch movement in the distance. There is a figure moving, and his scythe catches the reflection of Luna's moonlight. Skathen is here, but he stands removed, a spectator in the affairs to come. His robes of darkness ebb and flow in the winter winds. The blackness within his hood is all-consuming. A chill runs over my nonexistent body when I unintentionally stare at the void where his eyes should be.

"This is not the first time we have fought to the death, Marduk, but it will be the last," Lysander says, drawing my attention away from the reaper in the distance. "I left you for dead in the North two years ago, your body skewered with a dozen wooden stakes. But somehow, like a weed, you survived, so the gods brought me back to finish what I started, and this time I've planned for every contingency."

Marduk stands idly by, contemplation on his face. The demon is scheming, always scheming for a way to survive. That is the essence of the Blackblood virus—it has the willpower of a cockroach. But there is something hollow in Marduk's eyes now that he stands opposed to Fervent's new wielder. Is it regret? Does he remember being the last person worthy to wave this holy blade? Does he contemplate whether trading his soul was worth it? He merely traded one death for another. Put off Syrex killing him quickly for Lysander savoring every second.

Lysander reaches inside his breastplate and retrieves two items, pulling them out so Fervent's light can reveal them to Marduk. In his padded palm is a vial of red blood beside a small wooden box shaped like a miniature coffin.

"Sealing my soul in a Dybbuk Box won't kill me," Marduk growls, knowing exactly what these items are for. "It is a quick fix to a problem you can't solve. It may take months, decades, perhaps centuries, but I will escape that prison, and I will walk this earth once more."

"You were once Sylvian, it is said," Lysander answers the threat with calmness in his tone. "Savrian Sylvian, the weakest of his generation's Culling."

"That name has no meaning to me anymore," Marduk growls.

"But it has great meaning to me," Lysander laughs like a lunatic, the adrenaline of battle getting the best of him. "Because of you, the Sylvian family is bound by blood to the curse you've created. And so I wonder, if your spirit were to enter a Sylvian descendant, would it be canceled out by their powers? It is an interesting theory I've been working on, one I think I'll have my descendant's explore if you ever escape this box. Mark my words, Marduk, my descendants will infiltrate the Sylvian bloodline and produce a child. It may take decades, it may take centuries, but the gods have shown me the future, and it ends with them righting your wrongs. Your existence will be canceled out once exorcized into the chosen Sylvian designated as Bloodbound. The freewill you sought to put an end to tyrants will be overcome by the predestination of the gods, and they will punish you for all eternity for the abomination you've created. This is the life-blood of the woman I loved most on this earth," Lysander says, holding up the vial of Jezebel's sacrificial offering.

He continues, "Do not question the lengths I will travel to put an end to you. I used to be a dreamer like yourself—used to think we humans have the freewill to make something of ourselves. But I know now the gods have greater plans for us than we can ever imagine; plans that cannot be overcome by our decisions to rebel against the natural order of creation. I am their instrument, and they have chosen me to put an end to your rebellion."

"You are nothing more than a fool," Marduk spits. "You are the one to be pitied, Lion Knight, if you truly let the gods convince you to kill everything you love so you can put an end to my evil. You will seal my soul because you sacrificed the one you love, but I implore you to ask yourself when this deed is done—was it worth it? When you grow old with no one by your side, when you look in the eyes of another woman and know she will never provoke emotion in you the same, when you bear children out of duty instead of passion... You did not sacrifice the one you love because you are strong, Lion Knight. You sacrificed her because you are a coward. You would rather kneel before the gods and let them choose your future than stand up and forge your own destiny. That is what I fight for, and that is what makes us different. You've let the gods convince you I am the tyrant, and in the process you've become blind to the leash they tied around your neck long ago. Ask yourself, was it worth it? I fear in retrospect the one known as Bloodbound will find that answer in his searching, and he will not be so willing to sacrifice all he loves as you were."

Lysander screams, then drives Fervent into Marduk's heart with a single hand, its blinding light separating the demon's chest in two and illuminating his body from within like a Jack-o'-lantern. The burning blade sizzles as it sears away the flesh it comes in contact with. Marduk makes no noise as he drops to his knees.

Lysander releases the hilt, causing the steel to lose all color instantly, as if its radiance was a mere hallucination. Black blood trickles from the lethal wound like pus from an infection. Lysander opens the coffin-shaped box and collects the black blood, Marduk watching the seance happen before his eyes. Lysander opens the vial of Jezebel's blood and pours it along the edges of the box, tears streaming down his face. The black blood inside the box begins to bubble, as if it is in a cauldron set to boil.

As the blood becomes sealed, Marduk's appearance starts to shift. His flesh twists, shrivels, morphs. The black hue fades away. The bones that protrude from his body retract. His wings shrivel up and disappear. Muscles diminish. Size lessens. The demon retreats, and by the time Lysander shuts the Dybbuk Box, only Savrian Sylvian remains, his chest impaled with a blade he once wielded faithfully.

Savrian gasps, the monster that possessed him finally gone. Jezebel's blood drips from the lips of the Dybbuk Box, slowly solidifying to trap the curse within. Savrian whispers something as his life leaves him, "Skathen mori vere…" Lysander pulls the blade from Savrian's chest and beheads him with a single blow, no longer interested in what his opponent has to say to him.

Skathen mori vere. Our demons conquer us.

The vision fades, my eyes lingering on the reaper smiling in the distance. Although Marduk was his soldier, I can't help but feel like this is the result the devil wanted. I'm left to contemplate what I've just seen.

# 30

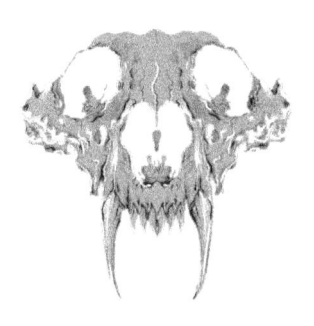

## MY TRUE ENEMY

It's all beginning to make sense.

*You were once Sylvian.*

Savrian Sylvian, the weakest of his generation's Culling.

Because of you, the Sylvian family is bound by blood to the curse you've created.

If your spirit were to enter a Sylvian descendant, would it be canceled out by their powers?

*Mark my words, Marduk, my descendants will infiltrate the Sylvian bloodline and produce a child.*

*It may take decades, it may take centuries, but the gods have shown me the future, and it ends with them righting your wrongs.*

*Your existence will be canceled out once exorcized into the chosen Sylvian designated as Bloodbound.*

*The freewill you sought to put an end to tyrants will be overcome by the predestination of the gods, and they will punish you for all eternity for the abomination you've created.*

I am that child, I realize.

My mother was the last known descendant of Lysander the Acolyte.

My father was Silenius Sylvian.

In me, the bloodlines have made Lysander's threat a reality.

I am the product of lineage manipulation. The gods have been carefully crafting my existence for eons, waiting to spawn me for Marduk's reincarnation.

Because of Savrian's sin, I am bound by blood to this curse.

The vessel that can cancel out its existence.

Bloodbound.

In me, all this evil can finally come to an end.

That is why Bloodlust wants me dead. Not because I stand in his way of ruling the kingdom, but because I am the one foretold to come—the one who can finally destroy his existence.

Still though, Marduk's final words pierce my heart.

*You did not sacrifice the one you love because you are strong, Lion Knight.*

*You sacrificed her because you are a coward.*

*You would rather kneel before the gods and let them choose your future than stand up and forge your own destiny.*

*That is what I fight for, and that is what makes us different.*

*You've let the gods convince you I am the tyrant, and in the process you've become blind to the leash they tied around your neck long ago.*

*Ask yourself, was it worth it?*

*I fear in retrospect the one known as Bloodbound will find that answer in his searching, and he will not be so willing to sacrifice all he loves as you were.*

Was Marduk right?

When the time comes, will I be able to sacrifice all I love to put an end to this evil?

No, I answer inwardly.

Everything I've done, all the death I've enacted, has been to protect the ones I love. Vesper. Sephora. Crixus. Creon. Scar. Lockjaw. My unnamed son.

If the price for destroying this evil is submitting myself to the will of the gods, I fear Marduk was the one who had it right this whole time. I've had enough of the gods meddling in my life; I won't let them take away the people I love most.

I asked Enchantress to show me my enemy, and now my eyes are open to who my true adversaries are. It is not Bloodlust, it is not Ventur, it is not Skathen. It is the Creator, and I'll be damned if I bend my knee to his will.

# 31

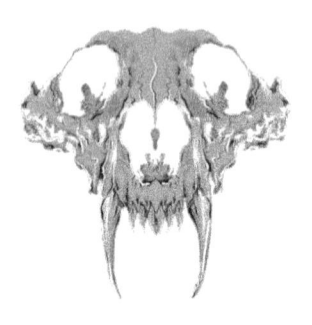

## THE TEMPLE OF THE ACOLYTES

"It exists," a voice calls out from the darkness as Enchantress's vision displays before me. The voice is like seeing home on the horizon after a long journey. It belongs to my childhood mentor, a man I never thought I'd see again, even in long-forgotten memories. Lundis repeats himself, "It really exists..."

It is nighttime in Nightfall, and the snow and ice are as plentiful as my other visits to this hell-forsaken island. Through the darkness, I see Lundis's purple eyes glimmering, illuminating his porcelain face. The elements, though ideal for an Undead, have their impact on Lundis and his companions. Ice forms in my tutor's thinning hair, the remaining wisps collecting the falling snow.

Accompanying Lundis is a band of Black Knights, three in total. No more, no less. Their armor squeaks in protest with every movement; the environment threatens to rust their joints if they stand too long in the same place. Their pitch black armor blends in with the night but stands in stark contrast with the snowy background.

Before them is a monument like nothing I've ever seen—a pyramid erected in the middle of flat earth. I take a look around and realize I'm familiar with this portion of Nightfall. Though trees have been cut away and ground has been leveled, this is where the Acolytes made their stand against the Blackbloods centuries ago.

Its base covers a span a kilometer wide and a kilometer long, its sides traveling up in slants to reach a single point tall enough to kiss the heavens. The clouds above swirl around its spire, cutting them off from my view. The outer walls are made from a mixture of frozen limestone and ice, making the monument look like an igloo-pyramid hybrid.

Lundis takes a moment to marvel in its beauty. It is the sort of creation only gods could have built. If this is the Acolytes' Holy Temple, I would consider it a miracle humans were capable of building such a structure. They have no superhuman strength, nor do they have the ability to fly like the Undead. Erecting this temple in these conditions required sacrifice, and lots of it.

"Several weeks we've searched for the lost Temple of the Acolytes, so long that I was beginning to lose hope," Lundis admits aloud. "But that view... Take it in, men. We will never see anything like it again."

The Northern Lights of Nightfall sway in the sky, converging on the pyramid's spire. I, too, am in awe. I am not a builder, nor am I an architect, but sheer common sense is enough for me to know this is the single greatest monument in modern history, and it was made centuries ago, eons ahead of its time.

I know where I am in history now; I have my bearing through space and time. Enchantress has shown me many things so far—her inception in the graveyard; Savrian's fall and Marduk's rising; Lysander and Jezebel's love story; Lysander's vengeance on behalf of humanity... But now I am in a place and time I understand.

What seems like an eternity ago, I spoke with Bloodlust about his origin. Though he tricked me into thinking he was Lundis this entire time, I see Ventur told a fraction of the truth: *"We studied the histories together. It was written the Acolytes had cut Marduk's heart from his chest and drained his body of every drop of black blood left in his veins. But what happened to the heart was uncertain. Xander's histories said it was burned. Canterbury wrote it was frozen in rem-ice. Lysander's journals said it was locked away in a crypt within the Acolytes' ancient temple. Each record further contradicted what we believed to be the truth of the matter. And still, the black heart called to your father every night.*

*"So he sent me on a mission to find the Acolytes' lost temple. The rest is history,"* Bloodlust said, gesturing at his body once more.

*"You found Marduk's heart?"* I asked in disbelief, staring at the corrupted figure.

*"And with it, the Blackblood virus found me,"* Bloodlust whispered. *"By the time I was infected, your father was dead and the Undead Empire had taken the throne. Everything Marduk's heart had shown him came to pass, and I was forced into exile as the virus took over my body."*

But half of this was a lie. Though Lundis was the one to discover the lost Acolyte Temple, I have a feeling I will soon learn the truth of what happened. Bloodlust has framed Lundis as being his host this entire time to preserve the Undead Emperor's reputation all along, but I have a feeling Lundis was never infected in the first place.

The band of vagabonds approach the temple's front gates. The Black Knights get to work chipping away the thick ice that seals the doors. They bring out icepicks, something Lundis must have ordered them to pack in anticipation of this discovery. While the three of them get to work, Lundis walks around the temple's perimeter, still flabbergasted by its appearance.

"Silenius's nightmares were right all along," Lundis gasps to himself. "If Marduk's spirit still exists, this must be its final resting place. I'm sure of it."

I admire my former teacher from afar. So many admirable qualities in him; the fact that he is Undead never made him pompous like the rest of his kind. He was always searching new ways to learn, always admitting his ignorance when the opportunity presented itself. Being proved wrong was one of his favorite occurrences.

I can read his mind without him speaking it. If humans were capable of building this, what more are the Undead capable of if they get their heads out of their asses? The ice cracks at Ventur's feet while he stares at the Northern Lights above, then gives way without warning.

Ventur falls, plummeting into the depths of the earth without so much as a yelp of surprise. I follow him, diving into the hole to find an icy tunnel slanted in a forty-five degree slope. Though Ventur could fly if he wished, he slides down the tunnel like a laughing child, his purple eyes dispelling the darkness as he falls.

After several seconds of following him, the tunnel opens up into a cavernous pit, the floor covered with upward facing stakes ready to impale intruders caught unaware. Ventur employs flight to avoid being lanced up the arse, his laughter shaking the surrounding cave walls.

Torches light automatically, revealing the skeletons that line the cave floor like flies caught in a spider's web. Lundis has somehow stumbled into an ancient trap set by the Acolytes, likely one of many outside the Temple's domain. The snow and ice from Lundis's fall hits the ground atop the dead bodies from long ago.

"Oh Lundis," my tutor laughs at himself, "How many times has your curiosity almost been the death of you, old man?"

He levitates a few short feet from the wooden stakes that would have put an end to his life. The torches light his way as he floats to the opposite side of the pit, landing peacefully on a flat tunnel walkway that delves deeper into the earth. Torches light without Lundis's doing, igniting the path for Lundis to explore.

There's no telling how long it's been since someone maintained these tunnels, but the abundance of cobwebs and floating dust indicates it's been quite some time. Histories don't give a definitive answer when the Acolytes went extinct. They were born from necessity, a fighting force created to hunt the Blackbloods to annihilation. After accomplishing this, it seems they lost their purpose, and after Lysander's death, they lacked sufficient leadership to find their way in this world.

Leaders rose—Xander, Canterbury, Artileas—but without a common line of succession, the knights bickered over who was worthy to lead humanity's cause. Elections became more contested, and after several generations, the Acolytes became so dissociated from their origin that they no longer could agree what they stood for.

It has likely been several hundred years since this Temple has been explored by the living, and its many secrets will require excavation and research before answers can be found. Lundis steals a torch from its mount on the wall and continues onward, his excitement palpable in a way only I can understand.

## 32

## THE MAN BENEATH THE HOOD

"Gods be good," Lundis exclaims, dropping his torch at the sight of what awaits him. Several hours he has navigated the Temple's underground tunnels and hidden chambers, finally to discover the cause for his search.

Torches light themselves throughout the ominous chamber to expose something entirely unholy. The fire at Lundis's feet does not die out, but instead burns brighter. I, too, am rendered speechless at the contents of this chamber. Unlike Lundis, I have now seen the moment Lysander sealed Marduk's soul within a Dybbuk Box. But there's no telling how many years ago that was, nor what the Acolytes have gotten themselves into since.

I stare at a vast room located somewhere within the heart of their Holy Temple. The walls are spread far apart, and the ceiling spans so tall not even twenty men standing on each other's shoulders could reach its surface.

Here, stacked and packed so tightly there is hardly any room to walk, is an entire chamber dedicated to storing Dybbuk Boxes, all of them sealed with the sacrificial blood of some long forgotten soul. The boxes stretch as far as I can see, some sitting on altars, others on stone pedestals, and others stacked atop others like abandoned cargo. The number of boxes is incalculable. Hundreds, thousands, perhaps tens of thousands of souls sit silently trapped within this room, their number knowing no end.

Lundis stands there, shocked at what he's found.

The histories fail to report on the Acolytes' missions after defeating Marduk, but none come even close to suggesting they collected a genocide of souls from this world. Lundis shifts uncomfortably, all sense of joy fleeing his body. "Gods be good," he repeats himself, "What atrocity have I just discovered?"

The boxes each vary in size, no two the same as the other. Some are actual coffins, others are so small only a single coin could fit inside them. All of them drip the dried blood of their sacrificial seals, their outsides inscribed with the name of whose soul they entrap.

Lundis takes flight because there is no room for him to walk. It appears there was once some orderly system for storing and stacking the cargo, but that system was later abandoned in favor of throwing the boxes untidily atop the other. It is like being in the hut of some hoarder, only it isn't meaningless trinkets that fill this room, and the implication of these boxes means many died so they may be here.

Involuntary tears stream from Lundis's eyes. He whispers to himself, "There aren't enough demons in this world to have deserved treatment like this."

I glimpse at the inscription on a few boxes myself. *Heralt, Lycan*, says one. *Thymir, Treason*, says another. It appears each name is followed by the offense that caused their soul to be disbanded from their body. *Jenny, Promiscuity. Renade, Tax Evasion. Lyzome, Lycan. Hymen, Lycan. Joffir, Drunkenness. Felthi, Fornication. Rudox, Lycan. Mishem, Lycan. Seldym, Petty Thievery.*

Gods be good, I curse inwardly. These Acolytes, whoever they were, were trapping the souls of mortals for committing petty offenses—for even being born a Lycan, something outside their control. I'm suddenly nauseous. This is not what Lysander stood for. This is not why the Acolytes were created. Not even the Bloody Tower is as egregious a punishment as this. Stealing souls to discipline people for misbehaving? To steal one's soul is to deprive them of the afterlife...

This is worse than the death sentence, for this punishment deprives its victim of even life after death. The Acolytes went from doing the work of gods to decreasing the workload of devils.

The further Lundis flies across the room, the more manic he becomes. Today, his ignorance tears him in two. It is like he has stumbled onto a great graveyard of dead bodies no one knew existed, an entire population obliterated without so much as a whimper of protest.

My childhood mentor sifts through the boxes, at first fearful of touching them, then less cautious as he realizes there is nothing particularly dangerous about them. He is careful to not alter them in any way, knowing if one of them breaks, the soul within will seek refuge in his body. Lundis, too, sees the names and crimes that doomed these people to death, and he comes to the same conclusion I have.

The Acolytes, created to put an end to evil, became the greatest evil on earth before their extinction. Lundis spins in panic, whirling in the air, searching for an end to the madness. He finds none. It is as bad as it seems, he realizes.

"So many souls," a voice calls out to him. It is ethereal, bouncing off the chamber's walls in every direction.

Lundis freezes in flight, his nose twitching in search of some scent. He finds none. He calls out, "Who goes there? Show yourself!"

Darkness gathers at the base of the boxes and a figure forms from the mists. I am not surprised to find him here, but it is evident Lundis has never seen spiritual properties such as this. A robed figure levitates from the ground, rising to meet Lundis where he hovers. Inside the hood of the figure is palpable darkness, darkness not even Lundis's purple eyes can peer into. Here, introducing himself to Lundis for the first time, is Skathen.

"My name is Skathen, and I am here to present you with a choice, Lundis."

Lundis backs away from the demon midair. "How do you know my name, dark spirit?" Lundis is riddled with emotion. The circumstances have boiled his emotions over the edge, and now this mysterious figure only further perpetuates the inevitable. Lundis is getting violent, provoked to anger at the injustice he sees. His mustache twitches as his lips quiver.

"I have known you since my inception, Lundis, though your mortal body cannot recognize my immortality. Be still, for this will all make sense with time. I am here as a cautionary warning; I come as a friend. The Black Knights that came with you—one of them is a traitor, a sword hired by Ventur."

The words Skathen speaks unlock some chord of trust in Lundis. Lundis is one of two people that knows Ventur's plots to upend and betray Silenius Sylvian. The fact that this figure of darkness knows the reason behind Lundis's journey earns a tinge of patience from the tutor.

"Whether or not you trust me is up to you, Lundis. But what I speak is the truth. In your absence, Ventur has made his move for the throne, after decades of plotting. Under the guise of the full moon, he has slaughtered the Sylvian family and framed it on their eldest son, Syrus."

Lundis shakes his head, violently refusing to accept the meaning of these words. His tears are unending, knowing Skathen shouldn't have knowledge of these events. Ventur's plotting was known to Lundis, closely confided to him by Silenius himself, but Lundis traveled here in an attempt to disrupt these plans. The very utterance of Skathen's words means this journey was for naught.

"You don't have long, Lundis," Skathen whispers, his voice echoing all around. "Silenius is dead. The Queen is dead. Princess Selena is dead. And Syrus is now on the run, wanted for the murder of the royal family."

"No... No!" Lundis screams.

"Silence," Skathen interrupts. "These occurrences were inevitable, Lundis, even Silenius knew that. You mortals are fleshy fodder in the hands of bored gods. But hope has been secured in Syrus's preservation—there is still a way to defeat the Fates in their meddling. That is what Enchantress showed Silenius, all those years ago in Queensmyre."

"How do you know these things?" Lundis screams, his brain unable to understand the plans of an infinite being.

"I am one of many beings with plans to overthrow the gods, Lundis. I have harnessed the powers to defeat death, and I have risen to the rank of god-dom. My reign on earth is near, and I seek soldiers to herald my cause. That is why I'm here, Lundis, as a friend, but also as a leader of the coming age."

"You... you are a god?"

"A god only receives their title when people come to believe in them. This time hasn't come to pass for me, but it will be here soon. Soon, all will see me for my extraordinary powers, and the whole world will come to know me as the man who defeated death."

A queer look possesses Lundis's face. He stops his retreat from the shrouded figure. Lundis speaks, "I recognize your voice... It... It can't be... Show yourself, demon!"

"Be careful what you wish for, Tutor Lundis," Skathen replies slyly, bringing his robed hands to either side of his hood. Slowly, the shrouded figure removes his hood of darkness, revealing to me and Lundis his true identity.

The torch light illuminates his features, and my entire world shatters in the balance.

No.

No no no.

No!

I scream inwardly, wanting to thrash my fist through the boxes beneath me so hard that I crack through to the core of the earth itself.

It can't be.

It makes no sense.

All answers I've received are outweighed by newly spawned questions.

I want to scream. I want to cry. I want to rip my soul in two.

There, floating before Lundis, is me, Syrus Sylvian, the man destined to destroy the will of the gods and all of creation in the process.

## 33

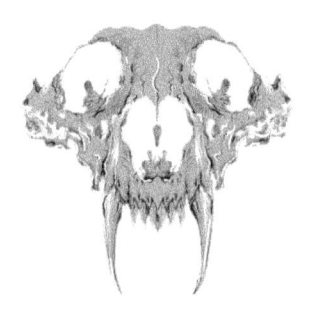

### SCARED LITTLE BOY

"Suh-suh...Suh-hyrus?" Lundis stammers, unable to get the words out of his mouth. Through space and time, Skathen has traveled to reunite with his childhood tutor once more. And although Lundis will die before getting to see me grow old, he recognizes the man I grow to become, and staring at Skathen's face is like looking into a mirror at myself.

I don't have time to react, though it's all I want to do. I want to cling to Enchantress's shoulders and shake her until this bad dream disappears. I want to beg her to tell me this isn't true, to reassure me that I'm not the one responsible for all this death and destruction. The creation of the Blackbloods, the deaths of so many humans, the rise of the Acolytes, and the Dybbuk Boxes created in their downfall's aftermath. All of it is my doing, I come to realize, though my mind is only just beginning to scratch the surface.

"It's me, Tutor Lundis. Albeit much has happened since we last met. This is the night you die, my friend. One of the Black Knights up there is Ventur's confidant. He murdered one of the men father sent to join you on your mission. He waits for the Temple door to be opened, then he will kill his companions and come for you."

"What has happened to you, Syrus?" Lundis asks, ignoring Skathen's words altogether. "What is this monster you've become?"

"I am no monster, Lundis. This world is only kind to those powerful enough to force it into submission," Skathen says. "I have merely become what the world has made me. I have finally harnessed the powers to disrupt the gods, and all I've done has led to this exact moment."

"But... You claim you're a god, but you are just a boy... I—"

"When you left the Areopagus, I was a child. But much has happened in only a few short decades. There is not enough time for me to explain to you the order of events yet to happen. All you need to know is that you are a part of a much larger plan, Lundis. A Black Knight will kill you tonight, and there is nothing you can do to stop it. He will retrieve Marduk's Dybbuk Box and deliver it to Ventur's hands. With it, Ventur will raise up a new era of Blackbloods as he simultaneously crowns himself Emperor of an Undead Empire. This is the world Syrus Sylvian will be raised in, believing he is the one to blame for his family's death. And this is the world Syrus Sylvian will defeat death in, so he can put an end to the tyrannical reign of malevolent gods."

"You look so much like your father, but speak so much like a scared little boy," Lundis says, straightening his back and puffing out his chest. An aura of confidence overcomes him; this is the man I knew and loved growing up.

"I did not come here to exchange insults, old man," Skathen snaps.

"Then why did you come here? You talk down to me as if being a god is an honor. I know no gods who became such through happy endings. Dagon and Damon ascended after tearing each other's throats out. Sylvian the First was betrayed by everything he knew and loved, his inner circle only using him for power. Luna and Solis have been condemned to spend eternity apart from each other, and don't even get me started about The Creator.

"Have you learned from nothing I taught you in my time on earth? Even if I die tonight and we never meet again, did all that I teach die with me?"

"I am not the child you knew, Lundis. The gods took everything from me. Mom and dad. Selena. My wife. My daughter. My son. My throne. My kingdom. My *Crixus*!" Skathen screams the final words with a tremble in his voice, anger swelling inside him. "My whole life, everything I came to love perished!"

"You fool!" Lundis shouts back, "Regardless of how you lost these loved ones, did you not know they were destined to die the moment they were born? Have you really become so lost in arrogance and unwillingness to die that you think we all deserve to be immortal?"

"They deserved much longer on this earth than they got!"

"I'm so sorry, Syrus. Not for the loss of your loved ones, but for the monster you've become. You lost too much at too young an age, and I am partly to blame for that. Your parents and I did all we could to delay Ventur's betrayal, but you've let pain and grief consume you. It's turned you into a personification of Death, yet here you are telling me you've defeated Death. Take a look at yourself, Syrus. You wear the robes of a Grim Reaper, and you expect me to believe you defeated death?"

"Shut up, old man!" Skathen screams, as if the sound of his voice will lessen the void in his chest. I am in pain watching this. Is this really my destiny? Have these premonitions truly been leading to this moment? When I wake up from these visions, I will have defeated death, and I will be a god in my own right.

All of it makes sense. The cosmic order of my being. It did not start at my birth, rather my birth was crafted by the almighty hands of my own being. If Skathen's words can be believed, I have existed since the dawn of creation. I did not exist within the linear chronology of humanity. I was not restricted by space or time.

I am the one who raised Enchantress, protecting her from the injustice of her curse. Because of me, she lived, and because of me, her spirit watched over my life in the flesh. All of this—everything—was scripted by me, Skathen, Death-Defeater. I am the one who combats injustice throughout the world. I am the one who saved Savrian Sylvian from being slain by his tyrannical brother. I am the one who let Marduk die when his spirit became unruly.

Enchantress said it herself, though it feels like I heard the words ages ago:
*I tell the future, and the price is costly.*
*Men pay for my prophecy by submitting themselves to its haunting consequences.*
*To know the future is to know what Death has in store for you.*
*There are many possible outcomes, but those who hear my oracles are gifted the ability to choose the best possible outcome, even if it means they must die as a consequence.*

I now know the future, and the price I must pay is any semblance of happiness I hold in the prospect of a better future. Here Skathen is, a version of myself that knows the past, present, and future, telling Lundis I will lose my wife and daughter in the coming war. That I will lose Crixus.

That I will lose my kingdom. That everything I fight for, that the very war I died for, is a lost cause.

I have nothing to fight for.

I have nothing to live for.

I have nothing to die for.

"I may have been your teacher in some past life, but you are no student of mine," Lundis mocks, no longer mesmerized by his reunion with me. The words break my heart, but they send Skathen into a rage. From thin air, his scythe appears in his hand. One moment it wasn't there, the next it was. The same scythe that slaughtered Syrex, the same scythe that has likely slain millions.

"Life is the greatest teacher," Skathen hisses, his eyes glowing violent silver. "And it taught me the lessons you were too weak to ever learn yourself, Lundisssss." The hiss is like that of a serpent, accentuating the end of Lundis's name. Seeing Skathen like this makes me afraid. Afraid of myself. Afraid of my potential. Afraid of what I'm to become.

Skathen rolls his head, forcing himself to regain composure. Lundis is not fearful of this demon; the scythe does little to deter his resolve. He looks Death in its silver eyes and doesn't bat an eyelash.

"I came to ask you for a favor, Lundis. In this room is a Dybbuk Box—one that is near and dear to my heart. It belongs to Enchantress, the spirit of the woman my father met in Queensmyre, the woman Alabastur wrote *Equinox* about. She is the reason I am the way I am. She is responsible for making the monster before you. She is the one who took everything from me."

I look around the chamber. Enchantress's spirit is nowhere to be seen; she makes no attempt at rebutting the accusations Skathen speaks. I am still missing a tremendous piece of the puzzle. Skathen is the one who found Enchantress as a child, laying haunted by the dead in a graveyard. He saved her, he raised her. Why does he hold so much animosity toward the woman who's saved me my whole life?

*"You* are the reason for the monster you've become, Syrus. You have no one to blame but yourself," Lundis spits back, unapologetically.

"Regardless of your view of me, I am asking you a final favor. Find her box and hide it, before Ventur's servant arrives. Ventur has instructed him on the extraction of more than Marduk's spirit. Ventur wants power, and he knows so long as Enchantress's spirit is trapped, she can continue to destroy my life. Please, Tutor Lundis, I'm asking you as my father's son. Find her box and hide it. Hide it where Ventur's soldier will never find it. Only then can I send someone to destroy it, once and for all."

"If you are so almighty, then you already knew my answer before coming. So tell me, *Skathen*, why speak to me if you know my answer?" Lundis asks, dancing around the request with another question.

"To give you the chance to be the hero of this story, so I no longer have to be the villain."

"I was the one who taught you there is no such thing as heroes and villains, Syrus. Your rhetoric won't work on me. There are only people doing what they've convinced themselves must be done."

"You can save thousands of lives in this very moment," Skathen pleads, reminding me of myself for the first time. "You can change the outcome of history! You can prevent me from becoming this monster. Please, Lundis, I'm begging you."

"You're so afraid of the things you can't control," Lundis whispers, more to himself than anyone else. He shakes his head in disappointment, realizing how much he's failed me. "You Sylvians... You have the power of gods coursing through your veins and it still isn't enough. You would go to the end of the earth to find control, thinking you are the ones fit to dictate what happens in this world.

"Don't you realize what you're doing? You sit here and beg for me to help you shatter the chains of predestination, not realizing the fallacy in your argument. My actions today won't change anything. I'd merely be giving the chains Enchantress holds over to you. Replacing one tyrant with another. I'm sorry for whatever it is Enchantress has done to you. I know the gravity of her actions in meddling with your father's life. I've counseled him many times on their repercussions. This is not the first time I've encountered her. But there is no amount of death you can defeat to override her plans, Syrus. Your father chose this path for you, knowing it was the only way through.

"If the things you say are true—if a portion of her soul has been sealed off in one of these boxes—we have much bigger problems at hand. Now I know why her wrath has been provoked. It is not because the gods cursed her. It is because you oppose her. You, Syrus. You are the one who brought death to your family's doorstep. Time may be a construct, but no amount of you starting over and intervening can stop what she's planning."

"Then why won't you help me!" Skathen screams.

"Because..." A single tear falls from Lundis's weary eyes. "After all this time, you're still the scared little boy I left behind in Areopagus. If I help you, I fear far worse will happen in this world than what Enchantress has planned."

"Gods be good," a voice calls, the walls of the chamber illuminated by a new torch light. "I've been looking for you," a Black Knight calls out, looking at the unending room of Dybbuk Boxes. The initial shock hits him the same way it did Lundis.

"Say, good knight, where are your companions?" Lundis replies, seeing the Soulless is unaccompanied. He pries to see the validity of Skathen's words.

"They are keeping watch at the Temple's front door. Or what's left of it. Took us forever to break it down. We were worried you didn't make it. Saw you fall through one of the traps."

"Takes a lot more to kill me than a primitive trap door," Lundis sighs, reaching for the hilt at his hip.

"Let's hope not," the Black Knight chuckles, drawing his sword.

Without another word spoken, Lundis knows the Black Knight's intentions, and the Black Knight knows Lundis won't go without a fight. Skathen still floats behind Lundis as the old man turns to face his foe. The demon is seemingly invisible from the knight's sight, his appearance going unnoticed by the duelist.

"I'm sorry Lundis," Skathen whispers. "I wish our friendship hadn't ended on these terms."

"No need to be sorry, child," Lundis replies, drawing his sword. "There is no greater privilege in this world than to finish out our destiny."

"Huh?" The knight twists his head in confusion, unsure who Lundis is speaking to. He isn't given the time to ponder long. Lundis dives through the air, sword ready for its final battle. Skathen vanishes from his midst, unable to watch what's to come.

Swords clash and blood is spilled.

I know how this story ends.

I have all the pieces of the puzzle now.

Lundis will die on this day.

Ventur will claim Marduk's box.

He will use it to create Bloodlust, then use Lundis's death to make it seem like Marduk's reincarnation is someone other than Ventur himself.

A new age of Blackbloods will be born.

Lycans will become Muzzled.

War will wage between Undead and Blackbloods, marshaled by the Undead Emperor in the guise of two bodies. With Saunter's blood, Ventur will be able to shift back and forth between his body and Bloodlust's. With Skillah's aid, he will be able to sever Marduk's soul into numerous boxes so he can wield Marduk's curse at will. He will control both sides of the war, and me and my family will become consumed by its destruction.

The vision fades as Lundis is impaled through the heart by the Black Knight's merciless sword.

*Show me my enemy, so I may know my enemy.* These are the words I spoke to Enchantress.

She was right. I don't like what I've seen.

If these visions have shown me anything, it's that I don't have one enemy. I have many. And now, I don't know who I can trust. Bloodlust and Ventur, sure. They will need to die for what they've done. But Enchantress? Skathen?

I no longer know if I can trust the devil who holds my leash. Don't even know if I can trust myself. There is much more than what I can wrap my head around. Too much I don't know. I thought Enchantress was on my side, but seeing Skathen's identity changes everything. Even more, seeing Skathen's identity frightens me. Am I truly the villain of this story? What possibly happens that turns me into such a monster?

*I tell the future, and the price is costly.*

The price is costly indeed.

*Men pay for my prophecy by submitting themselves to its haunting consequences.*

I will be reborn unsure of what I must do. The lives of many will hang in the balance.

*To know the future is to know what Death has in store for you.*

Lundis was right. I may have defeated Death, but Death has also defeated me.

*There are many possible outcomes.*

Too many to count.

*Choose the best possible outcome, even if it means you must die as a consequence.*

I would gladly die at this point, but death won't have me. It has chewed me up and spit me out, all so Enchantress can come one step closer to accomplishing her hidden agenda.

# PART THREE

# 34

## DEFEATER OF DEATH

I wake, gasping for something that isn't there. My body seizes uncontrollably as it fights to buck my soul from its midst like a bronco. My chest heaves so hard my spine nearly snaps. My fingers claw at the solid ground beneath me. My eyes roll back in my head. My skin crawls like I'm wrapped in a python's chokehold. My legs kick like I'm falling through thin air. Everything burns as my senses come back to life. Touch, taste, smell, sight, hearing. Coming back to life feels like dying a thousand times over. Everything feels wrong.

I'm no longer weightless. Instead, I'm weighed down by this sack of meat and bones. There is no sense of tiredness in the afterlife, but I feel it snare me like a sinking anchor. I can feel hunger in my gums. I shiver despite it being a midsummer night. Everything is loud, the sounds of warfare piercing my brain like black powder exploding next to my head.

After a few moments, the initial shock subsides. I roll over slowly, a dead heart lying on the cold ground beside me. It lays quietly, no body to supply it with a beat any longer. I grip my clammy chest. It beats somehow, as if Enchantress managed to grow a new one inside me like a weed in place of a dead tree. Nausea swells up my ribcage and through my esophagus. Warm, bloody vomit exorcizes itself from my mouth and flows around the dead heart, turning it into an island amidst bloody waters.

"Nikolai! Over here! He's alive!" a woman calls from several feet away.

"Well I'll be damned," Nikolai's familiar voice echoes. "You can hate the man all you want, but you can't say he doesn't have heart!" Nikolai cackles, his voice slurring his words like he's half drunk. "Get it? Heart?"

I collapse flat onto the ground, my muscles still writhing with the effort of living once more. The world spins so fast I can't register where I am. My brain is useless. Memories are no help. Everything is a blur after existing outside a linear timeframe. Thoughts of Lysander and Marduk and Lundis and Enchantress impair my thinking. I'm caught between the now and infinity. I've never felt pain like I do now. Emotional, physical, mental, spiritual pain. It hooks me like bait and casts me to hell's eternal waters, reeling me back in for the faintest of breaths.

"Well, what are you doing? Help me get him up!" Nikolai shouts, this time much closer. "We've got a war to fight and a general napping in self-pity!"

Hands wrap themselves around my naked body and haul me from the ground. Vertigo seizes me as my feet touch down. I stagger as my weight buckles my knees. I want to vomit again but my stomach has no bile left. I dry heave, hyperventilating while reality sets in. My vision narrows on Nikolai's purple eyes, then expands to his wrinkled face, then his armored body.

"There ya go, easy does it," he whispers, slapping my cheek lightly to get the blood rushing back to my head. "Thought we lost ya. Coulda sworn that was your heart lying on the ground next to you. Was about to call it quits and head back to the pub for a final drink before we all die!"

I look beyond him into the eyes of several dozen armored Undead, all staring up at me like I'm some spectacle they've paid to see. The capital square is filled with the slain bodies of a hundred plus Lycans, their naked bodies ravaged by the war that's washed over this land. Their blood flows down the capital's steps to join the flowing waters below, the streets utterly flooded from the erupted dam.

"Syrus!" Wolfsram squawks, fluttering from a nearby rooftop when he sees me standing.

"Oh here we go," Nikolai sighs. "Damn bird has been protecting your body like he owns you. Nearly pecked my finger off when I tried to check your throat for a pulse."

Wolfsram lands on my shoulder and nuzzles his neck feathers into my ear, rejoicing in the fact that I'm still alive. The dark sky above reveals the silhouette of several thousand ravens going to war with Undead and Blackbloods. Their dead bodies float down the city streets in the Wirewood River's overflow.

"Wuh-l-f-suh-raaam," I croak, the word making my esophagus feel like shattered glass.

"He speaks!" Nikolai shouts, "Huzzah!"

The surrounding fighters cheer, not knowing that my resurrection will likely mean their deaths.

"Water, water! Someone fetch this man some water!" Nikolai orders, then grumbles, "Lord knows there's plenty of it to go around." I can smell the alcohol on his breath. I briefly wonder what that's like, being so confident in your fighting abilities that you show up to war piss drunk.

A page fills a bucket with the Wirewood's gracious gift and almost trips on his sprint up the capital's steps. Nikolai pries my mouth open and the page ladles an uncontainable amount of water down my throat. My body absorbs it before it can even rehydrate my mouth. Another ladle follows, then another, and I continue drinking until my gut feels as though it will burst.

"Wuh-what have I missed?" I ask, my memories slowly coming back to me.

Saunter's betrayal.

Crixus and Vesper fighting.

Sephora commanding the Lycans.

Vesper attacking Saunter.

My body hitting the ground, my heart ripped from my chest from behind.

"Well, you were certainly right when you said evil was coming for this kingdom. Come it has, and come in many forms. As soon as the sun set, I rallied these forces," Nikolai says, gesturing at the few dozen armed Undead around us. "Others who defected from the Undead military after your family's demise. We came searching for you, but found only your corpse. There are wars within wars happening. The Lycans are engaged in a bloody civil war on the ground. The Undead and Blackbloods suck each other dry in the sky. And to put the cherry on top, there's an absolute ogre of a man running through the streets yelling, 'Purple eyes. Black wings. Mammoth kill.' I'm assuming that's somehow your doing?"

"You forgot the most important part, sir..." the page interrupts, no water left in his bucket to ladle.

"The Creator's Prophecy... The second moon..."

"Ah, yes, it slipped my mind with the initial shock of you coming back from the dead," Nikolai muses. "I certainly have never seen anything like it, though I am far from a religious man."

My eyes follow the page's trembling finger to the sky, beyond the orbit of warring ravens and bloodsuckers. There, shining bigger and brighter than Luna ever has, is a second moon, its orbit breaching through the atmosphere like a frozen meteorite stuck in purgatorial limbo. It shines on me as a silver shade takes over my vision. Strength returns to my bones and ligaments. I no longer need to lean on Nikolai's patrons for balance. My body shakes no more. I straighten, shunning the weakness from my body with violence. My throat clears itself, any pain I felt before a dissonant chord from a past life.

I stare at the second moon, and the second moon stares at me. The Creator's Prophecy... Just another religious text I've disregarded my whole life. It's said when the end of the world is near, the Creator will send an omen to his Creation to warn them Death incarnate has come. If the prophecy is to be trusted, no one will survive the destruction on the horizon.

I realize now this has everything to do with Enchantress—the Summoner. This is just another step in her holy war against the universe. At birth, Solis cursed her to be haunted by Death. Somehow, some way, she has been granted the ability to become Death itself. It haunted her for so long that it became intertwined with her soul. And I? I am now the Defeater of Death, alluded to by Skathen's afterlife projection of my soul. A god in my own right, resurrected by Enchantress so she can continue to use me as her instrument.

Whatever she has planned for this kingdom, for this world, I realize it isn't good. I, like Nikolai, am not a religious man. But no atheist can deny the presence of the second moon that now peers down at us with murderous intent.

*But there is no amount of death you can defeat to override her plans, Syrus,* Lundis spoke to Skathen, spoke to me. *After all this time, you're still the scared little boy I left behind in Areopagus. If I help you, I fear far worse will happen in this world than what Enchantress has planned.*

I will prove Lundis wrong. I am not the scared little boy he left behind. I am Syrus Sylvian, Defeater of Death, heir to the Areopagus Throne, Commander of Lycans, Hellhound of Sygon, the man gods cannot kill because I am a god myself.

"Where is the Lycan Civil War?" I ask, stretching my muscles and cracking my neck.

"One half is commanded by Princess Saunter, My Lord," Nikolai whispers, almost as if he fears the unnatural change in my demeanor. *So the bitch is still alive?* I think to myself. I should have killed the cunt when I had the chance.

Nikolai continues, "The other half is Lycans that arrived Muzzled with Bloodlust's forces. The bats loosed their muzzles and dropped them from the sky like raining demons. Their alpha is like no Lycan I've ever seen before. It's a she-wolf whose fur is silver, as silver as an Undead of Celestial descent. And her eyes... They too are silver. Like yours. Like your father's."

"That's my daughter," I reply through a thinly pursed smile.

"No kidding," Nikolai chuckles. "You raised quite the little savage. My scouts told me they saw her choke a Blackblood to death with its own wing."

"Like father like daughter," I sigh, instantly relieved to hear Sephora made it out of the capital's bloodbath alive. That still leaves Vesper though, but something tells me she is the least likely to die in this war. I have known her for over half my life. I know what she's capable of, and not even I would want to face her in battle.

"Do your scouts have eyes on the Emperor?"

"No sight of him or Bloodlust since the carnage began."

That's because they're the same person, but I don't have time to explain that to these soldiers now. Good, I reflect. That means I injured him badly in our altercation. He is likely holed up in the castle making plans for my arrival. I will deal with Saunter first, then march on Ventur before the sun rises. I look back at the second moon, weary of its gaze. It, like Luna, calls to the beast within me. Double moons, double the power of Lycans. If I can reconcile the warring wolves and submit them to my cause, there isn't a goddamn army in this world that can stop us from claiming the throne tonight.

"Take me to the Lycans, it's time to put an end to the Princess," I order, taking flight into the night.

# 35

## VALOR'S VENGEANCE

I take in the carnage from my aerial view, the second moon bathing me with its power as I float like Death incarnate ready to take back all of Creation. Nikolai and his battalion of Undead surround me, their purple eyes accenting my silver. The Undead and Blackbloods avoid this airspace, knowing their dead bodies will become Lycan fodder if they fall wounded to the ground. They collide in the distance, black wings met by pale opposition, their bodies dancing in combat like kites in a tornado's wind.

There is no way to discern the identity of the warring Lycans below. From up here, all I can see is a patchwork of diverse fur converging on itself. Snapping jaws, gnashing teeth, tearing flesh, snarling, yelping, howling. They go to war in the Areopagus's vineyard, but the red substance that flows at their feet is not grape juice. Miles and miles of open fields envelop them, separated by thinly spaced rows of upright grape vines and blueberry, blackberry, and raspberry bushes.

I used to chase Selena through this maze of berries as a child. On our mother's birthday, we would pick as many of the ripe berries as a wicker cornucopia would fit and present it to her as a gift. Mother and Selena are long dead now, and so too are my beautiful memories of these fields.

I spot Sephora amidst the genocide. She is the only Lycan with silver hair and silver eyes. The moon behind me singles her out from the blacks and browns and grays of her army's neutral fur color. She commands the Muzzled slaves brought to Areopagus for the sole reason of causing havoc, and they commit themselves to their cause masterfully.

The Fang Clan is renowned for its fighting prowess—they've spent their time since Dagon's demise practicing the art of hand-to-hand combat. But they've never faced anything like the Muzzled before, slaves starved to the brink of death and sustained by the blood of their brethren. There is nothing more dangerous than a hungry wolf, and these wolves are the hungriest of them all. Though the Fang Clan fights composed and strategically, the Muzzled are chaotic and willing to lose it all. They have tasted wolf blood many times before, and they have become addicted to its taste.

Saunter stands safely behind her ranks of devoted Lycans, her face grimacing at their savagery. She detests Lycans. Raised by Ventur, she's been raised with the impression their inability to control the beast within makes them worthy of such a miserable ending, forced to rip their companions to shreds under the light of two full moons.

I can delay no longer. This chaos must be put to an end, and only I can reconcile the damage that's been done.

"Nikolai," I growl, anger building in my chest.

"My Lord?"

"I am going down. I will put an end to this madness. Princess Saunter dies here. If she tries to escape by air, I command you and your battalion to apprehend her and send her back to hell so me and my Hellhounds can deal with her."

"Your will be done," he replies, his voice suddenly stone-cold sober.

Time for you to take over, beast, I speak inwardly. The beast within hears me, and I feel him rise to accept the order graciously.

*That bitch dies tonight*, he growls, his voice rife with feral hatred.

I move my body directly over her, behind her safety net of Lycans. I close my eyes and release the wind's hold over my body. Gravity accepts my body graciously while I begin my transformation. I plummet toward the earth like a falling comet, bones breaking, fangs emerging, claws extending, fur sprouting, muzzle expanding. By the time I land, I am fully Lycan once more, rising from the crater in the earth I've created to face Saunter for our long-awaited reunion. I rise, a god reincarnated in my mortal flesh, here to bring Death's doing to someone well deserving of its embrace. My frightening figure blots the second moon's glow, shrouding Saunter in darkness as I watch her face become horrified at what she sees.

"You… I… You're supposed to be dead…" she stammers, her fear apparent in the way her legs buckle beneath her.

*Who says I'm not?* I ask telepathically, my voice a growl sinister enough to give demons nightmares. *Truth is, sister, hell was not strong enough to hold me back from my vendetta. I will repay Death for my resurrection by sending you back in my place.*

"Brother, I beg you… Don't do this!" She cowers from me, instantly admitting defeat when her only other prospect is standing to face me in a fair fight.

*You beg for mercy? Where was my mercy when you sent your psychotic boyfriend after me? Where was my mercy when you ripped my heart from my chest? Huh?*

"I'll exile myself!" She pleads, "I'll run away and let you rule in peace, I swear! Just let me live, please! You'll never see me again…" Tears fall down her cheeks at the thought of dying. She's younger than me, much younger. Her silver eyes do all they can to convince me of their innocence.

*Right before you killed me, you fed me some bullshit sob story about the wolf pup Ventur made you kill*, I growl, slowly closing the gap between us as Lycans tear at each other's throats behind me. *I was sorry to hear about Valor. But if you expected me to feel sad for you, you were sadly mistaken. I have no tears to shed for your sorry excuse of wasted Sylvian genes, sister. No, instead I feel sorry for Valor, for it was your mistake in believing a wolf can be domesticated. I assure you, we are not the same Saunter Sylvian. We are creatures of our environment, and my environment has taught me how fatal a mistake it can be to put a leash on a wild animal.*

I see her fingers inching for the silver dagger at her hip. She thinks she is sly. This is the second time in the same day she's begged for forgiveness with the intent to betray me. Fool me once, shame on her. Fool me twice, I'll rip her fucking head off. "Ventur is yours—Bloodlust is yours! I just want to live, brother," she doubles down. "The crown is yours, take it… It isn't worth my life. I'll hand over this Lycan army and go to the Neverglades—I'll go to the Thoren Mountains—anywhere you command me to go, and it will be done."

It's comical to watch her beg like a dog while her fingers wrap around the hilt. She rips it from its sheathe and lunges for my heart. I grab her wrist and snap her arm in two, my ears ecstatic to hear her scream of pain. We have switched places since Queensmyre. There, she held all the leverage. Now I am the one with the power. I squeeze my paws tight, shattering the fracture so it won't heal in time before her death. The dagger clatters to the ground at our feet.

*Help!* Saunter screams telepathically to her army. Members of the Fang Clan stop what they're doing and turn to face their endangered alpha. *Kill this man! Someone!*

The Fang Clan identifies me as their new enemy. Meanwhile, the Muzzled army continues their onslaught, attacking the Fang Clan while their back is turned.

*Enough!* I scream, enough to still the bloodshed. *All of you, bow!* The Hellhounds immediately obey. Muzzled and Fang drop to their knees in submission at my command. Sephora stands in the distance, her beautiful silver coat covered in the blood of others. She was not strong enough to override Saunter's control over the Fang Clan, so she took command of the Muzzled. I, however, am strong enough to unify these forces. I am their alpha.

I lock eyes with Sephora in the distance. She saw me die, but now she sees me more alive than I've ever been. Though Saunter sent me to hell, I have come back for my daughter, for my wife, for my family.

*No!* Saunter screams, trying to overcome my authority over these wolves. She opens her mouth to command them once more. "Stand up and—" her voice cuts short as my claws reach in her mouth and rip her tongue out by its root, blood spitting itself onto my jet-black fur. She opens her mouth to scream, but her lack of a tongue dilutes the howl into a dulled moan of desperation. The feeling of hot blood rushing over her lips and onto my claws is euphoric. Though she could hypothetically order these Lycans telepathically, the agony she feels clouds her thinking. Her reign here is over, and mine is just beginning.

The Fang Clan has front row seats to watch me torment their alpha—the same alpha they followed into battle—the Sylvian who hates Lycans so much that she refused to shift into one.

I pivot my body so the second moon's light is no longer blocked by my looming figure. It shines brightly on Saunter's bloody face. It exposes every inch of feeble weakness she projects. She cannot hide under its glow. Luna watches from afar as I make an example of this coward for the whole kingdom to see.

*The light of the moon makes it easy to see how pathetic you look*, I growl, quoting some of Syrex's final words to Savrian. Saunter's lip quivers as she sobs. No temper tantrum she can muster will save her from what's to come.

*No one is coming to save you*, I whisper violently, quoting Lysander. *That second moon you see, that is the Creator's omen of my Master's coming, and I am the reckoning she's sent to prepare the way for her.*

*Syrus, please,* she begs one last time, speaking telepathically because her tongue lies dormant on the cold ground. *I know where Vesper is... I can bring you to her...*

*Keep my wife's name out of your fucking mouth*, I snarl. *Wherever she is, I can guarantee it's a much better place than where you're going. In blood, you are my sister*, I quote Savrian's final words to Savannah Sylvian. *But so many of those who were related to me by blood are now dead. Now, you will join them. Pray to your gods, and allow me to show you the power of my Devil.*

I lift her frail body by the neck and feel it crack and dislocate between my claws. *Hellhounds! Strip this body of its meat, then suck its bones dry of marrow!* I throw Saunter into the fray of the civil war she's started. For a brief moment, I see her body hover, as if she's trying to take flight. This is put to an end as several Lycans leap on her, claws hooking into her flesh. I hear a gurgled moan of pain and fear escape her mouth before it's snuffed out by the sound of snarling and tearing. My Hellhounds pile atop her fallen body until I can no longer see pale flesh; she is covered by a tumorous mass of vicious fur.

This is the first justice of many to come tonight. Somewhere in the heavens, Valor looks down and thanks me for avenging her death.

## 36

## THE HELLHOUNDS

Enchantress told me of this occurrence, but I didn't know what her words meant when she spoke them. *The fates have hidden what is to come, though I know what outcomes are possible from reading your father's future. Because of his bold decisions, the Sylvian bloodline lives on in you, and in your daughter. And because of his bold decisions, there is a third. This is the way it had to be, for the Undead Empire to be defeated.*

The third was Saunter all along. She was the necessary evil to aid me in transcending Death. Without her, I would not be all I am. She killed me, and through this act of hatred, she has made me stronger. This is the way it had to be, for the Undead Empire to be defeated. I could not take on my enemies as a mortal man. I had to be more. I *will* be more.

But now I have no use for Saunter in my life's story, so I watch the ravens pick her bones clean of their flesh now that my Hellhounds have feasted on her morsels. She is food for the birds and fertilizer for this vineyard. In years to come, I will gather these berries and savor the wine that sprouts from her death.

I embrace Sephora as she runs through the crowd of panting Lycans. My arms wrap around her silver fur and squeeze her so tight I fear I may break her ribs. Her wolfish figure whines as she nuzzles her snout against my chest. This war has changed her more than it has me. She has never witnessed death like this before. She has never had to kill to protect herself. Her whole life I protected her from this unfortunate outcome, yet it has found her nonetheless. For a brief moment, I am not Death Defeater and she is not commander of the Muzzled. We are just father and daughter. We let the war run its course as the world ends around us, and my arms refuse to let her go a moment sooner than I must.

*I watched you die,* she whispers telepathically, her throat whining like a pup who misses its mother. *I watched her rip your heart from your chest.*

*Death cannot take me away from you, my daughter,* I reply, unable to explain what's happened. *Where is your mother?*

*They took her, the Blackbloods. She was fighting Saunter one second, and the next she was gone. They swooped down and carried her away—three of them. They made off for the castle. She tried to fight back but they knocked her unconscious. That's when I retreated from the capital and ran into the Muzzled. Saunter sent Fang Clan after me. That she-wolf from Sygon almost caught me—Crixus—she was about to kill me, but one of the Muzzled intervened. I joined their ranks as they raided the city and commanded them to my will. That's how we got here.*

*How long has it been since I fell in battle?*

*I don't know,* she pants, a deranged look in her brows. *An hour? Maybe less? It has all happened so fast.*

*Syrus,* Crixus calls, emerging from the crowd. I hardly recognize her Lycan form anymore. She is covered with so much blood I can no longer see her fur's color. The feral look she had in her eyes as she fought Vesper is gone. Saunter's hold over her is gone. She is free of this curse, but the damage she's done in this war is irreparable. *I'm... I'm so sorry... I didn't mean to—*

I hold out my paw for Crixus to take. I can sense Sephora is frightened by her presence, still traumatized by the she-wolf's attempt on her life. Still though, I insist on Crixus taking hold of my hand.

*No, Syrus... I don't deserve your forgiveness...*

*You of all people, Crixus, deserve my forgiveness*, I reply. Now that I am her alpha again, she has control over the beast within. But I know how it feels to wake from some feverish dream and recount the atrocities I've committed as a Lycan. I spent my whole life dealing with this pain. She feels she is a monster, and so I must be the one to remind her we are more than our worst mistakes. We are not inherently evil. I love this woman despite her flaws and sins. All I can do is thank the gods she wasn't able to harm Sephora, or else we'd be having a different conversation right now.

*Savior...* Another voice calls to me from the fray, a wolf stumbling forward through the ranks to interrupt me and Crixus's mediation. This wolf, like Crixus, is covered in blood from snout to tail. But unlike Crixus, this Lycan is covered in his own blood. His body is ravaged beyond repair. His ears have been ripped from his skull. His scalp is split open and hanging from a loose thread of fur. His left arm is more skeleton than flesh, like a cooked chicken wing sucked of all meat. Guts and bowels hang from his abdomen. His jaw is dislocated from its socket and hangs unnaturally low. There is no amount of healing Dagon's Curse can do to fix this beast as he falls to his knees before me. As he dies, his body shifts back to its human form, retaining the injuries he can't repair. I know this man. Twenty-four moons I was a prisoner to the Muzzled, ten of which this man was the only company I had. He kneels across from me as he did a month ago, staring at me with the optimism of a child. From the smile on his face, it's almost like he doesn't know he's dying.

"I... I knew I was right," he moans without his lower jaw able to move. "Dagon's visions... Sent a savior... I knew it was Syrus. Watch-watched you fru-from across the cave. Day-Dagon has not for-sake-en us... Suh-I-Rus is our save-yor..."

I cringe as I realize I recognize this man's voice.

*Dad.* Sephora grips my arm tightly. *This is the Lycan that saved me. When Crixus was chasing me, he cut her off so I could get away.*

"Duh-otter of my suh-ave-yor... Suh-ilver eyes like her fuh-ah-ther." I see the dead skin around his mouth and know he was Muzzled. The scars on his cheek cut deep from many moons of his basket muzzle being tied too tight around his face. Crixus hears Sephora's words and looks at the damage she's done to this Lycan—someone from her own species. She shrinks away in fear of what she's done. Crixus has done much worse than kill this man. She has left him to suffer.

*Ophy,* I speak his name with a tone of adoration. I leave Sephora's side and kneel in front of him, wrapping my arms around his dying, human body. Here kneels the man I once regarded as a lunatic—the man responsible for seeing my potential long before it was apparent to myself. He wasn't crazy after all, I realize. All he prophesied has come to pass. I have risen as this species' savior. I have liberated the Muzzled. I have unified our forces. I am the most powerful of us all.

A month ago, this epiphany seemed impossible. But Ophy prayed for me daily, asking Dagon to give me the strength it takes to do what I've been destined for. Sometimes it takes a stranger to remind us who we are. Sometimes they can see something in us we're too afraid to become.

*You saved my daughter, Ophy. For that, I can never repay you.*

"Yu-ooo can, sayorrr," he groans happily, his tongue doing all it can to speak without assistance of his jaw. "Ree-memba me, Son of Day-gawn..." His hand trembles as he points his remaining arm at the second moon. "Suh-ine of Cree-aye-tor... Chosen one... Yu-ooo are Chosen One, Suh-I-Russs..."

*Find Skathen in the afterlife, Ophetus*, I command, speaking his full name with reverence. *He will be waiting for you. He will protect your soul in Death.*

"Skuh-skuh-aye-th..." His voice trails off as he goes limp in my arms. Ophy died for what he believed in. There are few ways more honorable than this in passing. I will see him in the afterlife. Devout, loyal, unwavering faith. He believed in me more than I believed in myself. I will have need for Hellhounds like him in whatever comes next. I lower his fickle body to the vineyard's ground. Whatever grapes spring forth from this patch of grass, I will make sure their wine is drank in remembrance of my most loyal servant, Ophetus.

Two more wolves approach Crixus's side. I instantly recognize them as Creon and Scar, both of their bodies actively healing wounds incurred by Muzzled opponents. Creon speaks, his words humbled now more than ever, *I am sorry for mocking you all those moons, Ophy. You prayed for me when no one else would. You were patient with my ignorance. I now realize the error of my ways, for doubting your visions. I only wish you were alive to forgive me.*

It is the sincerest apology I've ever heard from Creon. He is not the sort of man who asks forgiveness regularly, and I know his heart is shattered to see one of his fellow Muzzled fallen from this useless battle. Creon and Scar, like Crixus, were subsumed by Saunter's false leadership. Because of their nature as Lycans, she perverted them into killing their own kind needlessly, and their defeated demeanors reflect they are disturbed by their actions.

The entire Fang Clan recognizes the error of their ways. The Muzzled, on the other hand, see no abnormality in this civil war. They have spent many moons killing their fellow Hellhounds. They've accepted it as the way life is. This war has merely been a larger scale iteration of every full moon they've endured under Bloodlust. We need unity now more than ever. And I'm going to provide it.

*Hellhounds*, I speak, leaving behind Ophy's body for all to see the consequences of their actions. I am not here to lecture them. They are not children who need a scolding. They need a Lysander to direct them to victory, and I know now I can be that for them. *Members of the Fang Clan, you saw me stand before you and listened to my words. I told you that tonight, we must endure bloodshed a final time. I said to you that together, we will usher in a new age of peace, one where Lycans and Undead live amongst each other in fellowship. And I said to you, Hellhounds, that we will not let the monsters inside us dictate our abilities to love one another. I said these words to you, and I meant them. But that was before my heart was ripped from my chest. Now I stand before you as Defeater of Death. And now I say to you, any dream I had of peace died with the dormant heart laying on capital square. The new moon above us orbits as a testament to my resurrection. I am the Defeater of Death, an omen foretold of for thousands of years. Fear not, my Hellhounds, for you are on my side. Have fear only for those who stand opposed to us, for they are the ones who will soon meet their demise with the gnashing of our fangs. Change can come with time, but it can also be forced through violence. Truly, I say to you, I don't give a fuck who sits on the throne. We must be our own kings tonight.*

I quote Lysander's words because no words of my own will do this moment justice. *Tonight, no one is coming to save us. It is only us. We are the only thing standing in the way of the Lycanthrope's extinction. Let that sink in, Hellhounds. You who are Muzzled know what the Blackbloods will do if we lose. And you of Fang Clan know we will live in exile so long as the Undead reign supreme. We can only force change through bloodshed. The old ways must die for the new to prosper. Death is coming for this kingdom, but we are on its side. We are Death's facilitators. We are the hounds that guard hell's gates, and tonight we will welcome all who wish to burn in its eternal fires. So, I say to you, my Hellhounds, rise! Rise, and follow me to the Areopagus Throne! Tonight, we purge all who stand in our way!*

The Lycans rise and let out a synchronized howl pitched in a way that shakes the earth's foundation. The new moon above welcomes us. Luna shrinks in the distance. This is not the first time she's seen Lycans storm a kingdom for the throne. She knows what will come. Many will pay the price for the gods' choice to oppose me.

Memories of Skathen opposing Enchantress fade in my mind. I feel too powerful to consider the consequences of what I've done. I owe my life to her. She is the only reason I have these powers. Her words come to me now: *It's so humorous, watching you humans speak as if you know the meaning of life, as if you have all the answers.* I won't pretend to know why Skathen hates her, nor will I pretend to have the answers.

If she was so evil, she wouldn't have let me see Skathen, nor would she let me know his true identity. Seeing myself in the afterlife was cryptic—it was like seeing the past and present all at once. On the one hand, I saw those who came before me, those who are long dead now. On the other hand, Skathen is a vision of what I'm to become. But the future isn't certain. It's always changing with every decision I make. Maybe she showed me him as a warning, or maybe she wants me to become him. There's too much uncertainty. I can't waste time reflecting on it now.

The collective howl of our unit vibrates through my body and into my newly loaned heart.

"My Lord," Nikolai shouts as he descends from the sky with his Undead battalion. He lands behind me and I watch as my Hellhound army prepares to attack. Their hackles raise on their backs and their snouts snarl at the sight of Undead. Nikolai staggers back, afraid of the Lycanthrope forces. Not all the booze in the world can comfort Nikolai as they prepare to lunge at him.

I raise my arm and speak telepathically to my wolves, *Be still, Hellhounds! Take in these Undeads' scent, they are on our side! Not a single one of them is to be injured by you. They oppose the Emperor and have joined us in our cause.* The wolves pause and their demeanor changes at the snap of fingers. Their nostrils lift to the air and sniff the aroma of Nikolai and his companions, memorizing their scent.

Nikolai regains footing and stands his ground as he sees the Hellhounds relent. "My Lord," he repeats, ignoring my army's reaction to him and his species. "The Blackbloods and Undead heard your howling and see you're unified. They left us alone when you waged war against one another, but they're coming now."

I nod to acknowledge his words, looking to the sky to see thousands of silhouettes coming to stamp out the sparks we fan. Black wings and purple eyes blot out the stars above. This is the moment we've all been waiting for, and as Death's instrument, I can't help but smile at their arrival.

*Let's go get your mother back, Sephora*, I growl, flexing my claws at my side as I prepare to show these demons why I am the one fit to rule this empire.

# 37

## WOLFSBANE WARFARE

The Undead have the Black Knights, and the Blackbloods have the Dread. The Black Knights are the kingdom's elite force of police power sworn to protect the crown. Also known as the Soulless to commoners, they kill without remorse. Their reign of terror has kept this kingdom in fear for decades. They were a gift from the Celestials to my father when our kingdoms merged, and they were the same knights responsible for killing my family when I was ten.

And then there is the Dread—Bloodlust's chief executioners and vicious fiends dedicated to leading the Blackblood armies in war. Designated by bat wings branded into the back of their hands, the Dread are easy to spot out of a crowd of Blackbloods. They are substantially larger and their bodies are more rotted than the average Blackblood. The longer an Undead is infected with the Blackblood virus, the more it perverts the nature of their body. At first, the virus makes itself known with black varicose veins rising to the flesh's surface. Then, wings sprout from their back. Slowly, the black blood seeps from their veins and dyes the color of their skin. Their bones turn to spears and rip from their skin. Their silver hair falls out and their flesh corrodes until they are walking skeletons. The Dread are amongst the oldest members of the Blackblood regime, and the virus has impacted their bodies beyond those who've recently joined their ranks. They've sworn their lives to protect Bloodlust in the same way the Black Knights have sworn to protect Ventur, though neither fighting force knows their master is the same.

Both forces descend upon the vineyard with the intention of slaughtering us Lycans before we can formulate an organized attack on the Areopagus Castle. The Dread and Black Knights set aside their differences and land amongst us with lethal intentions. There are few things Undead and Blackbloods can agree on, but killing Lycans is one of them.

My hackles raise as the first knight touches down. The royal guard was responsible for killing my father, mother, and sister. The vision Enchantress showed me from childhood is still fresh in my memory. I can still picture them decapitating mother as she made a final stand to protect me. I can still see them stabbing father mercilessly as he guarded Selena's body from their attack. Ventur will pay, but his precious guard will pay first.

I utter a single word command to my legion of Hellhounds as the Dread and Blackbloods make contact. *Kill*, I whisper, like a hunter sending his dog after prey. They obey their master with utmost devotion.

Crixus, Creon, and Scar surround me and Sephora like a protective triangle. *Till our hearts beat no more*, Crixus growls. Creon and Scar finish the sentiment simultaneously. *We will cherish the sacred hunt*.

There are no front lines to this battle. It is not the same as an army charging another, shields raised and spears pointed. Instead, it is much like the war I witnessed between Lysander's Acolytes and Marduk's Blackbloods.

Black Knights and Blackbloods crash to the ground between us Lycans, greeted by the sound of snapping jaws and slashing claws. It is just a sample of what's to come.

The sound of fangs on metal is not one I'm particularly used to, but I will never forget it after tonight. Nor is the sound of Blackbloods begging for mercy, but I will savor and memorize its harmony tonight.

A Dread demon approaches me and meets my own royal guard. Crixus familiarizes him with her claws. Scar introduces him to his fangs. Creon stares in his eyes as he severs his rotting skull from his shoulders. It's enough to make a grown man smile. All those months we spent prisoner to these demons, and I now see we had the power to defeat them this entire time. That is the problem with bondage—it is a mindset, not a reality. Once one gathers the courage to defy what keeps them captive, they learn the price for freedom is not one they cannot pay. Rather, fear keeps them dormant and submissive.

As my Hellhounds go to war for me, I watch Nikolai and his fellow Undead go blow for blow with their own kind. I can hear the Black Knights mocking Nikolai as a traitor, shortly before he pierces their hearts with his cold steel staff. His weapon is not one I'm familiar with. It's a double-tipped spear effective for blocking sword strikes, yet Nikolai can detach it in the middle, allowing him to wield each half like dual short swords. Though I've never seen a weapon like this before, I see now it's bloody efficient at killing.

I can say many things about Nikolai. He's a drunk. He's a gambler. He's a cheat. He's an addict. But despite those flaws, the man is a damn good swordsman. Twenty years it's been since he left the Black Knights and the man hasn't lost a step. They don't make soldiers like him anymore. The Black Knights can't keep up with his rapid blows and vicious strikes.

And his fellow Undead traitors aren't far behind in skillset. Their weapons—a mix of swords and spears and axes—ring out in the night like instruments playing a concert for Luna above. There is so much disunion, so much chaos, yet Nikolai and his band of fighters maintain composure through it all. Other than Sygon, this is my first time taking part in an official war. I can see how it would be easy to lose your head. So much happens so fast. We are surrounded by enemies on all sides. Swords fall. Jaws reply. It's easy to get lost in it and fail to see more opponents pouring in to strike you down from behind.

My Lycans continue to do what Lycans do best. There is no method to their madness. They leap from prey to prey, some dying in the process, others prevailing against numerous enemies before their hunt is put to an end. Crixus yelps as a sword skewers her shoulder. Hearing her in pain tears at my heartstrings and provokes me to wrath, but before I can do anything, she severs the hand responsible for the attack and forces the knight's body to kneel before her, blood gushing from his arm stump. She sends him to his death swiftly, then rips the sword from her shoulder and throws it atop his corpse. *Till my heart beats no more*, she grunts inwardly.

I examine the blade she's thrown to the ground, worried it is forged from silver. I wipe the blood away to expose the metal and breathe a sigh of relief. Thank the gods, it is steel.

Undead normally bring silver to the battlefield, but they had no idea they'd be fighting Lycans tonight. It's the luck of the draw whether a Black Knight wields silver or steel, likely up to the wielder's preference. Crixus's wound will heal, but I have no one to thank but Enchantress that Death won't claim her this time around.

Scar and Creon are like brothers separated at birth the way they rip through their adversaries. Without speaking a single word, the two double team everyone that stands in opposition. Creon grabs a Black Knight's leg in his maw and Scar bites down on his opposite arm. The two pull away from each other until the Undead's body is torn in two at the torso, his bowels stretching like the gooey cheese of a fried mozzarella stick. A Dread opens Scar's back from shoulder to hip with a swipe of its claws, instantly regretting its action as Scar turns to face it. Scar's jaws are big enough to clamp down on the demon's entire neck. He violently removes the Dread's throat from operating, reminding me of a crazed surgeon. The black blood flies in all directions, some of it landing at me and Sephora's feet. I pull her close, unwilling to lose sight of her again.

Creon seems to be in his natural environment now that he's loosed from his human bondage and able to take part in a proper moondance.

Just this morning, Enchantress warned me Creon would betray me—in fact, she showed Creon a vision of the future revealing such. But as I watch him kill for my cause, it's hard to imagine him ever being capable of turning against me. Him betraying me wouldn't be the same as Saunter doing so. Forgiving Saunter was poor judgment on my part. But Creon? Creon has never done me wrong whatsoever. On the contrary, he has bled for my cause. He has made my objectives his own. And now, he spills blood in my name like an Acolyte on behalf of Lysander.

Creon is an equal opportunity killer. He fells Black Knights and Dread alike, neither doing much to deter him from his rage. With every kill he gets under his belt, he seems to grow with power, loosing himself to his bloodrage. *That the best you got, bloodsuckers?* Creon howls at the top of his lungs, his enemies not able to hear his telepathic wrath. Instead, the inward taunt manifests itself as a deep-throated growl.

Two Dread to my right pin Scar to the ground and paint their bodies with his red blood. Crixus launches herself onto one of their backs and carves it like a sculptor expressing displeasure with a botched clay sculpture. Creon goes after the other, tackling him off Scar's fallen body and rolling through grape vines in a mass of fur and rotten flesh. Creon arises victorious, and Crixus helps Scar to his feet as her prey lays broken beneath them. They step over his corpse and launch themselves at their next target.

*Wolfsbane torches!* a Lycan shouts from the distance. My ears snap in their direction and see a troop of Black Knights on the horizon with torches blazing in their hands. They soar through the night sky with pillars of smoke leaving a trail of wolfsbane ash floating behind them. Among them, several Undead fighters carry a crate filled with various weapons forged from silver, the cargo suspended by chains held by four separate warriors. This is how the Undead managed to drive Lycans to the brink of extinction. Silver and Wolfsbane are lethal to our kind, and our adversaries leverage these weaknesses against us every chance they get.

If permitted arrival, these Black Knights will smoke us out with their fiery torches and supply their army with silver swords. My Hellhounds will be slaughtered with little protest. The Fang Clan likely has exposure therapy to Wolfsbane like myself, but the Muzzled hasn't had contact with the toxic herb in many moons, and neither Tribe is able to defend against silver. The tides of war will shift exponentially against us and leave us defenseless against the reaping.

I lock eyes with Nikolai and point at the torch bearers, then drag my index finger in a slit across my throat. Nikolai puts the pieces together and leaps into action. "Undead, with me!" He and his soldiers rip into the atmosphere like arrows aimed for the oncoming threats. Ironically enough, the Soulless see their purple eyes approaching and assume Nikolai's forces are on their side, not comprehending the treachery Nikolai plans to enact. They make no attempt to intercept him until Nikolai drives his spear into the leader's chest, knocking the burning wolfsbane torch from his grip. It plummets to the ground a hundred yards short of the battlefield. The other

Black Knights see their leader drop from the sky and scramble their flight patterns to avoid Nikolai's raiding party.

"Traitor!" they scream in hysteria.

"Tell me something I don't know," Nikolai chuckles, hiccuping from his drunkenness as he drop kicks an Undead carrying the cargo container of silver weapons. The chain drops and the cargo box tips over, spilling its contents onto the ground below, far short of where the Black Knights need it for it to be accessible. Nikolai makes short change of the other cargo holders, their hands unable to drop their chains and draw their swords fast enough to defend against his rain of blows.

The remainder of the torch holders die quickly at the hands of Nikolai's army, all of them plummeting to the ground long before the smoke of their wolfsbane can breach the perimeter of Lycans it was meant to kill. We got lucky this time around, but that won't be the last attempt the Undead make at putting a quick end to us. The Undead will do anything to snuff out our fire. We need to keep moving if we're to reach the castle in one piece. We are sitting ducks in this field, our forces tightly packed together. We need to spread out and mobilize.

*Hellhounds!* I shout, my voice traveling directly to my soldiers' minds to be easily heard over the bloodshed. *Make for the castle! If the Undead and Blackbloods want to fight us, we will make them chase us through the city streets!*

I grab Sephora and guide her off the battlefield. My soldiers finish the kills they're currently working on and drop to all fours, following my lead as I leave the vineyards behind to be watered by Undead and Dread blood alike.

# 38

## THE BIGGER THEY ARE, THE HARDER THEY FALL

The city landscape of Areopagus separates us from charging uniformly, but it also forces our enemy to pick us apart separately. If the Undead want to smoke us out with wolfsbane, they'll need to cover the whole city with its smog. They stand little chance at stopping us. Without a centralized commander to direct their actions they are like a headless snake writhing to adapt. The war with the Blackbloods has distracted them from the real threat, and neither Bloodlust nor Ventur has made an appearance to mitigate the damage of this war.

It has been twenty years since I've ran through these streets, but I still know them like the back of my hand. The Areopagus was built with its Castle as the centerpiece of it all. The Castle's wealth trickles into its nearby fiefs, flowing fief by fief until there is little prosperity left to be spread. Four military sectors are built on the city's perimeter—one in the north, a second in the south, and one in the east and west, forming a cross-like shape with the Castle at their equal radius. Four military sectors, four times more firepower than any fief across this land.

When I was a child, these sectors were the pride of our kingdom. A place of integration between humans and Undead. A place where boys and girls came, but graduated as men and women, their fighting skills honed and recruited to one of the Areopagus Military's unique branches. Now that this place belongs to the Undead Empire, only Undead make up the military, and humans have been forced into positions as bloodbags. So much has changed in such little time. The lack of human optimism has struck this kingdom with destitution.

This kingdom is a shadow of its former glory. Inns and taverns and bakeries are empty shells. Most buildings are skeletons, the Undead instead burrowing underground to build crypts safe from the sun's exposure. Nature has risen to consume the empty streets. Grass grows between cobblestones, and vines of ivy eat whole buildings. The Wirewood's residual flooding is enough to topple over whole structures, wiping them from existence and carrying their rocky fixtures down the city streets as we wade through the rough waters.

We Lycans no longer run on all fours, the waters around us surging at our waistline. The Wirewood Dam erupted in the northeast, and we are in the south. Its roaring waters flow wherever there is no resistance, and its tsunami has worked its way from the northeast to our marching path in the south, pushing against us as we fight against its riptide. We shoulder through the rapids together, our fur soaked as we move north.

I make sure to keep Crixus close, knowing she can't swim. If she loses a single step the waters would suck her up and consume her completely. The she-wolf marches on my right side, and Sephora on my left. Scar is ahead of me and Creon tails us with the rest of our wolfpack.

The light of the new moon lights our way like a second sun. Little darkness fills these streets with its added illumination. Because of this, I'm able to see shadows soar over us as winged demons circle above. I curse, wishing we could make more progress before our next attack. A pack of Blackbloods crash to the ground in front of us, splashing a plume of river water like a child cannonballing into a swimming pool. Our path is effectively cut off, either side of us surrounded with wall-to-wall buildings. Can't go over them, can't go under them. We'll have to go through them.

Their leader is a member of the Dread, and damnit if he isn't the biggest and ugliest bastard I've ever seen. He is twice my height and his shoulders are nearly wide enough to touch the buildings on either side of us. His wings spread and scrape against the mortar walls, breaking what little remains of the glass windows in these abandoned buildings. His fellow Blackbloods trail behind him, like my army around me, each of them large in their own right but dwarfed by the presence of the Dread monstrosity. His fangs are the size of a wine bottle, long enough to go in one side of my neck and out the other. His hands end in talons sharp enough to split air in two. The batwing branding on the back of his hand marking him as Dread looks as small as a freckle. His face is so rotten I can see chunks of his skull beneath the shriveled tapestry of his head. His ribs have outgrown his chest and protrude like a mountainous range of valleys and ridges. His eyes are black and silent, exposing their emotionless gaze beneath the moon's radiance.

*Since when were Blackbloods this bloody big?* Creon shouts, passing me and Sephora to approach Scar's side. *This guy's about half the size of your schlong, Scar. What do you think of that?* Creon laughs at his own joke. Scar growls in response, spreading his feet in a wide base.

"I am Vorgoth the Dread. I've been sent by Bloodlust, King of Blackbloods," the Dread bellows, foul phlegm flinging from his decomposed lips. "I've come for the Sylvian leader. You there, silver eyes," he points at me. "We've come for you. No harm need come to your Muzzled if you follow us."

*Till our hearts beat no more*, Creon laughs.

*We will cherish the sacred hunt*, Scar finishes. Turning me over to our enemy is not even a thought in their minds. These two would sooner die for my cause than see me be taken captive by bloodsuckers. I smile inwardly. A moon ago, we were mere strangers. Now, we are closer than blood relatives. We've been bonded through trauma and adversity. Molded by life's many sufferings. We've lost loved ones together, been betrayed together, conquered death together. I doubt this Dread knows what force he reckons with.

"We have your bitch wife captured," Vorgoth shouts as Creon and Scar sling themselves at him.

*They have mom, dad!* Sephora calls from my side.

*We knew that, Seph. Your mother can handle herself. We will be with her shortly*, I reply, watching as Vorgoth's fist splatters Scar's wolfish body into a wall to our right like a fly hit with a swatter. Scar's enormous frame breaks through the rubble and the dilapidated building collapses atop him.

*Scar!* Crixus yells, jumping into action. Creon howls as he lands on the Dread's arm and sinks his fangs deep in the rotting flesh. Only now do I see the disparity between Creon and the Dread's figure. The Dread's arm itself is longer than Creon's Lycan form and nearly thick as his torso. Whoever chiseled this demon from clay forgot to complete the work until he was normal proportions.

Creon's bite is like a paper cut on a demigod's pinky finger. It does nothing to deter Vorgoth from ripping Creon's jaws free and submerging his head in the roaring waters.

Creon's body thrashes like a fish out of water as his oxygen leaves him bubble after bubble. He's drowning, helpless against Vorgoth's almighty hold. That is, until Crixus arrives on the scene, ducking under Vorgoth's arm and sinking a mouth full of fangs into the demon's gonads. All men have their weaknesses, and no matter how big they are, their ballsack remains their ultimate shortcoming. Vorgoth hisses in pain, releasing Creon's head to retrieve Crixus from his privates. Her canines rip his genitalia clean off as she retreats behind him, black blood spurting from the space between his thighs. This Blackblood will never make love again, nor will he have the pride of calling himself a man. This war has impacted us all, but it will impact Vorgoth in ways few can understand.

Creon emerges from the brink of death, gasping and panting. Black blood from Vorgoth's ballsack splashes on him and gets in his mouth. Creon looks at the source of the bleeding, disfigured member and throws his head back into the water, spitting and screaming for all us to hear, *Ball blood! Ball blood in my mouth!* Crixus climbs up the brute's back, severing his thick wings at their root.

Wolfsram and an entire army of ravens descend from the sky.

"Revenge!" Wolfsram caws loud enough for the Dread to look to the sky. Wolfsram's beak impales Vorgoth's eyeball, causing it to explode upon impact. Another raven plucks the opposite eyeball from its socket. The host of ravens accompanying them go after the other Blackbloods behind Vorgoth, consuming them with a tornado of black wings. Wolfsram retreats from Vorgoth's swatting hand as it slaps his bleeding eye. It triggers my memory of ravens attacking a thyrops in an attempt to save me. Fond memories, but now it's time to make more for future reflection.

Wolfsram lands on my shoulder, his beak covered in black blood.

Crixus does what Crixus does best, enacting violence on her victim like Vorgoth is her lifelong mortal enemy. The legion of Blackbloods behind are dazed and frustrated as ravens tear into them like insects picking apart a corpse. Creon lifts from the water, his fur sufficiently soaked yet washed clean of black blood. His claws are paintbrushes and Vorgoth's body is Creon's canvas, opening his midsection with lines of obsidian blood with every masterful stroke.

The demon swats in every direction possible, but he is blind, and all he can do is react to the places he feels pain. Crixus hops from spot to spot, attacking at his most vulnerable pressure points, but she is never in the same spot by the time Vorgoth strikes, and now he has Creon to worry about as well.

"My lord!" Nikolai calls from overhead, "Undead archers with silver arrows!" I look to the sky and see a unit of archers land on the rooftops surrounding us. We are sitting ducks for them to open fire at. Without being told, Nikolai and his battalion attack the archers, but they can't be everywhere at once, and there is no telling how many arrows will be loosed before they're put down.

*Hellhounds!* I yell, *Scale the walls!*

My army scatters to both sides and sinks their claws into the brick and mortar buildings as the arrows take flight. Sephora and I remain put, undaunted by the silver arrows because they hold no lethality over us. We are Sylvian; these archers will need much more than silver to put either one of us down. The fur on my upper back and neck stands as I hear wolves get hit with arrows during their climb. I watch in fury as several of them fall, splashing into the roaring waters to never be seen again. Creon and Crixus take shelter from the volley of missiles under Vorgoth's wingspan. Silver arrows smack into the Dread's massive frame like splinters into a calloused hand. Still, the arrows are enough to get a reaction out of him, distracting his attention while Crixus slits his achilles tendons from behind, then opens his thighs along the sciatic nerve, causing the great behemoth to fall to his knees.

Wolves yelp as arrows continue to pierce their bodies, but most have made it to the rooftops now, greeting the archers with their fangs and claws. Nikolai's soldier's cut the bowstrings and kick the Undead from the rooftops, causing them to fall directly onto the host of Blackbloods behind Vorgoth. Lycans jump from the rooftops onto the Blackbloods as the archers' numbers dwindle. Everything is utter chaos, and I haven't even lifted a finger. I am the heartbeat of my Hellhounds, and they go to war for me like extensions of my vengeance-filled mind.

For hundreds of years our species has waited for this day. Exiled, beaten, enslaved, deprived of life's many joys. We have been told we are monsters, and we have been treated as such. Vengeance hasn't been ours since Sylvian the First led Dagon's pack against Cardone, and since then we have sulked in the shadows, judged by the content of our curse rather than the quality of our character. No more. If the Undead and Blackbloods want to call us monsters, we will show them what kind of monsters we truly are.

I hear Lycans whispering from all around me in synchronization. *Till our hearts beat no more.* Gnashing fangs, snapping jaws. *We will cherish the sacred hunt.* Slashing claws, dying breaths. *Till our hearts beat no more.* The river at my feet has turned black from the blood of our enemies. *We will cherish the sacred hunt.* Vorgoth's body collapses, Crixus and Creon standing atop his back like conquerors of some foreign land. *Till our hearts beat no more.* Wolves howl all around me, provoking wolves in the distance to howl as they advance toward the Areopagus Castle. *We will cherish the sacred hunt.* Creon and Crixus join a pack of Lycans who dig at the rubble of the collapsed building, uncovering Scar's fallen body. They pull him from the destruction and submerge him in water, the cold chill bringing him back to consciousness. Scar jolts to life, welcomed by his brethren howling victoriously. We have won this battle, screaming at the new moon with our howl as we let Ventur know both his armies have failed yet again at quashing our rebellion.

*We are coming for you, Emperor*, I whisper inwardly.

# 39

## A True Leader

Over and over we Lycans show the Undead we are the superior species, and Nikolai shows them it is better to be on our side than a subject of our wrath. We could have existed in peace, but these demons chose violence. They killed my daughter in front of me, making me believe she died for my faults for two years. They've stolen my wife after ripping out my heart. They've enslaved my baby boy, a child I didn't know existed until hours ago. They murdered my parents. They replaced Selena with Saunter, a delinquent psychopath in place of an innocent, kindhearted girl. This coupe is personal, and my Hellhounds communicate my rage with their massacre.

But as we arrive to the castle's doorstep, I see why we've been so successful up to this point.

*Take cover!* I howl to my remaining soldiers as a volley of silver arrows launches to exterminate us once and for all. It was a mistake to come from the south. The castle's front entrance faces south, and Ventur's entire army of Black Knights and infantry stands posted along the perimeter of the castle like pawns and rooks on a chest board preparing for war. An entire row of infantrymen stand with wolfsbane torches in hand, their collective column of smoke rising around the Areopagus Castle like a shroud of fog. I can smell its potency from the central courtyard, the path my league of Lycans chose for launching our attack.

This is the same courtyard Ventur once carried me over his shoulder through after my family was massacred. I can still see the Bloodmaple he nearly burned to death under. It stands slightly taller and wider, aged by twenty years in my absence. Its crimson leaves rustle in the violent summer breeze.

The castle's front courtyard was once a thing of beauty. People would travel across the kingdoms just to get a glance at its maze of gardens and wildlife, its labyrinth of hedges and stone statues dedicated to knights and rulers of old ages. But the Undead do not cherish the beauty of nature during the day and have paid little attention to this sanctuary's former glory. It is now a miniature jungle of its own, overgrown with weed trees and wild grass. The statues of Sylvian kings have been decimated to rubble and consumed by poison ivy. An onlooking stranger to this kingdom would see this land as nothing more than an eyesore, never knowing it was once a slice of heaven on earth.

I suppose it was nostalgia that made my subconscious mind choose this as my path for attack. The way I see it, I was chased out of this kingdom through this courtyard, so there's no better place for me to arrive to retake my throne. But the Undead won't go down without a fight, so me and my Hellhounds dive for cover as arrows blot out the new moon above, intent on striking us dead before we can even reach the castle's doorstep.

A host of ravens, led by Wolfsram, passes over like a dark cloud, intercepting the flying arrows with their bodies. I watch everything unfold as Wolfsram catches an arrow with his beak, while other ravens are skewered completely and fall to the earth, another painful sacrifice heaped atop the others that have died in this war. We will avenge them, like we will avenge the long list of heroes that died too soon for my cause.

But first, I need to find a way to disrupt the Undead Empire's front lines. My army of Lycans can go no further without something changing. The infantry is armed with silver swords and daggers, each of which requires only one well-placed cut on a Hellhound to poison their blood and discharge their souls from earth. And the air around them is filled with the particles of burned wolfsbane from their torches. Its smog is so thick it will kill my soldiers before they can even break free from its haze.

Nikolai's forces rendezvous with the other Lycan branches that arrive to the east and west of my position, telling them to remain put until I've devised a plan. But the truth is, I am at a loss for ways to overcome this foe. When I arrived in Areopagus hours ago, I had no idea I'd even make it this far. Sephora and I are the only Lycans present with a tolerance for silver, but two cannot take on an entire army, and I won't let my daughter be put in harm's way for a war I started. It's only now that doubt starts to creep in. So many are relying on me. So many have died to get us this far. Damn our species' curse! I don't know what to do.

Arrows continue to fly and ravens continue to drop, sacrificing themselves by the hundreds. My mind is panicking. Think damnit, think! Enchantress wouldn't have brought me this far for it to all end in failure. I refuse to believe that. She has guided me every step of the way. So what do I do? How can I disrupt this army long enough for my Hellhounds to besiege the castle?

There is no answer that awaits me.

No one is coming to save us.

We have failed.

The Blackbloods will soon flank us from behind and the Undead will advance with their wolfsbane torches and silver weapons. I've single-handedly doomed my army and signed their deaths with my own blood. Even with all my power and strength, I won't be strong enough to save Sephora, to rescue Vesper, to retake my throne. Atlas would have thought this through, he was the one with enough charisma to draw thousands of Acolytes to his cause. I am an imposter. I wasn't fit for leadership as a child, and I'm certainly no different now.

*How long will you continue to doubt yourself, human?* the beast within growls inside my head. *How is it your army has more faith in you than yourself?*

Because they think I have a plan, when really I've just trapped them between a rock and a hard place.

*Is that how you view this? Do you think Sylvian the First cringed as Damon's Clans went to war against Dagon? Do you think he feared the outcome as brother clashed against brother, reducing an entire city to smithereens? Do you think he counted the many lives lost that bought him power over this kingdom and secured his line of royalty until your father's death? Don't be so naive, Syrus. You came here for power, and this is what power costs. You have died for this cause, and you have been resurrected to see it through. Everyone here knows you are the Defeater of Death. They saw your heart ripped from your chest. These Hellhounds do not follow you because you promised them life. They came to support your cause because you promised freedom. So stand, coward, and take back what is rightfully yours.*

Fire burns inside my veins as I stand before thinking my next step through.

*Syrus!* Crixus calls from behind me, lurking behind the rubble of some long forgotten statue.

*Dad!* Sephora calls.

My silver eyes shine on their fragile bodies as I make up my mind. *Crixus,* I growl, *Protect my daughter with your life.*

*Till my heart beats no more,* she responds, fearful of what she sees in my eyes.

Scar and Creon stand, ready to follow me.

*Down, soldiers,* I bark, ordering nothing short of obedience. *You two have gotten me here. Now it's my turn to pay back all you've done.*

Creon mutters, *But Syrus—*

*It was an order, not a question, Creon.*

I leave them behind, trudging through the thickets of the courtyard I once ran from to save my life. No more running. No more hiding. If the Undead Empire wants me dead, now is their chance. But if they mess this up, all the power they've stolen will finally be back with its rightful owner. The beast within was wrong in one regard. I am not the same as Sylvian the First. The lives I lose matter to me. And unlike Sylvian the First, I do not watch this war from the city's outskirts, reaping its benefits from afar. I am on the frontlines, and I will sacrifice as much as my army has sacrificed for me. A true leader leads by example, and I intend to set the bloodiest example this world has ever seen. I leave my Hellhounds behind, and that's when I hear a thunder of footfall storming in the distance.

My heart drops as the ground beneath me shakes. Surely the Blackbloods aren't here already. No, that can't be Blackbloods. They wouldn't flank us from the ground, they would attack from the air. I look to the sky and see only the wings of ravens in close proximity. I twist my head around to see what is able to cause such a commotion. And that's when I hear the voice of a demon in mortal flesh bellow, "Purple eyes! Mammoth kill!"

There, only a hundred yards away, is a man the size of Vorgoth, the chains that once held him hostage now wrapped around his fists as he leads an army of freed prisoners from the Bloody Tower. There are few people in this world who hate the Undead Empire more than me, but this battalion is composed entirely of warriors who wish to see the Undead be put to extinction once and for all.

The orders I gave Mammoth were simple. Purple eyes, black wings, Mammoth kill. And here, displayed in organized fashion, is an entire army of purple eyes waiting for Mammoth to make good on his promise.

I smile, then charge toward the castle.

# 40

## REVENGE. REVENGE. REVENGE.

All the silver weapons and wolfsbane torches in the world can't stop Mammoth from what he's come to do. I was there when the Emperor briefed the Black Knights, but they were not prepared for the events of tonight. Unlike Lycans, Mammoth has no weaknesses. And at first glance, Mammoth and his small retinue of prisoners from the Bloody Tower may seem like a suicidal pack of lunatics, but I know better. This is the warrior from Greylock my father sent entire armies to vanquish. A man so large he once used a mammoth's tusk as a spear. A man who took a stand for all he knew and loved and fought till his last breath, then spent decades imprisoned for defying the hierarchical order of this world.

The ogreish man pays us Lycans no attention as he runs past us lurking in the shadows. After all, his orders were simple. *If you see any wolves, leave them be. The wolves are on our side*, I instructed. Purple eyes. Black wings. Mammoth kill. I can appreciate his devotion to simplicity.

Behind Mammoth are dozens of prisoners he's freed from the Bloody Tower. I know none of them, though I'm sure they each have equally terrifying backgrounds to supplement their sentences. They carry with them weapons they've stolen from the dead they've killed and wear armor they've stripped from corpses. They scream like bloodthirsty demons as they charge their captors. Tonight is a night of revenge. For me. For Enchantress. But especially for these men.

The Undead panic as they divert their attention from lurking Lycans to the oncoming threat. Archers ready their arrows. Knights form a shield wall, digging their feet in the ground and bringing spears to bear.

"Fire!" an Undead yells. A volley of arrows is unleashed, no longer aimed for Lycans and ravens but instead aimed directly at Mammoth and his rebels. Mammoth twirls his chains like a cyclone in front of his body and knocks the projectiles away, then leaps into the air with supernatural strength. A man that big shouldn't be able to jump so high, I reflect in wonder as he closes the several dozen feet that stand between himself and the front lines. When Mammoth lands, he does so with a maelstrom of blows, his chains knocking shields and spears aside to create an opening for his fists to follow.

He shouts, "New Greylock!" as he obliterates an entire section of the Undead's frontline defense, giving his fellow prisoners time to catch up and launch themselves into the fray. His fists are the size of three skulls, and every chain-wrapped punch he throws dents Undead helms inward to shatter the face they shield. "Purple eyes, Mammoth kill!" he yells as he whips his colossal chains around, breaking breastplates and ribs in the process. There are hundreds of Undead, but this won't be the first time Mammoth has faced unwinnable odds and prevailed.

My silver eyes shine through the veil of wolfsbane smoke as I approach the front lines. My enemy doesn't even notice me, too concerned with their collapsing defense to spot a ghost among vapor. All the better, I think to myself as I cut a knight nearly in half with my claws, then disappear in the mist. Strategically, I bob in and out of the transient smoke, claiming more souls with my bloodied fangs and claws with every advance and retreat. I aim for archers first, who point their bows at Mammoth and pay little attention to the demon lurking in the shadows. After all, the Undead suppose they're safe from Lycans for now since this wolfsbane smoke will kill any who advance. But I am no ordinary Lycan, and I have been preparing myself to face this smoke since my time as a teen wolf under Mordecai. I cut them down one by one, ensuring the target they aim for will never be hit.

Before I know it, I've slipped behind every row of defense the Undead form. They're so preoccupied with death that they don't notice it sneaks behind them. I am quiet in my killing, snapping necks and slitting throats with such speed it looks like they are dropping dead from fear itself. I take them out one by one while Mammoth takes them out three by five. Swords pierce his flesh and add to his rage. Every strike that doesn't kill him makes him stronger. He wraps his chain around the torso of a Black Knight and flings the man's body against his own teammates, crippling their ranks with the corpse of someone they once knew.

Mammoth's fellow prisoners die noble deaths, each taking several souls to the afterlife with them. I watch one get stabbed through the stomach, then watch the prisoner thrust his dagger through his attacker's heart as a final goodbye. I have no idea what these men have been through, but it has made them worthy to conquer the kingdom's greatest fighting force, the Black Knights. Talent can only take the Soulless so far in this world, and talent is never enough to overcome a vendetta. These prisoners have been given a second chance at life, but they are more than willing to throw that away for a chance to kill their captors. Crixus said it best nights ago, they wish to fuck the world before the world fucks them. For some men, it's not about living with freedom. For some, it's about dying with purpose.

Some knights try to escape the bloodshed by taking to the air, but Mammoth's chains are long enough to reach them there. He drags those escapees back down to earth and heel stomps their brains into the ground. Logisticians could not calculate the odds Mammoth overcomes with every passing second, and I use this to my advantage, killing distracted warriors before they can even know they're under a subsequent attack. The lines of Undead are now scrambled and discombobulated. They've lost all composure. They swarm Mammoth by the dozens in an attempt to put an end to their fear, and I attack their exposed backs. In this moment, Mammoth is the meat in the cage, these Undead are feral dogs, and I am the butcher.

Wolfsram leads his ravens to aid Mammoth's cause. There is no stranger sound than lumps of feathers bulldozing into unaware knights. Knights are trained to face mortal enemies, not to defend against raining, piercing beaks. The archers have thinned the ravens significantly, but not so much that they don't wreak havoc. They're impossible to see through the smoke until it's too late.

I watch a knight lift his visor to look at the sky, only for a beak to strike his eye a second later. The noise is indescribable. Cawing of various volumes and noises echoes everywhere, drowning out the noise of Undead screaming. The ravens chant a single word, led by Wolfsram's urging. Revenge. Over and over, without any synchronization in their method, the word rises from the abyss and surrounds us. Revenge.

Revenge.

Revenge.

Revenge.

Thousands upon thousands of ravens cawing the word in violent protest as Mammoth rips their bodies in two. He tears peace to pieces. Over and over Mammoth announces his kill count. Mammoth kill! Mammoth kill! Purple eyes! Mammoth kill! The death toll is incalculable. I look up and see Nikolai's retinue of soldiers watching from the sky, attacking any Undead who dare to flee this genocide. He is smart enough to remain up there. Nikolai knows there's no protection for purple eyes in this hellstorm.

Wolves howl in fury around us, encouraging us to prepare this battlefield so they may join. Their vocal cords tremble with excitement. I focus my energy on finding the torch bearers and dispose of them one by one, snuffing out their flames by ripping off their helms and shoving the torches down their throats. They scream as hot ashes are put to sleep. The last thing they see before death are my burning silver eyes staring down my snarling wolf nose.

Smoke rises, and soon, after I've rid this area of all wolfsbane torches, the veil of smoke will dissipate and lift completely. It is only a matter of time, and my claws have rid this castle's front steps of all archers. Silver arrows are no longer a threat, and Mammoth has made sure those who wield silver swords do so as their last action in this land of the living.

Mammoth's body is covered in his own blood. He has more cuts than a beach has sand. Whatever indomitable willpower within him keeps his chains swinging and his enemies falling, I silently envy it. I see now why father's armies failed to conquer him. There is a fire inside his heart that cannot be quenched. A rage unable to be subdued. He is a demon wrapped in human flesh, fueled by the loss of the ones he loved and his inability to save them. Mammoth is the sort of man you do not provoke. All these years the gods preserved him so he may have his revenge. He shouts, "Mammoth wins!"

All these years the gods preserved him so I may prevail.

Blackbloods land amidst my howling wolves, meddling in affairs that will be the death of them. My Hellhounds are baying for blood, and black blood is better than no blood. While the smoke rises from the Areopagus Castle's southern entrance, more and more Undead soldiers try to flee by air. I watch them plummet back to the ground as Nikolai and his warriors make quick work of them.

Before long Mammoth tackles open the barricaded doors of the castle. If I remember correctly, father once said the doors were thick enough to withstand twenty battering rams. Twenty battering rams, but they cannot withstand one Mammoth. His chest heaves with manic breaths. There are Black Knights waiting behind the collapsed doors for him. Mammoth meets them with renewed vigor. He is propelled forward by some inexorable destiny. The knights shout in unison as they try to stop him, their shouts shortly turning to screams as Mammoth's chains crash into them.

I stood amongst these knights hours ago, pretending to be one of them. I heard the Emperor's marching orders. *That is why I have called you all here, Black Knights. You are to be the last line of defense should we lose the battle. Tonight is the night. Bloodlust has come for the Dybbuk Box.* Even on the cusp of Ventur's demise, he lied to his soldiers about the reason for Bloodlust's arrival. It is easier to motivate an army from fear than to tell them the truth—that this war was planned and provoked by the same man who wears two skins. Power corrupts, and it has corrupted Ventur past the point of redemption. Marduk's spirit has accomplished everything Skathen asked of it. A new species, a final evolution, and one last war to solidify their claim to this new world.

Ventur had said: *Every Undead archer and calvary man has returned to the Areopagus for this long-anticipated battle. We will leave nothing to chance. They stand ready and await the coming of our enemy. No flood or criminal horde can deter our resolve. No enemy known to man can taint our conviction. No demon sent from the Devil himself can tarnish our Empire!*

Ventur may have meant these words when he said them, but someone forgot to tell Mammoth in the process, just as they forgot to tell him Black Knights are the kingdom's greatest fighting force. His chains tear into them as he lashes the knights inside the castle incessantly. The knights' brave shouts turn to cowardly screams. Their swords and shields make little difference. These chains are slick with the blood of thousands, and they don't plan on stopping now.

I enter the castle behind Mammoth and the knights see my silver eyes. "Retreat!" one of them screams as the sight of my shadowy figure is enough to break their will. They scatter like flies before a swatting hand, taking flight in all directions within the castle's lobby. *No demon sent from the Devil himself can tarnish our Empire!* These were overly optimistic words, I reflect. An inaccurate appraisal of the situation at hand.

The wolfsbane smoke has lifted. My Hellhounds storm the castle and tear into its innards, chasing the retreating foes through the dark corridors of the castle. Crixus, Sephora, Creon, and Scar are back at my side. Wolfsram lands on my shoulder, cawing for further bloodshed. The raven will get what he wants, and his army of carnivorous birds fill this cavernous entrance with the echo of flapping wings and snapping beaks and tearing flesh.

# 41

## Selena & Sephora

All the Undead and Blackbloods in this kingdom couldn't stop me from taking back what's mine. But I take no time to revel in this victory. There is much to do and little time to accomplish it in. But first thing's first. I will get back my wife and find my son. Then, I will kill Ventur, or Bloodlust—but certainly both. Then I will deal with the aftermath of the war I've started.

Sephora and I set our noses to searching for Vesper's scent. She has been here, but the lingering aroma is weak. It is like trying to sift through sand to find a trail of bread crumbs. Crixus, Scar, and Creon don't leave my side. They have all briefly met Vesper and know what she smells like, so they sprint through this castle's corridors ahead of me and narrow my search scope. All other Hellhounds dispose of the remaining Black Knights that hide.

Orton, a Muzzled I knew well in my time imprisoned, reports we have seized the throne room and cleared it of adversaries. No sight of the Undead Emperor anywhere, Orton reports. Doubt slowly creeps in that I don't know this castle as well as I thought I did. Hallway after hallway we search and there is no sign of the Emperor or Vesper anywhere. I return to my childhood bedroom, the place where Vesper was held prisoner. Nothing. I go to my parents' old chambers, the condition severely dilapidated and dust-ridden. Nothing.

I pause for a moment, looking at a portrait of Silenius hanging opposite their old bed. Claw marks have ripped the painting corner to corner, but his looming gaze still remains. I linger, my silver eyes illuminating his features. I pull Sephora close by my side, forcing her to set aside her search. I realize she has never seen what her grandfather looks like. This is a moment I can't pass up, as my past life collides with my current.

"Syrus!" Wolfsram squawks, fluttering from the bedpost to examine the portrait. He repeats, "Syrus Sylvian!" He thinks the man inside the frame is me. I can't blame him. It's been twenty years since I've seen my father's likeness. I look more like him than I ever realized.

*This is your grandfather, Seph. Silenius Sylvian.* Her wolfish figure straightens next to me, her silver eyes joining mine to fully expose the details of my father's likeness. He is dressed in military garb, his chest and shoulders decorated with honorifics of military prestige. Sephora extends her paws and touches the canvas, straightening its folds out to view it completely.

*You look just like him*, Crixus says, approaching my other side. Her fur rubs against mine and arousal jolts up my arm.

*You do*, Sephora agrees.

*Our appearance is our only similarity, I fear*, I reply. *His ghost turns in its grave at what I've done tonight.*

*You are twice the man he was,* Crixus dismisses my doubt immediately, coming to my aid. *He was not strong enough to save the ones he loved. You have sacrificed everything to keep Sephora safe, to save Vesper, to protect your wolfpack, to reclaim your kingdom.*

I search for Crixus's hand while Sephora's back is turned. Crixus interlaces her clawed fingers with mine. Even as Lycans, we are more human than monster in this moment. Our snouts turn to face each other. Our eyes lock. The space between us creates a tension more violent than black powder ignited by an ember. My heart is beating fast. I want her more than I want to breathe in this moment. As a human, as a Lycan, her form doesn't matter, because my soul is called to hers in the same way it is to Vesper's. She doesn't speak aloud, and neither do I. We don't want Sephora to hear the thoughts of our hearts. Not while her mother is missing. Not with so much uncertainty surrounding this night. Maybe in another life we found each other first. Maybe in another life she is my Vesper, and Vesper is my Crixus. The heart is a tricky, deceitful thing. It is always searching for love in places it should never be found. And all the love in the world will never be enough for it to feel full.

I release her hand and turn back to my father. He cheated on my mother for Saunter to be born. He is not the man I thought he was as a child. Time has perverted his character as I gradually learn of his misdeeds. The shadow of his portrait stretches into dark places.

*Is this lil squirt you?* Creon calls out from across the room. I nearly forgot about the paintings mom made me and Selena do. We had to sit in the same spot for hours as the painter sketched our likeness. Sephora and Crixus follow me to the corner by the bed frame. I blow on the dust and sneeze as it attacks my nostrils. I let out a howling cackle at the sight of my former self. I haven't seen this thing in decades. It's like traveling back to a time I forgot existed. But my laughter cuts short as I see Selena's caricature next to mine. I wipe the dust off carefully with my padded palms, clearing a circle of dust just wide enough to see her face and hair.

*It's... It looks like me*, Sephora gasps. *Well, she has black hair, but everything else is so similar...*

Sephora walks up to Selena's picture and touches it as if it will come alive. The painter made Selena's eyes outward looking, almost as if she is in this very room staring directly at us. It looks so real, so lifelike. *You have always reminded me of her, Seph. You have more than her looks. You have her kind heart.*

Seeing Sephora in front of my sister's painting is nearly too much for my new heart to bear. There is so much that was taken from Selena. She would have been such an amazing aunt, such an amazing mother, such an amazing wife to some lucky man. She died before she ever felt love, before she ever felt true grief, before she ever experienced the world. It's in this moment that I realize how beautiful life can be, despite how much suffering it has put me through. I cannot count the times I wish it had been me that died on that horrible night, but if I had, I would have never met Vesper or had Sephora. All this suffering and pain I've endured, and I would experience it all again for the chance to have the life I live.

I died a few short hours ago, and I am lucky to be here. Just last month, I wanted to die more than anything. How foolish could I be to cheapen life like it's something unworthy of fighting for? There are many who've passed on so I can be here, in this moment. How on earth could I ever throw that away? I realize the error of my ways. It makes me want to do better, to be better. For Vesper, for Sephora, for myself.

And it's upon this epiphany that my nose scrunches as I catch a scent on the air. It twitches and sets off alarms in my mind. I leave the portrait and my wolfpack behind as my nose leads me toward a scent I never thought to look for.

*The bloody hell is he doing?* Creon asks as my nose leads me to my parents' bed. I dig my claws under the mattress and rip it off the mahogany frame, throwing it aside as the scent grows stronger. Splinters fly as I strike the frame and break it to pieces. The hair on my neck stands as the familiar scent lifts into my nostrils. Without asking questions, Scar leaps to my aid and rips the wood apart like his missing tongue will be found beneath it. Creon stares at us like we are mad men, twisting his head in confusion. But when the frame is reduced to smithereens and we kick it out of the way, there lies the method to my madness.

A trap door under my parents' bed. I thought I knew this castle like the back of my hand, but I stand to be corrected. The draft of air that lifts from the door's cracks is potent with the scent I detected. My fellow wolves smell it now too. It is not Vesper's smell of cloves and cinnamon like I'd hoped, but it is the next best thing.

*Is that...* Creon sniffs around the trap door as his whiskers twitch. *Is that piss?*

I push him out of the way and lift on the handle, exposing a cavernous tunnel that delves into the earth below. *That isn't just piss,* I reply coyly. *That's my piss.* I turn to Crixus and pull her close. *There's something I didn't tell you, but now you must know.*

*What is it?* Her eyes are reluctant, fearful almost. The words float in my head for longer than they should. I don't know how she is going to react. I've spent this whole day knowing this moment would come, but now it's finally here.

*Your father is here.*

# 42

## GHOST OF THE FUTURE

We have searched for Vesper's scent to no avail but we've found the next best thing—Chimel.

I've filled in my wolfpack on what transpired before their arrival tonight. Told them I tracked Crixus's father, Chimel, down in Varne in order to procure in ally in collapsing the town atop the Blackbloods. Creon nearly coughed up a lung from laughter after I told Crixus I peed on her dad as a way of marking him as my territory. She wasn't surprised when I got to the part about him betraying me. He has only ever done what was in his survival's best interest. To be fair, even after threatening him, I wasn't surprised myself when I discovered his treachery.

Now we follow Crixus through the twisting tunnels that dive into the earth's subterranean embrace, following a scent of ammonia that becomes stronger with every corner we navigate. It's my hope finding this rat will bring us closer to finding the Emperor, and hopefully Vesper and my son.

Fear swells in the back of my mind that there's something I haven't prepared for. With the help of Enchantress's visions, I have a better context of what the Emperor may have planned. There is more than one Dybbuk Box Ventur harbors in this secret keep. He had Lundis killed so his Black Knight could retrieve a whole host of boxes from the Acolytes' Temple in Nightfall. That, coupled with the fact that there are weapons capable of killing Sylvians hid in some secret armory causes me to doubt myself. The Deicides, Enchantress called them—Fervent, Fang, Exile, Reclaimer, and Sun Piercer.

As a kid, Ventur drove Fang into my heart in an attempt to kill me. He failed, but today he will try to correct his past oversight. Now that I have unlocked the powers of Sylvian the First, any one of the five Deicides has the power to kill me, to kill my daughter. I can't falter. There is no room for mistakes. If it comes down to it, I must be ready to sacrifice myself for those I love most.

Lower and lower we dive into the earth. These tunnels are dark and damp and haven't seen foot traffic in decades. Cobwebs cover every nook and cranny. Spiders glare at us and hitch rides along our fur as we destroy the homes they've built. I'm silently glad I sent Wolfsram to regroup with Nikolai above ground. The raven is great company, but spiders are like dessert for my feathery companion, and he can be a loud glutton. Give the little troglodyte enough grub and he'll give away our arrival before we ever make an appearance.

Creon moans about claustrophobia whenever the tunnels narrow. Scar's shoulders are nearly too wide to continue onward in some places. I cling to Sephora like a secondary shadow, unwilling to let her leave my cloak of protection.

It's evident Chimel didn't use this entrance to enter the network of caves, which means there are other entrances all throughout the castle. I'm just lucky enough the scent of my piss was strong and familiar enough to be detected from this far away. It is like a dog after an encounter with a skunk—there is no remedy Chimel can seek that will ever truly cleanse him.

The floor beneath us turns from slick rock into a chiseled staircase. We're led downward for several flights of stairs and spit out into an actual cave wide enough for all five of us to walk abreast.

Crixus is dialed; she is a cat on the hunt for a filthy rat. She hasn't been the same since I informed her of her father's presence. She's slipped into a dark headspace that none of us can comprehend. Through the brief time I've known her, I've received small glimpses into her past. She did not have a father-daughter relationship with Chimel, the man who whored her out to make a quick profit on her ability to shift into a Lycan.

It was Chimel's rearing that turned her into a monster by necessity. Crixus wasn't afforded the posh childhood I was, and even though I thought I had it bad after my forced exile, Crixus has seen and done things to survive I'll never comprehend. These memories infect her mind now like a virus. It is intimidating to see her like this. She is like a bloodhound tracking its master's kill through the forest. She hasn't spoken a word since I explained the circumstances to her. She won't let me in her head. Whatever memories haunt her are wrapped in barbed wire and sealed tighter than a Dybbuk Box.

The cavernous tunnels themselves are carved with elegance. They are not like the jagged walls and floors inside the Blackbloods' mountainous siege. Whoever cut out these corridors did so with refined artistry. If anything, it looks like this bunker's construction was done with twice the attention to detail the castle received, which is saying something. The Areopagus Castle is the finest architectural testament throughout the entire kingdom, other than the Acolyte Temple of Nightfall which remains a mystery.

Hieroglyphic images sprawl along the walls as we walk, though Crixus's determination doesn't grant the time for close examination. Images of wolves and bats and knights. Astrological signs—the sun and moon and stars. Comets crashing to earth like Phobos, Solis eclipsing Luna, Luna eclipsing Solis. It's like seeing this kingdom's entire religious history depicted for wandering eyes to ponder.

I nearly trip over my feet as I see a reaper standing before a collected mass of stick figures, his scythe raised in his hand like he is Sylvian the First ushering in a new age. Next to this image is that of a queen seated on a throne, her eyes glowing purple. Then boats docking along a coast, millions of soldiers swarming the globe, followed by an image of the world on fire as two moons cloud the sky.

What in Sylvian's name is all this?

And how has all of it somehow come to pass?

The reaper's image frightens me. *Skathen*. The demon's name flashes through my mind.

Is this what's to become of me?

*I am no savior, as Ophy once said. I am the reaper, culling all who stand in my way at redeeming what little I have left in this world.*

*All saviors must befriend the reaper. They must be okay with death. They must embrace it in their soul, so that they are its chief executioner. It is the very nature of saving someone that guarantees death. Saving implies killing. Every victim has a captor, and every captor must yield or die as a result of their oppression.*

These are the words etched on my heart from some distant life. I've known this truth all along, and yet knowing it provides me no comfort. I've seen my future, and I'm not sure it's something I want to embrace with open arms. Skathen attempted to alter the course of time itself to submit it to his will.

And I am Skathen, or at least the soul that leads to his inception.

I have seen the future, and I know its price is costly.

I'm hesitant to make it a reality, especially if it means losing all I am to become the savior the world needs. Twenty years I've run from this destiny as it closed in on my heels. Should I be grateful for the time I was able to avoid it, or fearful that it has finally caught up to me?

All of this will make sense soon, and I'll be less reluctant when Vesper is back at my side.

All I can do is hope Chimel will lead us to her.

As we get closer to whatever chambers these tunnels lead to we encounter sentry guards patrolling. Unfortunately for them, they are the only things standing between Crixus's long-awaited revenge with her father, so they meet their deaths swiftly and silently. Now that there is no light to shine on Crixus, I'm forced to watch her shadowy silhouette and listen to her determined grunts. It gives me some sense of twisted admiration to know Sephora can observe Crixus as a she-wolf. Vesper may be her mother, but Seph had no role models as a she-wolf until Crixus.

When we were Muzzled, Crixus's name was the only one feared more than mine. Most wolves didn't know if they would make it through the next full moon alive, but it was almost guaranteed rumors would bring news Crixus was victorious. She kills like a priest prays; the hunt is her religion and the beast within is her goddess. I would not be who I am without her. We have been through a lifetime of pain and trauma together in only a single month. Our wolfpack has bonded through innumerable tribulations. We've walked through fire and emerged unscathed.

We turn another corner as the scent of my piss becomes so potent it makes my eyes water. Light appears at the end of the tunnel, but there is a shadowy figure blocking its full radiance. I slow my stride instinctively, but Crixus barrels forward. The hooded man pulls a scythe from thin air and slams its pommel into the rocky ground. On his shoulder is the skeleton of a raven, its feathers and flesh deteriorated by afterlife. It sits silently perched, eyeing Crixus with hollow eye sockets.

*Crixus, wait!* I scream. My heart is swallowed by my stomach as fear and anxiety floods my mind. What is Skathen doing here? Of all the times and places for him to appear in my life, why now?

Scar, Creon, and Sephora slow down at my side, but Crixus presses on and flexes her claws, intent on removing the obstacle from our path. So I'm not the only one who can see Skathen after all... He has made himself present to all of us, but I won't let whatever lesson he's here to teach endanger Crixus.

I sprint to Crixus before she can reach Skathen, who stands menacingly opposed to her purpose. I grab the she-wolf from behind and tackle her to the ground, fighting her protests as she screams to be let free. I know how she feels. We are so close to Chimel. So close to vengeance. It is within her grasp. She can feel it, yet I am stopping her from reaching it fully.

*Release me!* She howls, *I must kill my father!* There is so much pain in her voice. A storm rages violently within her.

Holding her body down is like taming a wild stallion. Her midsection arches in an attempt to throw me off. My silver eyes do little to force her submission. The vendetta and bloodlust clouds her reasoning. Thoughts of Chimel dead make my leadership as alpha moot. But Skathen is an astral projection of my future soul, so I fear what he's capable of after losing everything he loves. I cling to Crixus's retaliation like her life depends on it, because it does.

"Crixus," Skathen speaks into the night. The sound of his voice is enough to make her body go still immediately. After all, it's a voice she recognizes instantly. It's *my* voice. Crixus's ears prop up and her wolfish head twists in confusion. Skathen continues, "Release her Syrus. I am not here to cause her harm." It is like hearing me talking to myself.

"Release!" Wolfsram's skeleton caws, mimicking his owner's words even in the afterlife.

*What the shit is happening?* Creon shouts.

*How does that thing know your name dad?* Sehphora panics in the distance.

"Be still, Hellhounds. I am not here to harm anyone," he speaks comfortingly as I release Crixus's body. The tension melts from her. Oddly enough, she submits herself to this demon's will without protest. It's like she can sense it is me—or some future version of me—her Lycan ears can pick up the similarities in Skathen's voice.

The reaper continues, "Revenge only leads to pain. What you will find beyond this tunnel is only pain. I am here merely to issue a caution, though I know you won't listen. If you choose to pass me, that is your decision. But if you pass, you must abandon all hope, for what awaits you is tragedy. All paths lead to the same ending if you enter this chamber, but if you turn and leave you can save what little of this life you have left. Take Sephora and Crixus and start anew. I have traversed the bounds of space and time to alter the events of today. All of my toils have been useless. Enchantress cannot be defeated. She cannot be overcome. Her spirit is indomitable."

*The fuck is this guy talking about Syrus?* Creon calls.

"I should have appeared to you earlier in life, Syrus, but the hold she has on you is too great. Now that she is in the flesh, this is the only opportunity I have..."

Now that she's in the flesh?

What is Skathen talking about?

None of this makes sense. It's just one mystery after another, a great tangle of knots I'm unable to pull apart. The only way to find answers is to proceed in this journey. Moving forward is the only solution that makes sense. If I leave with Sephora and Crixus, I lose everything I've fought so hard for. Vesper; my unborn child; my chance at revenge... I'll be haunted by the prospect of what could have been if I run from my problems once again.

"Hear my words, Syrus Sylvian. Trust my words," Skathen quotes Enchantress's address to me from Queensmyre. "If you leave now, you will be haunted for the rest of your life. But if you go forward, you will be haunted for all eternity."

The darkness that composes Skathen's body combusts and vanishes as Wolfsram's skeleton echoes, "Eternity!" The shadows absorb his spirit and the mists swirl to the ground like they were never there. I'm left feeling confused and dazed from the interaction. Crixus nuzzles my side, no longer a captive to her blind lust for revenge. I'm left to face my wolfpack, who is even more confused than myself. But I don't have the answers they search for. I have no idea why Skathen seeks to prevent my inexorable advance, no idea what waits for us outside this corridor. I'm torn into three pieces as past, present, and future rip at my body for a way through this daunting decision.

*Who was that dad?*

*He sounded just like you,* Crixus whispers to herself.

*I'm sick and tired of not knowing what's going on,* Creon adds. *Since when did we have demons communicating to us from the afterlife? And where does he get off acting like he knows what's best for us?*

*How did he know the future?* Scar interjects.

*Silence,* I growl, their questions only echoing a fraction of the confusion that toils internally. *His name is Skathen,* I explain, more to myself than to my pack members. *He is me... Or, he's some future version of myself. I'm not entirely sure. But I met him after Saunter ripped my heart from my chest. I don't understand it fully, but he's existed for all eternity. He's seen the world from its inception to its demise. He's... he's the one responsible for creating the Blackbloods—*

*You mean to tell me you're the one who creates the Blackbloods?* Creon scoffs. *Let's be serious...*

*It makes no more sense to me than it does to you,* I stutter, trying to make sense of it piece by piece. *But it's the truth. Enchantress showed me after my death. There are things I don't know, that I don't understand. But the only way to gain answers is to confront Enchantress herself, and I can only do that if I do her will. She's orchestrated all of this. My entire life. My enslavement. This whole fucking journey we've been on—Sygon, Areopagus—all of it.*

*We can still turn back,* Crixus whispers, rubbing the fur along my forearm. *If I can give up the chance to confront my father, you can give up your hunt for the Emperor. We can heed the reaper's words and start anew, just the five of us.*

*No,* I growl. *Do you know how many have died for us to make it here? I'm not leaving without Vesper... I'm not leaving without...* I almost mention my newborn son, then think better of mentioning his existence. I want Vesper by my side when Sephora learns she has a brother. This is news to be celebrated, not announced in dark circumstances like this. He doesn't even have a name yet. I don't even know what he looks like. He was born in a time of chaos against impossible odds. Life won't be worth living knowing Vesper and him are still out there. I need answers, and I need them now.

*Hellhounds, advance,* I order, making up my mind in a split second. *I won't run anymore. Today we make our stand; we will finish the sacred hunt until our hearts beat no more.*

# 43

## Bloody-Eyed Monster

"Welcome wolves," Vesper grins from her throne. The tunnel we've raced through dumped us straight into a vast cathedral of carved stone. Stalagmites three times my height loom before us and stalactites hang from the ceiling like upside down mountain ranges. From the cracks in the rocky ground grows a thousand different species of purple nightshades. Amethyst ore litters the cathedral's walls and glows brilliantly as torches burn brightly. Down here is a separate kingdom in and of itself, separately distinct from the throne room where Ventur assembled his Black Knights to protect him.

The stretch of stalagmites rise on either side of us and provide a clear walkway to the altar where Vesper sits. In her arms she cradles a baby that can't be older than a few months. Its frail body is swaddled in dark linens as it sucks from her exposed teat. I cock my head in confusion as I see the crown on Vesper's head. It is the crown my father once wore, the one Ventur stole from him.

She wears it upside down, and it is too big to sit atop her head. Instead, it straddles the bridge of her nose, covering her forehead and eyes, its jagged top hanging over her cheeks like icicles. It is like a mask that makes it so I can no longer see her beautiful eyes, the first feature of her face that made me fall madly in love with her. I don't know how she sensed our arrival—there's no way she can see through that metal

*Something isn't right*, I whisper to my pack as we freeze amongst the sharp, rocky spears around us. I've known Vesper the majority of my life, I know her better than I know anyone. She was my first love, my soulmate, my twin flame. But this... This woman seated on the altar's throne... This is not Vesper.

*Dad... What's wrong with mom?* Sephora steps beside me but I hold her back with my arm. *Who is that baby she's feeding?*

"Tonight is about revenge," Vesper declares, her voice a deep perversion of what I've known it to be. Though her eyes are blocked from view, it feels like she is staring straight into my soul. "Each of you has endured many hardships throughout your life, and tonight is the night you will see the fruits of your labors. Gathered in this underground fortress is something each one of you desires. For some of you, that is revenge. For others, it's redemption. And for one of you, I will grant the power of restoration. My name is Enchantress, and I have claimed this body as my own. I once walked this earth, cursed by the Creator to kill everything I touched. Death haunted me. But finally, after thousands of years, I have returned to seek revenge, and you Hellhounds will do my bidding, until your hearts beat no more."

Vesper...

No...

It can't be...

All of this... This whole night... It was all a ploy...

Worse than that... I am the one responsible for delivering my wife's body into my master's hands...

The weight of this news is enough to make my knees buckle beneath me.

My heart sends pain jolting up my neck.

How did this happen? Everything was going in my favor!

I did everything this demon whore asked of me and more! And what did she do in return?

Resurrect me and steal my wife's body?

Why!

I demand answers.

My unconsolable rage won't rest until I've ripped Enchantress's soul from Vesper's body and sent it back to hell where it came from!

Skathen was right, and he tried to warn me. Now I know the reason for his eternal rebellion. Enchantress has been playing me this entire time. Since childhood, since my slavery, since Sygon, since I arrived in Areopagus. I have single-handedly aided her in claiming my throne.

This is my origin story—today is the day I become Skathen.

As a Sylvian, I am familiar with our family creed.

Vere mori skathen. We conquer our demons.

But today, I must be more than a man who conquers his demon. I must become a demon in my own right. I must submit myself to the darkness that wells inside me, and I must let it burst forth like the Wirewood River at the collapse of its dam. Enchantress has no idea what she's just started. I am informed enough now to put the pieces together. I will hunt her until my last breath, and if that is not sufficient, I will hunt her across all eternity. I will present myself to her when she's a child, when she is vulnerable, and

I will pretend to be her friend if that's what it takes. I will earn her trust and then bury her with it.

There must be some way I can save Vesper... Enchantress herself has showed me through visions of the past how to make a Dybbuk Box. There must be some way I can exorcize Enchantress and preserve Vesper's soul. There must be! Even if I can't figure it out, I can recruit Skillah's help. She knows more about Dybbuks than me. She will help, I know she will. And if she refuses, I'll force her. I won't take no for an answer.

*I'm here*, the beast within growls, interrupting my descent into madness.

She betrayed us, I quiver inwardly.

*The gods have been preparing us for this betrayal since our inception*, he responds. *It's time to show them you've learned your lesson.*

I can't lose her, I reply.

*You won't. I won't let you.*

*Dad,* Sephora whines at my side. *What's happened to mom? Who is Enchantress?*

*Syrus!* Crixus shouts as my ear twitches. *Watch out!*

I smell Bloodlust before I see him. The air carries his putrid scent as he falls from the elevated ceiling with one goal in mind. He is here to put an end to me. His wings catch his fall and I have just enough time to push Sephora away and brace for impact. The collision sends me into the closest stalagmite and reduces it to an explosion of rocky dust. In the blink of an eye I'm on my back and face to face with hell's favorite demon. Oh buddy, you picked the wrong fucking day to pick a fight with me.

I look up into Bloodlust's eyes, which are now covered with his repulsive Lycan skull mask, further adding insult to injury. I am no longer intimidated by this monster. A month ago, I was too afraid to even speak his name aloud. Now his existence is a joke to me. I have destroyed his army. I have watched Lysander—a mere human—kill Marduk. And I am so much more than a mere human. I wrap my claws around the back of Bloodlust's neck and anchor them in his rotten flesh, then thrust my forehead into his own, snapping his mask in three pieces. It falls away from his face and clatters on the ground around me.

Last night, just before I fought Atlas, the red-haired Sylvian told me the Lycan skull once belonged to his father. Bloodlust raised Atlas, and he wore the mask as a reminder of what happens when mortals defy demons… Atlas's father can rest in piece now knowing his skull is no longer used as a symbol of fear.

Bloodlust hisses in my face and douses my fur with his putrid saliva. There is little I can do from this position to protect myself from his blows, but I know how to stop this fight before it can even begin. I sink my claws even deeper into the back of his neck and pull him close to me—shoving his hissing mouth into my carotid. I feel his fangs penetrate my fur coat and draw blood. Bloodlust writhes uncontrollably but I wrap my legs around his waist and my free arm around his back. There is nothing he can do to shake my grip. My blood gushes from my lacerated neck into his mouth and forces its way into his throat.

It is his fault for revealing Sylvian blood as the cure to the Blackblood virus. My family is bound by blood to this curse—we are the reason for its inception. Enchantress may have betrayed me, but she certainly revealed my enemy's weakness so I can defeat him. I feel Bloodlust's figure contort in my grip as the virus leaves his body all at once. His wings shrivel to dust. His mass shrinks back into human proportions. The black flesh melts away like a butterfly emerging from its stale cocoon, or a serpent peeling its skin to reveal something newer. In mere seconds, Bloodlust has been defeated and all that remains is Ventur's weak, old, decrepit body in my grasp.

I twist our positioning so he is on his back and I am on top. I take a long moment to stare at the man who's ruined my life and destroyed my father's kingdom. There is no longer anything remarkable about him. The once great man I knew died long ago. With no robe to cover his horribly scarred figure, I gaze down at a half-senile, power-obsessed tyrant. My silver eyes burn into his glazed, glaucomatous irises; purple retinas that are probably too blind to see the demon I've become. His silver hair is withered to a few wisps; his scars and wrinkles make his flesh a canyon of valleys and ridges.

"I suppose it's time for my last words, is that right?" Ventur chuckles as blood bubbles from his mouth. "Twenty years of plotting; twenty years of power; twenty years of treachery. An entire Empire built on a masterful lie. All for it to end with my death at the hands of a miserable brat too scared to face his past. Well done, Syrus. Your father would be proud. You've become a man strong enough to finish what he could never do. I've always said only the gods have the power to destroy me, and I see now you have become a god in your own right. I was wrong to underestimate you. I pushed you past the point of breaking and created a monster in the process. But I am proud to take credit for the despicable being you've become. An abomination in the eyes of gods, you are. They say to seal a soul in a Dybbuk Box you must do so with the blood of something you truly love... It's a good thing there is still one person left on this earth I love more than all else..."

I flinch as Ventur grabs a splintered piece of his Lycan mask from the ground and drives it into his own heart, grunting in pain as he kills himself. His eyes don't leave mine as he whispers, "Mysssselffff..."

Creon shouts, *Move away from him!*

At the same time, I'm reminded of Saunter's words: *Ventur's mortal body is failing, Syrus. When he saved you as a child to protect his reputation, the sun nearly killed him. He will not make it to the next age without a new vessel. Ventur knew the only way to save himself was to insert his soul into the body of a Sylvian. He fooled all of us, but he didn't plan for you killing Atlas. Now the only male Sylvian left is you, Syrus.*

Oh fuck, I think to myself as Ventur's blood leaps from his chest and a smile spreads across his face. I've seen a Dybbuk Box be created firsthand. I watched Lysander slit Jezebel's neck, then use her blood to trap Marduk's soul within a coffin-shaped box. But what if there had been no box available? What if the soul was free to leave Marduk's body and search for a new host immediately? It would be cutting out the middle man… Is it truly possible for a soul to leave its body and possess another? If anyone knows, it is Ventur, seeing he has splintered Marduk's soul into several boxes and used them over the course of twenty years to resurrect the Blackbloods. Maybe, just maybe, he plans on trapping his soul in my body as a form of a living Dybbuk Box.

Shit, I think to myself as Ventur gathers his blood along his palm and reaches for my chest. I have been played, and this time, it is too late for me to realize my error before being consumed by its consequence.

A force grips me from behind and pile drives me out of the way. My body is thrown sideways and crashes into another stalagmite as I hear Creon howl. My vision goes blurred as the back of my head reverberates against cold rock. I hear Crixus and Scar screaming in the distance. I crunch up enough to see Ventur's bloody palm leaving its print on Creon's chest. My throbbing head puts the pieces together. Creon sacrificed himself to push me out of the way. A mixture of black and red blood drips from his fur as he rises and writhes like a headless snake. He stands above Ventur's body as it breathes its last breath. Shadows contort in the space between their two vessels as Ventur's soul claims its new home.

Creon lets out a desperate howl as panic fills his mind. He is scared. I can sense it. It's palpable. He is losing control of his body to a new beast, one that will not return control to him when the full moon sets.

His Lycan form thrashes against an enemy it cannot hit. His claws reduce surrounding stalagmites to smithereens, then claw at his own face to free himself from this demon taking over. Long gashes rake over his eyes and snout as he tries to escape the unavoidable. His panicked whines echo within these walls. Creon clenches his eyes shut, then open to reveal purple irises. Tears are falling down his furry cheeks. Tears and blood.

Crixus tries to restrain him but he backhands her away, sending her sprawling. Scar jumps on him but Creon grabs his throat and throws his companion's body atop a stalagmite, the rocky spear ripping through Scar's back and out his belly.

Vesper's mouth smiles as another one of Enchantress's visions come true. Everything is starting to make painful sense. *The hag showed me the truth of things. Showed me how I will soon betray you. Showed me how I will die the villain of this story*, Creon admitted vulnerably what feels like a lifetime ago. Where Enchantress showed me and Crixus our pasts, she elected to reveal to Creon his future.

*And Creon's vision of the future? What was the point of that? Was that some attempt at scaring him into subordination?* I asked Enchantress this very morning.

*No*, she shook her head, *That was the truth, Master Sylvian. Just as Ventur betrayed your father, so too shall your right-hand man betray you. The war you fight in the physical world is far more than flesh and blood. The Creator resents me and the death I carry with me. He has failed so many times in putting an end to me, so therefore he does his best to kill my best soldiers.*

I sob inwardly as Enchantress's vision comes true. Ventur has just claimed his new vessel, and though he intended for it to be me, Creon's loving sacrifice will now be his undoing.

*No...* Creon had said, just after we had set fire to Queensmyre's amphitheater. He had explained his vision of the future to me: *It felt real. Like dejavu... Like I'd lived through it before. I could feel the dagger in my hand as I drove it straight through your heart. The emperor—Ventur—he made me. I had no choice.*

Ventur will make him do it, alright—only Creon won't be the one responsible for driving the dagger home. What Enchantress showed Creon was the future—but it wasn't a future where I prevailed... It was an alternate universe where I let revenge drive my impulsiveness, effectively damning Creon to die the villain.

Skathen tried to warn me. *Revenge only leads to pain. What you will find beyond this tunnel is only pain. I am here merely to issue a caution, though I know you won't listen. If you choose to pass me, that is your decision. But if you pass, you must abandon all hope, for what awaits you is tragedy.* I didn't listen to him, and now I've lost Creon as a consequence of my insubordination. Creon, and Vesper as well.

I jump to my feet and try to capture Creon's body but it's too late. He shoves me aside and takes off for the exit we entered through. Ventur is a survivor, so he will flee to fight another day. My body fills with despair as I watch his figure disappear through the exit. This won't be the last I see of him. This is merely the Fates getting one step closer to the plan they've devised. My body lands atop Ventur's limp corpse. I can barely see his face through the tears that fill my vision.

Revenge truly is a bloody-eyed monster.

## 44

## CRIXUS VS. CHIMEL

Scar is unable to lift himself up from the rock that penetrates him. He is like a turtle laying on its shell. His feet cannot touch the ground to gain leverage and his arms aren't strong enough to lift himself up from the slick, bloody rock that protrudes from his stomach.

Crixus and I gather ourselves from the despair we feel and squat beneath Scar, lifting him up and over the stalagmite's pinnacle. The solid black Lycan doesn't whine in the slightest despite the fact that it is likely excruciatingly painful. Scar has been buried by an entire building and stabbed straight through his gut, yet doesn't complain whatsoever. He looks at me with pain in his eyes, *We will get Creon back... Till our hearts beat no more.*

*Till our hearts beat no more*, I reply. Creon and Scar have become long-lost brothers over the span of a single night. Creon was the heartbeat of our pack. Losing him is almost worse than losing me. The only thing I provide this pack is leadership, but Creon... Creon was the only reason we had the strength to endure at times. I owe Creon a happier ending than that. Whether or not it's Ventur's soul who controls him, I will see him again, and I will win back his body.

But first, there's Vesper.

Vesper, and the overwhelming scent of urine...

Crixus's head lifts up as we lay Scar's body upright against a stalagmite. His gut will heal with time, provided the moons are still aloft in the invisible sky. Crixus's snout twitches as she sniffs the air violently. I smell it too. Enchantress has trapped Chimel in this labyrinth of rock as well. And if I know Chimel, he's been watching this whole time, waiting for us to be distracted enough for him to escape.

The rat emerges from the shadows along the opposite row of stalagmites. The only thing stopping him from escaping is Sephora's frozen body, her eyes glued to Vesper's figure seated on the throne. In Chimel's hands is a spear like none I've seen before. Its entire body is made from chiseled blue gemstone—shades of aquamarine and sapphire—which extend into double-sided spearheads bigger than daggers. The entire staff looks as if it is made from pure energy, like fire if a flame's color was blue. The only weapon I've seen that comes close to this spear is Fervent, which—

*Fuck*, I curse inwardly as I realize what Chimel possesses. I am no genius, but it doesn't take one to recognize this spear as one of the Deicides, the only weapons capable of killing a Sylvian. I hadn't thought about the fact that the armory that contains them is likely down here. All I know is that the light from Sephora's silver eyes clashes midair with the glowing spear. My daughter has full access of her Sylvian powers now, so if that spear pierces her there will be no healing that can save her.

I sprint into action to intercept Chimel's charge. To him, all he sees is a single obstacle standing in his way of freedom. He is a cockroach; the only thing that matters to him is scuttling back to the shadows before my heel can crush his head.

*No!* I hear Crixus growl as she shoves me out of the way, shouting at the top of her lungs, *This is my fight!*

I trip, stumbling out of her way, then catch myself on a stalagmite. I watch Crixus's slender, she-wolf figure throw caution to the wind. Revenge is a bloody-eyed monster. This is the man that sold her into slavery. That let others rape her for a quick profit. He is responsible for the monster she's become, and now she will show him the consequences of his actions.

Chimel sees Crixus coming for him. I smile as I see true, guttural fear dilate his eyes. The burning blue aura of the spear illuminates it for all to see. Chimel cocks the spear back and aims blindly for Sephora. My heart sinks. Crixus sees what her father is doing. If he dies, he will take my daughter with him. And what's worse, he knows Crixus's heart better than most. She is his daughter, after all. She has always put others before herself. In Queensmyre, she rushed into a burning building to save a baby she didn't even know. Outside Sygon, she stayed behind and nursed me back to health when it would've been easiest to leave me to die. And when I faced Atlas and Saunter, she was the first Lycan to rush to Sephora's side in order to protect her. Crixus has always shown compassion for the disenfranchised. As her father, Chimel knows this. So now Chimel will expose her weakness and turn it into his strength.

I gasp miserably as Chimel releases the spear on a forward trajectory toward Sephora. Sephora is too young and naive to register what's happening. She doesn't even know about the existence of Deicides; doesn't know weapons exist that can kill her. In a matter of minutes, I've lost my wife, lost my friend, and now I will lose my daughter.

But not if Crixus has something to say about it...

I watch in horror as Crixus kicks off a stalagmite to redirect her momentum, diving through the air to intercept the flying projectile. I push off in pursuit of Crixus but know there's nothing I can do to save her or my daughter. I feel helpless, as helpless as the day Blackbloods captured me and snapped my daughter's neck before my eyes. Crixus grunts as she glides perpendicularly between the spear and my daughter. The spearhead makes impact with her stomach and tears into her mercilessly. A desperate yelp exits her mouth as the weapon bites into her. The spearhead rips from Crixus's back. Chimel smiles as his attacker becomes temporarily subdued with pain. Gravity throws Crixus's body to the ground in defeat.

Sephora stares at what's happened in shock. Crixus's blood has sprayed itself on Sephora's face, covering her wolfish snout and eyes with war paint from her protector's sacrifice. Seeing Crixus go down is enough to provoke something in my daughter, snapping her out of her transfixed paralysis. She has only known Crixus for a single day, but in that day, Crixus has been like a second mother to her. It was Crixus who broke her chains and guarded her when Atlas came for me, and it was Crixus who protected her on the journey to Areopagus.

Sephora snarls at Chimel and moves to finish what Crixus started, but as her trembling body steps forward, something makes her stop. *Dad*, she whimpers, looking to me. *I don't feel so good*, she whines. I push off a stalagmite and rush to her side. I place my Lycan claws at the base of her neck to feel for a pulse. Surely enough, it is low. Deathly low. Sephora collapses to her knees in my arms as I search her body for the cause of this reaction.

She holds out her arm for my examination and I see a single scrape across her forearm, a wound so shallow it could be confused with a score across baking dough. I grab hold of her arm and examine the cut, then stare at the spear that protrudes from Crixus's back. No... It can't be. There is no way that spearhead protruded enough to make contact with Sephora... There's no way, I tell myself, my heart hyperventilating in my chest.

*I feel so weak*, Sephora whispers telepathically as strength leaves her body. No... No!

I scream, the fur on my back standing as chills crawl across my body. It is only a mere scratch, I tell myself.

Surely a scratch from a Deicide is not enough to kill a Sylvian... Right?

There is no way; I refuse to believe it!

But the silver light slowly fades from Sephora nonetheless, and my blood chills as panic possesses me.

There is no way.

My daughter can't be dying.

She can't!

Not after everything I've been through.

Please, gods, not after everything I've been through.

Why must the gods be so cruel?

Surely they wouldn't reunite me with my daughter just to take her away from me like this, by a mere scratch.

*Daddy*, Sephora pleads as death takes over her body. *What's happening to me? Why do I feel like this?*

I blink away a tear that wells in my eye. I need to be strong for Sephora in her final moments. If I'm to cry, I will do it when she is no longer around to see my pain. There's no telling how much time she has left, and I won't spend it grieving the inevitable.

*Shhhh*, I whisper, wrapping my Lycan arms around her wolfish body. *Everything will be fine*, I lie to her, rubbing my claws along her furry back.

*Am I... Am I dying?* she asks in a strained voice.

*No*, I lie again, trying to protect her from the truth as I have her entire life. *I have defeated Death, and as your father, I won't let it claim you.* I put a finger under her snout and lift her eyes to meet mine. *You are so strong*, I reassure. *I couldn't have asked for a better daughter than you, do you know that?*

She nods her head weakly as the silver light continues to fade. *I want to go home with you and mom. I want to go home now... So... so tired...*

*We are going to go home... I promise*, I lie a third time, my heart breaking as her body shudders in my hands. *Just stay with me for now, okay? I know you're tired, but I need you to stay awake...*

Sephora's eyes start to roll back in her head and I gently tap her cheek to bring them back to me. *I... I can see that reaper again dad*, she whispers fearfully. *He's... he's standing behind you...*

I swivel my head and look behind me. There is no one there. Skathen is nowhere to be found.

*He's... he's offering me his hand dad...*

*Don't take it, Sephora. For the love of the gods, don't take it...*

*I... I can see his face*, she mutters as her face twists in confusion. *He's... the reaper is you, dad...*

*Don't take his hand, Sephora. You have to stay here with me.*

Crixus whimpers by my side as she rips the spear from her belly, her entrails falling out as she does. Chimel brushes past my shoulder as he sprints for the exit. Everything in me wants to go after him, but I won't leave my daughter's side in her final moments. I won't leave her to die alone. I have failed her enough as it is, but I won't fail her again.

*I love you dad*, Sephora cries as her remaining composure crumbles in front of me. I can see her invisible soul leaving her mortal body.

*Don't do this, Sephora... Don't you leave me here all alone... Don't you leave me here!* I scream as her body collapses in my arms, dead. I cradle it as she leaves me for the afterlife, and I mumble to her corpse over and over, *I love you too, but don't leave me here alone. Please, gods, don't leave me here alone. I can't lose you again, please don't leave me here alone!*

Saunter may have physically ripped out my heart, but now, it has been ripped from my chest a second time. Crixus's blood-soaked body wraps around me from behind as I mourn my daughter's death, but I no longer have a heart to appreciate her comfort. I rock back and forth with her body, muttering indistinguishable gibberish. Now, the tears fall freely, no longer contained by false composure. My jowls quiver uncontrollably. My claws dig into Sephora's body as if their sharpness will wake her from the dead. I lift my muzzle and let out a howl powerful enough to shake the stalactites above, as if screaming to the heavens will convince Sephora's soul to return.

There is only so much pain you can feel before your body goes numb, and I have now transcended agony in favor of emptiness.

My daughter is dead.

My wife is possessed.

Ventur has escaped.

My daughter's killer is at large.

This is my origin story—today is the day I become Skathen, I remind myself.

As a Sylvian, I am familiar with our family creed.

Vere mori skathen. We conquer our demons.

But today, I must be more than a man who conquers his demon.

I must become a demon in my own right. I must submit myself to the darkness that wells inside me.

Enchantress has no idea what she's just started.

I don't care what it takes.

I will hunt her in this life; I will hunt her in the afterlife.

She has taken my wife's body and allowed Chimel to kill my daughter.

She will answer for her sins.

*Dad*, Sephora's memory whispers to me, *What's happened to mom?*

I push Crixus off me and stand to face the queen who sits on a hollow throne built from Death itself. Vesper snickers at me, my son still suckling at her exposed tit. He is mine, that much I'm sure of. He already possesses his silver eyes, and their light shine upward to reveal Enchantress's malevolent features.

I have been her pawn this entire time, but pawns can kill queens when queens are careless. And Enchantress has just committed every careless act in order to provoke me.

*Syrus*, Crixus mutters from beside me, *We need to leave... We aren't strong enough to take her on...*

*There is no longer any 'we,'* I growl in response. *It is only me, and I will have my revenge.*

*But the strength of the pack*, she pleads.

*What pack?* I snap at her, my muzzle snarled. *Look around you, she-wolf! Our pack has been decimated! Creon is gone; Scar is half dead; your entrails hang from your belly like dead snakes.*

*I am sorry about Sephora, Syrus, I really am. I did everything I could to—*

*Well it wasn't enough!* I scream at her, staring at the hurt in her eyes. Those who are hurt themselves often hurt others as if it will make them feel better, but seeing the pain in Crixus's eyes only makes me feel worse. This is the woman who just took a spear to her gut in an attempt to save my daughter and I've just lambasted her.

*Stay out of my way*, I growl, pushing her aside as I walk toward Vesper with renewed vengeance. I am now Death Defeater; it's time for me to live up to that title.

# 45

## REMEMBER WHO YOU ARE

My fur recedes and my beast retreats with every step I take. Stalagmite by stalagmite, I transform from Lycan to human. I come to Enchantress demanding answers; I want her to see the hatred in my face as she supplies them.

Cold air attacks my naked flesh. The tension between us is palpable. Everything else is drowned out. It's just me and her; no baby, no Hellhounds, no tangible world beyond these rocky walls. Never in all my life have I stared at Vesper and felt the contempt I currently do. But this isn't Vesper; this queen is a perversion of the woman I fell in love with at first glance.

I was too tense and confused earlier to take in the throne platform's content. Splayed before Enchantress are more Dybbuk Boxes than I can count offhand. So this is where Ventur stored the select cargo his knight stole from the Acolyte Temple. All this time, he has been hiding them in secret in a place the kingdom didn't know existed. Dozens—no—hundreds of souls; all of which have been forgotten yet preserved like the mummified remains of a captive corpse. Who these boxes conceal, I may never know. But I do know one thing; Enchantress's soul will soon be joining them if there's even a remote chance of saving Vesper's body from possession.

Strapped to the throne's sides are the remaining Deicides, each one of them more lethal to me than the last, though some are missing—their dust covered mount sitting vacant for my eyes to examine. Fervent is gone, its cold blade likely still in Sygon's castle from last night's fight with Atlas. Another mount, this one much longer than Fervent's, is also missing. It is the one which belonged to the spear that pierced and killed my daughter. Then there is Fang, the dagger I was acquainted with as a child that failed in killing me. Above that is a bow that looks as if it's been carved from bone and strung with dried blood vessels.

And lastly, mounted closest to the floor is a weapon I've seen before. With its blade closest to me and its staff facing away is the same scythe Skathen wields in the afterlife. All those times I saw it I had no idea it was one of the five Deicides, but if it had the power to slay Syrex in Nightfall then it makes sense that Skathen has chosen it to be his chief tool for executions. I avert my attention from the weapons back toward Enchantress.

"It's just you and me," I call out, raising my arms to either side.

Enchantress smirks at me, then replies, "It's *always* just been you and me."

"I hope betraying me was worth it, because I'm going to make you pay for what you've done."

"Me? Betray you?" Enchantress scoffs, her shrill voice far from the loving tone I'm used to hearing from Vesper. "Mortality has made you forget, Syrus Sylvian, but you are the one that started this war…"

"Whatever Skathen did to you in a past life is between you two. My wife and daughter and son have nothing to do with our quarrel, yet you've taken them from me nonetheless."

"On the contrary; your wife and family have everything to do with our quarrel. They were the reason you decided to kill me when I walked this world in the flesh, Syrus."

I spit on the ground, "I have no idea what the fuck you're talking about."

Vesper smiles, the old hag's wrinkles raising on either side of her previously unblemished face. "No, you don't, but I will show you. Maybe then you will remember; maybe then you will understand."

"No. I'm not interested in another one of your visions of the past. All that matters to me is here and now."

"Do you remember being a fugitive to Bloodlust a mere month ago?" Enchantress asks. "I came to you in this appearance; I pretended to be Vesper to instill hope in you, hope to endure. And do you remember what you asked me that final time I appeared?"

I rake my brain for the conversation. It all seems so long ago. My time in that dark prison cell is rife with delusions and hallucinations. Seeing Vesper's ghost—even if it was Enchantress after all—was the only thing that kept me going so long. I remember the conversation now. "I asked why you had returned after all those months leaving me to suffer in isolation."

"And I answered truthfully," Enchantress replies sympathetically. "Because you've forgotten who you are, Syrus. I have come back to remind you. That may have had a different meaning to you then than it does now, but it is still true. You were Skathen before you were Syrus, and you have forgotten the sins you committed before this life—run away from them as if I wouldn't find a way to catch up to you."

"Whatever I did to you as Skathen, I know now it was justified. My daughter is dead because of you; you have claimed my wife's body as a host for your corroded soul! I can confirm I will repeat Skathen's actions with even more malevolence than before!"

"You don't mean that," Enchantress laughs. "You humans are just too emotional. I suffered from the same emotions when flesh plagued my spirit too. I did not claim your wife's body to punish you, Syrus Sylvian... I did it so we can finally be together! Finally, after all these eons, we are reunited! I have claimed Vesper's body as an act of love, because I knew you wouldn't want to be with me if I was anyone else!"

"Are you fucking mad?" I snarl. My human lip quivers like I still have the snout of a Lycan. The slur is enough to send me over the edge. I leap onto the platform's stage and charge Enchantress with no plan in the back of my head. Maybe it's the beast within speaking, but I want to tear this woman apart piece by piece—but that will harm Vesper's body, so I'll have to settle for opening one of these Dybbuk Boxes and trapping her soul in it with my own dying blood.

To make a Dybbuk Box, I must use the blood of someone I love or someone I hate to trap a soul.

I may not love myself like Ventur did, but I certainly hold enough contempt in my heart for myself to forever seal Enchantress's soul where the sun never shines. Even if I'm to die, my soul will rest easy knowing I righted at least one of my many wrongs on this earth. Then, just maybe, Sephora's spirit will be waiting for me in the afterlife, and we can await Vesper's arrival together.

I act impulsively even though I know little good has ever come from acting on emotion. My eyes fix on the scythe at Enchantress's side. If it is good enough for Skathen, it is good enough for me. I didn't trust his warning before, but I will trust his judgment now.

I will only have one chance. This scythe has the power to deal a killing blow to myself, which means my blood will be able to rip Enchantress's soul from my wife's body. There is no room for error. Each stride I make toward her is filled with a thousand calculations in my brain. I ready my slick palms for the scythe's presence. I eye the Dybbuk Boxes for a suitable container. I will only have seconds to kill Enchantress after I've dealt myself a lethal blow. I'll need to drain my blood around the box's creases sufficiently.

And what of my son?

What world will I be leaving him alone in if I do this?

I can't let his consideration become a variable that deters me. If I do this properly, Enchantress will die and Vesper can raise him. And if I fail, Enchantress will die and take Vesper too, but Crixus will raise my son. I know she will. She loves me, and the boy will have the best adoptive mother possible despite these circumstances.

I close the distance and dive for the scythe, grabbing its hilt with a death grip and arcing it behind me. All that's left is for me to cut myself open with it, then my fate will be sealed.

"Remember who you are," Enchantress whispers from my side as her hand touches my shoulder. I don't remember her standing from the throne. One second she was seated, now she is hovering next to me. It is almost as if she teleported through time and space to prevent me from completing my plan, as if she has watched this transaction of events an infinite amount of times and readied herself for my attack.

The scythe falls from my hands as Enchantress's spirit subdues me.

My eyes become heavy and darkness consumes me.

# 46

## Equinox

When I open my eyes, I'm no longer in Areopagus. Enchantress's touch has once again teleported me through space and time to a foreign land, one I haven't seen in many years.

I visited this place before, as a child, I realize. This is Cardone—the City of Ghosts, the same ancient kingdom reduced to rubble by Dagon and Damon clashing forces until neither prevailed.

I see Enchantress standing amidst the wreckage of a once great empire, staring at the vast destruction with tears in her eyes. But this isn't the old hag I've grown accustomed to seeing, nor is it Enchantress in the form of Vesper's body.

Once again, I'm seeing a vision of Enchantress when she inhabited the earth in her own flesh, as I did when she laid alone in that fearful graveyard as a child.

She is beautiful in her youth. She is no longer a timid and scared child as I saw before. She is now a young woman who's grown into her body in ways other women would envy. Her hair is no longer dark but has lightened into dirty blonde. It is a mix of wild, loose flowing strands that end in dreadlocks. There is a primitive allure to her. She wears little clothing, and the little she wears clings tight to her body. She looks as if she's been raised by apes; her breasts and privates are covered with a sewn tapestry of dead, withered leaves. She is dirty in a way that suggests she sleeps most nights on the ground by a campfire, but it only adds to her wild elegance. The woman reminds me of a lean lioness, a look of hunger in her eyes as she consumes Cardone's remains with her gaze.

The ground she stands upon dies gradually as it fails to withstand her curse. Blades of grass shrivel and turn to dust. Skathen stands at her side, leaning on the same scythe he will someday cleave Syrex's head with. They stand shoulder to shoulder and an army of dead spirits stretch behind them as far as my mortal eye can see. Nature has taken over Cardone's crumbled ruins, turning it to a beauty few people are brave enough to behold. Spirits claw forth from the ground, rising from their eternal rest to join Enchantress's ranks. Ancient soldiers—both Undead and Lycan—from Dagon and Damon's war that have long been forgotten. People say Cardone is haunted by ghosts, that's why no person in their right mind travels within miles of this destroyed city. I now see people are right to hold such beliefs as dead spirits rise to meet Enchantress, called from their sleep by her mere presence alone.

"There's so many," Enchantress whispers to Skathen, her voice in shock. "So many beautiful lives sent to their deaths. For what? Just so Sylvian the First could reign supreme? It's disgusting..."

"You grow too attached to the dead, Enchantress. A wise teacher once told me people are destined to die the moment they are born. We mustn't become so lost in arrogance and unwillingness to die that we think we all deserve to be immortal."

The words Skathen utters are the ones Lundis spoke inside the Acolytes' Temple in Nightfall. Though chronologically, that event won't happen for a thousand years, Skathen is not constrained by time. He exists outside this moment, constantly knowing the past, present, and future.

"Your teacher was a fool," Enchantress scoffs. "Those that died, all the dead that follow us, they all deserved much longer than the time they got."

Skathen laughs, not in a mocking manner, but with a light heart. "That was nearly my same response. But still, they fought for what they believed in and died as a consequence. Now they will commit themselves to your cause, and death cannot take what has already died."

Enchantress pauses, meditating on the reaper's words. She bites her lip as she contemplates asking a question, represses it, then lets it come pouring out all at once.

"How did you die, master?" she asks, averting her attention from the thousands of souls that rise from the earth.

"You know I won't answer that. You've asked more times than I can count, why do you continue to waste your breath?"

"I don't know… It's been years since I've asked. I guess I just thought we've grown closer as I've grown older."

"You thought wrong. I don't speak about my mortal life. Not with you, not with anyone."

"Just thought you might trust me after all we've been through."

"Drop it, child."

"I'm not a child anymore, Skathen!" Enchantress shouts. "When will you see that I'm a woman grown now? Stop treating me like some daughter you have to protect from the world!"

"I had a daughter in my past life, child," Skathen growls in response. "And I assure you, all my protection wasn't enough to save her from death. I'd never be so foolish to think I can protect another from the same outcome."

"Let me in, Skathen," Enchantress pleads, tugging at his sleeve. "Twenty years you've raised me. I'm twenty-seven now, and you've been at my side this entire time. You raised me. You protected me. You taught me life was worth living. You turned my curse into a blessing. Without you I would have given up. I was too weak to shoulder this burden alone. Without you, I am nothing."

"Don't do this... Not again," Skathen pleads.

"If not now, when? You've led me all this way. We've resurrected the dead from the Thoren Mountains to Cardone. Half the kingdom we've called to our cause. Millions follow us. All so we can reign supreme, together. I, as queen, and you, as my king. Twenty years we've dreamed of this. We've cursed the gods and manifested our own destiny. I love you, Skathen... Not as a father, as more... As a partner... I want to be more than what we are... Please... Why can't you love me back?"

"Enchantress, don't..."

"Why the fuck not? Everything I fucking touch dies, Skathen! I'll never know what the touch of a mortal man feels like without watching him die! But you are no mortal... You've transcended life and defeated death. My touch cannot kill you, because that which is dead cannot die. You said so yourself! We are perfect for each other... My whole life I've strived to please you. Everything you've commanded, I've done. I've raised the army of dead you wanted, I've marched them across creation come, I've plotted an attack on Areopagus... What more can I possibly do to please you?"

Skathen turns to face her, the darkness of his hood consuming her rebellious gaze.

He speaks, his voice trembling with passion, "I had a wife, in my past life. At times, she was the only good thing I had going for me—the reason I got out of bed in the morning. She meant everything to me. She, and she alone, is the only reason I know what love feels like. And then she bore me a daughter, Enchantress, and that itself redefined how much love I thought my heart could store. My mortal life was no longer about myself, it was about protecting them. Everything I did, every decision I made, was for their safety. If you think you can mean to me what they did, you are gravely mistaken."

"Look around, Skathen!" Enchantress waves her hands like a lunatic at her army. "There are millions of dead who follow us, but I don't see your wife or daughter here! Sylvian's sake, you refuse to tell me what happened to them but if they truly loved you like I do they'd be here! They would search for you in the afterlife like I would! They would—"

Enchantress's voice catches in her throat as Skathen's hand shoots around her neck. A crackling gurgle echoes as she's picked off her feet with ease. Her pale skin turns red as a rose. "My wife and daughter died for me; their souls owe me nothing more. You'd be wise to keep their memory from your mouth." Enchantress's feet kick under her. She holds on to Skathen's wrist with her frail fingers. He squeezes her neck hard enough to burst, but not hard enough to snap her spine. He pulls her close to the darkness of his hood, then whispers, "Tell me, would you die for me?"

Tears well from her bulging eyes as she nods frantically. Enchantress collapses to the ground gasping for air as Skathen releases her. She massages her already bruised neck as she fights the urge to pass out.

"Do you ever wonder why I came to save you as a child?" Skathen asks, averting his eyes back to Cardone's hollow shell. Enchantress is too busy gasping for air and choking on saliva to answer.

"Did it ever occur to you that I never came to save you as a child, but instead, to make you fall in love with me... Fall in love, so you can know what it feels like to lose everything you've ever cared about?"

Enchantress looks up at him with betrayal in her eyes, the stinging in her neck a pain she's never felt before. For the first time in twenty years, the man she's grown to love has hurt her in ways she didn't know possible. "You stupid bitch, all of this was a ploy. Eternity is a long time, so sacrificing twenty years to win your heart was merely a flash in the pan. I didn't come to you as a child to save you, Enchantress. I came for revenge, because you are the reason I am the monster I've become. You ask me why I can't love you in return, and to that I say, there is nothing you will ever do that will overcome the hatred I feel for you in my heart. You want to know why you don't see my wife or daughter here? It's because you are the one who killed them, you miserable cunt, just like you killed everything else in this world I loved."

"What are you talking about?" Enchantress coughs uncontrollably.

"Because you live here, you exist also outside the realm of time and space. You exist at the beginning of time, and you exist thousands of years in the future, when my mortal body is born on this earth. And like the dead that haunted you as a child, you are the spirit that haunted me my whole life, Enchantress. Your jealous obsession over me is what destroyed everything I loved in the flesh. As a mortal, it took me too long to realize your wicked intentions—that you would rather see those I love die before I get the chance to love anyone other than you. You say you would die for me, but I know the truth. You wouldn't die for me. You'd sooner make everyone else die so you can be by my side, and that isn't love. That's obsession."

"No!" Enchantress screams. "I refuse to believe that... Don't do this, Skathen, I'm begging you. Please, I can fix whatever it is I've done. Don't punish me for sins I haven't yet committed. I can right my wrongs... If the things you say are true then let me fix them. Let me prove myself to you. I can change my destiny; I can—"

"You are the one who killed my wife and daughter, whore of the dead!" Skathen backhands Enchantress so hard she falls to the ground, nursing her superficial wound yet unable to heal the emotional turmoil within. "You ruined my life. You made me a monster. You raised me from the dead just so you could rule the kingdom by my side. You claimed my wife's body as if it were your own—convincing yourself that was the only way I'd love you. You stand here and scoff at Cardone's demise as if it was all a waste, as if these people died for nothing, but truly I say to you, Enchantress... The amount of people you kill in my lifetime alone is enough to make Cardone's fall look like a drop of water in the ocean! That is why I came to you as a child, and that is why I've lied to you all these years.

"You lied to me my whole life, just so you could end up with me, so I have lied to you in yours, just so I can show you we will never be together!"

Skathen gathers his scythe in both hands and swings it back, ready to put an end to the cause of his eternal suffering.

"Don't do this!" Enchantress pleads, tears streaming down her face.

"Silence!"

Millions of dead souls surround them, and all will bear witness to their leader's death. They have all been enchanted by the Summoner, but none will dare to defy Skathen. Enchantress raises her hands in a desperate attempt to defend herself. Shadows bubble in her palms as darkness materializes. Without trying, her soul manages to pull something from the realms of existence into reality, conjuring it from pure emotional fear. As Skathen's scythe falls, I see the shadows take shape to form a small, wooden doll in Enchantress's hands. It is the doll Skathen once gifted to her as a child two decades ago. Its face is precious and innocent, like Enchantress's face as a little girl. But it's too late. The sight of the doll does nothing to slow Skathen's scythe.

Blood splatters. Enchantress's head is cut in one swift blow. Her red blood paints the face of the wooden doll, covering it from head to toe, the perfect symbol of their relationship coming to an end. For this is how Skathen won the Summoner's trust and love, and now that trust and love has led to her inexorable death.

This is the price of revenge. Twenty years Skathen spent winning Enchantress's trust so he could show her what it feels like to be betrayed by that same person. But I see now this will be the beginning of the end for him—his complete undoing. Because just as Enchantress's body begins to topple over, I watch her spirit lift from her body and retreat into the doll's wooden enclosure, sealed within by the blood of one Skathen truly hates. In seconds, Skathen's act of pure hatred has unintentionally turned the doll into a Dybbuk Box, and before he can grab the doll from Enchantress's dead hands, the darkness consumes it from reality, causing it to vanish into thin air.

Skathen stands over her headless corpse, bloody scythe trembling in his fury-filled hands. The millions of souls surrounding him vanish into thin air, no longer compelled to obey his orders now that their Enchantress is dead and gone. In the blink of an eye, only Skathen remains. Skathen, and the lifeless body of the girl who single-handedly ruined his entire life.

Silence permeates the atmosphere as he realizes what he's just done. As with any person who dedicates their life to revenge, he will now be forced to spend an eternity grappling with the hollow void he feels inside his chest. Twenty years he's spent waiting to kill Enchantress, and yet it was his act of showing her kindness that will now preserve her soul to one day walk among the living again.

This is what Alabastur based *Equinox* off of, I realize...

Caspian never existed at all…

He was just a fictional character written to represent Skathen, the man who made Enchantress fall in love with him with a single act of kindness. And like the Thanatos rose that was Caspian's undoing, this doll will now be what destroys Skathen's mortal life when he's born in flesh as Syrus Sylvian, the child destined to lose everything. It has all come full circle, and I've known this story without knowing this story all along. I am Skathen, and Skathen is Caspian, and I've always known Caspian's betrayal led to his own undoing.

Revenge is a bloody-eyed monster.

I am bound in blood by my own actions, those of this life and those of my eternal soul. I am the one to blame for losing Vesper. I am responsible for the monster Enchantress becomes. If I hadn't meddled in her affairs, if I hadn't been so stupid to fuck everything up, none of this would have happened to me. It is up to me to right my wrongs. It is up to me to fix the linear timeline. It is up to me to beg Enchantress for forgiveness.

# 47

## TILL MY HEART BEATS NO MORE

But as I wake from Enchantress's vision and stare at Vesper's perverted body, I know there is no possible way I can forgive her for what she's done to me. I lay on the ground at the foot of her empty throne, my scythe loosely splayed to my side on the ground. I stare at the throne and see a bloody doll staring back at me. It is the Dybbuk Enchantress miraculously formed before Skathen killed her. It is one of the many boxes Ventur's soldier recovered from the Acolyte Temple and stashed in preparation for this day.

While I was dead, Vesper was captured and brought here so Enchantress could claim her, just as the Fates drew me here so Ventur could claim my body. But no one was here to save Vesper like Creon was here to save me, and so now the devil I want dead the most resides inside the woman I can't bring myself to kill. And to make matters worse, she holds my son captive in her arms.

Enchantress did all this so we can be together. In some sick, twisted way, this is her way of showing me she loves me. Because of Skathen's actions, she gravitated to me like a parasite, leading me through time and space so we can end up together in this moment. We are each other's opposites—Death and its Defeater incarnate—forbidden love like Luna and Solis eclipsing to create gods against the Creator's wishes.

The future is a fickle thing. So many ways it can end based on what I decide to do next.

If I kill Enchantress, I may lose Vesper forever. But if I submit to her plan, I will spend the rest of my life obeying a shallow mockery of a woman I once loved.

"Rise, my love," Enchantress whispers from above me. She looms over my naked carcass with eager anticipation. I have finally received the missing puzzle piece. I know everything required to make an informed decision.

She loves me because I raised her, and I hate her because she killed everything I love. How does she think this is going to end? I have seen countless visions of the past, but I have no way of knowing how this is supposed to turn out. Am I to rule this kingdom by her side?

Why did my father choose this path for me?

He died so I may live.

He lost his throne so I may gain mine.

Of all the moving pieces that make up one's destiny, everything has finally converged to one distinct moment.

The stone hallways that led here depicted premonitions of my future—a Grim Reaper leading a nation to war. A reaper stood before a collected mass of stick figures, his scythe raised in his hand like he was Sylvian the First ushering in a new age. Next to this image was that of a queen seated on a throne, her eyes glowing purple. The illustration was of me and

Enchantress, I realize. The seated queen was Vesper's possessed body, and I was depicted as her chief executioner in the coming age.

*I tell the future, and the price is costly,* Enchantress once told me. *Men pay for my prophecy by submitting themselves to its haunting consequences. To know the future is to know what Death has in store for you. There are many possible outcomes, but those who hear my oracles are gifted the ability to choose the best possible outcome, even if it means they must die as a consequence.*

I grip the scythe beside me and use its handle to help me stand. I rise to face Enchantress, then close the gap between us. Her cold, inverted crown still hides her eyes. I'm silently thankful I can't see behind it, afraid of whatever perverted gaze lurks beneath.

I stare down at my son. His silver eyes gaze up at me innocently as he suckles his mother's exposed breast. Now that Enchantress has taken Vesper's body as her own, she is no longer cursed by the Creator. The things she touches no longer die. For the first time in eternity, Enchantress can live out her prolonged fantasies... She can be a wife and mother without killing her husband and children. Grass will no longer wither as she walks upon it; ghosts won't follow in her footsteps; nations won't exile her for existing...

I hold out my arms for Enchantress to hand him over, and she smiles warmly as I accept him. He is swaddled in crimson cloth. His body has already grown so much; he's heavier than I expected. I want to cry over this interaction but my body no longer has any tears to spare. All this time I've been imprisoned I've had a son. It kills me to know Vesper is not here to share this moment with. It kills me even more to know her body is here with her soul in some prison I can't reach.

When I first met Vesper, I helped free her from the chains that imprisoned her. But now, she is bound by chains I cannot see, nor can I break.

I stare down at my nameless son. He is the product of love expressed in a forbidden place. I can still remember the moment he was conceived, just before I went to war with the Blackbloods. My top half laid in the sunlight of a new day while Vesper rode me in the shade of a cliffside cave. This boy is the product of two beings expressing their love through impossible odds. His innocent silver eyes stare up at me, wondering what his father will do when he's been backed into a corner.

"Don't defy me, my love," Enchantress whispers. "I know every future, and they all end with you by my side in this life. I've moved every piece through space and time to make sure of it. What is a queen without her king? I have done all of this for you, my love. It is time for you to take the mantle."

"What is a queen without her king?" I repeat the question to myself, then answer it coldly under my breath, "A royal bitch with an empty fucking throne."

"Huh?" Enchantress mumbles.

"Crixus!" I shout, "Catch!" I twist around and throw my son through the air directly at the she-wolf. Crixus's eyes lock with mine, then dial in on the silver-eyed child that soars through the air. The female Lycan removes her claws from her bleeding stomach and sprints toward the babe. Enchantress gasps, then moves to intercept our child. Her movement ceases as my arm catches her by the throat. "I love you Vesper, but this is not you," I growl.

Her crown-covered eyes stare at me through the metal. Her lips mouth a single word to me. "No."

I look over my shoulder and watch my son land safely in Crixus's arms. I look to her and issue my final order as her leader, "Run."

Although it is one she will not want to comply with, my Sylvian powers remove any ability she has to defy me. I can see the sadness in her eyes as she slowly sulks away like a dog that's just been disciplined.

I can't do what needs to be done with Crixus here. *Don't do this Syrus*, she screams at me through the air between us. I reply, *Save my son. Let it be known to him today is the day I defeated the will of the gods.*

"Release me," Enchantress croaks.

I turn to face her as Crixus grabs Scar and runs off for the same exit Ventur escaped through.

"You made one fatal mistake," I tell Enchantress as my body takes flight with Vesper's neck in my fist. "You may have helped me defeat Death, but Death is not worth defeating without Vesper by my side."

The air beneath us accelerates as I soar toward the stalactite-infested ceiling above. There is nothing she can do to stop what's coming. Now that she has embraced a mortal body, all her scheming and intervention is useless. Together, we slam into the rocky overhang above, soliciting a loud crack to echo throughout this cave. The shock of impact is enough to make us bounce back toward the ground, but I fight gravity's pull and lift us back up again, throwing us into the ceiling a second time. This time, it's enough to make the rocky fortress around us shudder as cracks spread across the ceiling and down the glowing walls. Stalactites fall around us, breaking from their comfortable perches, then smashing to smithereens on the ground below.

The crown is knocked from Vesper's head, finally revealing the ghastly white, glazed eyes that rest beneath. They are devoid of all color, the eyes of someone who's stared at the sun for an eternity. Seeing this is the only reassurance I need to follow through with my destiny. This is not the woman I married. She no longer smells of cinnamon, no longer sets my soul ablaze with her amethyst gaze, and no longer makes me feel as though I have everything to lose...

"I love you, Vesper," I say to her, not looking in Enchantress's eyes, but looking far beyond them for some reminder of the woman that resides within. Enchantress chokes and squirms in my grasp, begging for air to rebut my purpose. For someone who claims to know the future, this demon sure seems worried that nothing is going according to her plans. I release my chokehold on her and wrap her in my arms as I throw us back into the ceiling a third time, this time hard enough to destroy all structural integrity the fortress has. A chunk of rock dislodges from above, pushing us both toward the meaningless throne so many have clung to. Above us is the Areopagus Castle, and it comes crashing around us as the ground caves and the space beneath it implodes.

Enchantress and I thud to the ground as boulders rain around us. Soon, we will both be dead and this will all be some distant memory.

The gods make plans and men laugh. Devils scheme, and Hellhounds howl.

This is the only way to stop Enchantress. She can see the future, but she cannot see a future that doesn't exist. It is up to me to create that oblivion, a destiny where all that awaits us is an eternity of darkness.

But Enchantress was right about one thing. Gathered in this underground fortress was something each one of my pack members desired. For Crixus and I, there was revenge. For Ventur, there was restoration. But for me, and me alone, there is redemption, and it is mine for the taking.

If she wants me to play king so bad, I will wear the entire castle as my crown.

"Don't do this," Enchantress squawks as the world around us crumbles. "You need me!"

Rocks fall all around us. Enchantress is on her knees begging for me to hear her out. I stare at her coldly, but it's hard to look at Vesper's face without feeling some shred of emotion.

"The Creator's Prophecy," she croaks, alluding to some biblical event I don't believe in. Enchantress has stalked me all my life; she should know by now that I am not a religious man. Still, she persists, "They're coming! Syrus, they're coming for us!"

"I've had enough of your lies," I scoff aloud, unimpressed by whatever attempt this is for me to preserve her life.

"You have to trust me, Syrus! The Creator is sending his army as we speak! The only way for this nation to stand is if we are the ones ruling it! I have seen it! Hear my words, Syrus Sylvian! Trust my words!"

The earth's trembling drowns out her words more and more as time passes. I scream at her, partly in rage, but partly because I can barely hear myself speak. "What army!"

"Wendigos! An army of Wendigos!"

Too late, I think to myself as the roof collapses atop us. Falling rock crushes us as I huddle over Sephora's fallen body. Enchantress's voice dies off as we are consumed. In my final moments, I think about my father guarding Selena from the Black Knights as they attacked her. It was his love for her that led to his death. Like him, I too failed in saving Sephora. But I am happy to spend my final moments on this earth huddled with her body.

Still though, in my final moments, I can't help but wonder what the fuck a Wendigo is...

# 48

## Retreat

*Hellhounds, retreat*, I order, making up my mind in a split second.

Skathen was clear in his words, *Revenge only leads to pain. What you will find beyond this tunnel is only pain. I am here merely to issue a caution, though I know you won't listen. If you choose to pass me, that is your decision. But if you pass, you must abandon all hope, for what awaits you is tragedy.*

Skathen has now vanished, but he has left me with a vision of what is to come if I proceed through this tunnel. What waits for me is only pain. Pain, and loss. Loss, and failure.

I did not storm the Areopagus just to lose my wife and daughter. Nor did I assemble my Hellhounds to leave them leaderless.

I stare vacantly at the end of the tunnel. Past its entrance, Enchantress and Bloodlust await me. But past its entrance, the destruction of an entire nation lurks.

*The bloody hell do you mean, retreat?* Creon scoffs, gripping my shoulder from behind.

*My father is in there, Syrus,* Crixus growls at me. *Your own wife is in there!*

*Only death waits for us in there,* I reply. *The reaper has shown me what's to come if we proceed. It will lead to our last stand, and we will fight until our hearts beat no more.*

*That's what we signed up for,* Crixus rebuts. There's pain in her voice. I know what it's like to be so close to revenge that I can smell it. So close that I can taste it. And now, I am denying Crixus the one chance she has at redeeming her dignity. But I know her heart, and it is made for much more than killing those who've oppressed her. This she-wolf is strongest when she fights out of love, not hatred. Leading her to realize this will teach her that she is more than the oppression that's shaped her.

*We can handle whatever awaits us,* Scar asserts, still clinging to hope I'll reconsider.

*No, my brave companion. We can't,* I reply, placing my paw on his shoulder.

*But what about mom, dad?* Sephora whines beside me.

*When your mother and I brought you into this world, you became our priority, Seph. I will not fight to save your mother if it means losing you.*

*I'm not a little girl anymore, dad. I can fight!* Sephora snarls.

*Sometimes fighting cannot delay the inevitable.*

*And neither does yielding,* Creon shouts.

*That is your first mistake*, I reply coldly, turning from the light at the end of the tunnel and walking back from where we came. *This is not us yielding, my Hellhounds. This is us buying time to fortify for what's coming.*

*Oh, here we go,* Creon moans inwardly. *And what terrifying enemy could be coming for us now that is worse than what waits for us in that cave?* His voice suggests he has little trust in my leadership, but then again, this is the same man who'd be willing to die for me if we went in there.

I brush off his comments, listening to my wolves trudge behind me skeptically as I lead them back down the dark corridors. When I reach the point of murals painted on rock, I stop to examine them a second time. A reaper stands before a collected mass of stick figures, his scythe raised in his hand like he is Sylvian the First ushering in a new age. Next to this image is that of a queen seated on a throne, her eyes glowing purple. Then, boats docking along a coast, millions of soldiers swarming the globe, followed by an image of the world on fire as two moons cloud the sky.

But I examine the images closer, looking particularly at those who charge from the docked boats. I wipe the thick coat of dust away to reveal things I may have missed. What I previously neglected to see was their features, writing them off in my mind as the same as the stick figures under Skathen's control. But after further examination, I see they are anything but human. In a primitive image like this, no detail included is to be ignored. The masses that storm my kingdom are demonic, emaciated figures with antlers sprouting from their skulls. With legs and arms longer than their torsos, and faces of pale ash that glare with red eyes, they are unlike any Blackblood, Undead, or Lycan I've ever seen.

On the outskirts of the mural is a single apple, and its surface drips blood like drops of condensation sweating after an orchard's been hit by rain. I don't know what this image means, but I tuck it away for future reference, committing it to memory.

"Wendigos! An army of Wendigos!" Enchantress screamed in an alternate future.

An army raised by the Creator in order to bring chaos to my kingdom—a final attempt to snuff out Enchantress's dominion. It's too late for me to switch sides. Despite my renewed hatred for her, I have already aligned myself with Enchantress's mission. Whatever hate I harbor toward her, I will need to set aside for the moment. Similarly, the Lycans and Undead can no longer afford to go at each other divided if we're to survive what's coming.

*The hell is that?* Creon growls, moving closer to the wall's portrait. His claw points at the hooded figure with the scythe, then eyes me. *Is that the bloke that just convinced you to change your mind? The one you said was actually you?*

*That's me alright,* I reply, letting the realization set in.

*And those?* Creon asks, pointing to the devilish monsters that storm my army.

*I have no idea...*

Enchantress's words echo in my head. This war is much larger than flesh and blood, but what she failed to mention is that flesh and blood will be all that's spilled to fight it.

*We must leave this place, now,* I command, turning from the haunting mural. *This is not a war that can be won today, but I have a pretty good idea how we can shift the advantage in our favor.*

*I'm with you, Syrus,* Crixus whispers inwardly, placing her hand on my back. *Till the end of time, I'm with you.*

*As am I, Scar* echoes.

*Oh what the hell,* Creon sighs. *It's just one giant, mysterious adventure after another. I don't have much better to do, so you can count me in.*

*I can't leave mom,* Sephora shouts, pulling away from us.

*Sephora!* I yell.

Crixus sprints to cut her off without me ordering her to. Sephora moves to push past Crixus, which elicits a sharp growl from the she-wolf's daunting figure. Crixus grabs Sephora by the scruff of her neck like a misbehaving pup, then throws her back toward me.

*Bitch!* Sephora howls for all of us to hear. *You aren't my mother!*

*You're right, I'm not weak enough to be captured, so thank the gods for that,* Crixus spits.

*Woah!* Creon shouts, ripping Sephora back as she lunges for Crixus with her claws out.

Sephora screams violently, unable to detach herself from her inner emotions. *You're just going to let her talk about mom like that, dad?*

*Enough!* I scream, taking Sephora from Creon's grip and pinning her against a nearby wall. *You will listen to me as your father, understood?*

Sephora snarls her teeth at me, her throat vibrating so much that I can feel it in her chest. Her silver eyes are almost frightening to look into. All the trauma and aging has turned her into a beast I hardly recognize. *And you*, I turn to face Crixus and continue, *Speak ill of my wife again and it will be the last thing you ever say.* Crixus stares at me with vacant eyes.

*We are supposed to be a unified pack, you all! While we bicker, our enemies laugh. Get that through your heads. Your mother would be ashamed of you, Sephora. Do you think she sacrificed herself for you to turn on me? She put her trust in me, and it's time for you to do the same. Creon, Scar, get her out of here.*

*Wait, no!* Sephora screams at me.

*Where are we taking her?* Scar asks.

*Go to Cardone. Take as many Hellhounds as you can and rendezvous there. If I'm successful, I will meet you there.*

*Successful with what?* Creon mutters, grabbing hold of Sephora's flailing limbs.

*I am going back to Sygon. Crixus, you're coming with me.*

*What's in Sygon?* Crixus asks, confused.

*We need strong soldiers,* I reply. *We are going back to resurrect Atlas.*

Silence settles, then is interrupted by Creon moaning, *Ah, hells, I had a feeling you were going to say something I didn't like.*

## Epilogue 1

A lone man stands alone upon the Areopagan coast, watching the waves crash against the sandy shore. The tide crawls across the beach, reaching for the man's feet, stretching so far, but not quite far enough. The ocean pulls the dying waves back into its body, then sends a successor to accomplish what their predecessor failed to do. All the while, this man skips stones across the water's face, strategically aiming for the space between waves. With a calculated flick of his wrist, he's able to hit the same spot no matter the water's tendencies.

He's been here for hours, reveling in the destruction of the Areopagus from detached neutrality. In all his life, the man has never smiled so much in such a short span of time—there is a soreness in his cheeks, and his lips twitch in their corners from overuse of the muscles. The sounds of war have gone on all night, and he's had a front row seat to witness it all. The screaming, the howling, the explosions, the flapping wings, the drawing of swords, and so much more...

The Areopagus has stood for millennia as a testament of order and control in this world. First, it was ruled by the Sylvians, then, the Undead. But now, after tonight, this kingdom is left confused and broken. Its people will no longer know who to follow. Rumors will spread, further sowing discord among the masses. Alliances will scatter across the realms like wildfire, each city bound to declare where their loyalties lie—there will be no mercy for those who sit straddled upon a fence.

This world is one step closer to its end, and the Creator's Prophecy has been brought to life in a single night.

"From life, comes death," he whispers to himself, reflecting on the carnage of the night. Many times over the span of this night he's muttered under his breath, "Creation cannot thrive without destruction," as thousands died in the distance. "The Creator will send an Omen," he says, looking up at the starry sky. Above him, looming in the atmosphere amongst the clouds, is a second moon, this one much larger and much closer than Luna's meager silhouette in the distance.

A silent shadow descends upon the man, followed by the spastic flapping of leathery wings. A tremendous figure lands behind the no-longer lonely man with a thud, but he doesn't turn to face his newly arrived guest. The demon's fanning wings kick up sand and send it whirling in the stranger's direction. As Bloodlust, leader of the Blackbloods, Emperor of the Undead, killer of Sylvians, master of the Muzzled, rises behind him, the strange man flicks another stone across the ocean. The rock manages to skip eight times before being subsumed by a colossal wave, then disappears from sight.

Bloodlust growls, "It's done. Everything you've asked, I've delivered to you. Death has claimed her mortal body. The kingdom is in disarray. The populace is leaderless. The Undead, the Lycans, the Blackbloods, have all shown their true colors. Now please, I beg you... Stay true to your word... Deliver to me a new body, so I may shed this carcass..."

The man replies, agitation in his voice, "Creation's light has tempted death to come." He pauses to skip a stone, then continues, "Come she has." Again, he skips another stone. "Life has had its turn to reign. The cycle of Death is all to remain." As the words come from his mouth, it becomes increasingly apparent that he is angry, though his smile remains.

Bloodlust is able to see his throwing hand is empty, no longer able to skip rocks any longer. Still, the strange man rears back and flicks his wrist again, and a rock releases, skipping across the ocean until a wave puts an end to its momentum.

The man flattens his palm and wipes it on his pants, showing to Bloodlust once more that there are no rocks left in his possession. "From life, comes Death. And from Death, comes life," the man whispers, his voice maddening and ethereal. He flicks his wrist, and sure enough, a rock is flung into the ocean's wake.

"Please," Bloodlust pleads, sensing the man's vexation. "We had a deal..."

"Indeed we did," the stranger replies coldly. "Tell me, Bloodlust, do you truly believe you held up your end of the bargain?"

"I did everything you asked," the demon replies, his voice hollow and unconvincing.

"We met quite some time ago, Ventur, when you attended my play in Queensmyre," the man says, finally turning to face his demonic guest. Unlike most mortal men, the stranger doesn't so much as flinch as he takes in Bloodlust's appearance. "You watched *Equinox*... Tell me, did Caspian survive his encounter with Enchantress?"

"This isn't a play," Bloodlust asserts defensively. "This is real life."

"Life imitates art, and I am this world's artist. I gave you a simple task, Bloodlust, but you are **FUCKING UP MY ART!**"

The ground shakes beneath the man's feet, and suddenly, after hours of the waves failing to reach him, the water crashes around the man's calves and manages to entrench Bloodlust with its collateral reach. Veins bulge from the man's neck as his voice ranges somewhere between an authoritative whisper to a blood-curdling scream, "Kill the Sylvians, that was my order to you twenty years ago, and how many remain?"

"I killed Silenius. I killed—"

"You've allowed Syrus Sylvian to be immortalized, you fool! Look at that moon, cretin! With Enchantress's help, people will now think he is the Death-Defeater!"

"I can only do so much with this failing body," Bloodlust argues, not willing to concede to this man's attack on his achievements. "You promised me a new body, and once I receive it, Syrus Sylvian will be neutralized."

The stranger laughs at Bloodlust, as if the demon's words are a joke only a god can understand. "My final play is nearly finished, Bloodlust. My life's greatest masterpiece, a story that's taken eons to write. But because of your failures, there are now characters bleeding into the script I never accounted for—their existence is like pesky editor notes written in red ink, and I assure you, I fucking hate relinquishing control to extraneous editors. It is your fault that Syrus Sylvian is still alive; you had him right in your palm and yet you let him go—for what? So you could make him suffer a little longer for what he did to your body when he was a mere child? My Death-Defeater is coming, Bloodlust, and so help me gods, if Syrus Sylvian and his children are still alive when he arrives, no body I give you will protect you from his wrath."

Without warning, the stranger turns to face the ocean and rears his empty hand back, flicking his wrist a final time. A rock shoots forth from his grasp, but this time it does not skip across the ocean. This time, as the rock collides with the endless sea, the water parts before the stone's trajectory. There isn't much that can surprise Bloodlust in this world, given the supernatural spectacles he's encountered, but as the tide splits in two down the center, opening a pathway for mortals to navigate, the Blackblood is left speechless.

"You truly are him," Bloodlust says, equally amazed and terrified by what he's seen.

"Twenty years you've served me, and the parting of an ocean is what leads you to this conclusion?" the man asks whimsically.

"Men have claimed to be the Creator incarnate before... You could have just been another false messiah, a crazed prophet destined to die like the rest of them."

"I am Alabastur the Almighty, the incarnation of the Creator. The things I write are my creation, and I have orchestrated this entire world by breathing it into existence with the Word. Every life that's ever existed has played a part in my play, and the grand finale I've alluded to since *Equinox* is nearly here. Soon, the whole world will testify to my splendor," he says, quoting a portion of the Creator's Prophecy.

"And what part will I play?" Bloodlust asks. "Will you deliver to me the new body you promised?"

Alabastur stares at the parted ocean, reveling in the waters' ability to obey his omnipotent will. "No, I won't," he answers after several seconds of reflection. Bloodlust clenches his fists so hard that his claws cause his palms to spill black blood on the sand. "You've fucked up royally, my servant. Syrus Sylvian is still alive, along with is daughter and son. The Sylvians were Luna and Solis's ultimate defiance to my holy order, and I have sought their extinction for eons. In truth, I should kill you for failing me. Be thankful I've spared you thus far."

"Death doesn't scare me," Bloodlust says confidently, almost as if he actually believes the words. "It's not that you have spared me, Creator... You couldn't kill me even if you wanted to."

"Is that what you think?" Alabastur replies, amused.

"It's what I know, fearmonger. You have cursed this creation a dozen times over—yet every curse you've cast has only bit you in the ass. Damon and Dagon turned creation against you with the curses *you* gave them! Then Luna and Solis outsmarted you with Sylvian the First's inception! Creation bleeds because of your ill-tempered actions, Alabastur, and yet, you've done nothing to rectify it... I know your secret, Creator—I know you have a curse of your own, and that curse is precisely the reason you won't kill me—why you *can't* kill me." Bloodlust knows he cannot take on a god wrapped in mortal flesh, so he takes his anger out on the stranger with his words. Where weapons fail, words will always prevail.

Alabastur stands there, almost as if Bloodlust's words have washed over him entirely. His eyes are tired—they are the eyes of a being who's seen the rising and setting of too many suns. He mulls on his servant's defiant words, strangely intrigued by the demon's gall to speak to him in this manner. Then, as their ears are consumed by the surging of the sea being parted by some invisible barrier, the Creator says, "This path through the ocean leads to the Deadlands, and my Death-Defeater, Steppenwolf, is now on his way. When he arrives, gods will die and devils will perish.

"You are right, Bloodlust... As a Creator, I lack the ability to destroy that which I've created. That is my curse, and it has nearly been my undoing. For millennia, I've been forced to look upon my creation and watch you mortals destroy everything I once cared about... I am the Creator, and my ability to create is both my greatest power and weakness. I cannot destroy, but I can create beings who can destroy. At first, I thought Enchantress would be the answer to all my solutions—the plan seemed to be flawless...

I created Phobos to seduce Luna, and she fell for the bait. It was perfect, and even Solis fell into my trap. He cursed the girl to kill everything she touched, effectively doing my dirty work *for* me.

"It was a thing of beauty," Alabastur says, staring longingly at the ocean. "If the plot carried out the way I intended for it to, the cursed bitch would have destroyed all of creation without me having to lift so much as a finger, and I would have gotten the blank canvas I've desired for so long."

"Well that cursed *bitch* is now occupying Vesper Sylvian's body like a parasite," Bloodlust says, informing the Creator on the events that have transpired. "I don't doubt you already know the threat that poses to us."

"The bitch has always been an unruly variable, which is precisely why my plans for her failed the first time. But I assure you, she's exactly where I want her this time around. Even though you failed in killing Syrus Sylvian, the next best thing happened—he fled from her when she needed him most. Without her white knight there to protect her, she's ours for the taking. She thinks by resurrecting her Sylvian lover she's made a Death-Defeater of her own. But I assure you, the true Death-Defeater will be here soon, and I will finally have my blank canvas by the time he's unleashed my wrath upon this half of the world."

"And you expect me to stand by and watch you destroy this entire kingdom? Everything I've worked for? It was all for naught, and I was just another pawn in your metaphysical war?"

"Be glad I let you survive to the main act, Ventur. You were right when you've said I've cast many curses in my time. Though you may not realize it, the curse I cast upon you is one of my most diabolical," Alabastur says, twisting his head to glare at Bloodlust with amusement. "By the time I'm done with you, you will know what I speak of... For there is no greater curse than selling your soul to gain the world, only to have a malevolent god pluck it from your palm, piece by bloody piece."

## Epilogue 2

*Crixus*, I call out after her as we stow away from Areopagus like thieves in the night. Her wolfish ears twitch as I order, *Stop right there.*

We have reached a zone of safety I once retreated to as a child. Here, on the outskirts of the Areopagus, there is no threat of being discovered by Blackbloods or Undead as they nurse the mortal wounds incurred on this night.

This is the same place I fled to as a child, after Ventur saved me and Scouts from the castle hunted me. It was here that I collapsed, the weight of the moment becoming too heavy to bear as the death of my family sank in. We stand in a grove of ferns amidst towering oaks, and it was here that I cried myself to sleep for the first time in my life.

It was here I turned the page on my old life and started a new chapter, and it is here I will do so a second time.

*What is it?* she asks, turning to face me. The two moons above light our surroundings as we cross the outer limits of the kingdom. I close the gap between us, taking in her appearance as a Lycan fully for the first time all night. She is slender, as most she-wolves are, but there is something about her figure that intimidates me. Like her hair as a human, her fur is jet black.

Dried flecks of blood are matted all across her body, revealing without words how dangerous she truly is.

*Back there, in the caves,* I begin, not able to think through my words before saying them, but knowing if I don't tell her now, I may never gather the courage to. *The reaper... Skathen... He showed me what would've happened if we followed through with our mission...*

*Syrus... Are you okay?* she asks, seeing the tears that build in my silver eyes. She closes the gap between us that I'm too afraid to cross myself. Her blood-soaked claws caress the side of my muzzle as I stare down at her.

*No... I'm not okay,* I reply, placing my hands on her hips so I can feel her body once more. Shivers jolt my fingers as I grab her, then run up the course of my forearms, causing my fur to stand. *We've just been through hell and back, Crixus, and you... You are the only reason I wasn't consumed by its fires. I need you... I need you more than I need revenge, more than I need peace, more than I need a happy ending... When I learned Vesper was still alive, my whole world changed... It made me realize you and I can never be together... But after seeing Skathen's vision—after having to make a decision where I lose in every possible outcome... I'm done denying myself a chance at happiness...*

*Then let me make you happy,* she replies, cutting me off as she licks the tears from my muzzle. Her claws scrape down my chest and abdomen, then reach for the space between my legs. She has been waiting for this moment since the moment we first locked eyes, and I've just given her permission to rip down the walls around my heart.

I dig my claws into her hips, causing her to jump with excitement, then fondle her breasts through her bloody fur. I lean down and inhale her scent, euphoria injecting itself into my veins as my body trembles. She nips at my neck and collar bone with the same canines that removed hundreds of jugulars hours ago.

*When Saunter ordered me to attack Vesper,* Crixus whispers telepathically as she grips my cock through my fur. *I didn't even try to hold back—didn't fight to resist Saunter's control over my mind... There was a part of me that was glad I could fight her free of blame... After years of fighting to survive, fighting to earn your love was the easiest decision I've ever made.*

*Fuck,* I whisper inwardly, goosebumps rushing across my body as my fur falls away. Together, slowly, we shift back to our human forms. Her claws break away from her nails as she scrapes them against my naked skin. Our bones crackle and shift as we hold each other tight, our bare skin joining like we are long lost lovers finally reuniting.

Her muzzle disappears as she licks mine, our lips converging to make contact for the first time. We fall to the ground together as our tongues acquaint themselves with one another. Steam rises around us as the last of our wolfish features recede, leaving us to explore our humanity together.

I lay atop her, pressing my hips into hers as she digs her nails into my back. The pain feels good—the best damn pain I've felt in years. I bite her lower lip, drawing blood, then revel in its taste. I feel the skin along my spine open as her nails scrape to communicate her pleasure. Because I'm a Sylvian, the flesh heals almost immediately, but because she's Crixus, she reopens it just as fast.

Our mouths consume each other, not because we are inexperienced, but because we have never been so hungry for another human. Blood seeps from my back, over my ribs, then drips atop her breasts. My chest presses into her, smearing it. I lower myself down her body, licking her bloody chest, flicking my tongue over her nipples as she grips my hair so tight I fear it will rip from my scalp.

I place my mouth between her legs, driving my tongue into her as my fingers rub the space above. Her legs stiffen over my shoulders as she whimpers involuntarily, moaning loud enough to alert the Undead of our whereabouts. Luckily for us, night retreats over the horizon, and the day is ours for devotion.

She is the most feared Lycan I've ever known, but in this moment, she is completely submissive to me. My eyes peer up her body, across her lean stomach and perky breasts, directly into her powerless eyes. She lays her head against the ground and arches her back as my tongue flicks back and forth rapidly, then slowly, then rapidly. I feel her legs tremble around me, choking my neck with her thighs as she stiffens. She cries out, convulsing helplessly as her love becomes overwhelmed by lust.

Her hand pulls at my hair, and I obey her guidance. I creep back up her body, kissing her wildly, letting her taste the fruits of my tongue's labor. Her hand grips me, then pulls me into her, causing me to curse with joy. She whispers in my ear, "My turn," as she flips me onto my back, then sits upright atop me.

The early morning sun peaks through the foliage, glistening against her tone upper body. Several veins are exposed where her flesh hugs her hip bones. I place my hands over them as she slowly rises, then falls, then rises, then fall. "We owe ourselves this," she whispers, placing her hands on my chest to support her weight. "Say her name," Crixus growls as she locks eyes with me.

"Vesper," I moan, cupping her boobs in my palms. She bites her bleeding lip as a bead of sweat falls from her forehead onto mine.

"Again," she orders as her pace quickens.

"Vesper," I croak, stiffening with each utterance.

"Louder!" she screams, her ass echoing as she bounces violently.

"Vesper!" I howl as we climax simultaneously, her body twitching uncontrollably as I shudder beneath her.

The sun rises in the distance as two moons disappear over the horizon. We embrace one another as we spasm, an unquenchable fire ignited in our hearts after years of drought.

Crixus was right…

We owe ourselves this…

After leading lives of misery, we of all people deserve a chance at happiness.

I have seen the future, and there is no outcome where I emerge alive.

No matter what I do, I will die as a price for my actions.

But as the sun shines upon our bodies, welcoming a new day, I smile.

The gods will soon take everything from me, but at least in this moment, I can finally appreciate everything they've given me.

## Epilogue 3

"I wan' my mommy," the little girl cries out, tears streaming down her cheeks. She squeals, "I wanna go home!"

"Shhhh," Chimel whispers comfortingly, putting his hand over the toddler's mouth to muffle her scream. "Mommy and daddy entrusted you to me, my darling..."

He removes his hand so she can speak.

"But I don' know you, and dey always said to not tawk to stwangers."

Chimel has his hands wrapped around the girl's waist, bobbing her up and down on his knee as the fire he curated crackles. He's far enough away from the Areopagus Castle that he can no longer hear the audible bloodshed, and he's bathed himself three times in the Wirewood in an attempt to remove the smell of urine from his skin.

"I told you, darling, I'm not a stranger... I'm mommy and daddy's friend, and they asked me to look after you while they rebuild their home. We've been over this, some real bad people came to town and got in a tussle... It's not safe for you at home right now."

"Den why did dey not come wiff us?" she asks, tears still welling up in her eyes. Chimel doesn't mind the tears so much, but it was the damn screaming that drove him up a wall.

He would only be safe so long as he remained untraceable, and that required an immense amount of silence. He only made it out of that forsaken kingdom by the skin of his teeth, and he'd be damned if he let some snot-nosed brat give him away.

Still though, he was a business man at the end of the day, and business men were always on the lookout for opportunity. It was almost too perfect when he found the abandoned girl wandering the streets of Areopagus on his way out, screaming for her mother and father. Truth is, her mother and father were likely dead. If there was anything Syrus Sylvian had managed to accomplish on this night, it was hurting the innocent civilians of Areopagus, who never asked for any part in this war.

The streets the girl wandered were decimated by the Wirewood's flooding. Houses and huts were torn down from the impact of the tsunami, and if Chimel had to bet, he'd guess this girl's parents had sacrificed their lives in order to save hers.

"Don't worry, sweetheart. You will see mommy and daddy again, but in the meantime, you need to stay with Uncle Chimel. Now, lets get those wet clothes off you, you must be terribly cold wearing that!"

Chimel sets the girl on the ground in front of the fire and reaches to unfasten her ratty shirt. The girl, whose name Chimel hadn't bothered to ask, raises her hands to block the buttons that hold her shirt together, whispering timidly, "I don' wanna take off my cwothes."

"But you'll catch a cold wearing those soaked rags, darling. We can take them off and hang them by the fire, that way they'll be dry by the morning. Doesn't that sound nice?" This wasn't Chimel's first rodeo gaining a child's trust. In his line of business, he'd learned how to manipulate the damn brats into doing anything he asked. The first days were always the hardest, like separating a pup from its bitch. They'll whine in the night for their momma, but he'd come to learn that after a few days, they accepted their new life whether they wanted to or not.

The girl shakes her head, still refusing to uncover her shirt buttons. In truth, Chimel didn't care if the tike froze to death or died of pneumonia, he just needed to see what he was working with. Her innocent face was cute enough, but his kind of clientele cared more about what a kid looks like once their clothes were off. If she was underdeveloped enough, Chimel could charge twice as much for men who wanted to cut her hair short and pretend she was a boy.

Chimel reaches over and forcefully removes the girl's hands from her shirt, ripping the first button off in the process. The interaction causes the girl to scream out fearfully, her voice echoing through the dark forest. Chimel instinctively backhands her, almost knocking the vulnerable girl into the fire. If it wasn't for his other hand catching her, she could've easily been burned, and then no man would have wanted to pay for her services.

"See, why must you make me get angry?" Chimel asks, pulling the trembling girl in close to his body. Her cheek bleeds from where his ring made contact, so he wets his thumb and wipes it away. Her lower lip quivers as she fights the urge to cry out once more, then thinks better of it and decides to silently sob in Chimel's embrace. He brushes her hair with his hand as he whispers, "I don't want to hurt you, little one, but I told you we can't scream out here. The bad men might find us if you scream, and then they'll hurt both of us. Do you understand?"

"Let the girl go," a voice calls from the darkness, causing Chimel's blood to freeze with fear. He pulls her in tighter so she can't squirm to freedom, then looks around for the voice's owner. It's still dark out, still a few more hours until dawn, and staring at the fire has eliminated Chimel's ability to see in the dark. His head swivels and his eyes flicker, scanning his surroundings for some sign of an unexpected guest.

He hears a chain rattle behind him, which causes him to rotate on the tree stump he sits upon. "Who goes there?" he calls, trying to keep his composure. The odds of this being someone who knows him are low—so long as he pretends everything is okay, this intruder won't know the difference.

Again, a chain rattles, this time on the opposite side of the fire. It's sound makes Chimel's skin crawl as he spins quickly to face it. His body is so tense that he has to force himself to loosen his grip on the little girl, realizing he's suffocating her with his embrace. Still, he can feel her diaphragm sobbing silently as she realizes she's powerless to break free.

Through the haze of night, Chimel sees two distinct yellow lights shining through the trees. He squeezes his eyes shut, massaging them for a moment, then peers past the fire once more. The lights are gone, and he convinces himself they never existed in the first place.

"Don't make me tell you twice," the voice calls from beside him, causing him to nearly jump out of his skin. "I said let the girl go." Somehow, some way, the voice is now on the other side of him, almost as if there are two separate people taunting him, even though they have the same voice. But it would be impossible for a single person to cover that much ground in such short time. Surely there must be two who lurk in these woods, and that is why he continues to hear noises all around him.

"Please, whoever you are, you're frightening my daughter," Chimel exclaims. "Just come out from those woods, there is plenty of room around the fire for all of us!"

"I know who you are, Chimel, just as I know that girl is not your daughter," the voice growls, a tone of hatred making Chimel feel unsettled.

Chimel grinds his teeth, his fear turning into rage at the current circumstances. He did not just escape a Sylvian and his army of Lycans to be mocked by some stranger in the darkness. Instincts of flight instantly turn into instincts to fight. Chimel releases the girl from his embrace and holds her out, picking her up like a shield as she lets out a desperate cry for help. "If you know who I am, then you know I'll kill this little girl if you so much as threaten me! Don't think I won't, coward! Now come out from hiding and face me like a man!"

The chain rattles once more, this time from behind Chimel, and before he can even think about moving to face it, a piercing agony tears into his shoulder, causing him to drop the little girl and wail at the top of his lungs. He instinctively grabs his right shoulder with his left hand, then screams a second time as he feels a spearhead protruding from his severed socket.

"It would be quite difficult for me to face you like a man," the voice calls, a chain rattling as Chimel's body is pulled to face its attacker. She snickers, "But I will come out and face you like a woman."

As Chimel's body is forced to rotate, he sees now that the chain he heard rattling is attached to the spearhead in his shoulder, anchoring itself to his body like a hook caught in a fish's lip.

A slender, feminine body exits the shadow-laden forest, a cowl covering her face, hiding every feature but one—her glowing yellow eyes. Like some demonic hellcat, the woman who holds Chimel's chain has eyes more yellow than the scorching, midday sun.

Her wrist flicks, causing the chain to dance around Chimel's body in a single coil, then again, and again, and again, until the chain is wrapped around his torso so tight that he can't move. She pulls the chain, causing him to fall to his knees as his tears mix with the slobber that drools from his mouth.

"Please, I'm begging you," he pleads between sobbing breaths. "There must be some mistake! I don't know how you know me, but you must be mistaken!"

The little girl flees from her captor and rushes to her savior's side, hugging the yellow-eyed woman around her leg. The woman squats beside the child and examines the cut on her cheek, then whispers something in her ear. The little girl laughs, which only adds to Chimel's anxiety.

"Oh, I know you alright," the woman replies, standing from the little girl. Slowly, she grabs each side of her cowl and removes it, revealing her pale face and jet-black hair. Her mouth is covered with a mask that cuts off at the bridge of her nose, which explains why Chimel confused her voice with that of a man's.

The woman tightens her grip on the chain and speaks, "My name is Huntress, and I have been searching for you for quite some time, Chimel. We have unfinished business, and your life depends on how you settle your debts with me." Huntress lowers her eyes to the little girl, then whispers just loud enough for Chimel to hear, "Look away, little one. I will deal with this monster..."

# ABOUT THE AUTHOR

I used to think I was a werewolf—I think that's why I've always been so fascinated by them.

Now, before you write me off as some weirdo, let me contextualize. As a child, I suffered from many peculiar sleep disorders. First, I was an avid sleep walker. But I wasn't your average, run-of-the-mill sleep walker who went to the fridge for a glass of milk and returned to bed. I can recount one time in particular I slept walked out of my parents' house and managed to walk nearly a mile down the road before being discovered. You can likely imagine how disturbed my neighbors were to find a half-naked boy stumbling through the dark.

Because of this, my childish mind could only explain such instances by attributing them to Lycanthropy. Since I didn't know what sleep walking was, this seemed to be the only plausible explanation. I mean, I'd fall asleep in my bed fully clothed, then wake up in random and unexplainable places with nothing but my Fruit of the Loom boxer briefs. To me, there seemed no explanation more rational than to believe I was transforming into a blood-thirsty wolf every night.

It didn't take long for me to learn what sleep walking was, but my fascination with werewolves persisted, as did my deranged sleeping habits. I ended up developing sleep paralysis and night terrors as I entered high school. Dealing with dreams where I would see demons in the night, I coped in ways that would give most psychiatrists heart palpitations. I avoided sleep by overstimulating with caffeine, sometimes going several nights without sleep. One time I fell asleep on the school bus, only to be woken by a demon whispering my name in my ear.

All of these experiences culminated in creating this universe, where I get the chance to use you, the reader, to express my fascination with werewolves and give them the screen time they've always deserved.

Thank you for reading, and I hope you enjoy living in my nightmares.

Milton Keynes UK
Ingram Content Group UK Ltd.
UKHW020050061124
450708UK00006B/704